With part of her mind [...] Sithli. . . . And the other par[...] was beautiful. As she though[...] her. "Come sit near the fire." [...] pulled a chair in front of the flames, and came and took her hand, intending to lead her there. Without conscious will they were in each other's arms again.

What is wrong with me? Rilsin wondered, just before she kissed him.

After a few endless moments, they broke apart.

"We can't do this, Sola." Her voice sounded breathless and high, even in her own ears.

"No," he agreed, "we can't."

Why was she so unhappy that he agreed with her?

THE
SWORD
OF THE
LAND

NOEL-ANNE BRENNAN

2003
50TH
ANNIVERSARY

ACE BOOKS, NEW YORK

THE SWORD OF THE LAND

An Ace Book / published by arrangement with
the author

PRINTING HISTORY
Ace mass-market edition / March 2003

Copyright © 2003 by Noel-Anne Brennan.
Cover art by Michael Herring.
Cover design by Rita Frangie.
Text design by Julie Rogers.

For information address: The Berkley Publishing Group,
a division of Penguin Putnam Inc.,
375 Hudson Street, New York, New York 10014.

Check out the ACE Science Fiction & Fantasy newsletter!

ISBN: 0-441-01031-8

ACE®
Ace Books are published by The Berkley Publishing Group,
a division of Penguin Putnam Inc.,
375 Hudson Street, New York, New York 10014.
ACE and the "A" design
are trademarks belonging to Penguin Putnam Inc.

PRINTED IN THE UNITED STATES OF AMERICA

10 9 8 7 6 5 4 3 2 1

1

SHE WAS EiGHT YEARS OLD, AND SHE KNEW THE POUNDING
at the door was bad. She knew it because they had been running for weeks, sneaking through the countryside, through
this cold northern wilderness, hiding from the soldiers. She
missed her home and her friends, and Bet, her hunting cat,
but she understood that she might never see them again. She
tried not to cry, but sometimes she couldn't help it. At least
she tried not to let Mama see, because Mama said saedin
don't cry, and Mama had enough to worry about.

Every time they found shelter, they could not stay for
long, because the warning came that the soldiers had found
them again. Mama said they must leave, or their friends
would be hurt. Rilsin knew it was that, and more. Their
friends would be killed, and so would they. Papa was killed,
and so was Grandma. Grandma Wilna, the SaeKet, the
queen. That made Mama the SaeKet now. That was why the
soldiers would kill them, because the soldiers didn't want
Mama to be SaeKet, and they wouldn't leave anyone alive
from the Sae Becha family, the family that had ruled the

land for time out of mind. So when the pounding at the door began, Rilsin was afraid.

A young woman rushed into the room.

"They are here!" she gasped. She was obviously frightened, but she was carrying their travel cloaks, and she looked determined. "My lady will try to hold them while you get out the back. Hurry!"

So Mama picked her up and wrapped her in her cloak. Rilsin tried to cling to her, but Mama put her down.

"You will have to walk and ride yourself, my sweetheart." Mama took something from her finger, a ring. She took the cord from around Rilsin's neck, the cord that held her naming amulet, and tied the ring onto this. Then she put the cord back over Rilsin's head. The amulet and the ring clinked together. "Come," she said.

The pounding had stopped. For a moment there was silence, but then the screams began. Mama grabbed Rilsin by the hand, and they ran through the house. It was a big house by the standards of the north, but not to Rilsin, who grew up in the palace. The young maid took them through the kitchens, through the warmth and the rich smells, and out into the cold of an early spring night in the north. The bite of the frosty air made Rilsin gasp.

There were horses waiting and a few of their own soldiers, who had been with them all along. Rilsin saw Witki, who had been a friend to her, and who often let her ride before him on his horse. But not tonight. Tonight there was a horse just for her. Rilsin knew why. Even though she was only eight years old, she could ride well. If the worst should somehow happen and all their soldiers should be killed, or if they should somehow become separated, Rilsin knew she was to try to reach Hoptrin, where she could find help. In Hoptrin, people were still loyal to the SaeKet. She and Mama were trying to get there together. There was a sudden flare of torchlight.

"There they are!"

People were running toward them, and others on horseback were blocking their way. Witki drew his sword, and other soldiers did, too. Someone boosted her up onto the horse. Rilsin grabbed the reins and looked for her mother. But her mother was not on horseback. Her mother was surrounded by enemies.

"SaeKet! Behind me!" cried one of their soldiers as she tried to come forward to protect her SaeKet. But there was the thunk of an arrow, and she sprawled forward across the neck of her horse.

There were more cries and more flying arrows. Rilsin's horse reared, but she controlled it somehow. She could see that her mother had drawn her sword. There were enemies all around her mother, but they hadn't shot her. They seemed afraid, as if caught in a spell.

"Go, Rilsin," Mama cried. "Go!"

That seemed to break the spell. One of the enemy soldiers drew his sword and advanced on Mama. Rilsin screamed and kicked her horse forward. Not away from the fight, but toward it. They couldn't hurt Mama!

There was the clash of weapons, and people screaming and shouting, and horses screaming and rearing. One of the screaming horses was Rilsin's. The gelding had been shot, and Rilsin just managed to roll free as he stumbled and fell. Witki was shouting at her. He was still on his horse, and he was holding out a hand to her.

"SaeKetti! Here! Rilsin, come here!"

But Rilsin didn't, not fast enough, and then Witki was shot, too. The blood that gushed from his throat was black in the torchlight. Her mother was fighting a soldier. It didn't look the way it did in the practice sessions Rilsin had seen. There was an intensity to this that just wasn't there in practice. Her mother spared a glance and saw that Rilsin was still there, on foot.

"Run, Rilsin!" she shouted. "Run!"

At last Rilsin turned to run. But the momentary distraction had cost her mother her life. The enemy leaned in under her guard and thrust the sword deep into her breast. Rilsin saw it happen.

"Mama!"

She ran forward and somehow barreled her way through the surprised soldiers. She was beside her mother, clutching her hand as her mother's blood poured over her. Her mother reached up to touch Rilsin's face, to smooth her hair, but then her hand fell back, and she made a strange noise in her throat.

"No!" Rilsin screamed and caught up the sword from beside her mother. It was huge, way too big for her, but the soldiers stared at her and didn't try to take it away, even though it was obvious she could do nothing with it. One of them, a young woman, looked horrified and sick.

"Stay clear of the blood!" The enemy captain had come forward. The gold slashes on his sleeves gleamed. "Remember the curse of saedin blood!"

Rilsin knew about the curse. As a member of the saedin class, it was one of the first things she learned. Saedin blood was noble because it came from the land, from the Mother Herself. If it should fall on a member of a non–saedin class, especially an enemy, it could cause pain, madness, even death. Sure enough, the soldier who killed Mama was rolling on the frozen ground, gasping and ripping at the skin of his hand and arm. Suddenly he took his sword, still wet with Mama's blood, and plunged it into his own heart. One of his comrades, who had been going forward to help him, pulled back.

"I'll kill you! I'll kill you all!" Rilsin's eight-year-old voice sounded weak and thin, even in her own ears. But she took her mother's sword and sliced a gash in her arm. She cried out in surprise at the pain of this, but then she leaned forward as the blood began to well, and tried to smear it on the soldier nearest her. The soldier shouted and drew back, and Rilsin crawled forward, madly waving her bleeding arm, screaming and sobbing.

"Stop her!" said someone.

Rilsin saw a soldier fit an arrow to his bow. But another soldier, the same one who had looked sick when Mama was killed, knocked his hand aside. She took off her cloak, walked up to Rilsin, and threw it over her, bleeding arm and all.

"There, there, child, don't struggle," she said. She hugged Rilsin tight through the cloth. "Poor child!" she said.

2

THE ROOM WAS COLD BECAUSE it WAS NOt YEt FULL spring, and it got cold even in the south, but also because the walls were stone blocks with too many spaces between them and did not keep the heat in. There was only a fireplace for heat, anyway, and the fire in it was never very big. The room was high up, in a tower of what used to be the old palace, long ago, hundreds and hundreds of years ago. It was not a palace anymore, though, and it hadn't been for a very long time. It was a prison instead. There were bars on Rilsin's window, the window that looked down on a courtyard that only the pigeons and the squirrels ever visited. This was fine with Rilsin. She didn't want to see people, but the birds and squirrels were amusing and hurt no one.

Every day the old jailer took her down to this courtyard, where no one else could see, and let her sit there in the chill air. He was not supposed to do this, but he did not think that children should be locked away, whatever their parentage. He thought children should run and play outside, the way his grandchildren did. But Rilsin did not run or play. She just sat there, staring at the squirrels, until one day it occurred to her to give them some of the bread that she got twice a day. So every day she saved a little of this for the squirrels and the pigeons, and when the old man brought her to the courtyard, she parceled it out to them. The jailer shook his head over her, but she never spoke to him or even to the animals, and she never moved from the spot where she sat, so eventually he simply left her alone for a short time before bringing her back to her prison room. It did not occur to him that there might be another way out or another way in.

It was during one of these times in the courtyard that Sithli appeared. To reach the courtyard she would have had to negotiate the outer walls of the old castle and then a labyrinth of inner walls and courtyards, but that was what she did, since the jailer did not let her in and did not know she was there. Sithli obviously knew her way around the castle prison. She watched Rilsin for a day before she actually spoke to her. But when the old man had gone muttering back to his other duties, for the prison was full of captured officers and saedin loyal to the old SaeKet, Sithli came out into the open. She did this dramatically, but Rilsin did not react the way she expected. Rilsin merely looked at her and said nothing.

Sithli was a year older than Rilsin. Where Rilsin was dark-haired and dark-eyed, with a fair, pale skin, Sithli's hair was a deep honey blonde that streaked lighter in the sun. Her eyes were gray as rainwater, and her skin was golden. Rilsin was pretty, and might someday, if she lived, be beautiful, but Sithli was already beautiful, and would one day be breathtaking. Sithli and Rilsin were cousins, and before the war they had been friends. In those days, not that long ago, and irretrievably lost, Sithli had treated Rilsin as the younger sister she wished she had.

"Aren't you cold?" Sithli asked.

Rilsin merely shrugged. She was wearing the clothes in which she was captured, washed by one of the jailer's apprentices, but tattered and still stained with her mother's blood and her own.

She had no cloak for protection against the wind of early

spring, which whipped through the courtyard, but she did not shiver.

"Take my cloak," said Sithli. She had tied it into a knot around her waist to keep it from interfering with her climbs and dashes, and she untied it now. "Mama makes me wear it, but I don't need it." The cloak came free, a flash of green and gold, the colors of her family. When Rilsin saw this, she flinched back. For the first time since her capture, she spoke.

"Get it away from me! I don't want it! Get it away!"

Sithli pulled it back quickly. "Sh! Rilsin! They will find me here!" She looked around hastily, but there was no one. "Do you want them to find me?"

"I don't care what they do, or what you do, Sithli sae Melisin. Why don't you leave me alone."

"Sithli SaeKet Melisin." Sithli looked at her intently but without hostility. "I am the SaeKetti now, and one day the land will be mine."

"Your grandmother claims to be SaeKet now, since she had my mother killed." Rilsin did not cry, and she stared the other girl straight in the eyes. "But she is not. I am the true SaeKet."

"Don't let them hear you say that! The only reason you still live is because they think you are too young to understand. Grown-ups!" She sniffed and tossed her long braid, from which long wisps of blonde hair had escaped. Then she looked at Rilsin curiously. "They must not tell you anything in prison. My grandma is dead. Your soldiers killed her, before we beat them. My mama is SaeKet." Sithli had not been close to her grandmother, the way Rilsin had been to hers.

"Then go home, SaeKetti," Rilsin packed more scorn into the title than should be possible for a child her age, "and leave me alone. If you were a true SaeKetti you would know that the land will *not* belong to you. You will belong to the land." Rilsin turned away from the other child.

No matter what Sithli did or said, Rilsin did not speak to her again, or even look at her, so eventually Sithli left. The jailer returned and took the silent Rilsin back to her tower.

But that was not the end of it. The next day, and the next, and the next, Sithli returned. The jailer never caught her, the new heir to the throne visiting the old, and Rilsin never spoke. But every time she came, Sithli brought something for Rilsin, usually food that she had saved from her own supper or breakfast. Rilsin always took this, without a word, and fed it to the squirrels. She did not seem to know or care that she herself was growing painfully thin. And then one day Sithli brought a flower.

It was a wild spring-rose, the kind that grew in the fields and on the slopes of the hills when the snow was just melting, rather than the cultivated ones that grew huge and brilliant in the gardens of the saedin. Its fragrance filled the little courtyard. Rilsin took it and inhaled deeply. It reminded her of last spring, when Mama took her riding out into the hills with their hunting cats, Mama with huge golden Dek, and she with the smaller golden Bet, Dek's daughter. They had left their escort behind, and Bet and Dek together had brought down a fat deer. There had been blood on the patchy snow, and spring-roses everywhere.

"It's time to go, Rilsin." Sithli was looking at her. "You have to leave with me. We'll sneak out, and I'll hide you. I can keep you safe. They won't find you; they'll never know where you are."

Rilsin said nothing, did not acknowledge this. She only continued to smell the spring-rose.

"Rilsin! You have to come! They're going to kill you, I heard them! At first Mama didn't want them to kill you; she said it's a shame, you're so young, but she's going to agree because you're Sae Becha. I can tell. They haven't come here yet because Papa is still trying to get them to change their minds. But he won't win; he never wins when Mama has decided something. Rilsin!"

But Rilsin still said nothing. She was not yet nine years old, but she had known this was coming, ever since Mama died.

"Rilsin, they're going to cut your throat in the Mother's Square and catch your blood in the crystal goblet! They can't!" Sithli was near tears.

This was what made Rilsin finally look at her. Sithli had cared for her passionately ever since she could remember. Why this should be, she didn't know, but it obviously hadn't changed. It wasn't Sithli's fault that her family had seized the domain. And more than that, Rilsin had a sudden vision of the knife and the crystal goblet in the Square of the Mother, where saedin died and gave their blood back to the land and to the rulers. She had never seen this, but she knew how it would be. She remembered cutting her arm with the sword, and imagined the knife at her throat. She swallowed, and held out her hand to Sithli.

"Good!" Sithli jumped up, grabbing her cousin's hand. "This way! Hurry!"

That was when the jailer came back. He was old, but he was not stupid. He took it all in at once, the new SaeKetti holding the little deposed SaeKet by the hand. He was sorry for them both, but he did what he must. Despite Sithli's protests, pleas, and useless commands, he sent them both back to the palace under guard, "an escort, SaeKetti," he told Sithli unrelentingly. And he sent a message ahead to her mother. In the courtyard, a spring-rose lay forgotten and crushed on the packed earth.

3

THE PALACE WAS JUST AS RILSIN REMEMBERED it, but it was also completely different. The rooms were the same, but the hangings and crests were the bright green and gold of the Sae Melisin, not the deep blue and gold of the Sae Becha. In some places they had made a sloppy job of the replacement: the old crests had been hacked off the walls, leaving the wood raw. Many of the people she had known all her short life were gone, replaced by others, who whispered behind her as she passed. She was under the guard of soldiers, although only three of them, and Sithli was no longer with her. She had been taken away from her cousin as soon as they reached the palace grounds. But the biggest change of all came when she entered the SaeKet's Hall. Instead of Grandma Wilna in the huge carved chair there was Fraelit Sae Melisin, Sithli's mother. Fraelit, daughter of Bellinama Sae Melisin, Bellinama the Rebel, Sithli's grandmother.

Sithli was there, too, beside her mother, sitting on a stool beside the SaeKet's chair. It was a Sithli changed into clean clothes and scrubbed, at least somewhat, and with her hair freshly braided. It was also a Sithli whose golden skin had paled, and who would not look at Rilsin. Behind them both was Dinip dira Kelli, Fraelit's husband, Sithli's father. He was a dira, a member of the honored class, not a noble, but he was respected by all. Sithli loved him, and he had always been friendly and kind to Rilsin.

The soldiers brought Rilsin to the foot of the huge chair. When they did this, Rilsin noticed for the first time people that she knew. There was a small group of saedin standing to the side, guarded by soldiers. Their hands were tied behind their backs. One man, a general in her grandmother's defeated army, was trembling and couldn't seem to stop. Chella sae Lettin, a young woman with long gold hair, who was one of her mother's closest friends, was leaning against her husband. When she saw Rilsin, she burst into tears. Her husband whispered something to her, but she did not stop crying.

"Rilsin sae Becha," said Fraelit. She sounded tired. "Do you know why you are here?"

Rilsin shook her head no, although she did know. And since she did know, she decided to say something.

"SaeKet Becha," she said. "Rilsin SaeKet Becha." When she said this, Sithli finally looked at her. It was a look of despair, so Rilsin knew she was right.

"Not anymore," said Fraelit. She nodded to a man draped in green cloth, her first minister, it seemed, the one responsible for the protection of the realm. Rilsin couldn't remember who he was, although she had seen him before. He stepped forward and cleared his throat. He unfolded a paper.

"Rilsin sae Becha," he said, reading, "you stand here for the crimes of your family, for all the years of their evil. For this you are sentenced to death. Your blood will be returned to the land, that the Mother may cleanse it. On the morning of the day of the dark moon you will be taken to the Square of the Mother, to give your life to the land."

He looked up, but he did not fold up the paper. He put it down on the table near the SaeKet's chair and lit a candle that was there. Then he drew a knife and ran it through the flame. He put the knife down beside the paper and looked at Rilsin.

Rilsin knew what she was supposed to do. When saedin felt death calling them, they were said to hear the song of the land. It had been described to Rilsin as a hum or a vibration, something felt as much as heard. The SaeKet and members of her family were supposed to be able to hear it any and all the time, if they wanted to, although Rilsin wasn't sure if she'd heard it or not. The legend said that if saedin were sentenced to death for any crime, but especially for treason, they would hear the land calling for them to purify their blood. Saedin were supposed to agree to this, to prick a finger or a palm, and seal their death warrants with their own blood. That was what the knife was for.

When Rilsin made no move to go to the table, the others became uneasy. The first minister, whoever he was, obviously felt he should help her. He was saedin himself, of course, but Rilsin realized that even so, he did not want her blood on him, the blood of the SaeKet, the true SaeKet. He looked to Fraelit in appeal, and then back to Rilsin.

Rilsin ignored him for a moment. She was busy listening, trying to hear the song of the land, but all she could hear was the shuffle of feet and the shifting of garments, the sputtering of the candle, and the continuing sobs of Chella sae Lettin, softer now. It seemed to her that if there was any time to hear the song, this was it. She cocked her head, but she still wasn't sure. Could that faint hum be it? As she did this, she caught Sithli's eye again. Sithli knew what she was doing, and it looked like Sithli wanted to know if she heard it, too. This confirmed something for Rilsin: Sithli hadn't heard it either. The minister realized he had no choice and stepped forward to help, to coach Rilsin in the etiquette of death. But before the minister could reach her, could take her arm, there was a crash.

The huge window behind the SaeKet's chair had shattered. Glass was flying and people shouted and screamed and the soldiers rushed forward toward the SaeKet to protect her, but it was already too late. It happened so fast that to Rilsin, thinking about it later, it all seemed to happen at once. Someone wearing black, even over the face, had jumped through the window. It was not easy to get this far, across palace grounds guarded by soldiers, not without being caught, but this person had done it.

"Assassin!" people were screaming. Soldiers drew their swords. The prisoners in the corner, the saedin of the old regime, straightened up, beginning to look hopeful and horrified at once. But everyone was reacting too slowly.

Dinip was the first: the assassin sliced at him with a sharp two-edged knife as Dinip turned to face the intruder. Dinip cried out and threw up his arm and stepped back as blood gushed, and it was this that saved his life. The assassin was not interested in Dinip but in Dinip's wife Fraelit, the new SaeKet. Even as the soldiers surged forward, even as Fraelit started to rise from the great carved chair, the assassin reached around the side of the chair, grabbed her by the hair, yanked her head back, and cut her throat. He, and Rilsin had the definite impression the assassin was a man, did not seem to care that the SaeKet's blood was falling all over him. Almost casually he next stabbed the screaming, green-clad minister, who fell moaning to the floor. He stabbed next to the side, killing the soldier quickest to respond, the only one so far.

Then Sithli screamed. The sound cut through the air, rising above the shouts and screams of everyone else. The masked face turned toward Sithli, and quick as thought he was beside the child, reaching for her.

The only person in the entire room who had somehow anticipated this was Rilsin. Even as the assassin reached for her cousin, she was there first. She threw herself between the towering figure and her friend.

"No!" she shouted. "Not Sithli!" And she kicked the assassin as hard as she could in the shin.

That was all it took. It distracted the assassin just the necessary seconds to allow the soldiers to grab him. And grab him they could, since he was hopping on one foot. Rilsin wondered if she had caused the capture of a Sae Becha partisan, one of her own. She supposed she had, but she didn't regret it; she couldn't let him kill Sithli. But she was wrong about this, as it turned out.

"Death to all saedin!" cried the assassin. His accent was foreign. Rilsin had heard it before. It was the accent of Runchot, the merchant state to the south. He glared around him and at Rilsin in particular. "Curse you, small saedin!" he said. Then he bit down on something in his mouth. There was a bitter smell, and he slumped forward into the arms of the soldiers.

The soldiers ripped off his mask. It was a man, a pale man with long white hair, which some of the Runchot had. A little foam trickled over his lips.

"I want answers!" shouted the soldiers' captain, but he was not going to get them from the Runchot assassin, who was very definitely dead.

Rilsin looked around her. Dinip was holding his wounded arm, trying to stop the spurting of blood and at the same time somehow put his wife's head, which the assassin's cut had taken almost completely off, back on her shoulders. He was crying as he did this, but he didn't seem to know it. The prisoners, Rilsin's own friends, had been pushed back into the corner by two soldiers, as if they had anything to do with what happened. Someone was shouting to get the doctor. Sithli had stepped over the body of the first minister to get to her mother. Her eyes were huge.

"Mama?" she said. "Mama?"

Rilsin felt a lump in her throat. She put her arms around her cousin just as Sithli began to shudder, and she held her as Sithli gasped out great sobs. Then Rilsin began to cry, too; she couldn't help it. The two girls clung together in the midst of the blood and corpses until the soldiers' captain came over to them and grabbed Rilsin, yanking her up by the shoulder.

"On the day of the dark moon," he said to Rilsin, "that is what you will be like." He nodded at Fraelit, lying in her blood. "Damned Becha brat!" He dragged her up.

Rilsin didn't struggle. She couldn't because she was crying too hard. It was all too much, all the blood and hatred and violence, and Sithli's mama dead, and her own mama, her own mama . . .

"You leave her alone! Put her down right now!" Sithli was still crying, the tears streaking down her face. But her voice carried over the pandemonium in the hall, and there was a note in it that commanded attention. "She is not going to die!"

The captain looked confused, and he stood with Rilsin' dangling from his grasp, but he didn't put her down. It was clear he didn't want to.

Sithli ran over to the table, which miraculously still stood, with the candle still burning. She smashed the candle to the floor and stamped on it. Then she snatched up Rilsin's death warrant and ripped it into little pieces. The pieces of paper floated across the room on the breeze from the broken window.

"I am the SaeKet!" Sithli's fists were clenched, and her face was turning an odd shade of brownish purple. "Put her down!"

The captain did. This was when Dinip came over to his daughter. His arm had been tied with a belt around it, and the bleeding had stopped, but he was holding it as if it hurt a lot. He put his good hand on Sithli's shoulder and spoke over her head to the captain. He had to sniff and clear his throat.

"I am regent for the SaeKet," he said. "You may obey her command and release Rilsin sae Becha to my custody. Come here, Rilsin."

Rilsin went, carefully avoiding Fraelit's body. Dinip put his good arm, somehow, around both Sithli and Rilsin, and drew them to him.

"The Civil War ends now," he said. He looked around the room as if daring anyone to contradict him. "Rilsin sae Becha will live. She will be the right hand of the SaeKet."

"When we are grown up," said Sithli to Rilsin, "you can be my first minister."

Rilsin looked at Sithli, looked up at Dinip. She was only eight, but she knew a political compromise when she heard one. Then, finally, she looked at Fraelit. Her face hardened and her tears stopped.

"All right," she said clearly, "I will. And I will see that the land is kept safe. No more killing. Only peace."

"Only peace," said Sithli.

It was then they realized there was silence in the hall. Everyone had been listening to them. For a moment no one moved. Then the doctor, who had finally arrived, came to look at Dinip's arm.

4

It was a beautiful day in summer. The flowers were blooming in all the vast palace gardens, and birds were teaching their fledglings to fly. Iridescent insects droned everywhere.

The late afternoon sun lay golden along the old pinkish stone of the palace and along the well-kept paths. It also lay golden on the SaeKet's woods, in the near distance. Rilsin knew the moors and plains would be golden, too, but she also knew there was not enough time for her to escape to the moors and be back again before dark. The woods, and only the edge of the woods, was the best she could hope for today, and only if she hurried. She brushed her hand through her short hair. It was kept short to show that she was not a free citizen but a prisoner of the SaeKet. At first this bothered her, but it had been kept short for so many years now that she preferred it that way, especially in the summer, and she felt sorry for Sithli, whose long golden tresses were always getting in the way and getting her scolded.

At fourteen years of age Rilsin had just undergone a growing spurt. She had gained some of the height for which

the Sae Bechas were known, and although she did not realize it, she had the grace and the wiry aura of power that
were also family trademarks. She was also beautiful in a re-
mote, almost austere way, a way that was at first not as no-
ticeable as her cousin's stunning good looks. If anyone were
to tell Rilsin that she was beautiful, she would have
laughed, but no one told her. Sithli was often told.

Rilsin ran through the gardens behind the palace and
quickly darted down a side path that led past the huge and
rambling servants' quarters. As soon as she was well along
this path, she tied up her shirt into a knot that exposed her
midriff to the little summer breeze. It was a trick she had
seen the serving women do when they did not have formal
duties in the palace. She also rolled her trousers up above
her knees. None of this was considered appropriate dress for
a saedin and the cousin of the SaeKet, free citizen or not,
but it was much cooler and more comfortable in the summer
heat.

Around her neck on a thong was a pendant, her only or-
nament. It was made from her naming amulet and her
mother's ring, which had been melted together. Sithli had
this done for her years ago, saving the two items when they
were taken from Rilsin, and having them molded into a new
form. The pendant was all that remained of Rilsin's early
childhood and of her mother. She fingered it unconsciously
as she walked.

She waved at some of the servants who saw her as she
darted past, and they waved back, but Rilsin was not stopping to talk today. She wanted to get away from the palace
and her lessons as fast as she could, and get out where she
could breathe.

The sun was much lower by the time she got to the
SaeKet's woods. This was only to be expected. But what
disturbed Rilsin and altered her plans was the presence of a
group of saedin, out for a summer ride and a picnic. It was
the snorting of their horses that first alerted Rilsin. Normally she would have seen their signs of passing in the
fields and parklands, but she was so intent on getting away

from the palace that she had not been paying attention, and she was lucky they didn't see her first.

She had learned tracking from the first huntsman, who once let slip that he wished she were not who she was, so that she might become his apprentice instead. It was a rare compliment. And because Rilsin prided herself on her wild-sense, almost running into the recreational party of saedin was especially annoying. Adding insult to injury was the fact that she must creep along on her stomach through the tall grass to avoid being seen, getting scratched and hot in the process. But since she didn't want to be found, she wasn't.

When she emerged from the grass, so far away from the picnickers that she could no longer even hear them, she was outside a portion of the woods she had previously avoided. She had avoided this portion of the woods for one major reason and one minor reason. The minor reason was that these woods were not tended as the woods closer to the palace were. They were overgrown with thickets and bram-bles, which made riding in them impossible and walking in them difficult and unpleasant. The major reason was that this portion of the woods was once her mother's favorite place to take her when they wanted to get away from the palace. Then it was better tended, kept clear of the choking secondary growth that had overrun it now. Rilsin had avoided it diligently for years, ever since her capture and her reprieve from death. But now, looking at it in the light of late afternoon, Rilsin felt drawn to go into the shade of the trees, to see if anything was as she remembered it from the misty long ago. Pausing to tug down her pant legs and her shirt for protection against the brambles, she forced her way in.

It was much cooler under the trees, and once slightly deeper into the woods, the brambles thinned out. Rilsin found a path she was sure she remembered, and she began to follow it. She was certain it led to a stream, and some-where along the course of the stream should be a cabin, a forester's shelter, for use in bad weather. But the stream was not where she remembered, and she wandered for a while,

confused and vaguely upset that her memory, which she had
carefully tried to repress for so long, should have done what
she wanted it to and failed after all. She climbed a rock out-
crop in the hope of seeing a little into the surrounding
woods. She couldn't see far, but while she was there, there
was a pause in the birdsong as a hawk swept overhead. In
the silence, Rilsin was sure she heard the sound of a stream
over rocks. She hurried down to follow the sound.

It was there, much diminished by summer, and not where
she remembered. But she was sure it was the same stream;
it had just altered its course. She walked along the bank,
noting where the wildflowers grew and a little pool where
there might be fish. Perhaps she could come back here
again, to this place where she could be away from everyone.

It was pleasantly cool after the heat and stuffiness of the
little room where she had spent most of the day at her lessons with Sithli. Sithli was still at her lessons, while Rilsin
had been let go. She knew Sithli would give much to be
with her now. But Sithli was not only the SaeKet and one
year older than Rilsin, she was a much poorer student.
Rilsin already knew geometry, history, religion, and spoke
the two languages of the Runchot and the three dialects of
the northern barbarians fluently (the latter because she spent
time talking to northern prisoners), while Sithli struggled
with her mathematics and mangled any language but her native Saeditin. Rilsin tried hard to coach her, but it seemed to
make no difference in Sithli's progress or lack of it. Today,
out of heat and frustration Sithli lost her temper, snapping at
both her tutor and the innocent Rilsin. So Rilsin was sent
out into the air while the SaeKet was held inside to conju-
gate Runchot verbs.

Rilsin kicked off her old leather shoes and slipped her
feet into the water. It felt wonderful, and she sighed and
wiggled her toes. The pool here might even be big enough
for swimming. She decided to try it out and hastily stripped
off her clothes. Yes, the water was deep enough, and Rilsin
splashed happily. It occurred to her to keep this place secret
even from Sithli, and she felt a pang of guilt. Not only did

she owe everything to Sithli, but Sithli was her best friend, her only friend.

The noise of the explosion caused Rilsin to freeze motionless in the water. It came from nearby, and sure enough, within moments there was a white and gray cloud puffing up into the treetops. Rilsin scrambled out of the water and into her clothes without attempting to dry herself. She crammed her wet feet into her shoes, shook her head like a dog, slicked her hand over her hair, and set off to find out what was going on.

It was the old forester's cabin. She couldn't mistake it, the place where she and her mother and sometimes their guard would stop to rest on their woodland rides. It was run down, after all these years, which was only to be expected, but someone recently had been trying to fix it up. And from the open window issued the cloud, or what was left of it. Steam, Rilsin saw. Also from the open window issued the sound of heartfelt cursing. It occurred to Rilsin that whatever it was that exploded might have harmed whoever it was who was inside cursing. Without hesitation she shoved open the wooden door and stepped in.

Inside it was more humid than anything had a right to be, even at the height of summer. Condensed steam dripped down one wall. A fire burned on the floor where it had been scraped bare, and wood was piled around it. Over the fire was a strange contraption: cast-iron containers fitted one above the other, with iron tubes connecting them. The lid had apparently blown off the top container. There was also a small water tank sitting on a high carved shelf, with a pipe that connected it to the top container. There was water everywhere; everything was wet. In the midst of this mess stood a boy of about Sithli's age who regarded her with alarm.

"Are you badly hurt?" Rilsin peered at him.

"I'm not hurt at all. What are you doing here?"

"I saw the explosion, so I came to see if anyone was hurt. What are *you* doing here? And what is that thing? That is what exploded, isn't it." This last was a statement rather than a question, as it seemed obvious, and Rilsin went to get a closer look at the thing. The boy was too astonished to stand in her way, so Rilsin got to examine it for a moment.

"You shouldn't be here," said the boy. While Rilsin examined his contraption, he examined her. He determined, from her clothing, her hair, and general appearance that she was the daughter of a political prisoner or more likely a war captive, probably a barbarian from the north, and therefore a prisoner herself. She undoubtedly worked at the palace and had somehow gotten the afternoon off. "You're pretty far from the palace. If they catch you, you'll be in big trouble." This was true. A captive servant who shirked was severely punished.

"Oh!" Rilsin had been paying no attention to him. "Oh! You heat the water in here to make steam, and it rises to here through this pipe, and that blew the lid off, right?"

"Right. I—"

"Why does cold water come in here?"

"It's supposed to condense the steam and pull the piston down."

"What?"

"The lid. It's a piston. I attach it to a weight over there—" he pointed, Rilsin looked, "and it will move a pump. Or it should, when I get it right. It's not right yet."

Rilsin stared at him, first in surprise and then in awe. "Do you know what this can do?" She was too excited to wait for an answer. "After you get it to work right, you could heat the whole palace with this! Just run the steam through pipes, the pipes could go right on the walls—"

"I thought it could it pump water out of the mines."

"Of course! This is wonderful! Did you tell anyone about it yet? Where did you get the iron pipes? And the containers? They look as though they were specially made."

"They were. My mother knows I'm doing this, even though she doesn't think it will come to anything. She doesn't think I'll ever get it right, and even if I do, she doesn't think anyone will care. It's only steam, she says. But she got the blacksmith to make me these."

"You've almost got it right now. It won't be long. Who's your mother?"

The boy looked at her for a moment and then shrugged. "My mother is Kerida dira Mudrin. I'm Sola dira Mudrin. I just returned from two years' fostering with my aunt in the east."

A member of the honored class, not noble but certainly high-ranking. All the same, he looked a little embarrassed. Rilsin realized all at once why this was, and what she must look like. Sola dira Mudrin did not want to make a palace servant, a captive, feel awkward. She warmed toward him, and as she did she realized she knew the name.

"Your mother," she said, "she's the keeper."

"The royal keeper of the cats," he said. "Yes. She takes care of all the hunting cats for the saedin, and breeds them, too. Have you seen them close up? The cats?"

"No," said Rilsin shortly. For a long time she had grieved for her own cat, the sweet Bet. But only the SaeKet's family was allowed the golden hunters, so Bet was taken from her and given to Sithli. Sithli treated Bet like another toy, and it was obvious to anyone that she did not really care about the animal. Despite this, Sithli would try to sneak Rilsin in to see the cat, and vice versa, but they were usually caught. Sithli stopped trying, and Bet pined away, refusing to eat, and died. Rilsin had stayed away from the cats ever since, even though she had been offered a choice of the striped hunters the dira and most saedin used, or even the rare silver ones the nonroyal saedin coveted.

"There's no need to be afraid of them." Sola had misinterpreted her. "They're gentle when they're properly bred, and when they know you. My mother lets me help her sometimes."

Rilsin was not really listening to him anymore. She had glanced out the window. "I've got to go," she said. "I've got to get back. The sun is setting."

She went to the door, Sola with her, and he saw she was right. The summer afternoon was over, and evening was beginning to cool the land.

"If I don't get back, they'll have the cats after *me*." Rilsin laughed, but there was an edge to it. She did have to be back, and they probably would set the cats after her.

"Good luck with your steam machine, Sola. Can I come back sometime and see it?"

"Yes! I'd like that! Don't tell anyone about it, though. I came out here to keep it secret. Will they let you out again?"

"Oh, yes. Sometime." Rilsin shifted her gaze. She realized that she couldn't keep this secret from Sithli, not if she planned on coming back. "I may have to bring a friend. She can be trusted," she added. She was out the door in a bound.

"Wait! You didn't tell me your name or where you serve! Who are you?"

But it was too late. Rilsin had vanished into the shadows of the forest and the evening.

5

It was after dark when she got back, even though it was the soft gray early dark of summer, and she had to sneak into the palace. She knew there would be questions, and she wanted to avoid them as long as possible. She took the secret way she and Sithli had, a way disused and long ago forgotten, the old passage from the kitchens to the room that was now Sithli's parlor, which once had been a SaeKet's private dining room. The room Rilsin lived in was just off of this, a small space with one high window where servants would wait to attend the SaeKet. No one needed to point out to Rilsin just how appropriate this was.

The room was stifling, despite the open window. It was also dark. Rilsin squelched in and kicked off her sodden shoes with a grunt, and reached to yank her shirt off over her head. It was then that she became aware that there was someone in the room. Without a perceptible pause, she converted her motion into a sideways dodge. She grabbed the knife she had hidden under the pile of folded shirts on top of the small dresser, and in another second had grabbed the person who was waiting at the head of her bed. She guessed correctly, and had her knife at the throat in less time than it took to draw breath.

"Rils! Rils, it's me!" The voice was squeaky with surprise and fear, but recognizable, as was the shape under Rilsin's hands.

"Sithli! What in the Mother's name are you doing?"

"Don't swear! Waiting for you."

"In the dark? Damn it, Sithli, I'll swear if I want to! What if I'd killed you? Or even cut you? A cut, even a scratch would give that slimy Zechia just what he's been hoping for." She groped for a match, a new invention in Saeditin, and held the sudden flare of light high as she reached for the oil lamp. Before she could light the lamp, Sithli leaned over and blew out the match.

"There's a reason, stupid!" said the SaeKet. "I wanted to warn you. They're looking for you, and you're in trouble."

"Who's looking? I'm not that late. I did get the afternoon off."

"Bilma and Nefit, right now. The doorkeepers have been alerted, and Zechia suggested sending out guards, or at least the cats. I talked Bilma out of it, at least for now, or Nefit did." Bilma was the first minister. In theory he reported to Sithli, the SaeKet, but in reality he reported to the regent, her father Dinip.

"Nefit! Oh damn! I was supposed to see her tonight!" Nefit was the doctor, the SaeKet's personal physician. "How could I forget! Oh damn it damn it damn it! I'd better go find her before it gets any worse. Where is she, in her rooms or her laboratory?"

"Rooms, I think. You can't get there without getting stopped."

"How could I forget it's slop night?"

"All too easily, if you ask me. I told them that's all it was, that you just forgot, that you weren't trying to escape the treatment, let alone the palace. But you know Zechia. A little overzealous, but he means well."

"He does *not* mean well, as I keep telling you. He's dangerous, and I don't just mean to me. He's dangerous to you.

I'm just a way to get at you." Rilsin sometimes referred to him as Zechia the Odious.

Sithli raised her hand to forestall argument. "Let's not talk about this again right now; you have to get to Nefit. I'll go with you; that way you won't get stopped or brought with an escort of guards. Zechia wanted you bound."

"That won't happen." For a moment Rilsin looked grim and much older than she was. Sithli was reminded again of just how good Rilsin was at arms practice. Rilsin was a natural, the instructors said. That she was allowed arms practice at all was still a cause of concern for some, and for Zechia sae Eanern in particular, it seemed, but not for Sithli. Sithli, and almost everyone else, had no doubt that Rilsin's growing skills would be used only in Sithli's defense or at her command. "Just let me go with you," Sithli said. "It's better that way."

They paused only long enough for Rilsin to put on dry shoes and a clean shirt. When she dropped the dirty shirt, her pendant went with it. She reached for it, but Sithli stopped her.

"Get it later," she said. "The guards will be here soon." Sure enough, they were no sooner out of Rilsin's room and down the corridor than they were approached by two guards, who drew back at the sight of the SaeKet.

"We have been sent to find Rilsin sae Becha," said one of them. He was a saedin himself, as were most of the palace guards.

"Well, here she is," said Sithli. "As you see, she is with me."

"She is to be brought to Nefit sae Culli."

"That's where we're going," said Sithli.

The guards looked uneasy.

"No one needs to bring me anywhere, Zeltin," said Rilsin with a grin, "but you can come along if that helps."

Zeltin grinned back at her. He had seen her practice, and he had a great respect for her abilities. He had also heard how quick she was at her lessons and how loyal she was to her cousin. In short, Zeltin liked her. And he knew it was reciprocated, and that she had no desire to see him get in trou-

ble with his superiors for not following his orders. So he
and his partner fell in on either side of the girls and escorted
them down the palace corridors, past startled servants,
guards, and the occasional official, to the rooms of Nefit sae
Culli, physician to the SaeKet and her family.

Lamps were burning outside the door, and there were
more guards waiting. Rilsin didn't wait for them to open the
door and announce them but stepped ahead of Sithli and
pushed through the door first, with Sithli and the two guards
right behind her.

The doctor's outer room was bright with light and
crowded with adults. Bilma sae Grepsin, the first minister,
was there, deep in conversation with the regent, Dinip dira
Kelli, and with Zechia sae Eanern, Zechia the Odious.
There were also several guards and servants, and the doctor's assistant and apprentice, Maltia sae Dofrit, a young
man of nineteen years. All of these people looked up as
Rilsin burst into the room. Only the physician herself was
absent.

"I am sorry to be late, Uncle." Rilsin wasted no time, addressing Dinip before anyone had a chance to recover and
speak. "I didn't mean to cause you any worry; I just forgot
what night it was."

"Oh, indeed! And you expect us to believe that?" It was
Zechia who answered. Although Zechia was only on the regent's council, he was more finely dressed than anyone
there. Others were dressed in linen and the new fabric, cotton, but his trousers were brocade and his long shirt was
thick maroon velvet, despite the heat. Jewels twinkled in his
long brown braid.

Rilsin flushed slightly but did not reply. Except for the
flush and the subtle clenching of her jaw muscle, it would
have been possible to think she had failed to hear him. She
continued to look politely at her uncle.

"You may believe whatever my cousin tells you." Sithli
stepped from behind Rilsin into clear view.

"SaeKet!" Zechia put his hand over his heart ostenta-
tiously and inclined his head. "I did not see you! Please believe I have only your welfare at heart!" He inclined his

head again, his hand still splayed across the velvet cloth covering his chest.

Rilsin glanced at Sithli briefly, and although she said nothing, the glance spoke for her. *Odious!* it said. Dinip read this as clearly as his daughter did. He frowned.

"Where have you been?"

"I went for a walk at the edge of the forest. I simply forgot. I meant no harm." Rilsin gritted her teeth. She didn't mind apologizing to Dinip, but she hated doing it in front of Zechia.

"You should take my advice," said Zechia to Dinip, "and not permit her to leave the palace. She cannot be trusted."

"Surely that is not necessary," said Bilma, the first minister, "although some punishment is appropriate." He was quite willing to dismiss the whole problem and get home to a late dinner with his wife and children.

"She is a danger to all of us, but especially to the SaeKet!" Zechia pulled at his long braid in agitation. "She should be sold to the Runchot!"

"Never! You touch her at your peril, Zechia sae Eanern!" Sithli stepped forward. "Your concern for me carries you too far!"

"Enough!" Dinip glared at Zechia, irritated. "She is still a child, and children forget. She meant no harm, just as she says. But saedin should not forget, and the future first Minister least of all. Rilsin, you will be confined to the palace for the rest of the month. In your free time you will help the SaeKet with her lessons or study, yourself. That should help you to remember." Dinip was sometimes overwhelmed, not by the government of the land of Saeditin but by the necessity of acting as sole parent to two girls.

"As you say, Uncle." Rilsin inclined her head very slightly to the regent, but her eyes did not leave Zechia. It was a calculating stare, cold and intelligent. It was a gaze that should have belonged to someone much older and more experienced than a fourteen-year-old child, and it said very clearly that Rilsin had his measure. Meeting it, Zechia shivered.

All of this ended when Nefit sae Culli strode into the

room. "A little late, hmm, Rilsin? Well, never mind." The doctor held a flask of purplish liquid. Rilsin fought a gag reflex when she saw it, and she swallowed quickly so no one would notice.

"Rilsin, come with me, and you, too, Maltia. Everyone else can go."

Dinip shepherded his daughter out of the room, followed with hasty relief by servants, guards, and First Minister Bilma. Zechia lingered.

"You also, Sae Zechia."

"I should stay, or someone should, to make sure the young traitor does not escape her sentence."

"Rilsin is the SaeKet's cousin, not a traitor. And do you mean to question my integrity or my capability, or both, Zechia sae Eanern?"

"Your pardon! Neither, Sae Nefit."

"Then, out!" Nefit gestured, and Maltia, a tall young man, made as if to escort him physically. Zechia left in haste.

"Such a to-do! See what happens when you are a little late, Rilsin." Nefit had carried the flask into the next room and set it down on a wooden table.

"Yes," said Rilsin. "It gets me stuck in this pile of stone for the hottest weeks of the summer with nothing to do but work. This is the first time I've been late. Ever. You would think they could grant me a little grace."

"Sit down, Rilsin." She nodded in the direction of a comfortable chair, the soft, overstuffed chair that Rilsin usually took. "It is because this *is* the first time, *and* because you are approaching the age of womanhood that they reacted as they did. You must not forget your importance. If nothing else, these sessions should remind you of that."

The physician's rooms reflected her personality. They were comfortable and serviceable, well-appointed but not ostentatious. The heavy velvet curtains of winter were down, replaced by the filmy new cotton that the Runchot imported from somewhere far to the south. But most of the hangings and coverings were traditional Saeditin embroidered linen, and the furniture was of native wood. Rilsin ran her fingers over the highly polished wood of Nefit's big table while she pondered the doctor's words. The decision to let her live, all those years ago, had been in large part a compromise, a compromise to satisfy Becha partisans and end the war. Rilsin was under no illusions. Her uncle and her cousin loved her, but she was a living token to the commoners and to the supporters of the old regime that the Melisins would keep the peace.

"Are you ready, Sae Rilsin?" Maltia had come up behind her chair. He held wide straps of softened leather in his hands. "Shall I use these?" he asked, as he did every week.

"Not necessary," said Rilsin, as she had ever since the first time, when Nefit herself was the physician's apprentice. She settled herself deeper into the chair, trying to make herself comfortable, although she knew it was a futile attempt. There would be no comfort until this was over. She held out her arm. Maltia took it in a grip that was gentle yet firm as a vise. He clasped her arm against his body, bracing himself, and held the small hollow needle ready. When he was in position, he nodded to Nefit, who handed Rilsin a clear glass filled with the purplish liquid that was in the flask.

Rilsin had endured this ordeal ever since her release from the tower prison, every week for six years. It was a major condition of her continued survival, one that the otherwise gentle-hearted regent insisted upon. The purple liquid in Nefit's glass was an intensely strong concentration of beltrip, an herb known to every Saeditin woman, whether of the noble, honored, or common classes. In lesser doses it was a contraceptive. In such a strong dose, and taken every week over a span of years, it destroyed fertility permanently. It was a crime in Saeditin to use it this way, except by order of the state. Nonetheless, prostitutes had been known to sometimes give it to their daughters from the time their daughters were small, but even they did not administer the dosages to which Rilsin had been subjected. In large enough doses, it could be fatal.

Rilsin took a deep breath and downed the contents of the glass in two great gulps. The resulting nausea was almost immediate. She broke out in a cold, heavy sweat, and her stomach cramped. She clenched her teeth against the urge to vomit.

"Keep it down, Rilsin, that's a girl!" Nefit made no move to help Rilsin. There was nothing she could do, but if Rilsin should vomit the mixture up, she would have to take it again, and again, if necessary, until it stayed down. That had happened only five times over the years, and when it did, Nefit had to be very careful. By order of the regent, Rilsin must have as high a dose as possible, but Nefit did not want to kill her.

Rilsin gripped the arm of the chair with her free hand as the convulsions began. This was what Maltia's straps were for, to keep her from thrashing too hard, but Rilsin had never needed them. She stiffened herself against the drug and breathed loudly through her mouth. It was now that Maltia inserted the little hollow needle into the vein in her arm and withdrew a tiny amount of blood. The blood had an odd bluish cast to it. He held it so Nefit could see.

"It looks right. Take it in the other room," said the physician, and Maltia went. Nefit would examine the blood in a few minutes. If it had small threads of blue in it, Rilsin must be watched to be sure she did not slip into a coma. But the solid blue tint was merely a sign that it was working as it should.

The cramps and the convulsions were easing now, and Rilsin knew it would be all right, she was not going to throw up this time. She closed her eyes as the nausea faded, and slumped back into the big chair. She had never resisted this treatment, even though she understood, even as a small child, just what it meant. Every Saeditin woman, it was assumed, would someday want a child, preferably a daughter, to carry on the family name. That was precisely why Rilsin, the last of the royal Sae Bechas, could not be permitted to have one. A Sae Becha must never attempt to regain the SaeKet's chair from the Sae Melisins.

Rilsin did not care. In fact, she preferred it this way. She had known from the time she was first given the drug that she did not want children. At nine years of age she had had plenty of experience in being a child, and she did not wish that experience on anyone else. Nothing in the intervening years had caused her to alter her opinion.

Nefit had gone into the inner room to examine the blood, and Maltia had come out to watch Rilsin. When she opened her eyes, he offered her a mug of warm, salty broth. She took it but made no attempt to drink it. She was still shaky and weak.

"I don't suppose you ate dinner," said Maltia. Rilsin didn't answer him. "I didn't think so. Well, it's too late now." He sighed. "I wish I could have been out in the woods today myself." He meant it. He was only nineteen, and was in the early years of his apprenticeship, which he sometimes found to be more work than he had imagined. He would have liked a little more relief from his duties.

Rilsin sipped the broth tentatively. It was supposed to settle her stomach, and she guessed it must do something along those lines, since she always felt a little stronger after drinking it. As she finished it, Nefit came back.

"It's all normal. You can go, Rilsin, whenever you're ready."

Rilsin put the mug down, smoothed back her sweat-dampened hair, and straightened her clothes. As usual she said nothing and offered no complaint, but Nefit couldn't resist a little sympathy.

"It won't go on forever, Rilsin. One year, or two at the most, just to be sure, after you begin to bleed. Knowing Dira Dinip, probably two years, but then it will be all over. It may seem like forever from where you are now, but it won't be that long."

"No," said Rilsin. She did not relish even thinking about years more of "slop night," as she and Sithli called it. And she felt an uncharacteristic flash of resentment. Surely the drug must have worked by now, after all these years, and she didn't need any more.

"Nothing," she said, quoting the proverb, "is forever except the Mother's love and the land of Saeditin, which will both last until the end of time." She didn't wait for Nefit's reply but went straight out the door.

6

RILSIN'S CONFINEMENT TO THE PALACE WAS IN SOME
ways worse for Sithli than it was for Rilsin. There were
other saedin children to play with, but none except Rilsin
treated Sithli in an open and unselfconscious manner. They
all, on various levels, remembered that she was SaeKet, and
worse, treated her as such. This made an impression on
Sithli, one that she told herself she didn't like. So at first it
was Sithli who tried to rebel. She declared that if Rilsin
couldn't leave the palace but must stay and work, then she,
Sithli, would do the same.

The declaration did not have the desired effect. Her tutors informed her that the additional study would be very
good for her, and that with a little diligence she could perhaps catch up to where she should be by the start of the cool
weather. It was to Sithli's credit that she tried hard to stick
to her promise, but it was not surprising that her temper
grew a little short. The summer was one of the hottest in
years, and the most humid. Even the stone bulk of the
palace soaked up the heat. After the first week of her vol-
untary confinement, Sithli was regretting her promise.

"You should have known that a threat like that would turn around and bite you, Sith." Rilsin was feeling a little short-tempered herself, after an afternoon of trying to speak Northern Runchot with her cousin. Sithli kept confusing verb tenses. "You don't have to stay here just because I do. Nothing is stopping you from going out." If Sithli would leave her alone, Rilsin would be able to choose between studying astronomy, which was a new art and not to be confused with astrology, the ancient art, and practicing unarmed combat. But if Sithli stayed, it was going to be Runchot all afternoon. She also wanted to look again for her pendant, which had been missing since the fateful slop night. Sithli thought it must have gone to the laundry with the dirty clothes. Rilsin wanted to question the laundry workers herself, to avoid getting them in trouble.

"You know I'm not going to leave without you."

"Well, then, we're stuck. Talk to me about how much you hate it. In Northern Runchot."

"We're not stuck. You will just have to leave with me."

"I can't, Sith. You know it. The guards won't let me past, and if I try—well—I'll be in worse trouble. Uncle Dinip won't forgive it. He'll forgive a lot of things, but not deliberate disobedience of that magnitude."

Sithli frowned. Although her cousin was one year younger, she was always using words like *magnitude*. It irritated her. "My father," she said, "won't mind. Well, all right, he will, if he knows. But he won't know." When Rilsin said nothing, Sithli went on. "We can sneak out through the old tunnel under the kitchens and come out by the horse pastures. And we can be back again before dark, the same way. I'll tell Sae Flotig that we're going to study in my private courtyard, and we're not to be disturbed. He can see us settled in there and close the door on us. We can even lock it. Then we go over the wall at the back, come around, and sneak back into the passage by your room—that's the tricky part—and then into the old tunnel. Come on, Rils. You promised to take me to see Sola. If we wait two more weeks, he may be gone, and I want to see the workshop. He may already be gone."

"I'll tell you how to find him. You can go by yourself."
Rilsin hated the thought of this. She didn't know why, but
she thought of Sola as *her* friend, someone who thought the
way she did. She was not sure just why, since she barely
knew him, but something told her this was true. He liked her
without knowing who she was or anything about her.

"I'm not going by myself. I'd get lost. But I *am* going,
and you're going with me." She raised her hand when Rilsin
opened her mouth to protest. "You don't have a choice. I
command you."

Rilsin stared at her cousin for a split second and then
laughed. She didn't take Sithli seriously. Her cousin had
never tried to command her before, and the truth of it was
that Sithli wielded no more power than Rilsin at this stage.
Her father did everything in her name.

The laughter hung on the sultry air like something tangi-
ble. All of the heat and the irritations and annoyances of the
past days, all of Sithli's unhappiness at having condemned
herself to share Rilsin's confinement seemed to congeal
around it. Sithli's eyes got small and hard, and the blood
rushing to her face darkened her golden skin.

"You . . . will . . . come . . . with . . . me." Her voice was
low and controlled and filled with such anger that Rilsin felt
the back of her neck grow cold. "If you don't, I'll tell Sae
Flotig that you refused to help me with the verbs, that you
told me to do my own work, and that when I complained,
you slapped me. He'll believe me. And you know what will
happen then."

The tutor would believe her, and for good reason. Less
than a year ago Rilsin had slapped her cousin. It was after a
quarrel when they both lost their tempers and Sithli kicked
Rilsin in the shins. They were both scolded, but Rilsin was
given a warning. If she ever physically attacked the SaeKet
again, no matter what the provocation, she would be
whipped publicly. Rilsin stared at her cousin, unable to believe what she had just heard.

"You won't!"

"Flotig will tell my father. By the time they question me,
I'll be sorry I said anything, and I'll beg them not to whip

you, but it won't do any good." Sithli looked at her cousin, who seemed not to be breathing. "So, which is it? Are we going to the woods, or are you going to the whipping block?"

For a moment Rilsin said nothing: The truth was that she couldn't. She felt as though someone had just pulled the earth out from under her feet, and she was floating in that vast nothingness the astronomers told her was the home of the stars. She had seen Sithli's temper before and been on the receiving end of it often enough, and she had seen Sithli manipulate others. But Sithli had never done anything like this to her. She had always trusted Sithli. It never crossed her mind that Sithli could treat her this way.

"Answer me, Rilsin. I'm waiting."

Rilsin could see that she meant her threat. Out of a vast emptiness, where nothing seemed to have meaning any-more, she said, "The woods."

"Well, then, let's go." Now that Sithli had gotten her way, the anger was gone. "No, wait. I'll go tell Sae Flotig. You stay here. I'll be right back."

It all went as Sithli planned. They climbed over the courtyard wall, sneaked back into the palace through the open doors near the regent's breakfast room, and scurried down the corridors to the tunnels near Rilsin's room. Twice they had to duck out of the way, once into a closet and once behind a wall hanging, as guards went by. Sithli was smoth-ering giggles after this, but Rilsin was quiet and grim.

The old tunnel was cool and dusty, and they surfaced back into the heat at the side of a brush pile outside the horse pastures. The brush pile was carefully maintained by the girls for the express purpose of hiding this secret door-way. After checking to make sure no one had seen them, Rilsin pushed brush back around the entrance. All this time Rilsin had said nothing.

"Come on, Rils, cheer up. We haven't been caught yet. We won't be."

They had to crawl through the long grass at the far side of the pastures, dropping down suddenly when a groom came out of a shed. If Rilsin had thought to talk about it first with Sithli, she would have suggested that they simply try to continue on their way, acting as normally as possible, and hope that anyone they saw would just ignore them, since there were plenty of children of all classes running around the fields in the summer. But it didn't occur to her to do this, so when Sithli dramatically ducked down at the sight of the groom, Rilsin had no choice but to follow. Luckily, the man didn't see them.

It seemed as though Sithli was right, for they had no problems after this and reached the fringes of the old wood without encountering anyone else at close range. It was cooler in the woods. Sithli caught her thin cotton trousers on a bramble, tearing them. She had not dressed appropriately for this excursion. Rilsin, hot in linsey-woolsey, felt a dull stab of apprehension. Since she must be along for this adventure, she wanted there to be no trace of it. Sithli's torn clothing now made that impossible. She realized that not only was her cousin wearing cotton trousers, but she was wearing a short-sleeved, lightweight silken blouse. It seemed an invitation to disaster.

Rilsin tried to lead Sithli straight to the old hunting lodge, but Sithli heard the stream and insisted on going to see it. She did not find Rilsin's pool, but she took off her shoes to wade in the water and sighed with relief at how cool it was. Rilsin did not join her but stood on the bank, staring into the treetops.

"So you used to come here with your mother." Sithli's voice made Rilsin start, and not just because she had climbed silently up behind her. Rilsin was remembering, out of the haze of the past, and despite herself, the face of a woman crowned with long dark hair, a woman who smiled at her and sang her songs. She had been fingering her neck for her lost pendant.

"I think so," she said shortly. "Get your shoes on and we'll go."

Sithli crammed her feet into her shoes and put her hand on Rilsin's shoulder. When Rilsin did not react, she moved to face her cousin.

"I'm sorry, Rils. Really."

Rilsin gently removed the other girl's hand and turned to lead the way.

"Rilsin, please! I didn't mean it. When I said I'd tell Flotig. I didn't mean it:"

Now Rilsin turned. "You did mean it. You meant it then." Her voice was perfectly calm. Inside, somewhere, there were tears, but Rilsin had promised herself a long time ago that tears, for any reason, would never come out.

They looked at each other. Sithli was the one who started to cry.

"Yes. I did mean it." She began to sob. "You made me so angry! I can't stand that; you know how I am. I wanted to see your face when they came to take you, but if they had really whipped you, I don't think I could bear it! I'm sorry, Rils, truly! Say you forgive me!"

"Of course." Rilsin accepted her cousin's embrace and returned it, putting her arms around Sithli. It was all true, she realized. Sithli had furious rages. For the first time, Sithli had turned one of those rages full force against her. Sithli wanted badly to see her punished, but—*and*—Sithli would have been wild with grief and self-blame if that punishment had been carried out.

"Of course I forgive you." She did, too. But she would remember, from now on, that she was not immune to her cousin's moods and tempers.

"Good! Let's go find Sola and his wonderful machine!"

The hunting lodge at first showed no signs of use. They looked at it from the trees, making no attempt to approach it. Maybe Sola had stopped his experiments, or maybe he couldn't do any more until he had new pipes made.

"Maybe it's just too hot," whispered Sithli.

"I don't know. Maybe we should go back." The silence of the hunting lodge and the miles of forest around it were making Rilsin nervous. She had just realized that she and Sithli—the SaeKet—were alone and unarmed, and that no one knew where they were. Children had been kidnapped for sale to the Runchot under just such circumstances. Although it was, of course, illegal, it did happen. And Sithli

SaeKet Melisin naturally had more enemies than anyone else in the land. It was just the way of things.

"We're not going back. Not until we at least look in the lodge." Sithli was determined. It was then that they saw movement, a quick flash of something around a corner of the old building. "Let's go," said Sithli, suiting the action to the word.

Rilsin grabbed her cousin, hauled her back beside her, and put her hand over her mouth. "Sshh! You wait here! Hide over there, between that boulder and the tree. Scrunch down and stay put! I'll call you if it's safe. If I don't come back soon, go back to the palace, but stay low and quiet until you get out of the forest. Can you find your way back?"

Sithli nodded, staring. The dangers that had already occurred to Rilsin were just occurring to her. She was about to tell Rilsin not to go, but she hesitated a moment too long. Rilsin was gone, vanished among the trees. Sithli blinked, but there was no sign of the younger girl, and she couldn't call out. So she settled herself between the boulder and the tree. Unfortunately, she couldn't see the lodge from this position, so she was left to wait and worry.

Rilsin got as close as she could to the little lodge without making a sound. Her woodcraft training enabled her to do this. Unfortunately, there was still an open space between the trees and the building, which she must cross if she were to be able to see inside. She waited for a while, silently, but there was no more movement near the building. If she had been alone she could have waited indefinitely, but she was afraid that Sithli would become impatient and break her cover. So at last she moved, making a quick dash for the building, flattening herself against the outside of it. Then she dropped down and squirmed along the ground until she was right underneath a window. The window no longer had any glass to shield it. Slowly and cautiously, Rilsin poked her head up and risked a quick glance inside.

Sola was inside, sitting on the floor, apparently drawing diagrams in the dirt. His back was to her, and there was no one else with him. Despite the insects of the woods, he had taken his shirt off in the heat. Rilsin could see the well-defined muscles on his back. She felt herself start to flush, although she did not know why. Nervously, she cleared her throat.

Sola jumped. He was on his feet, reaching for something on the table before he saw who it was. Then he stopped.

"You!" The concern and tension evaporated, leaving his face open and clear. He smiled, obviously glad to see her, and then suddenly remembered he was shirtless. He grabbed up his shirt from the floor and hastily jammed it over his head. "I didn't know if I'd ever see you again! You never told me your name or who you worked for, so I couldn't look for you. But you came back!"

"Yes," said Rilsin. She pulled herself up and over the old windowsill and dropped to the floor in one fluid motion. She smiled at him, feeling absurdly pleased, forgetting for the moment that she was not supposed to be here, and that she had tried not to come. "I wanted to see how your experiments are coming along."

"The blacksmith has been busy. I haven't gotten the new parts I need."

"Oh. Well, so long as you haven't given up. What are you doing here, then?"

"It's too hot. I like to get away from everything and come here to cool off and think." Sola shrugged it off. "I was worried about you. I thought you might have gotten in trouble after you came here."

"I did."

"But it's over now, because here you are."

"Well, no, actually." Rilsin grinned at him. She was feeling daring and she wanted to impress him, despite the fact that she was really there against her better judgment. "I sneaked out. If they catch me this time, I'll really be in for it. You have no idea." Thinking about it now, Rilsin shivered despite herself.

"Go back. You'd better go back now. Here, I'll come with you. They could sell you to the Runchot; they've been doing that lately with captive workers, even the children.

The Runchot pay a good price." Sola was grim; he obviously didn't approve.

"Zechia the Odious mentioned it, but they won't do it. Sithli would take a fit, and Uncle Dinip wouldn't permit it." She stopped, realizing she'd just given herself away.

Sola was staring at her, his mouth slightly open in surprise. He drew in a deep breath, put his right hand over his heart, and bowed his head. "SaeKet," he whispered.

Rilsin blinked at him. Something strange lodged in her throat, making it difficult, for a moment, to speak. But she did. "Not now," she said. "No longer, and not ever." She glanced around at the empty lodge. "Don't ever do that again, Dira Sola, don't let anyone catch you even thinking about it."

Sola straightened. "As you command," he said.

This reminded Rilsin. "Sithli! I left Sithli hidden out there! She must be ready to pop by now. Let's go get her."

Sithli had in fact come out of her hiding place, and she was not on her way back to the palace. She was sneaking through the woods toward the lodge, convinced that something had happened to her cousin and determined to find out what it was. She seemed disappointed in Sola, and certainly disappointed in the steam machine, since there was nothing much to see. She looked dubiously at what there was and listened to explanations, but she had heard it all from Rilsin. And Sola seemed both shy and defensive. He had smoothed back his long brown hair and retied it with a thong, straightened his plain linen shirt, and taken his sword from the table and strapped it back around his waist. At first he put on his best court manners, which Sithli found boring, but eventually he relaxed a little. In the end they went to wade in the stream and pick berries. It was while they were doing this that Sithli snagged her silk blouse on a berry bush and tore it, thus realizing Rilsin's fear.

As time passed, Rilsin became more and more edgy. Sithli could see this, but she insisted on staying, on picking more berries, attempting to engage Sola in more conversation, and cracking bad jokes. She accepted Sola's invitation for a special tour of the cattery, including the breeding pens, without so much as a glance at Rilsin. Eventually, Rilsin stopped suggesting they leave, since every time she did, it only seemed to prolong their stay. As the sun westered and the light grew gold and red, Sithli decided it was time to go back. Sola accompanied them most of the way, since he had discovered, to his horror, that they were both unarmed.

7

THE WOOD CLOSER TO THE PALACE AND THE OUTLYING
fields were much busier now than they had been earlier in
the day. There were children playing and adults relaxing,
come out for a stroll in the cooling of the day. There was no
longer any possibility of returning unseen. Rilsin proposed
her plan of trying to blend in with everyone else; if they
acted as though there was nothing unusual, maybe no one
would look at them twice. At first this worked, but before
they had come even one-quarter of the way, two saedin out
for an early evening ride recognized them. They smiled,
touching hands to hearts as they passed Sithli and headed
back toward the palace. After this, they were recognized in
succession by a courtier, a tailor who often came to the
palace, and an apprentice to Sola's mother, who had two
young cats out for exercise.

Rilsin was miserable, although she said nothing, and she
could feel Sola looking at her with concern. He hadn't forgotten that she would be in deep trouble if she got caught,
which now seemed a certainty. He gave Sithli an irritated
glance but said nothing.

Rilsin was thinking for the first time about the sale of Saeditin citizens to the Runchot. It was a practice that she understood had been on the increase in the past two or three years. The Runchot were willing to pay highly for Saeditin, who were generally healthy and strong. Only criminals convicted of serious crimes might be sold, with the money from their sale going, presumably, to the SaeKet's treasury. Rilsin wondered if the numbers of criminals had really been increasing recently. And all those commoner children, were they criminals, too?

Sithli was perfectly aware of the uneasy silence of the other two children, but she remained blithe. Rilsin believed she was trusting in her influence to somehow get them off the hook, or rather, to get Rilsin off the hook, since Rilsin was the one officially being punished. Rilsin did not have much faith in Sithli's influence.

By the time they were near the horse pastures, they had attracted a small following of other children, all of them saedin. Sithli and Rilsin exchanged glances. There was no need to speak; they knew they must not betray their secret passageway to anyone else. This meant that they must now approach the palace by one of its more public accesses, and with one accord they turned toward the regent's private entrance. *Might as well get this over with,* Rilsin thought.

The saedin children hesitated, and then followed along. A few of them were trying to engage Sithli in conversation. Chief among these was Sifuat sae Sudit. He was a year older than Rilsin, and one of the golden saedin, with dark blond hair and gray eyes. He was beautiful, and he knew it. He was also his mother Norimin's only child, and she was immensely rich. She never denied him anything.

"I am having a gathering," he said, "at my town house, of a few select young saedin. I would be honored if the SaeKet would come."

Sithli blinked at him as he elbowed his way past Sola to get next to her. She said nothing.

"We can swim in my pool, and there will be refreshments," he said.

"I'll think about it," said Sithli. "Rilsin and I have some matters to take care of first."

Matters, thought Rilsin. She was not looking forward to those "matters."

"I would be honored if *you* would attend, SaeKet. It is day after tomorrow." He shoved Rilsin aside now, to keep his place beside Sithli.

Sithli gave Rilsin a glance, which Rilsin read correctly. The glance said, *Handle this for me.* It was a task that Rilsin often did for her cousin. Right now Rilsin was glad to do it. She found Sifuat irritating.

"She said she'd think about it." She gave Sifuat a sharp glance and a sharper elbow. Even though she didn't like him and he undoubtedly knew that she was confined to the palace, she resented being left out of the invitation. Norimin sae Sudit's town house was renowned for its beautiful pool, complete with a small waterfall and hanging plants. She suspected that he had not been planning this party but simply made it up on the spur of the moment, in the hope of getting Sithli to come. "And it's your mother's town house, anyway, Sifuat, not yours."

"I am not speaking to you, Becha. I am addressing the Mother of the Land."

Rilsin snorted a laugh. She couldn't help it. *Mother of the Land* was one of Sithli's titles, but it was one it would take her a while to grow into. Rilsin could see that Sithli was suppressing a smile. But Sifuat was losing his temper. He didn't dare lose it with Sithli, but Rilsin was a safer target. He gave her a vicious shove with both hands. Not expecting it, Rilsin staggered against Sola, who grabbed her arm to support her and keep her from falling.

"Watch what you do!" snapped Sola.

"I know what I do." Sifuat had perfected the art of sneering. He looked Sola over carefully. "Cat keeper's child. You should know better than to befriend this Becha . . . remnant." He smiled. The two remaining saedin children snickered with a mixture of embarrassment and approval, but Sola flushed bright red.

"You may be saedin," he said, "but there are commoners—and Runchot—with better manners. There are cats and bears and toads with better manners! Yes, toads! And toads stare just the way you do now, Sae Sifuat, with big bulge eyes! You should have more respect for—" He stopped suddenly.

Sifuat stepped into the pause.

"Respect for what?" he said. "Or for whom?" He smiled at Sola, daring him.

Rilsin was aghast. She had been kept from much contact with other children except Sithli, and even from contact with adults except for those chosen by her uncle. She wondered how many people shared Sola's apparent loyalties. If there were many of them or if they were vocal, she doubted that either they or she would be alive. But obviously there were some. She glanced again at Sola, her thoughts in a furious whirl.

"Respect for whom, dira?" Sifuat made Sola's title sound like an insult. "Do you wish to teach me manners?" Sifuat prided himself on his sword skills, and he had reason to. Already even some of the adults could not match him. Sola obviously knew this, because his face turned from flushed to pale in a matter of moments. But he did not look as if he meant to back down. In fact, he put his hand on his sword. Rilsin had had enough.

"Respect for all the Mother's creatures, Sae Sifuat," she said. "And if you have any question concerning manners, you may take it up with me."

Sifuat stared at her. If there was a possible match for his sword skills anywhere among the children, saedin or dira, it was Rilsin. Sifuat knew this, and he also knew that if he challenged her, he would be in big trouble himself. She might be the last member of the defeated Sae Bechas, but she was also Sithli's favorite, protected by the regent, and she would be first minister in time. It finally occured to Sifuat that Sithli had said nothing during all of this, and he sneaked a quick look at her. She appeared fascinated and perhaps even thrilled at the possibility of a formal fight. Her face was flushed, and her eyes were bright. Belatedly, he realized that he might have already gotten himself into some serious trouble.

"There is nothing," he said haughtily to Rilsin, "that you can teach me." He was about to elaborate when the unexpected happened.

All of the children had been engrossed in the little drama; none had been paying attention to anything else around them. They had reached a little bridge over a stream in a landscaped garden. The stream was dry now, its rocky bed exposed. They were close to the palace, but the garden was still half wild, or it was made to seem so. There was a small stand of fir trees and two artfully placed boulders at the far side, the palace side, of the bridge. Since the other children hung back, Sithli was the first to cross this bridge. As soon as she reached the other side, a figure materialized from among the trees.

Rilsin saw it almost as soon as Sithli did. It was just a man in commoner dress, the thick-kneed, leather-reinforced trousers and the short-sleeved baggy shirt of a gardener, which this man had belted tightly. He had a gardener's sack in one hand, and what was probably a trowel in the other. Nothing alarming, it would seem, but Rilsin felt a flash of warning, as if the earth had carried a tiny pulse of lightning up through the soles of her feet.

"Sithli!" she cried.

As she cried out, the gardener dropped his bag. At the same time it became clear that what he had in his hand was not a trowel at all but a knife.

Sithli saw it now, but she was already across the bridge, and all the others were behind her. She glanced back with the obvious thought of retreat, but it was clear there wouldn't be time, and if she tried to go back, the others would be blocking her way. There was nothing for her to do but run and dodge and scream and hope to bring help. It seemed a vain hope. If there was anyone near enough to hear, they wouldn't come in time. The SaeKet's guards thought she was in her private garden, studying with her cousin.

Rilsin saw Sithli begin to run, and she also saw that the

slope of the land away from the bridge, the placement of the trees and the boulders, would bring her within arm's reach of the man. She didn't wait but climbed up on the railing of the bridge and launched herself forward, leaping the gap that separated her from the bank and from her cousin. She launched with enough force that she actually landed just inches behind Sithli. She also startled the assassin, distracting him in the act of reaching for Sithli. As she looked up into his gray eyes, she remembered that she was unarmed.

Sithli started to scream. She had an excellent voice, a carrying voice, with a lot of power behind it. She used it now, calling for help at the top of her lungs. The assassin hissed at the sound. He grabbed for her, trying to catch her around the throat, but she dodged as well as screamed, and he missed. He caught hold of her long hair and yanked back, trying to bare her throat to his knife. She twisted, and the knife cut a long gash down the side of her cheek. Her blood ran onto his hand, but he didn't flinch. He was probably saedin himself and was not one of those who believed in the power of the SaeKet's blood.

Rilsin was trying to get him away from Sithli. She grabbed at his arm, but he saw her from the corner of his eye and lashed sideways with his foot, a sudden powerful kick that caught Rilsin a glancing blow on her side. She felt a searing pain in her chest, and it became hard to breathe. This was one of the moves she was due to learn in unarmed combat, but she hadn't learned it yet, never mind how to counter it. It didn't seem likely now that she would have the chance to learn it.

There was a sound beside Rilsin, a thud. Sola had leaped forward beside her, and his sword was drawn. He lunged toward the attacker, who had Sithli's hair wound tightly around one hand. He had forced her to her knees to control her while he dealt with this new annoyance. Faster than Sola could blink, he darted forward with only his knife and slashed the sword from the boy's hand. Sola stared at the blood that poured from his hand. His little finger was dangling loosely. He screamed, and the assassin smiled.

Rilsin ignored the pain in her side and grabbed for the

sword that Sola had just dropped. The world seemed to spin around her, but she lunged forward, watching the knife. The assassin had made a mistake. With Sithli on her knees, he couldn't move far; she was his anchor. Rilsin's sword cut his knife arm and then his chest, a long slash, and it was his blood flowing now. He realized he had a choice. He could do what he came for and kill Sithli, and be killed himself, or he could let her go and try to escape. He chose to try to live. In one motion he shoved Sithli forward onto her face and threw the knife at Rilsin. Then he ran.

Rilsin saw it coming, but the pain in her ribs made her slow. She tried to throw herself to the side, but the knife caught her under her arm and stuck there. Despite all intentions, she sank to her knees. She saw now that Sifuat had come up, and his sword was drawn.

"Stop him, Sifuat!" Rilsin shouted, or tried to. "Don't let him get away! And don't kill him!" She thought he heard her, but she wasn't sure. She realized that she was lying on the ground, and she closed her eyes. She couldn't help it.

WHEΠ RILSOΠ OPEΠED her eyes again, it was dark. There was an oil lamp flickering. The lamp was on her dresser, with the pile of her shirts moved aside. So she had survived, and she was back in her own room. Perhaps the attack was only a dream, a nightmare. She felt terrible, though, weak and fuzzy, with an awful headache. And she was very thirsty. She tried to sit up, but the pain that lanced through her side put a stop to that and forced a moan from her lips. Her moan brought movement from a corner, where someone had apparently been sitting.

"You're awake. " Sithli's face loomed over her, confirming for her that the nightmare was real. Sithli had been crying, and her face was puffy and discolored from the tears. But worse than that was the long gash that ran down her cheek. It had been tacked closed with several tiny stitches and smeared with a healing ointment, but it was arrestingly ugly, especially in the flickering lamplight. It would be better when it had healed, of course, but never again would Sithli be the breathtakingly flawless, golden beauty.

"Don't make any sudden moves," said Sithli. "Nefit says your ribs are broken. The knife wound isn't much; it caught you in that fleshy part under your arm. It's bandaged, so don't poke at it. I have to go tell her you're awake."

Rilsin put out a hand to stop her cousin. "Sith, your poor face! I'm so sorry!"

Something flickered in Sithli's eyes. But all she said was, "It will be better when it heals, and time will help it, too. Nefit says I have to keep it limber when it starts to heal so it doesn't pucker."

"Did they get him? Did Sifuat get him? The assassin?"

"I have to get Nefit."

"Wait! Sithli, please!" Despite the pain, Rilsin levered herself up on an elbow. She could feel the sweat pop up on her brow, under her arms. Sithli paused at the door. "What about Sola? What happened to his hand?"

"He's fine," said Sithli dismissively. "He lost his little finger." She went out the door, and Rilsin sank back.

She wanted to ask more. But Sithli wouldn't come back, she knew, so she was left to wait. Perhaps she could find out from Nefit some of the things she needed to know, find them out before she had to face Dinip. *Poor Sola,* she thought. But at least Sola was free to be out in the woods and the gardens; he was not disobeying a command of the regent. *I should never have agreed to go,* she thought. Sithli would never have gone by herself, and none of this would have happened. She thought of Sithli's slashed face, and despite herself, she shuddered. Sithli had always taken great pride in her looks.

Sithli was not gone for long. She was back with Nefit, as promised, and with Maltia, the apprentice. But that was not all. More people crowded behind the physicians into Rilsin's tiny room: Dinip, and Bilma sae Grepsin, the first minister, and Zechia sae Eanern, Zechia the Odious. There were also two guards, making it a very tight squeeze. Rilsin felt a wave of cold wash over her. This was serious. She forced herself to sit up, and Maltia hurried over to help her. He propped pillows behind her and eased her back.

"You know that I think this should wait," said Nefit.

"Rilsin is not ready for this yet." She was speaking to Dinip with disapproval, but she obviously did not expect him to listen to her.

"It must be now," said the regent. He looked at Rilsin. "You disobeyed me, Rilsin. And your disobedience almost cost the SaeKet her life." He was calm but grim. Looking at him, Rilsin found it hard to catch her breath. It was not just the sight of Dinip that did this to her but the concern on Bilma's face and the slight, anticipatory smile on Zechia's. "Sneaking out with my daughter, unarmed and without guards, was not only dangerous, it was stupid. You are not a stupid girl, Rilsin."

"It was not stupidity, it was treason," said Zechia. "It was planned. And you will pay the price, Rilsin sae Becha. You have escaped this long by the mercy of the SaeKet, but no longer."

Rilsin could see it in his eyes, the square in the sunlight, the knife waiting for the traitor's throat. He wanted this for her. And from the way things looked, he might get it. She felt a sudden stab of terror, and she couldn't keep it from showing. She opened her mouth to speak, but Sithli shifted beside her father.

"Father—" she began.

"Quiet, Sithli! Not a sound! You have nothing to say!"

Rilsin paused in the act of forming a word, staring at Dinip. She saw something in his face, she was sure she saw it, and she heard something in his tone, in what he said to Sithli. It was not like him to deny his daughter the right to speak at all, and so sharply, before others. Was there something specific that he wished left unsaid? She felt something in the air. She looked again at Zechia, and she saw more than his hatred of her, his well-publicized, cultivated hatred. There was a certain frenzy there, and a certain fear. She couldn't look again at Dinip, not yet; she wouldn't risk it.

"It was not planned," she said. "I am no traitor, Sae Zechia! Believe me, please! I acted without thought, but that is all! I meant no wrong, I planned nothing!" The fear in her voice was real enough, and it fed Zechia and distracted him. Now she looked at the regent, as if in appeal, and what she saw confirmed her suspicion. Dinip was not looking at her at all but at Zechia.

"The blood of the last Sae Becha will go to the land," said Zechia. "The SaeKet lives, despite you. When you are dead, then she will be safe at last! She will have a first minister who is loyal!"

And who might that be? Rilsin thought. *You?*

"I did not attack her!" Rilsin put desperation into her voice. "It was the gardener! We all saw it! I tried to save her!" *I did save her,* she thought. *Again.* But now was not the time for this thought.

"The gardener was not a gardener," said Bilma, "nor did he work on his own. He was a saedin mercenary from a poor family. A poor family, Rilsin, because they lost everything in the Civil War. Someone paid him to kill Sithli SaeKet."

Rilsin was watching the first minister, since he was addressing her, but from the corner of her eye she could see Zechia's gratification and his relief. And she could see that Bilma saw it, too. She was sure now.

"I did not hire him! I could not! How could I? Ask him! Ask him, and he will tell you! He will tell you I'm not the one! Sifuat caught him, didn't he?"

"Sae Sifuat caught him," said Bilma, "but we can ask him nothing."

"He is dead, Rilsin." Dinip was looking at her now, "but he left a trail. He was paid."

Rilsin realized she'd been missing her cue. "I had nothing to pay him with," she said. Was she right about this? Was this what Dinip wanted? "I have nothing of any value, certainly nothing an assassin would take."

"Oh, but you did, you did!" Zechia was eager to prove her guilt. And the regent had tensed, watching Zechia. Everyone in the room had tensed, Rilsin realized, including Nefit and Maltia. They all knew. But Zechia didn't see it, so intent was he on making his point. "You had one thing of great value. You had this." One of the guards passed him something, and he held it out on his palm. Rilsin saw what it was.

"You have it!" she cried, and leaned forward to try to snatch it from his hand. Zechia's fingers closed around her pendant as Rilsin gasped from the pain in her ribs.

"He had it," said Zechia. "The assassin had it because you paid him with it."

Sithli had been fidgeting beside her father, and now she could contain herself no longer. "You know that to be Rilsin's?" she said. Dinip glared at her, and she subsided, but she was unrepentent.

"Everyone has seen her wear it," he said.

"Give it to me," said Rilsin. The tears pricking behind her eyelids surprised her, and she fought them back.

"It is very valuable." Zechia was pleased with himself, taunting her.

"To me it is." Rilsin intercepted a look from Bilma and hurried on. "I lost it three weeks ago, Sae Zechia, and I have been looking for it ever since. It is all I have left—" she stopped. This was too much; she didn't want to say it. She looked away.

"An assassin would have had such a thing valued before accepting it as payment, would he not?" Bilma stepped in.

"Of course." Zechia was slightly confused.

"Then no assassin would have accepted it." Dinip was staring fixedly at Zechia, who looked startled. "It is worthless, except to Sae Rilsin, as a remembrance of her mother." He glanced at her briefly. He did not smile, but his gaze was warm, and Rilsin felt the ice around her melting. "There is very little gold in this. It is mostly base metal, melted down from a ring Sae Pellata, Rilsin's mother, got from Rilsin's father before she married him. Sae Frema couldn't afford much gold at that time."

Rilsin knew what she'd heard; her father's mother was a gambler who lost the family fortune. Rilsin's mother didn't care; she married Frema anyway. Zechia never heard any of this, it would seem. He was staring at Dinip. Something occurred to Rilsin.

"Who killed the assassin?" she asked. "Did Sifuat kill him?"

"Sae Zechia killed him," Bilma answered. "Sifuat caught

him, but Zechia got there next. He claimed the assassin was getting away. And he found your pendant in the assassin's pocket."

Zechia made a lunge for the door. It was a stupid thing to do in such a crowded space. Bilma grabbed him, and the guards took him after that. They could hear him shouting that he was innocent as he was dragged down the corridor.

"Now that that is over," said Nefit, "you need to rest." She told Maltia to mix a painkiller and a sedative.

Rilsin looked up at Dinip. *It can't be over,* she thought. *There must be more to come.*

"It was a stupid thing that you did, Rilsin," he said, "but I know why you did it. Sithli told me of her threat. You have been punished enough." Before he left, he put the pendant in her hand.

8

By the orders of Nefit, Rilsin was confined to her room and her bed for most of the following week. She spent the time studying astronomy. Her dreams, assisted by Nefit's sedatives, were full of fiery suns. Toward the end of the week she became restless, but she found that there was a guard just beyond her door who would not let her out. Whatever Dinip had said about her punishment being over, he obviously did not intend that she have free rein to wander, or not just yet. She didn't blame him, and to be honest, she didn't feel much like wandering. Her ribs ached, and the wound under her arm alternated between burning and itching. Although she knew the itching meant healing, she didn't welcome it.

Sithli was a frequent visitor. The young SaeKet brought Rilsin her meals, cleared away the dishes, and, once, swept out the room. This was Dinip's idea, but Sithli undertook the work willingly. She knew that her insistence on getting Rilsin to leave the palace was responsible for the current state of affairs, and she was truly sorry. Or at least, thought Rilsin, she was sorry that the escapade ended the way it did.

But Sithli did not spend much time with her cousin, so
Rilsin had many hours of watching the light shift in her
small room as the hot days passed. Rilsin had plenty of time
to become bored, and plenty of time to think. She thought
about her life, her past and her future, and about her place
in Saeditin, and she came to certain conclusions.

She could no longer afford to be ignorant. Not in any
manner. She must know what was happening in the realm,
and she must understand the affairs of state. Sola, it would
seem, knew more than she did, and more than Sithli. This
must change. She would be first minister, and she could not
afford ignorance. She would listen and learn all she could,
from every source that came her way, and she would go out
of her way to learn more. Knowledge would be a shield.

And she would be Sithli's shield. Sithli would never be
able to defend herself the way she should, and Sithli would
never learn or know all that she should. She did not have the
patience, so Rilsin would have to do it for her. Whatever
was necessary for Sithli to know, Rilsin would learn.

It did occur to Rilsin to wonder about her own chances
to reclaim the SaeKet's chair. It was not an event that she
considered likely or even particularly desirable. It was obvious that Rilsin still had her partisans, but she doubted they
could have been many or well organized. The Sae Melisins
had long enough to entrench themselves. But beyond that,
Rilsin could not imagine herself betraying Sithli. In some
way that defied logic, Rilsin knew that Sithli depended on
her even more than she depended on Sithli, that they were
linked together in some powerful, indefinable way. And she
remembered her long-ago promise to Sithli: no more blood.
She could not bring strife and bloodshed back to the land,
not after these years of peace.

Toward the end of the week, Sola came to see her. It was
on an afternoon that promised rain and an end to the heat.
There was the subtle and indefinable hint of autumn in the
air. Rilsin was sitting on her bed, dressed in rolled-up
trousers and tied-up shirt. Her legs were tucked up, and she
was gingerly poking at the bandages on her ribs and at the
one under her arm. She didn't see Sola until he cleared his

throat from the doorway. Then she jumped and simultaneously yelped from pain.

"Sorry. How are you feeling? Do you mind if I come in?"

"Please do! But there's nowhere to sit. Sithli broke my chair standing on it to try to hang new curtains for me." Rilsin hastily yanked down her shirt. "You'll have to sit there." She pointed to the bottom of the bed. "How's your hand?"

Sola looked at his right hand, which was bandaged. "I lost my little finger, but Sae Nefit says it should heal cleanly."

"How does it feel?"

"It hurts like hell." He smiled ruefully, settling himself gingerly at the foot of the bed. "I think the rain coming is making it ache. And sometimes it feels like it's still there, which is very strange, although Sae Nefit says it's to be expected."

"I was very sorry to hear you were hurt. More than sorry." She thought about it. "It made me angry. You didn't deserve that."

Sola laughed. "No more than you deserved to get your ribs broken or a knife stuck in you! You were so brave! Sae Sithli has a true friend in you."

"And in you."

Sola frowned slightly. "I am your friend first, Rilsin SaeK—Sae Rilsin."

"Listen to me, Sola, please. The past is gone; what might have been is gone. I hope you are my friend; I have never had a friend except for Sithli. But if you are my friend, you must be a true friend to Sithli SaeKet first. For your sake and for my sake. And because she truly is my friend. You must watch what you say, and you must say nothing against her. Ever."

"I understand. As long as she is your friend, she will be my friend, Sae Rilsin."

Rilsin nodded at him. "If we are friends, then I am just Rilsin. Unless you wish to be Dira Sola?" She raised her brows, and he laughed. He laughed easily, and Rilsin found herself smiling back.

Close on his laughter came a long peal of thunder, and then the rain broke. Over the sound of the rain pounding on the palace roof they discussed the astronomy Rilsin had been reading and the further plans for Sola's steam machine. When Sithli came, bringing Rilsin's dinner, she found them still talking.

A FEW ðAYS later, Rilsin was permitted to leave her room and to leave the palace. Nefit had taken the bandages off her ribs, but she had warned Rilsin that her ribs would not be healed for months and that she must be careful not to injure them further by stressing them unduly.

"You must slow down and go carefully, Rilsin," she said. "And if something hurts you, stop doing it."

Rilsin was not pleased with this, as she had hoped to resume her armed and unarmed combat lessons as soon as she was allowed out of her room. She told herself philosophically that she needed to learn patience, which was a much harder lesson. She settled for long, vigorous walks. She spent many hours studying, both with Sithli and apart from her, and she also sat in many meetings and consultations among the saedin, a silent spectator whose presence the regent tacitly encouraged. Sithli was encouraged more openly, but she went less often, claiming she found the details of government boring.

The weather had cooled ever since the thunderstorm, and it seemed that fall would be early this year. A late litter was born to one of the hunting cats. One of the kittens was silver, and one was the rarest of all colors, SaeKet gold. Kerida dira Mudrin invited Sithli to the stables and the cat pens to see and claim the gold kitten. Rilsin was invited, too, and Sithli insisted that Rilsin go with her.

"You owe her the courtesy, Rils. After all, she is Sola's mother, and you seem to like Sola well enough." She waited for a reaction from her cousin, but there wasn't one. "I could almost think you hated the cats if I didn't know better. Don't tell me you have forgotten Bet."

Rilsin drew a steady breath. No, she had not forgotten. Sithli did not realize she had struck a nerve; Rilsin's expression did not change. "Surely no one will miss me," she said calmly.

"I will. I want you to come," said Sithli, and so it was settled. On a bright day with blue skies and a crisp wind that tugged at their clothes, they went to the pens to see the kittens.

The cattery was actually several buildings, a big, barn-like stable, a second building that was used for training, a small veterinary hospital, and breeding pens. There were also outdoor pens and enclosures. Sola was waiting for them at the end of the lane that led to this complex.

"Come and see them; they're beautiful! Three striped ones, and the gold and the silver. It's a big litter."

He took them into the main barn, where Kerida greeted them, touching her hand to her heart. She faced them both as she did this, and Rilsin felt a sudden tremor. She knew where Sola learned his politics. But perhaps she was wrong, for Sithli noticed nothing.

"Where are they?" Sithli said. "I want to see the gold one. It's been a long time since I've had a hunting cat!" She allowed herself to be directed toward one of the stalls. Sola went with her. The hunting cats could be touchy, especially with new offspring, and they had been known to occasion-ally attack those they didn't trust.

Rilsin hung back. The smell of the cat barn was familiar and brought a lump to her throat. She had no desire to coo over kittens. Besides, they were not alone. The place was full of saedin who were already looking at the kittens or who had "just happened" to come in to care for their own cats at the same time the young SaeKet was there. Some of these smiled and nodded at Rilsin. She saw a certain respect in their eyes and realized that her latest defense of Sithli had earned her some goodwill. She was just making up her mind to cultivate some more goodwill by making friendly re-marks when Sithli called for her.

"Oh, Rilsin, come look! Isn't she just the cutest thing? And she's smart! You can tell already. Where are you, Rilsin? Come and see!"

Rilsin obediently edged up to her cousin. The new

mother had been given her own quiet stall away from all the others. At least, it was quiet until Sithli arrived. Although the others were speaking in soft tones, Sithli's voice was shrill with excitement. It was to the credit of the mother cat that she endured the noise and the handling of her kittens with equanimity.

The mother cat was a huge striped animal. She lay on her side, showing the rich, soft brown fur of her stomach, in which the tiny kittens were nestled, nursing. All the kittens, that was, but the little golden one. Sithli had got hold of this one and was holding it up near her face. The kitten was squirming, emitting hoarse little meows of distress while the SaeKet nuzzled it. Sithli squeezed it a little too tightly, and the kitten yelped. The mother cat looked up and grunted in warning, baring her teeth.

"Look, Rils!" Sithli thrust the kitten at Rilsin, ignoring the growling whine of the mother cat. "You hold her."

Gingerly, Rilsin took the kitten. She didn't want to, but there was obviously no choice. As soon as her hands closed around the kitten, it stopped meowing. She stroked the soft golden fur between its eyes and behind its tiny ears. She felt her eyes start to blur with tears and quickly willed them away. In the pen below, the mother cat relaxed and half closed her eyes while the kitten, which Rilsin had reflexively cuddled, tried to burrow into her neck.

There was a sudden silence in the barn. The saedin who had been watching, commenting softly to one another, ceased all conversation. Rilsin heard Sola, who had come up behind her, draw in a soft breath. Rilsin knew Kerida was there, too; she came at the mother cat's protest, but she didn't dare risk a glance.

"She's cute, Sithli SaeKet, and she may be smart, but how can you tell? She's just a tiny baby." Gently, Rilsin leaned into the pen and deposited the ball of golden fluff beside the mother cat, who immediately began to lick it. "When she gets older, you can train her." Rilsin glanced around now, from the corner of her eye. Everyone had relaxed, now that she had put the kitten back. Everyone but Sithli.

"She liked you." Sithli was looking at her. "She stopped crying when you held her."

The saedin were listening again, straining to look as though they were not.

"You have to know how to hold them," said Rilsin. She felt a thin trickle of perspiration start at her hairline. What was Sithli doing? She glared at her cousin.

"Sae Rilsin has a knack." Kerida drew everyone's attention. " If she wanted, she could apprentice with me and become a keeper of cats." She laughed, and the others joined in. Rilsin smiled gratefully at Kerida. But Sithli was still watching her.

"Pick a kitten, Rilsin." Sithli's voice had an edge to it. "You have to pick a kitten."

"Thank you, but no. I—"

"Pick one!"

"I don't want one, Sithli." Rilsin spoke in an undertone. "You know why."

"The other kittens are all spoken for," said Kerida. "Perhaps another time."

"Pick a kitten, Rilsin." Sithli was adamant. She was not about to let this pass. "Someone will have to wait. If I get one, you get one, too."

Rilsin looked at the tiny balls of fur nestled beside their huge mother. She felt more helpless than they. And she was upset with Sithli, too, but she couldn't say anything about it now. She couldn't refuse. Suddenly someone stepped out of the crowd and came up beside her. It was Sifuat. He looked at her briefly, then reached into the cat pen to pick up a kitten. Surprisingly, the mother cat permitted him to do this. It was the silver kitten that he held. He held it gently, supporting its small body with more care and tenderness than Rilsin would have believed him capable of.

"This is the kitten I picked," he said. "But I no longer want him, now that I have seen him." He took Rilsin's hands and put the kitten into them. "Take him. I will wait for another litter."

Rilsin looked down into blue eyes that already had a hint of the green they would become. The kitten was really more gray than silver, but he was nonetheless rare. This kitten, too, was snuggling against her. Despite herself, she stroked him, and he began to purr.

"I can't take your kitten." She held him out again. But Sifuat backed away.

"I will get another one." He looked at Sithli, who had begun to frown. "If the SaeKet wishes you to have a cat, then here is your cat. He is only a male, and he is the runt of the litter. So you take him, Rilsin sae Becha!" He smirked and then swept a bow to Sithli, his hand on his heart. "I do as the SaeKet wishes!"

Sithli smiled back at him, amused, and moved to speak to him. But Rilsin frowned. It was true that the little kitten, *her* kitten, was the smallest of the litter, and it was true that he was male, but he was still very valuable. And more than that, she was sure she saw tenderness in the way Sifuat held him, and she felt how gently he placed the kitten in her hands. Despite his tone and despite his words, there had been no mockery and no taunting in his eyes. But there was no telling now. He and Sithli were laughing at something, and he did not look at Rilsin. So she turned away from them all, Sifuat and Sithli and the saedin, and even Kerida and Sola. She brushed her lips against the soft silver fur and felt the warmth of the little animal against her.

"I guess you're mine now," she whispered.

SHE NAMED HIM Chilsa, or Moonlight. He stayed with his mother, of course, although Rilsin went to visit him every day, far more often than Sithli went to visit her cat. She was visiting Sola as much as she was visiting Chilsa, but it was more than a week before Sithli realized this. She cornered Rilsin in her room early one morning as Rilsin was preparing to go to the cat barn again.

It was a foggy, chilly morning, an autumn morning that was quiet and muffled. Rilsin had a cloak wrapped around her for warmth, and under the cloak she was obviously carrying something. She almost ran into Sithli, who was waiting for her right outside her door. Sithli put one hand on Rilsin's shoulder and almost pushed her back into the room.

"Going to the cat barn again?"

"Yes," said Rilsin. It was a moment before she caught the tone in Sithli's voice. "What's the matter, Sith? Sit down and tell me." She sat on the bed and patted the mattress beside her, but Sithli didn't sit down.

"You go to the cat barn every day, and usually more than once, and sometimes you stay for hours."

"Chilsa needs me."

"It's not Chilsa!"

"Shh! You're going to bring someone in here! Of course it's Chilsa, he—"

"It's Sola!"

Rilsin looked at Sithli for a long moment. "It's both," she said.

Sithli stared at her. Her thunder had been stolen. She had expected an argument, denials, but not this. Rilsin was pulling something out from under her cloak. It was a book.

"I'm returning this to him," she said. "It's a text on natural science; he lent it to me."

"Natural science?" Sithli was momentarily distracted. "The new way of looking at the world? That stuff is boring, Rils."

"No, it's not. Not to me. Not to Sola. He's my friend, Sith."

"I'm your friend!"

"Of course. My oldest, first, and until now my only friend. I love you, Sithli. Sola can't change that. Nothing can."

Sithli looked at her and then finally sat down next to her on the bed, moving the book aside. She took Rilsin's hands and looked into her eyes. "I love you, too, Rilsin. You belong to me. Ever since the day Mama died, you have been mine. You know that. I can't live without you." She took a breath. "And you can't live without me, Rils. You know that, too. If Sola comes between us—"

"He can't come between us, Sith. He's my friend, is all. And he can be your friend, if you'll let him. He's asked me to bring you along." This was a lie, but Sithli didn't catch it. She was mollified.

"Some day you'll get married, Rilsin—when I say you can."

"Married!" Rilsin stared at her in horror. Sithli saw this and grinned.

"When I say you can."

"Well, don't ever say it, then! Is that what you thought?" Rilsin considered Sola in this light. *Marry him?* She was not as horrified as she had been at first. "We're too young to think of this, Sith!"

"I'm not. Papa has even talked about it with me."

Rilsin swallowed and said nothing. She had had no idea.

"I told him I didn't want to get married. I don't have to, and I won't."

It was true, she didn't have to get married ever, if she didn't want to. But most people did, even SaeKets. "Someday you will," said Rilsin doubtfully.

"Maybe. But I'm going to have lots of children anyway. Dozens."

"Ugh." Rilsin screwed up her face. "You're crazy, Sith."

"Maybe, but I will. Ten anyway, five daughters and five sons. I'll form my own hunting team. And you can help them train their cats."

The two girls grinned at each other. The bad feeling was gone, and the foggy morning seemed somehow brighter.

"It won't be long," said Sithli, "until I'm seventeen, and adult. They will confirm me in the SaeKet's chair, and Papa won't be regent anymore. On that day, Rilsin, you will be free. You will be a citizen again. You don't have to wait until you turn seventeen. And you can grow your hair as long as water weeds." She reached out and smoothed Rilsin's short hair. "On your seventeenth birthday you will become first minister. Do you still want that, Rils?"

"Yes. And I remember my promise, Sithli SaeKet: peace. I won't ever do anything to hurt you, Sithli. And I keep my promises."

Sithli nodded. "You will be an excellent first minister. And I will be an excellent SaeKet."

9

It was not long before Rilsin had an immediate experience of one of the duties of the first minister. Zechia sae Eanern, Zechia the Odious, had become Zechia the Pathetic. The assassin's wife had been found, and before she was sold to the Runchot, she confirmed beyond a doubt that her husband was hired by Zechia. Zechia had meant to kill Sithli, have Rilsin blamed, and throw the land into a confusion from which he could seem to rescue it. Zechia was guilty of treason and was condemned to die in the Square of the Mother and give his blood back to the land. He begged and pleaded for his life and tried to buy his way out, which he couldn't do: everything he owned, or more specifically, that which his family owned, was taken by the first minister in the name of the SaeKet.

He was brought from prison to see Sithli and confirm his death sentence. Sithli was seated on the SaeKet's chair, dressed in a formal long shirt of gray silk, with gray cotton trousers. A green and gold sash was around her waist. Her healing scar was heavily plastered with powder, despite

Nefit's disapproval. Bilma sae Grepsin stood beside her, dressed in green.

Rilsin stood to the side of the room, slightly separate from the other saedin, who were separate from the dira. She was dressed entirely in black, both formal shirt and trousers, which helped her blend into the shadows and which kept her from the least hint of ostentation. It solved a problem for her, too, since she could not wear the Sae Becha colors, and she would not wear the Sae Melisin green. She clenched her hands behind her back as Zechia was brought in.

He looked terrible, haggard and frightened, and he visibly flinched when he saw the candle, the knife, and the paper waiting on the table. It was at this point that Rilsin privately renamed him Zechia the Pathetic. She looked at Sithli, but Sithli's attention was fixed on the man who tried to have her killed. Rilsin, seeing her expression, found her breath coming short. Zechia's fate was already decided, of course, but Sithli was enjoying this. She couldn't blame Sithli for that; it was to be expected of any saedin. Nonetheless, she felt chilled.

Bilma read the charges and the sentence of death. Zechia sobbed through this and had to be physically dragged to the candle and the knife. Rilsin looked away, unwilling to see more of this. It was only what Zechia had planned for her, after all, to take the blame, but Rilsin was feeling sick. From the corner of her eye, she saw Bilma holding Zechia's hand steady for the prick of the knife. Bilma only pricked his finger, but Zechia screamed. It was too much, and Rilsin actually began to turn away. She couldn't leave until it was all over, but she was not going to watch anymore.

It was the silence that made her look back. Zechia was standing with his finger dripping blood onto the paper, sealing his death warrant. But he was not paying any attention to that fact. His head was tilted, his mouth slightly open in surprise. On his face was a look of amazement and something else. It took Rilsin a moment to realize that the something else was joy. Zechia sae Eanern was hearing the song, the song of the land. Suddenly he smiled, drew a bloody line on the paper with his finger, then put his hand over his heart and bowed to Sithli. He was still smiling as they took him out.

He was not smiling on the day of the dark moon, when they took him to the square, but he was not pathetic any-more, either. He looked afraid but strong, and he climbed the scaffold without any assistance. He stood quietly in the midst of his guard, not looking at anyone. Rilsin thought he was still hearing the song.

It was a cold day, bitter and cloudy, and the wind whipped fallen leaves around the square, tugged at the cloaks of the spectators, tangled the long hair of those saedin and dira who had left it free. Rilsin was dressed in black again—black shirt, trousers, boots, and cloak—which she held tightly around her. She stood on the platform behind the chair that had been set up for Sithli, a shadow in her cousin's splendor.

Sithli was dressed in green and cloth of gold, glittering in the somber light. Her cloak was gold shot with green, her blonde hair was long and loose, bound back from her face by a headband of gold. The scar on her right cheek was healing well and, covered by powder, was not very notice-able. Her gray eyes gleamed with excitement. Her father stood beside her, tall and pale. The green and gold looked somehow darker on him, more serious. It was Sithli who drew admiring bows, and hands-to-hearts from the crowd. There was a festival atmosphere; people were laughing, and there was a vendor selling little cakes. Many commoners were buying these cakes, and even some of the dira, who reached down from their own platform, which was adjacent to the saedin platform.

Rilsin found she was not quite as invisible as she would have liked behind her cousin; people noticed her. They mur-mured and smiled and nodded to her, but no one put hand to heart. Rilsin felt warmed, though, and nodded back, which pleased them. She heard comments: "The SaeKet's protec-tor," they said, and "Sithli's sword." And even more often, "the sword of Saeditin," or "the sword of the land." They meant her, she realized. She had a nickname and a legend already. She wondered if Sithli knew this.

Bilma sae Grepsin climbed the platform, and the crowd hushed. He was dressed in the green and gold of the SaeKet he served, but he was wearing a scarlet vest over his green shirt, a brilliant scarlet that flashed in a sudden weak shaft of sun when he threw back his cloak. The crowd sighed, and then there was no sound but the wind. In the midst of his guard of soldiers, Zechia straightened and swallowed. Sithli, too, straightened, sitting bolt upright in her chair.

"Zechia sae Eanern," said Bilma, "you are convicted of treason against the land of Saeditin and against Sithli SaeKet Melisin, its true ruler. You have admitted your guilt; will you proclaim it now to the land?"

"I do proclaim it." Zechia's voice was clear. It was not strong, but in the silence of the packed square it did not have to be. He could be heard at the back of the square. Somewhere, a crying baby was hushed. He looked as though he would say more, but he stopped.

"In the name of the Mother, and the land of Saeditin, and of Sithli SaeKet Melisin, you must return your life and your blood to the land. SaeKet, will you receive this gift?"

"I will receive it," said Sithli.

Now the priest climbed the steps to the platform. Rilsin had not paid him proper attention before, this important actor in the day's drama, where he waited on the ground, surrounded by other priests and by soldiers. A priest of the Mother's third aspect. "Death priest," the crowd whispered. He carried a long knife before him on a pillow. Beside him, a novice carried the velvet case that contained the ritual crystal goblet. He stopped before Sithli's chair and nodded his head slightly. As he did so, Rilsin saw his eyes: they were flat and cold. Despite herself, she shuddered, and the slight motion drew his gaze to her. For one brief moment the death priest looked at Rilsin, and she felt cold seep into her bones. Then his gaze moved on.

The priest removed the the goblet from its velvet case. It was old, heavy crystal: plain, dull, slightly chipped, and not a thing of beauty. But it was old, so very old, and it had held so much blood over the centuries. Rilsin wondered what would happen if Bilma dropped it, shattered the sacred, hor-

rid glass into a thousand fragments. Would they postpone
the execution, set Zechia free? But Bilma took it carefully
from the priest. Zechia's guards tied his hands behind his
back and took him by the arms. Rilsin knew that grip;
Zechia had no chance of breaking free now.

She felt slightly dizzy and wondered at herself. What
was wrong with her? Every person in the square or on the
platforms knew the necessity of what was about to happen.
No one was bothered by the prospect of the death of a traitor, and most anticipated it with pleasure, the commoners
most of all, to see a saedin die. She must be the only one to
feel as she did.

It was worse because there were no politics behind what
she felt. She was not of Zechia's faction, if he had one, and
she did not believe him innocent; she knew too well that he
was not. She simply did not want him to die, at least not this
way. She wondered what the people would think if they
knew the "sword of the land" was feeling nauseous. She
glanced out across the crowd and found that someone was
looking back at her. It was Sola dira Mudrin, standing
among other dira on the nearby platform. Their eyes locked,
and Rilsin was aware that there was someone else in the
land of Saeditin who felt as she did.

The death priest was chanting something in a loud and
surprisingly musical voice. Rilsin dragged her attention
back to him, to what was happening right in front of her.

"The Mother will purify your blood," the priest was
singing. "She will cleanse your soul and make you pure."

The soldiers had brought Zechia forward and forced him
to his knees. His hands were tied tightly behind his back,
but the soldiers kept their hands on his shoulders for good
measure. Rilsin could hear his heavy breathing, and she
could see the pulse in his throat. She wrapped her hands in
her cloak and clutched the material desperately, as if it could
somehow save her, save them all. The priest was still
singing.

"We send you to the land of light, not into darkness, but
into light."

On the last word, before the priest had quite finished the

long note, the novice grasped Zechia by the hair and pulled his head back. Zechia jerked, as if he would struggle now, but he couldn't. The priest leaned forward, even as he finished his chant, and drew the knife across Zechia's throat. Zechia spasmed, but the soldiers held him.

The spurting arc of blood was brilliant even in the gray light. It soaked the priest, spattered the novice and the soldiers, dripped through the planks of the platform down to the dirt beneath, going back to the land. But not all of it. The priest took the crystal goblet from Bilma and held it to catch some of the scarlet fountain. The ancient glass filled with thick ruby liquid. Bilma took this carefully, reverently, and held it up so the crowd could see it. The crowd, which had remained silent through all of this, now sighed.

"The blood of the traitor is purified," said Bilma loudly. Rilsin glanced at Zechia; his body was sprawled, discarded, on the platform.

"His blood returns to the land, to strengthen it. May the land be strengthened!"

"May the land be strengthened!" echoed the crowd.

"May the SaeKet be strengthened!"

"May the SaeKet be strengthened!" roared the crowd.

Bilma, his scarlet vest spotted with Zechia's scarlet blood, carried the crystal goblet to Sithli.

For the first time since the sacrifice began, Rilsin looked at her cousin. Sithli's golden skin had a gray tinge to it, and her eyes were wide and slightly glassy. Her lips were parted, and Rilsin could hear her gasping. Her scar showed livid even under the powder. Sithli was in shock.

Bilma put one hand on his heart, and with his other, proffered the goblet.

At first Sithli made no move to take it from him. But in the lengthening silence she seemed to come to herself a little and reached out tentatively with one slender hand. Bilma gave her the goblet.

It had been many years since a SaeKet actually drank the blood of her enemies. But the ritual was the same as it had always been in every other way. Instead of drinking the blood, the SaeKet was expected to merely touch the goblet to her lips. With a hand that trembled slightly, Sithli raised the goblet to her lips. The glass bumped against her mouth, and still-warm blood lapped over the brim and onto her lips.

Sithli gasped, a sound that was audible in the quiet of the square. Her hand shook even more, and more blood slopped out, darkening the brilliant gold of her cloak. Sithli thrust the goblet away from her, and it became obvious to everyone that she was going to drop it.

If she dropped it, it would be a disaster. Bilma, who had stepped back to allow the crowd to see the SaeKet do her part in the ritual, was not close enough to do anything. Dinip was close enough, standing almost touching his daughter, but he seemed stunned. Furthermore, he was dira, not saedin, and only a priest or a saedin might touch the goblet. The goblet began to slide through Sithli's fingers. It would fall and break, just as Rilsin had imagined, but too late to save Zechia.

Rilsin acted immediately. Later she could not remember even thinking about what to do, let alone making any decision to act. She simply acted. She leaned forward and caught the goblet as it left her cousin's hand, and then, before Sithli could completely withdraw, she grasped Sithli's hand and pressed the goblet back into it. She closed her hand over Sithli's and the goblet together, and gripped both tightly. The crowd was murmuring in surprise and alarm, and under the cover of this sound Rilsin whispered her cousin's name. Sithli looked back at her, drew a deep breath, and nodded. Rilsin withdrew her hand.

"Zechia sae Eanern is purified," said Sithli. Her voice was thin and thready, and the crowd hushed to hear her. "The land accepts his blood."

"The Mother accepts his blood," said the death priest. He had come forward, looking a little pale and shocked himself, to reclaim the goblet. He took it from Sithli and overturned it to let the rest of the blood drain onto the ground. There was nothing left in the goblet now, however, but a few thick drops.

Sithli rose to her feet, helped by her father. The priest and his novice took the bloody goblet and knife and left the platform. Soldiers bundled up Zechia's body; others surrounded the SaeKet and the regent to escort them back to the palace through the milling, dispersing crowd.

Rilsin stepped back from all this activity. She watched the other saedin leave the platform, but she made no attempt to go with them. She was looking at her sleeve and her hand. The blood spilled when she rescued the goblet did not show on the black of her sleeve, but it was red and sticky on her hand and wrist. She thought of the blood on Sithli's lips. The nausea she had been suppressing came back in a rush. If she didn't get off this platform right away, if she couldn't get to somewhere secluded, she was going to throw up in front of everyone.

She stumbled down the steps of the platform, feeling sweaty and thick-headed. The pain in her healing ribs came back as she bumped into a platform support. People were pressing around her now, touching her, calling her name. They approved of her; they admired her; they wanted to be near her. She was not going to make it. She wrapped her arms around herself.

Someone was suddenly beside her, fending people away from her. She looked up as Sola's arm came around her. He tried to wedge himself between her and the people, to force their way through.

"Come on, Rilsin," he said, "you can make it."

But they were not making it. They gained a little headway, but the word had gone out that Sae Rilsin, the sword of the land, the girl who rescued the SaeKet again, was still there, and people wanted to catch a glimpse of her. They were surrounded by people, all of them commoners, who shouted Rilsin's name and reached out to her.

"Out of the way! Get back!"

Rilsin looked up and saw someone swinging a sword, flat side out, beating a path to her through the crowd. It was Sifuat. Of course he was here; it made sense, the way he'd been fawning on Sithli, and Rilsin wondered why she had not seen him before.

"Get away from her! Come on, Sola Nine-fingered! Take her other arm! Get her between us. Sae Rilsin," he made a small flourish with his fingers, "can you at least walk?" He laid about him with the flat of the sword. People screamed.

"Of course I can walk!" Annoyance made her feel a bit better, Rilsin found. She straightened. "Stop hitting people, Sifuat!"

He glanced at her and raised his eyebrows slightly. "I had the impression you did not want to stay and be mobbed. Was I wrong? If you want to get out, this is the way."

It was true. With Sola and Sifuat on either side of her, and with Sifuat clearing a path, they were making good progress out of the square. When they reached the semiprivacy of the bushes that lined the road to the palace, Rilsin pushed away from them. She crouched down, wedging herself between two bushes. Turning away from the road, she vomited until there was nothing left to come up.

10

It was cold outside, a light crust of snow frozen onto the hard earth by the sleet that had fallen overnight. It was that miserable time of year when the weather couldn't quite make up its mind to be completely winter yet or to remain autumn. The trees were bare, but some leaves still remained in sodden lumps beside the roads. Rain froze, snow melted, and then refroze to a crusty glaze. But winter was winning, even in the south, and soon all of Saeditin would be locked into cold days and frigid nights, bitter winds, and snow.

Right now it was more than cold enough for Rilsin sae Becha, first minister of Saeditin. She had been out walking in the hour just before dawn. It was a habit she had formed in the three years since she took office shortly after her seventeenth birthday at the request of her cousin the SaeKet. It was a time when she knew she would not be disturbed, when she and Chilsa could slip like ghosts through the fields and the woods, when the big silver cat could run free, when they could hunt and roam in the solitary manner they liked best. If she walked or rode during later, more fashionable hours, someone always wanted to keep her company. But her walk was over now, and she was at the palace for an early meeting. She passed the guards, who saluted her by lifting their spears slightly. She nodded in return and entered the palace, stamping her feet to shake off the cold.

The surge of warm air was almost overpowering; the steam heating pipes, which Sola had installed, worked best in fall and spring, when the weather was not too severe. The pipes did not add positively to the palace decor. They ran up the walls to the height of the room and then punched through the ceiling to continue on the next floor up. They did this in many rooms all the way to the top of the palace, with the pipes for the return condensate matching them in parallel rows, and they could not be hidden by tapestries or hangings, which would have impaired their effectiveness at best and caused a fire hazard at worst. On top of this, the pipes banged and hissed at odd moments, causing visitors to jump. But they were a marvel that visitors came to see and one for which Rilsin was very grateful. She had a similar system installed in her own manor house.

She made her way now to the SaeKet's breakfast room, in the wing that she and Sithli shared as children. Guards saluted her and servants nodded to her, but no one even offered to accompany her. They were all accustomed to seeing the first minister anywhere in the palace, at any hour, and they knew to leave her alone. Rilsin prefered it that way. Sometimes, especially when she was tired, it was hard to remember that she no longer lived here.

Sithli was not yet in the breakfast room. No one else was yet, either, except for the servants who were laying out food and place settings. Rather than wait, Rilsin headed for the SaeKet's apartments. The guards there let her through, even though she was wearing her sword. Rilsin alone was permitted to wear a weapon in the presence of the SaeKet.

Sithli was sitting in the wooden-backed chair in front of her mirror, having her hair combed and braided. She was dressed in crushed green velvet with gold embroidery, velvet trousers with the new wide fashionable flair, and a long velvet overshirt over a cream silk undershirt, which showed at neck and cuffs. A maid was plaiting her hair with little emeralds. She turned when she saw Rilsin in the mirror, causing the maid to drop a string of emeralds.

"Rilsin! Early as usual. Have a cup of hot cider. There's toast and jam, if you want it."

"Thank you." Rilsin helped herself to the cider. "It's been hours since I ate, and I'm not likely to get much in the meeting."

"Hours since you ate." Sithli frowned. "Most people, decent people, have only just gotten up." She shook her head at her cousin in mock dismay. "But then I suppose you've been out with Chilsa again. And I can see it snowed again, or some such; you've tracked water all the way into my rooms."

Rilsin looked down at her boots in dismay. Sure enough, her wet footprints followed her across the SaeKet's cream wool carpet. She had obviously been tracking water all through the palace.

"It's only water." Sithli waved her hand in dismissal. "If it stains, I'll have it cleaned."

"I'm sorry." Rilsin spoke more to Flet, the maid, who would be responsible for the cleaning, than to her cousin. "I'm not in winter mode yet."

"How could anyone tell? You look the same no matter what the season."

It was true. Rilsin was wearing her customary black: black overshirt, black undershirt, black trousers of the narrower, less fashionable cut, black, ankle-high walking boots. Her black cloak was draped over her arm. She was wearing wool now instead of cotton or linen, but she looked the same as she always did, just as her cousin said.

"At least you could let your hair grow, like a saedin or any free citizen. I've pretty much given up on trying to make you fashionable, but it's not right to keep your hair short like a captive's."

"We've been through this before, Sithli. It's comfortable this way. I'm used to it, and I like it. It doesn't get in the way." Rilsin took a gulp of hot cider. She did not want to talk about why she wore black and kept her hair short. She did not even want to think about it. "I didn't come here early to discuss fashion or track up your floor. I wanted to see you alone, before the council meeting. I want to discuss the Runchot quota on slaves."

"Captives. Criminals. Not slaves." She held up a hand to silence her cousin and turned to let the maid apply powder to her face. The scar on her right cheek was faded but still visible, and Sithli was very conscious of it. She kept it covered by makeup and even carried a small container of powder with her wherever she went, for emergency repairs. "The Runchot pay well for them, and what else are we to do with them? Lock them in prisons and feed them?"

"They are Saeditin, our own people, most of them." She did not say that she doubted there were so many criminals in the land. "It is not right to sell them. As to what to do with them, we can use the labor here."

"Where their families and friends can get at them, to cause more trouble."

When Rilsin opened her mouth, Sithli held up her hand.

"Save it for the meeting, Rilsin."

"But Sithli, you need to hear this first. I have figures, numbers. The numbers of Saeditin sold, of Saeditin, not northerners, have been—"

"I said, save it for the meeting. For the meeting, First Minister."

Rilsin stopped. She knew that tone. It was not worth it to cross her cousin now; it would just put her in a bad mood before the meeting. She was frustrated, though; she had wanted to talk to Sithli alone, to get her cousin's undivided attention. She knew the council members would not want to hear her, and that Sithli would be distracted. But she had not forgotten her childhood lessons, and she knew better than to press her cause just now.

Sithli's hair and makeup were completed. She rose from the chair and smoothed down the front of her velvet overshirt, glanced at herself in the mirror with approval. "That's all, Flet," she said to the maid, who took her cue and left.

Rilsin put down her mug of cider; it was time to go. But as Sithli moved toward the door, there was a flurry from the inner chamber, Sithli's bedroom. A young man rushed through the door, smiling at Sithli. He stopped short when he saw Rilsin.

"I wanted to see you before you left," he said to Sithli. "I overslept."

"No you didn't, sweet; I let you sleep. And see, you are not too late to see me." She smiled at him but stepped back when he made a move as if to embrace her. Her hair and clothes were perfect, and she did not want to muss them. Rilsin suppressed a smile. She had seen this before.

The young man was wearing a loose silk robe of watery gray, which flowed and parted, showing off various portions of his magnificent body. He was incredibly beautiful, almost as beautiful as Sithli. He had the same dark blond hair and golden skin, but his eyes were a brilliant blue, betraying a trace of northern ancestry. He was a saedin of a minor family, somebody's third son; Rilsin couldn't even remember his name, let alone his mother's. She couldn't remember because Sithli had a new lover every few months, or so it seemed, and Rilsin could not keep track. None of Sithli's lovers had been memorable. Despite her active love life, however, Sithli had failed to become pregnant. Dinip, who disapproved of his daughter's flightiness, believed she would conceive only when she settled down with one mate. Sithli showed no signs of settling down, however, claiming that marriage was old-fashioned, and in any event, marriage did not matter. Children did.

"Later, sweet." Sithli sidestepped her lover again and was now definitely headed for the door. "Rilsin and I must meet with the council."

When they were out in the corridor, accompanied by two guards, Sithli shook her head.

"Time for a change, I think," she said. "Degil is sweet, and certainly good to look at, but there is not much here." She tapped her emerald-spangled head. "Not much elsewhere, either, it seems. It's been almost a year, and I still have not conceived."

Rilsin grunted noncommittally, glancing at the guards,

who were pretending not to hear. Then she decided to comment anyway.

"I don't know why you choose them," she said, "except for the obvious. Certainly there are enough good-looking saedin, and dira, too, who could offer you more. And you know what Dinip says."

"My father," said Sithli, "is old-fashioned. Like you." She smiled at her cousin to take any sting out of the words. Rilsin had had only three lovers since her seventeenth birthday. "Perhaps you should marry."

"Sithli! I'm not that old-fashioned!"

"I suppose not. I don't see you showing any great devotion to your choices."

True, Rilsin thought. The young men she chose, including her current lover, were all pleasant enough, all intelligent, and all quiet. Unremarkable. She chose them because it was expected of her to have lovers and because they would cause no comment.

"You need someone intelligent, Rilsin, to match you. Someone like Sola, perhaps."

Rilsin stiffened. "He's my friend, Sithli."

"So you have said for years. Or perhaps you need someone like Sifuat."

Rilsin laughed. "I thought you said intelligent!"

"There's more to our Sae Sifuat than first meets the eye."

"Then you see very deeply, SaeKet!"

Sithli chuckled. "Norimin still has hopes of marrying him to me, you know."

"I know. You could do worse." She grinned at Sithli. "He's as good-looking as Degil, at least."

"I won't marry, Rils, and you know why." Sithli had turned serious. "Too many complications. And certainly not to someone like Sifuat, who has lands and power of his own."

"His mother has them," interjected Rilsin. "What Sifuat has is an appetite for clothes, women, and sword fighting. The man is an annoyance. But I understand. Too many complications, and it's too soon. You need to stay free for a time."

"Forever, Rils. I won't ever marry. I will be free to the end of time. My children will be mine alone."

"Poor Norimin," said Rilsin lightly. "So much for her dynastic dreams."

They were at the breakfast room now. The guards took their position at either side of the door as Sithli and Rilsin entered. The members of the saedin council already in the room and seated at Sithli's huge carved table came to their feet, putting down mugs of cider and pieces of toast or fried bread smeared with jam or honey. There was even fruit from the SaeKet's greenhouses, oranges and pears in a glazed earthen bowl. The saedin put their hands to their hearts, some seriously, some with perfunctory brevity.

Rilsin looked round to see who was present. The whole council was there: the richest, most powerful saedin in the land or their representatives, women and men with vested interests in the Melisin regime. The lone representative of the dira stood slightly to one side. Despite her long tenure on the council, no one treated Mettit dira Jat as an equal, nor did she expect it. There were no commoners present.

Sithli and Rilsin took their places at the head of the table, Rilsin to Sithli's right. They were followed by a rush from the saedin to seat themselves. Rilsin smiled at Bilma sae Grepsin and received a smile in return. The former first minister was beginning to show signs of age. On cold, damp mornings such as this one, his joints hurt him, and it was becoming painful for him to walk. But he would not be remiss in his duties, and he was always one of the first to arrive at any meeting or function.

He held no grudge against Rilsin for taking his office from him. On the contrary, he was pleased to be alive, as the days were not long past when replaced officials would meet with an accident, if they were not executed outright. But Rilsin sought his advice and made it clear she valued his opinion. Deep in his heart, Bilma thought more kindly of Rilsin than he did of his SaeKet.

The only person of importance not present in the breakfast room was the former regent. Rilsin was uneasy. Her uncle would normally have been one of the first to arrive.

He, too, had been looking tired and drained lately. He knew it himself, but he said only that he was not looking forward to another winter. Rilsin thought of him as an ally, someone whose opinion Sithli must take seriously.

A servant put a mug of cider and some fried bread in front of Rilsin. She took several bites, chewing rapidly, trying to get it down before the meeting started. She regretted now not having eaten in Sithli's rooms. She glanced at the food placed in front of her cousin; Sithli wouldn't eat a bite, she knew, but only because she did not want to drop a crumb on her perfect green velvet.

"Sae Rilsin, good morning. I wonder if you have a moment before all this begins." A young saedin took the chair beside her. He smiled ingratiatingly.

Rilsin took a quick gulp of cider to wash down the bread. It had begun already. The young noble next to her was the eldest child of a progressive family with modern ideas. Despite the fact that he had a much younger sister, he stood to inherit half the family wealth, and he represented the family with complete authority.

"Good morning, Sae Essit. It's always a pleasure to see you. How can I help?"

Essit flushed, pleased at his rapport with the first minister. He was one of the old line of pale saedin, with fine clear skin, sky-gray eyes, and glossy black hair. He was also young. The holdings of his family, the Sae Tillits, were in the north, adjacent to Norimin sae Sudit's lands.

"We think we have deposits of coal. At least so my mother sends me word. She has the services of a natural scientist," he frowned slightly, "the ones that study rock formations."

"Geologists, they call themselves."

"Yes. He thinks there is coal, and a lot of it."

"Wonderful!"

"Yes, indeed, First Minister! Coal for heating and coal for Dira Sola's new engines!"

"And coal to fire the pumps to help mine more coal," said Rilsin dryly. "I don't see the problem, Sae Essit, excuse me."

"Roads, First Minister. The roads are atrocious. Not the roads of SaedTillit, of course, not our holdings, but in the saedholds of some our neighbors. Not only are the roads terrible, but they demand outrageous rates, or say they will, to allow us to ship our coal anywhere."

The last of Essit's words fell into a silence, the kind that occurred in any large group. This one was caused, Rilsin saw, by Sithli having raised her hand for order, a gesture that she and Essit were late to see. The timing was unfortunate, however. Essit's complaint rang out clearly in the lull. Norimin, who was seated with her son Sifuat near the end of the long table, lost no time.

"What are you implying, Essit sae Tillit? That the Saed-Sudit is governed by highwaymen?"

Essit flinched, more, Rilsin suspected, at the use of his full, rhyming name, which he hated, than at Norimin's sarcasm.

"I would never say that of you, Norimin sae Sudit," he said. Which, of course, was exactly what he *was* saying.

Good for you, thought Rilsin. She was watching Sifuat through this, and she saw him beginning to flush dangerously. She wanted to tell him to relax, that it was only politics.

"We keep up our roads as well as we ever have," declared Sifuat.

"Which is saying very little! And you Sudits have been overcharging us for any use of them!" Essit was beginning to warm up to a speech, and it was not going to help the council's mood. Rilsin glanced to her left and caught Sithli's eye.

"Saedin, please," she said, rising to her feet. "I'm sure no affront is meant. By anyone." She looked pointedly at each of the parties, including Sifuat. She knew full well the impression she made. She had the height of her Becha parentage, and she was strong from her daily arms practice with the guards and her runs with Chilsa. The austere black she wore accentuated these features, and beyond that, there was her reputation. She was the SaeKet's defender, the Sword of Saeditin, the commander of the Guards, as well as first minister. And her suggestions, most of them anyway, were taken by Sithli. Sure enough, the angry nobles stopped glaring at each other and looked at her.

"I believe that all Sae Essit meant to do was to suggest that we, the Council of Saedin, set standards for all the roads of Saeditin, improving them where necessary." She sat down to astounded silence. Essit was gazing at her with something akin to worship, for this was in fact the matter on which he had hoped to gain Rilsin's help.

"Each saedhold is responsible for its own roads now." Bilma spoke up, looking thoughtful. "How would you suggest that improvements be made and standards enforced?"

"Each saedhold would continue to provide what it can. The rest," Rilsin avoided looking at Sithli, "would come from the SaeKet's treasury."

Pandemonium broke loose. Rilsin sat back, smiling slightly at the chaos. Sithli leaned over to her.

"It's a good idea," she said, "but you could have warned me it was coming."

"I did warn you. I tried to discuss it with you last week. There is more than enough for this in the treasury." Rilsin kept her voice low and an innocent expression on her face. It served Sithli right for ignoring her attempts to talk seriously.

"I don't remember it." Sithli raised her voice. "It is an excellent idea. We need to make sure commerce flows smoothly all across Saeditin; that has became obvious to me. And with the sales of criminals to the Runchot increasing, the treasury can afford some expenditure."

Rilsin looked at her, dismayed. This was too many issues at once, and Sithli had turned the tables on her. Then she decided to make it work for her.

"We should be selling coal and steam machines to the Runchot, not citizens of Saeditin."

The saedin looked from the SaeKet to the first minister and back. Things were moving too quickly now.

"Our coal and our machines, all the inventions of Sola Ninefingered, are Saeditin's! And the SaeKet's! We should guard them well. It is better to sell our criminals, get them

out of our land, than to give away our resources and our se-
crets." Sifuat came to the rescue, saying as always what he
thought Sithli wanted to hear. He did not see his mother's
look of contempt.

"The Runchot will get the steam machines, anyway, Sae
Sifuat," said Rilsin patiently, "or they will get plans for
them, same thing. And they will get coal, if not from their
own lands, then from somewhere, or they will use all their
forests up first and then come after coal. I say it is better for
us to sell to them now, to get the upper hand in this. If we
trade with the Runchot, perhaps we need not fight them as
often."

It was the beginning of a debate that lasted all morning.
True to her prophecy, Rilsin got no more breakfast. She was
too busy advocating her idea. Essit was her partisan, of
course, and so, at least moderately, was Bilma. Sifuat was
vociferous in his opposition, but Norimin said nothing,
merely watched and listened, glancing occasionally at her
son. Many others were not sure what stand to take. They
wanted the favor of the powerful first minister, but the
SaeKet had not yet made her stand clear. It was almost noon
before Sithli called a halt. The weary saedin, and the dira,
who had not spoken once, filed out of the breakfast room.
Sithli took Rilsin by the arm and hurried her away.

"At least," she said, "eat with me now; I know you are
famished. We can get away from all this . . . business . . .
and talk about clothes for the midwinter festival. Or at
least," she gave Rilsin a sideways glance, "my clothes."

"It's a little early for that, isn't it? Guards, accompany us
to . . ." she looked at Sithli. ". . . the SaeKet's rooms, and
see that no one disturbs us."

"It's never too early to plan for the festival."

"Sithli, you haven't talked to Uncle Dinip about my idea
for trade with the Runchot, have you? I told him about it last
month. I thought perhaps he might have said something. It
upset him, and he has been so tired that I didn't bring it up
again, but perhaps he spoke to you."

"I haven't seen much of Father in the past few weeks.
I've been busy." Sithli had the grace to look away. "Don't

look at me like that, Rilsin! All right, I admit, I haven't seen him in two weeks, so he hasn't said anything to me! I will send for him now, if you want."

Send for him, thought Rilsin. "Invite him to eat with us."

But Dinip never came. They were met by a breathless servant, who had been sent to find the SaeKet, even as the council meeting ended.

"Dira Dinip is sick!" she gasped. It was obvious that it was serious.

"Send for Sae Nefit!" Sithli and Rilsin said in unison.

It was not necessary. The physicians, both of them, were already in the rooms of the former regent when the women arrived. The nature of the sickness was plain: Dinip had been stricken by an arrow of the Dark One. The left side of his mouth drooped, and he could not move his hand or his leg. He was still conscious, and he tried to whisper something to them.

"It does not hurt," they finally made out.

Nefit led them away while Maltia tended to Dinip.

"It is bad," she said, "but not as bad as it might be. Sometimes they recover from this, to an extent. He needs rest, and if he makes it through the next few days, he will need help and much work to regain some of his former capacity. Dira Dinip has never been one to give up easily, so I am hopeful."

They stayed with him in turns, Rilsin and the guilt-stricken Sithli. There was always one of them there, no matter what their duties were. A death priest came to watch by the bedside as well, but Sithli sent him away. Dinip was in good spirits, and Rilsin began to think that he would recover. Two days after he was first stricken, in the early hours of the morning while his daughter the SaeKet dozed in the chair beside his bed, Dinip was stricken again. When Sithli awakened, her father was dead. When Rilsin arrived, hastily summoned, Sithli was sobbing, and the death priest was back.

11

TRUE WINTER CAME. THE MOOD IN THE PALACE WAS somber. Ever since the death of Dinip, Sithli had been wrapped in gloom, and her temper had been erratic. Saedin quarreled among themselves and dira challenged one another. In one instance a dira challenged a saedin, with the result that he was sold to the Runchot without even a hearing.

The matter of the selling of citizens versus the sale of coal and steam machines became an issue debated not only in the palace and among the nobility but in the capital of Petipal and all through the countryside. Saedin whose holds were coal-rich were in favor of trade, but there were not many of them. Many more favored the status quo. The commoners, who were beginning to find work in mines and factories, were in favor of trade also, but no one asked them. More important were the dira, the honored class, who ran most of the business of Saeditin. Most were in favor of the new trade, since they stood not only to profit from the arrangement but to stop losing sons and even daughters sold across the border.

But the issue was far from settled, and the SaeKet herself

seemed to be leaning away from making a decision. The speculation was that she did not want the new trade, but she also did not want to disappoint her cousin, the first minister. Everyone knew that Sithli's Sword was the trade faction's most enthusiastic proponent. They also knew she was the close friend of Sola Ninefingered, the man whose magic was responsible for transforming the land of Saeditin.

Many saedin grumbled about the first minister. She was plain and severe, unostentatious, devoted to duty. There was no doubt that she believed her views were best for Saeditin, even if they were not best for the saedin. The nobles were slow to convince, but the commoners loved her. "True SaeKet," some of them whispered. It was fortunate for them that, as usual, no one asked what they thought. It was in this way that winter began.

Rilsin was awakened before dawn one frigid morning by the chiming of her mechanical clock, an import from across the sea. At the appropriate time, tiny hammers hit small bells. Most of the time, this was pleasing. Today, Rilsin pulled the pillow over her head. She moaned.

"You are the one who insists on keeping it in the bedroom." Tilda dira Sechit, her current lover, tried to gather Rilsin into his arms.

"That is so it can wake me when I need it to." Rilsin's mouth felt like thick cotton. She gently pulled away from Tilda. "Go back to sleep, sweet. No need for you to suffer." She flipped the lever on the clock to stop the hammer and was not surprised to see that Tilda was already asleep again.

She pulled on her thick woolen trousers and her fur-trimmed overshirt, and shoved her feet into her fur-lined boots. She tiptoed out of the room, cursing the bitter cold. The next moment she was blazing hot. She paused to wipe sweat from her palms and felt a slight wave of dizziness. She swallowed and found that her throat was sore. She leaned against the wall, annoyed.

She had no time to be sick. There were rumors, more than rumors, good intelligence, that the northern barbarians would attack the borders at spring thaw, and she must prepare the troops; it was not too early. The Runchot had sent a delegation to demand a restructuring of their treaty, so she must talk to Sithli. The time for procrastination had ended. There was a council meeting tomorrow, so she needed to apply some last-minute pressure today, and there was Sola, who had something on his mind that he needed to see her about. She had not had time recently, and it was a terrible thing when one must make an appointment to see a friend.

Something simultaneously hard and soft knocked against her legs, against the backs of her knees, almost collapsing her against the wall. She looked down, not far, but down, to scratch Chilsa behind the ears. Ever since Tilda moved in, Chilsa was exiled from the bedroom. He would have preferred to sleep with Rilsin, but not only did he take up a large portion of the bed, he made Tilda sneeze.

The silver gray cat was huge. When he raised his head, it was at Rilsin's waist level, and Rilsin was not a small woman. He looked at Rilsin out of wild green eyes and yawned, showing his impressive canines. Then he banged his head against her knees again. Chilsa was hungry, and he wanted to play.

"All right, all right." Her throat was indeed sore. She pushed herself away from the wall and headed toward the kitchen, actually considering not taking Chilsa out for a predawn walk today. Partway to her destination, another wave of dizziness halted her briefly. It was not going to be a good day.

The kitchen was large and warm and comfortable. As saedin manor houses went, Rilsin's was neither huge nor extravagant, and it did not require many staff. But she had not skimped on the kitchen, which had both wood- and coal-burning stoves and a huge table of white marble. It was arguably the most pleasant place to be on a nasty winter day, and most of Rilsin's small staff was already congregated there. The smells of warm cider and hot cinnamon muffins greeted her, but Rilsin did not find it as enticing as she normally would. Seated at the marble table with a muffin and a mug of cider was Sola. Rilsin blinked stupidly at him.

"What are you doing here?"

"I thought I'd meet you here instead of by the horse

trails. It's pretty nasty out. I thought I might talk you out of walking today and maybe save myself the unpleasantness. Had I known you would be so gracious, I'd have picked the cold." He grinned at her and took a gulp of cider. Rilsin's staff, accustomed to this sort of banter, simply ignored it.

Rilsin went to the kitchen door that opened onto a storage porch. Meat for Chilsa's meal had been put there the previous day to begin to thaw. Now she brought some of this into the kitchen, hacked off a piece, and gave it to the cat. Chilsa began to eat noisily, pausing occasionally to look at Rilsin and emit a loud purr. For some reason, the sight of this made Rilsin nauseous. Her staff, accustomed to this sight and already giving Chilsa a wide berth to go about their business, did not notice. But Sola did.

"You're ill." He went to her and caught her as she swayed. "Sit down right here. By the Mother, you're burning up." He rested the back of his hand against her forehead, and Rilsin fought the urge to grab it and keep it there. "Meffa, get some herb tea for Sae Rilsin; she's got a fever. Sit, Rils, don't try to get up."

Rilsin relaxed into the chair and the comfortable warmth of the kitchen. Meffa, her senior servant, and Sola fussed over her, and Rilsin closed her eyes.

"You should be in bed."

"I can't. Too much to do today. This is the worst timing. I have the guards, and the Runchot are here; I must see Sithli." She said all this with her eyes closed, then suddenly snapped them open. "You wanted to talk to me about something."

"It can wait."

"No, it can't. You are here and I am here, Sola, my dearest friend, so tell me." She was looking straight at him. When she called him "dearest friend," a strange expression crossed his face. It was an expression she had seen before, but she could not think what it was. In a moment it came to her. It was the way some men looked at Sithli. But no one looked at Rilsin that way, not even Tilda. *I am truly ill,* she thought. Sola was telling her what it was, what was on his mind, and she had not been listening, she had been thinking instead about Sithli SaeKet and her lovesick men.

"... so a better-educated people would be better for all Saeditin."

Rilsin blinked at him. What was he talking about?

"I don't see why we need educated commoners, Dira Sola." Tilda had come into the kitchen. He was wrapped in his fur robe. "They are useful as they are, don't you think? They can work the fields, carry burdens, even run the machines in your mines without knowing how to read." He yawned and glanced at Rilsin. "I couldn't sleep. I called for Meffa to bring me breakfast, but she didn't hear."

"Think, Dira Tilda." Sola was pressing his point. "If you and I were commoners, think how it would be."

"But we're not. Why are you still here, Rilsin?" He came and put his hands on her shoulders in a proprietary gesture. Rilsin had the urge to shrug them off.

"She is ill. She should be in bed."

"And why are *you* here, Dira Sola?"

"He was invited." Her throat was getting worse, and it was not improving her patience or her temper.

Chilsa had finished his meal. Now he wanted to go out, and he looked expectantly at Rilsin. He came to stand beside her, squeezing between her and Sola. Tilda he studiously ignored, as he ignored all Rilsin's lovers. When Rilsin did not immediately respond to him, he meowed, a high-pitched, raucous, somehow kittenish sound from such a huge animal.

"Not today, sweet cat. Meffa will let you out in the pen later." She looked toward her servant, who nodded.

Meffa had been there all along, ignored by them all as the commoners always were, listening to the talk about commoners. Her face was flushed, and not from the heat in the kitchen. Think, Sola had said, how it would be. Rilsin tried to think. Meffa had been running her household for three years now, doing everything from purchasing supplies to caring for Chilsa. But Rilsin didn't know much about her, except that she came from a northern family, somewhere near the border.

"I have to go." Rilsin pushed herself out of the chair. She left Tilda in the kitchen and somehow got her sword belted on, her cloak around her, her boots laced.

"You forgot to comb your hair, Rils. It may be short, but it still needs combing." Sola reached into his pocket and handed her his own comb. He accompanied her when she went out, striding along beside her. "You didn't hear a word I said in there, did you?"

"Some. Well, no, not really." She swallowed, and it hurt. "I'm sorry. I really will pay attention."

"Later." Sola was more concerned than he would admit. He could see how sick she was. "There is lung sickness in the south," he told her, "and in Runchot. There are even a few cases in the city. You should rest."

"I don't have lung sickness. And I will rest when I have done what I must." Her vision was watery. "I'm sorry. I shouldn't snap at you."

The snow-packed streets were almost deserted at this early hour. An icy wind funneled between buildings and stung their faces. Sola wished Rilsin had decided to take a carriage, but this was something she rarely did. She walked whenever possible, and the palace was not far. But now they both had pulled their hoods up to cover their faces as much as possible against the sleet that quickly turned to snow. Midwinter was almost on them, the great festival of Sunreturn, although the weather would not warm for months beyond that. If the SaeKet's mood did not lighten, this midwinter would be grim.

They reached the palace, were saluted by Rilsin's guards, and entered the main courtyard. Despite the early hour, the courtyard was filled with saedin, mostly younger ones, who were stamping their feet, cursing the weather. They were obviously waiting for something, and they were not pleased to be doing it. Rilsin stopped, frowning. She should have known why they were here, but the reason escaped her. It was a moment before she realized that all of the saedin were members of the faction that opposed the new trade with the Runchot. Worse than that, most of them were Sifuat's hangers-on, young men who banded together to drink and fight and follow the lead of the handsome Sae Sudit. Now they flashed and strutted in the falling snow. Sifuat himself preened at the center of this group.

"They want to talk to Sithli SaeKet about refusing the Runchot delegation." Sola's comment was soft, meant for her ears alone. Unfortunately, it was picked up and repeated by a young saedin.

"And you would give all away to our enemies. You do not own what you create in your mind, Sola dira Mudrin! It is not yours to give away, Ninefingers! It is the SaeKet's!"

Rilsin was distracted, in her fevered state, by a thought. Was it possible for an individual, other than the SaeKet, who owned all, to own an idea? The barbarians of the north owned songs and rituals, which no one could perform without the owner's permission, so why not ideas? The silliness of the thought made her smile. The smile was immediately misinterpreted by the irate saedin.

"You think it amusing that our enemies should have what makes us strong?" He planted himself directly in front of Rilsin. The snowflakes melted on his flushed cheeks. Elpi sae Dorn, Rilsin remembered, the youngest child of an old family.

"Stand aside, Sae Elpi," she said, trying to be patient. Her voice cracked. "No one will harm Saeditin while I can prevent it. Now let us pass. Please." Her firmness was unfortunately undermined by another bout of dizziness, and she swayed. Before anyone else could react, Sola had her by the arm.

"I've got you, Rils." His arm went around her shoulders. "Let's get inside."

The whole courtyard had become suddenly silent, filled only with the hiss of snow and the indrawn breaths of the young men.

" 'Rils'? That is Rilsin sae Becha, Sae Rilsin, the first minister." Elpi, who showed no sign of respect for rank or protocol only moments before, was suddenly outraged.

Sola stopped dead. Whatever the friendship between nobles and honoreds, in public certain forms of address must be followed. Even a married couple of mixed rank must follow the rules in public. The lesser rank must address the higher rank by title. Sola had made a mistake, not a particularly bad one, except in this company.

"I beg your pardon. But Rilsin—Sae Rilsin—is sick, and needs to get indoors." Sola tried to push ahead. He was aware that he'd done it again, and that his only hope was to get out of the crowd before he did something worse.

"Perhaps," Sifuat stepped forward, "you are her lover. That would account for your familiarity." Sifuat knew better, knew it was not his business anyway, and he was not quite sure just what made him say this. There had already been quarrels and fights between the two trade factions, and he knew he was inflaming his friends, but he didn't care. He felt obscurely but personally insulted by Sola.

"Try not to seem any more stupid than you actually are, Sifuat." Rilsin stepped in front of Sola. "Dira Sola is right; we must get inside. Stand back, please."

"Did you call me stupid, or did I imagine it?" Sifuat couldn't stop now. He could feel the focused attention of the men around him, and he was on the brink of losing control.

"If you can imagine something, Sae Sifuat, then that is more than I thought you capable of. Now stand aside!" Rilsin's patience was at an end, and standing in the snow arguing with belligerent fools was making her feel worse. She knew she was insulting Sifuat, something she had taken care never to do before in public, and she didn't care. He was an idiot.

Sifuat was taken aback. This close to Rilsin he could see that Sola was right. She was ill, undoubtedly more so than she herself realized. It was unlike her to insult someone so offhandedly. He was about to step back and accompany them into the palace, but he hesitated, unwilling to give up his posturing. It was now that Elpi, who had not enjoyed being overlooked, spoke up.

"Don't take that, Sae Sifuat! Not even from the first minister!"

These was a chorus of agreement from the other saedin, and a few more taunts. There were calls of "make her apologize!"

"If she will not apologize, then she must defend herself!" Elpi put his hand to his sword.

"Are you challenging me, Elpi sae Dorn?" Rilsin knew it must be fever. This was becoming absurd.

Elpi took a step backward despite himself. He paled and swallowed. "No!" When others began to smile, he flushed. "Sifuat sae Sudit challenges you!"

Sifuat looked confused. He had no desire to challenge Rilsin or anyone else right now. This was becoming absurd, he thought, echoing Rilsin's thought.

"That's enough, Sae Elpi," said Sola calmly. He began to walk, holding onto Rilsin, who shook him off. She knew she was very ill now, but she was determined to get into the palace, at least, without help. But Elpi was not going to let this go. If he did, he knew he would be the butt of jokes for days to come. So he stepped in front of Sola and shoved him back. Without a second thought, Sola responded in kind.

Elpi started to draw his sword. Rilsin, who had begun plodding forward toward the seemingly unreachable haven of the palace, bumped into Sifuat. She pushed herself away from him, in the process sending him backward into the snow. She turned, saw what Elpi was doing, grabbed his hand before he could get the sword free, and shoved the sword back into the sheath with her hand over his.

"If you kill Sola dira Mudrin," she snarled, "you kill the best mind in all Saeditin. Maybe you would like that, but I promise you, the SaeKet will not. Nor will I."

He was suddenly frozen, looking into her eyes. Deliberately, she shoved him. He slipped on the packed snow and sat down hard, next to Sifuat. It was only then that Rilsin realized that she had pushed Sifuat down, too. The other young men began to shout.

Sifuat looked around him, heard the shouts of his friends. He remembered what his mother Norimin had told him, in disgust: that they were not truly his friends, that if he showed any sign of weakness, they would be on him like hunting cats on a rabbit. He knew she was right, and he resented it with a sudden fury.

"Enough!" he shouted. "I challenge you, Rilsin sae Becha!"

Rilsin stared at him. "This has gone far enough indeed, Sifuat." She stopped. The world was shimmering as with the heat of summer, but snow was falling. She was far too warm, and she loosened her cloak. What was she saying? Oh, yes. "I am sorry for pushing you into the snow. It was unintentional. Now let us forget this."

There were boos and hisses. Sifuat knew what he had to do. "I will neither forget it nor let you forget it! Draw and face me!" He did not want this duel, and any other time he would have accepted her apology, halfhearted though it was. He knew they were closely matched in sword skills, perhaps too closely. But he could see how sick she was, and he thought he could disarm her or perhaps draw first blood with a minor wound, and then it would be over. He thought she would be slow, and he had time. Or that she would realize all this herself and make a fuller apology. He was wrong.

Rilsin saw that he meant to go through with it. "I accept," she said. She dropped her cloak and drew her sword in one fluid motion.

The saedin gathered around them in a large, loose circle. Sifuat dropped his cloak and drew his sword. He saluted Rilsin as she saluted him. Sola, forgotten in the escalating drama, edged out of the crowd and ran toward the palace. Either no one saw him or no one cared.

12

RILSIN KNEW SHE WAS VERY SICK AND GETTING SICKER,
but it did not seem to be to her detriment. It was bitterly cold
in the courtyard, but she was warm, so warm that it seemed
to her the falling snow must sizzle as it melted on her skin.
Everyone around her seemed to be moving in slow motion.
If Sifuat moved this slowly, the fight would be over before
it began. There was a faint shimmer around everyone and
everything. If she could only move fast enough herself to
win this before she felt dizzy again, all would be well. And
if she could avoid swallowing, too, since her throat burned
like fire. It would all be over before Sola could return with
her guards.

Sifuat had barely finished his salute before Rilsin was on
him. She wasted no time with flourishes but came in under
his guard, going for his heart. He barely managed to side-
step and escape. Was she really trying to kill him? As his
sword scraped along the length of hers, he realized that he
had miscalculated. Immediately she was on him again, and
this time her point ripped through the sleeve of his overshirt
at the shoulder, parting the woolen cloth smoothly. He felt

the prick and glanced down in astonishment at the spreading red. It should not be like this.

"Shall we stop?" Rilsin had backed away. She attempted to speak lightly, but he saw her wince. And she was not trying to kill him, that was plain.

It occurred to Sifuat that he might not win. He, too, had seen Sola leave, and he knew the guards would be coming. He revised his plan: if he could hold out until the guards arrived, he would count it a victory.

"Not yet," he said. This time he was ready for her, but he could not break through her defense. To the onlookers, it seemed that both combatants were moving faster than should be possible.

Rilsin was still smiling. She was no longer feeling connected, however. She felt as if she were floating, moving through a spongy barrier. Everything was happening in slow motion now; Sifuat's movements, her own responses, her own advances. She saw it all happening, but she could not react as she wanted to. The snow was falling more thickly now, and under the new snow portions of the courtyard were slippery with ice. She was moving forward again, on the attack, knowing she must get through Sifuat's guard quickly, when she saw the foot.

She was not sure whose foot it was, but she saw it from the corner of her eye, saw it come out firmly in her way. It was extended in slow motion; she had plenty of time to see it, to register what it was and why it was there. But in keeping with the dreamy atmosphere that surrounded her now, she did not have time to react. The foot was extended at ankle level. Sure enough, her ankle struck it, and she stumbled.

Time resumed its normal character. She tripped over the foot, skidded on a patch of snow-slickened ice. The sword flew out of her hand as she stumbled, slid, windmilled her arms for balance. She crashed to the ground and tried to roll, but it was too late. She was on her back and Sifuat had his sword at her throat. In disbelief, she twisted away from the blade, but the tip, which Sifuat had already pressed against her throat, cut a long gash across her throat and the side of her neck. She and Sifuat both gasped in concert. She stopped moving then, glancing at the blood flowing onto the snow, then upward into Sifuat's stunned eyes.

"Yield," said Sifuat hoarsely. He couldn't believe what just happened, couldn't believe his luck, but he had done this enough times, won enough duels; he knew the formula. "Take your life at my hands."

Rilsin stared at him for a moment. There was absolute silence among the assembled saedin. Then she laughed, but cut it short. The point of the sword was still pressing into her throat, and she felt like coughing.

"I guess you will just have to kill me, Sifuat," she said.

Sifuat blinked at her. She couldn't mean what she said. "Yield," he said again. *Do it, Rilsin,* he silently urged.

"I'm a very poor loser, Sae Sifuat. You will have to kill me."

Sifuat had told his coterie that he would love to kill the first minister. Now that he could, it was the last thing he wanted to do. He was just beginning to think what the consequences of such an act might be. Beyond that, he never meant it when he said he wanted her life; it was just another puffing to his friends. He felt no particular ill will toward her; on the contrary, he had a good deal of respect for her. Even the jealousy for Sithli's affection that some had ascribed to him did not really exist. So now he stared down at her. He could feel the saedin around them getting restless. He had to do something, but what? He couldn't just let her go, and he certainly couldn't kill her. It was then that Sola arrived with the guard.

To Sola it was not his worst fear, but it was bad enough. Rilsin was still alive but bleeding onto the snow from a nasty gash in her throat. The young saedin looked horrified, intrigued, and guilty. *Why guilty?* he wondered. And Sifuat looked as though he had just realized that he was in over his head. He seemed actively relieved when a guard grabbed him by the arms and wrested the sword from him. Sola wanted to get down on his knees beside Rilsin in the snow, but he didn't dare, not after all the previous comments. One of the guards did this, pulling the scarf from around his own his neck and pressing it against Rilsin's bleeding throat.

"A little deeper and he would have killed you." The guard was shaking his head, horrified at what had happened to his commander. Then he pulled back, startled. "You are hot!" He looked up at them. "She's got a fever! She's ill!"

The officer holding Sifuat gave him a little shake. "You challenged a sick opponent?"

Rilsin began to cough. It was a cough that wouldn't quit. She was sitting up, helped by the young guardsman, but now she pulled away from him. She leaned to one side and coughed up a surge of blood onto the snow. She stared at this new blood in astonishment.

"You were right," she said to Sola. "I do have the lung sickness after all."

Everything blurred. Rilsin was conscious of raised voices, argument, commands, someone urgently telling someone else to take someone into the palace. There was a dispute, something about bringing illness into the palace, and then Sola's voice invoking Sithli's displeasure "if she dies." She realized that she was the person under discussion and that for some reason she was lying down in the snow. Her chest hurt when she breathed, and she remembered the duel. Did Sifuat kill her after all? Was she dying? No, of course not. She was ill, that was all. Very ill, too ill to get up.

"Take me home," she said, her voice sudden and strong enough to break into their bickering. "Take me home, inform Sithli SaeKet, and bring Sae Nefit."

She did not remember anything after that, but they must have done what she said, because when she opened her eyes again, she was in her own bed. It was dark, and she had the impression that it was snowing in the room, but when she blinked, she realized that she was seeing spots. She was freezing cold. There was someone sitting in a corner of the room. She wanted to say she was cold and to ask for more blankets, but she couldn't seem to do it.

When she woke again, she couldn't remember where she was. It was no longer cold, but hot, and her chest ached with

such ferocity that she whimpered. She couldn't seem to remember anything, and her head was buzzing. The room
seemed to be full of people, talking, but she couldn't see
them. The only person she could see was her mother, sitting
in the corner of the room. With great effort, Rilsin raised her
head slightly.

"Mama?" she whispered. "Mama?"

The figure got up out of the chair, came over to her.
There was a cool cloth on her forehead then, wiping away
the sweat, and someone propping pillows behind her.

"Hush," Sithli said. "Don't try to talk. Nefit says you
should take this." She held something to Rilsin's lips.
"Drink it, Rilsin, please drink it."

Rilsin tried, but she couldn't. Her throat hurt too much,
and when she tried to swallow, her chest spasmed, and she
coughed. Blood came out of her mouth, bright red. Sithli
sobbed.

"Don't die, Rils, please don't die! I can't bear it if you
die!"

Rilsin tried to reach up to wipe the tears from Sithli`s
face. "Don't cry, Mama," she whispered.

When Rilsin woke again, it was dawn, or just after. She
could tell by the light seeping through the cracks in the curtains of her room. Sithli was asleep in a chair in one corner
of her room, and Sola was stretched out on the rug by the
door, snoring slightly. Maltia was in another chair, next to a
small table covered with vials and bottles and cloths. Beside
her on the bed, taking up at least half of the mattress, was
Chilsa. Chilsa opened his eyes and regarded her inscrutably.
He was the only one awake.

Rilsin swallowed. Her throat was still sore, but it was
manageable now, fading. Her chest still hurt, too, and she
didn't dare breathe too deeply. She saw a pile of fresh cloths
on the table beside her bed, and a basin and a pitcher of
water. She remembered coughing blood, remembered the
lung sickness. Sola was right. And there he was, sleeping on
her floor, the brightest mind in Saeditin, probably in the
known world, risking infection. And in the chair in the corner was the SaeKet of the land, risking the same.

"Damnation!" It was only a whisper, but it started her coughing.

Maltia was out of his chair in a flash, and at her side. He snatched up clean cloths from beside her bed and leaned forward as if to slap one over her face, but Rilsin pushed him aside and continued to cough. He stopped trying to hold the cloth over her mouth after he saw her eyes, and settled for just holding her while she spasmed. When she finished, she was so weak that she dropped back against the pillows. She was covered with a cold sweat.

"No blood!" said Maltia triumphantly. "And you are sane again." He put his hand to her forehead. "The fever has broken!"

The fuss had woken Sola and Sithli, who hurried to her side. Rilsin tried to wave them away, but she could barely lift her hand. Finally she caught enough breath to whisper.

"What are they doing here? Why did you let them in!" She was furious with Maltia. "They could have caught the lung sickness; they could have died!"

Maltia looked right back at her, then at Sithli. "I could not disobey the SaeKet," he said with an air of vindication. "I do not have that authority. But they did not catch the infection, praise to the Mother."

Rilsin had a cold thought. "Where is Nefit?"

"She still lives, but she is very ill. She took the illness four days ago, not long after you. If she lives through today, she will be safe."

"You have been ill five days, Rils." Sithli knew what she wanted to ask. "Five days since you collapsed in the snow after that ridiculous duel."

"And the SaeKet has been here the whole time," said Maltia disapprovingly.

Rilsin was speechless. Not only did Sithli risk infection, but there was the small matter of governing the land.

"The Runchot," Rilsin whispered, "and the council—"

"Later," said Maltia.

"Rilsin," Sola began, but Maltia cut him off.

"Later," he said again. "You see now that she will recover. It is time for you both to leave and let her sleep."

Rilsin had no desire to sleep, but to her surprise she felt her eyes closing. She felt Chilsa shifting his weight to lie closer to her, and then she was asleep.

It was two more days before Rilsin was back on her feet, and even then she was still weak. Nefit had survived, she was glad to hear, and was slowly recovering, and in her absence Maltia was doing a fine job. The sickness had spread throughout the city, but he took steps to stop it. On his recommendation, traffic into and out of the city of Petipal all but ceased. Physicians gathered the sick together to better care for them, and they insisted on airing out and scrubbing homes where the sickness manifested itself, despite the fact that it was winter and bitterly cold. There had been no new cases of lung sickness in three days, and Maltia was optimistic that the worst was over. Only three hundred died, as opposed to a thousand during the last epidemic, forty years ago, and he was very proud of the fact.

Business began to return to normal, and the city reopened to traffic two weeks after Rilsin became ill. It was only now that Rilsin was capable of returning to her duties. It was two weeks before midwinter. The city, relieved that the epidemic was over so quickly, began to decorate itself for the celebration.

"The Runchot delegation left," Sithli told her, "the same day you fell ill. They did not want to risk the infection, they said. I think they brought it with them." She frowned, looking sour, since there was nothing she could do about it even if it were true, which was unlikely, and then she brightened. "But you are well now, and back with me. We can deal with the Runchot later."

Rilsin hoped they could. Her intelligence told her the Runchot were furious.

They were sitting in Sithli's small parlor, her informal room, where she liked to relax. Rilsin spent almost as much time there as Sithli did. Despite the fact that Rilsin had not lived in the palace for years, Sithli liked to have her there, and the two women spent almost as much time together as they did when they were children.

"We need to invite the Runchot back; tell them we want to talk."

"They will be back; they are always back." Sithli dismissed the subject with a wave. "There are more immediate matters to be dealt with."

Rilsin frowned, tried not to. She expected a discussion of the midwinter ball and tried to compose herself. She was surprised and gratified when Sithli chose a more serious matter.

"We need to stop the unrest among the nobles. The lung sickness and the quarantine have temporarily put a stop to it, but it will start again now. I cannot have my saedin bickering. I will not permit more duels like yours and Sifuat's. One of you could have been killed." She frowned at Rilsin.

Rilsin knew that Sifuat had spent the past weeks in disgrace at his mother's town manor. Elpi sae Dorn was banished to the far west, his family's holdings, and he was lucky not to be a slave of the Runchot, since his was the foot that provided the near-fatal trip.

"You showed an amazing lack of judgment in accepting that challenge. It can be explained, I assume, by the fever caused by the lung sickness, but there can be no more of this. It is your duty to keep the peace, not to set a bad example."

Rilsin knew something was coming. She had apologized to Sithli, and she was willing to do it again, but it was obvious that Sithli had something else in mind, something a little more public, perhaps. She fought the urge to say that, had she been well, Sifuat would have stood no chance. The duel would have been over in moments, with a minimum of embarrassment. It was true, but it was not what Sithli needed to hear, and it didn't excuse Rilsin.

"Sifuat has become more and more unruly. It is his influence above all others that has brought about this mood among the saedin, Sifuat and his band. He thinks of it all as mere pranks, but there is true divisiveness here. I have tried to speak to Norimin about this."

Rilsin was surprised, but she began to relax. Perhaps Sithli had nothing planned for her after all and was laying all the blame on Sifuat. "What was Norimin's response?" she asked.

Sithli snorted rudely. "Norimin's response was to insinuate, as usual, that Sifuat will calm down if he is married. She meant, to me."

Rilsin sighed. Norimin had been singing this song for years. "Something else will have to be done." She was thinking that she would have to talk to Sifuat, make him see that, whatever their differences, he must behave reasonably.

"I have decided that Norimin is right. Once Sifuat is married, he will certainly calm down. A wife who outranks him, whose family is older, will be able to curb him. And he is too valuable to leave unmarried for much longer. So I intend to see that he is married indeed."

Rilsin blinked at her cousin. "You are going to marry Sifuat?"

"I? No, of course not! You know better than that."

"You said, a wife who outranks him . . ." Rilsin was confused, thinking aloud.

"I am not going to marry him. You are."

Rilsin stared openmouthed at her cousin and then began to laugh. Sithli smiled back at her, but when she didn't join in the laughter, Rilsin stopped abruptly. "You can't be serious!"

"Completely. *You* outrank him, and your family is the oldest—one of the oldest in the land. Norimin wants her son married to the SaeKet. Sae Becha is as good as it gets, for a northerner. And you are totally loyal to me. Once Sifuat is married to the first minister, the commander of the Guards, he will not dare to misbehave. It is a perfect solution."

"It is no solution at all! I will not marry him! You know what I think of him! It is a waste of time even to ask me to do this!"

"I am not asking you. Norimin has already been informed of the match. She seemed pleased. She had no choice but to seem pleased, of course."

"I won't do it, Sithli! I can't do it! I have a lover!" When she said this, Rilsin thought not of Tilda but of Sola.

"Get rid of him. It is not as if he is the love of your life, Rils, not that it would matter if he were. Nor are you the love of his. The whole time you were sick, Tilda stayed at the other end of your house. He would have left and gone back to his family, but I forbade him."

Rilsin hadn't seen much of Tilda since her recovery, either. The truth was that she was preparing to ask him to leave, but she would not admit this to Sithli. "Sifuat is an idiot!" was all she said.

"A gorgeous idiot, then, you must admit; which has its compensations." Sithli grinned at her. "Although I still maintain he is not as slow as he seems."

"I won't do it. And you have no right to ask me."

"I have every right. And I am not asking; I am commanding you. You *will* marry Sifuat. Your betrothal will be announced at Sunreturn, at the midwinter ball."

Rilsin stared at her cousin. For a moment, all words fled. Sithli was absolutely serious. And it did make sense; it was a solution. Sifuat could not be left at loose ends, he was far too valuable a match. Sithli could not marry him, and Norimin would not be satisfied with a wife of lesser rank for her son. Norimin was a northerner, and the north, Rilsin remembered, remained loyal to the Sae Bechas in the war, at least until it became obvious there was no hope for that cause. She was the only Becha left, and she could have no children. There was no threat to Sithli from Rilsin, but Norimin must seem satisfied. And Rilsin would control the rowdy Sifuat, his crowd of young saedin would melt away, and harmony would be restored among the nobles. All true. But Rilsin could not stand the thought of Sifuat. There was no reason on her side, so she decided to try pleading.

"Sithli, please, don't do this to me. There must be another way—"

"Stop now, Rilsin sae Becha. You will marry Sifuat sae Sudit, and there's an end to it. Give me your answer now."

Rilsin stared at her. "As you command, SaeKet."

"Good! I knew you would see the logic of it. It will be a magnificent wedding, Rils! All the major saedin families will attend, and many dira; you can have a procession through the streets! And for wedding clothes—ah! Sifuat doesn't know yet; I commanded Norimin not to tell him yet. The midwinter ball can be your betrothal ball. Don't get up, Rils; where are you going?"

"I have business I must attend to, Sithli SaeKet. A matter of commerce between two saedholds, which I have been asked to arbitrate."

Sithli found this boring. "I thought you might want to tell Sifuat. Or would you rather I do it?"

"You do it, SaeKet; it's your plan." Rilsin turned her back ungraciously and stalked from the room.

13

RILSIN CURLED INTO THE LOVE SEAT IN HER OWN INFORMAL parlor. Despite the hissing of the steam pipes, a fire burned in the fireplace, and she was seated before this. It was so cold outside that exposed skin froze, and even the steam pipes were not up to that. Rilsin had a thick woolen blanket draped across her lap and a pile of papers on the low table in front of her. On the rug before the fire Chilsa sprawled on his back, paws in the air, exposing the silvery fur of his stomach to the warmth of the fire.

Outside the thick windows, darkness had fallen, the early darkness of midwinter. Rilsin shuffled the papers in front of her, seeming to read them, but she was not actually seeing them. Occasionally she fingered the raw scar at her throat without being aware that she did so. It was a week before the midwinter ball, and the festival of Sunreturn had already begun. Despite the cold, people were out in the streets, well-bundled, and occasional laughter drifted through the night. But Rilsin did not hear the merrymakers, would not have joined them if she did.

"Sae Rilsin. Sae Rilsin!"

Rilsin came out of her trance to see Meffa urgently trying for her attention. Her chief servant was obviously distressed.

"What is it? Sit down, Meffa." Rilsin decided she wanted to talk to someone. But Meffa didn't have time for this; there was something important happening, right now.

"He's here again. He won't leave; he insists he has to see you. He came up to the kitchen door; I don't know how he got past Judri at the gate, and he pushed his way in. Killip is trying to stall him in the kitchen, but everyone else is gone. You gave them all the night free." Meffa was distressed. The house was understaffed on top of everything else.

"Damn!" Rilsin put the papers down, started to push aside the blanket.

"Killip failed to stall me," said a voice from the doorway. "You can't keep refusing to see me, Rilsin. Midwinter ball is in seven days!"

Sifuat stood in the doorway. He was dressed for the cold: thick woolen clothing, fur-lined boots, fur-lined, hooded cloak, which was over his arm. His golden skin was flushed from the icy night and from anger.

"If I must marry you, then I need to speak with you!"

"Good try, Meffa; it's not your fault. I might as well see him. Thank Killip for me. Tell Judri I need to talk to him later."

She was left alone with Sifuat, staring at him. One thing was never in dispute: Sifuat sae Sudit was amazingly good-looking. It was too bad he was such a fool, too bad she couldn't stand him.

"Sit down, Sae Sifuat." She motioned in the direction of a chair near the fire. She had no intention of sharing her small couch.

But Sifuat couldn't sit, not yet. Chilsa got to his feet and twined himself around Sifuat's legs, looking up expectantly. Sifuat reached down and gently scratched behind the big cat's ears.

Rilsin was annoyed, more than annoyed, although she was careful not show it. Chilsa had studiously ignored all of her few chosen lovers, who were glad enough to return the favor and ignore him, too. Of her equally few friends, Chilsa was friendly with only Sola and Meffa, both understandable choices. She considered this show of friendliness in extremely bad taste.

"So he does live with you and not in the cattery. That's what I heard." Sifuat lost some of his anger, dealing with Chilsa.

"And you don't approve."

"Oh, I approve." Sifuat was surprised. "It's what I would have done."

Rilsin remembered that Chilsa was hers only because Sifuat relinquished his claim on the cat years ago. He had never owned another. She softened slightly. Chilsa finally allowed the visitor to extricate himself and sit. Sifuat took the chair; Chilsa settled himself by Rilsin's feet.

"What is so urgent that you must see me tonight?"

Sifuat flushed again. She aggravated him. "We are going to be married," he said. "Not that I wish it."

"Nor do I. There is nothing to be done about it, if that's why you are here. Believe me, I tried. The SaeKet commands. We must just make the best of it."

It looked as though she was through with him. He couldn't believe it. She looked away from him, picked up the papers from the table in front of her. Was she dismissing him, just like that? Then she lifted a hand and slowly, briefly, rubbed the scar at her throat. It was plain she did not know she did this.

Rilsin felt Sifuat's eyes on her; he was not taking the hint, not leaving. She looked up, met his gaze, and realized what she was doing. Hastily, she dropped her hand.

"You were very lucky," she said.

"I know," he said. "If you had not been ill, if Elpi had not tripped you, I might have lost."

"You would have lost," she said. "Very well." She sighed, giving up, and put down the papers. "Just what is it you want, Sae Sifuat?"

"I—" He stopped. With her eyes on him, this was much

harder than he had thought. "I want, uh, to know what to expect. What you expect from this marriage."

Rilsin sighed again. "Oh, not much. It is more for show than anything else. It suits Sithli's policy. All she expects, and all I expect, is that you, that we both behave circumspectly. It's a marriage of convenience, Sae Sifuat, that's all; surely you know that."

"Her policy?" His brow furrowed. "I don't understand. I don't know why she wants us to marry."

"In part because she doesn't want to marry you herself." Rilsin tried to be patient. Surely he must have discussed this with Norimin, at the very least. Norimin was one person she must see soon, and she was not looking forward to it.

"And you are next best? I don't understand. My mother, Sae Norimin, thinks you are better."

Not really. Rilsin thought.

"That you would govern better."

Rilsin raised her brows slightly. If Norimin really thought this, then she made a mistake letting it slip to her son. He would tell anyone. But he surprised her.

"I know better than to say that anywhere else. But I still don't understand. Why is it so important I marry—you, Sithli SaeKet, anyone? It is so old-fashioned!" Sithli's attitude had caught on among many of the younger saedin. Sifuat was very unhappy. He quite obviously didn't want to marry at all. Rilsin didn't blame him.

"You are important, too, Sifuat. You stand to inherit Sudit saedhold. That will make you a powerful force." Why was she explaining the obvious to him?

"My mother says I will never amount to anything." It came out of his mouth before he could stop himself. He flushed red again, then went on with determination. "I imagine she wants to see Sudithold safe in someone else's hands before she dies."

Rilsin looked away. He was right, and she could see he knew it, and it hurt. She, who grew up desperately missing her mother, found it hard to believe that a mother would be so harsh with her child, any mother, any child, even Norimin and Sifuat.

"Norimin never got over not having a daughter." Sifuat didn't look particularly bitter about this. He seemed quite accustomed to referring to his mother by name, like any other saedin. "She can't wait to see everything safe in the hands of a granddaughter or two. She is fond of saying that at least one grandchild should inherit her brains."

Rilsin exhaled sharply. She felt as though she had just been punched in the stomach. She swallowed hard.

"I see. Do you want children, Sifuat?" Her throat was dry, and she swallowed again.

"I have several. I assume you mean legal children." He smiled faintly. "I never cared. Oh, I know you can't have them. Norimin knows, too. She just doesn't believe it."

Rilsin said nothing, digesting this. This, of course, was part of Sithli's plan, too. Rilsin had only what the SaeKet had given her, which was much, but all of it returned to the SaeKet, should Rilsin die without offspring. Which, of course, she would. The same fate would now befall Sudithold, which would become hers by marriage. For a moment she thought that Sifuat did not realize this. But he did; she saw it in his eyes.

"Norimin will eventually be disappointed." He smiled more broadly. He wanted this. "No daughter, no grandchildren. All to the SaeKet. I know it, and you know it, but Norimin can't admit it. Someday she will. Someday." He looked into the future with a dreamy anticipation.

Rilsin was shaken by sympathy for Norimin. No daughter, no grandchildren, only a son who hated her, who cared only for clothes and women and sword fights. *Sithli*, she thought, *if you only knew what you are doing to me.* But Sithli probably did know.

"There is something I expect from you." She waited for him to look at her, to stop dreaming of his day of revenge. "I expect you to show me respect and to behave with discretion in public. No more carousing with your friends, no more women all over Petipal. I understand you have a woman living in your apartment now. She goes."

"You want me to live without women?"

"I didn't say that. I said, *discretion.* I won't have other men living here, and you won't have other women living here. We *will* be living here after we're married."

"Here?" Sifuat was distracted. "But this house is so small!"

"You'll get used to it."

He thought about this. "Norimin won't like it," he said at last, "so perhaps I will get used to it. For a while." The advantages of marriage were beginning to occur to him. "Agreed. We will live here, and we will be the model married couple, in public, at least. I have a request."

"Yes?" Rilsin was not anxious to hear this. She was sure he wanted something tasteless at best.

"I don't want to be forced to sit on the council, to have to make speeches, to have to support things Norimin never fully explains to me."

Rilsin gaped at him. Perhaps it was the way the firelight shone on him, but for a moment she thought he had tears in his eyes, but he turned his head and then they were gone. He looked at her defiantly, awaiting her answer.

"You don't have to, Sifuat. At least not often. Occasionally you will have to sit on the council to speak for Sudit saedhold when Sae Norimin can't; there will be times when I can't do that, not and speak as first minister, too." She spoke gently, more disturbed than she would admit. He had always been loud and brash. She would never have guessed there was this side to him. "I'm sure you will understand any issue on which I need your support and help." She chose her words carefully, and the gratitude with which he regarded her embarrassed her.

"I hate speaking in council. I always sound like a fool. I will be glad not to have to do it."

Rilsin felt worse. She did not know that Sifuat thought of himself as a fool. It didn't matter that she thought him a fool; he should not think of himself that way.

"I am much better with my friends," he said. "They understand me."

"Most of your friends are not worthy of you," said Rilsin thoughtfully. Perhaps Sithli was right. There was more to Sifuat than met the eye. "You are not a fool."

"You have said so."

"Oh, indeed I have. And you have acted like one, you must admit. But I think we were both too hasty: you in acting, I in judging you. Shall we start anew? A truce, at the very least?"

He looked at her for what seemed like a long time. Then he smiled, a genuine smile. It lit up the room. "A fresh start," he said.

THERE WAS SOMEOɎE else Rilsin had been avoiding. She didn't see Sola until the day of the midwinter ball, the day her betrothal would be announced. Whenever she thought of him, she felt unaccountably sad. He had always been her friend, never a lover, and they never discussed marriage, although they did skirt the subject several times. She kept herself from seriously considering the possibility because she always felt a need to protect their relationship from Sithli's jealousy. She remembered how she thought of him when Sithli mentioned lovers, but it was too late for regret. Nothing could be done now, and anyone close to her was too much a subject of scrutiny, a target for schemes, or worse. Her lovers had been safe because Sithli, and probably all of Saeditin, knew she did not really care about them.

Sola appeared on the afternoon before the ball. Rilsin had shut herself up in her library, claiming work. No one else was working today, the height of the festival of Sunreturn, except for vendors and merchants who could not resist the profit. Rilsin was not working, either, but she was in no mood to join the festivities. Still, she badly wanted distraction, anything to take her mind off what would happen tonight. After Sithli announced her betrothal, there would be no altering it short of death. She and Sifuat would be as good as married.

To avoid thinking of this, she buried herself in a new geology text. Mythological and fantastic creatures, it seemed, had been found frozen in the rock cliffs of the eastern saedholds. The author was convinced that these were animals that froze to death thousands of years ago, when the Great

Cold was visited on the land by the Mother. Sola found her reading this.

Rilsin became slowly conscious of the feeling that someone was watching her. She looked up from the book, saw Sola, and actually jumped.

"Sorry." He didn't look it. "Meffa let me in. I told her it was urgent, and she thought you needed distraction." He smiled at her, took the book from her unresisting hands. "I've read this. I don't think I believe it."

"You don't think the animals are there?"

"Oh, I think they're there, all right; it's the explanation that's lacking. It's too simple. Too irrational, too supernatural, but don't let the priests hear me. But I didn't come here to talk about animals in the rocks."

Rilsin found she couldn't speak. She sank back into her chair, hoping he would say what she wanted to hear, even though she was not sure just what that might be, and hoping desperately that he would not say it.

"Don't cut me off, Rilsin. Don't cut me out of your life the way you have these past days. Not for the sake of Sifuat sae Sudit."

Rilsin found she had been holding her breath. "You have always been my friend. That won't change." Her voice wavered slightly, and she clamped her mouth shut. What was wrong with her?

"I am going to say this now, Rilsin, and then I won't say it again. I love you. I have since I first saw you, that hot summer day when my machine blew up. That won't change, either. I hoped, because we shared so much, because we were so close, always—I always kept hoping. I was sure you loved me, too, but you couldn't say it, were afraid to say it." He stopped and looked out the window. He couldn't actually see out of the window, which was covered with ice flowers and frost. "I know you deserve something more than me. And the Sae Sudit are one of the noblest of saedin families." His voice cracked.

"Sifuat is an idiot," she said, forgetting that she promised never to say that again.

"Sae Sifuat has more to him than you give him credit

for," he said, surprising her. "Sae Norimin would poison any well. All I can say, Rils, is that I will always love you. I can't marry you, but I want to be your friend. As I always have been. I knew this day would come, that you must marry another saedin. That that was why we could not— why you—" His hands clenched. "But don't refuse to see me. I can't bear it if you keep me away. Not for Sifuat's sake." He turned abruptly and almost ran from the room.

Rilsin jumped to her feet, the book on the rock animals tumbling to the floor.

"Wait! Sola, wait!"

He turned at the end of the passage.

"It would not have worked, Sola. It would not work! It did not matter, does not matter, how I feel, how you feel! Other saedin marry dira all the time, but I never thought seriously about marriage. Not to anyone. And I never seriously considered taking you as a lover. I picked those others I cared about less rather than pick you. Don't leave, Sola! It's not how it sounds! Don't you turn away, not now! I couldn't think about loving you when even having you as a friend was dangerous!"

He turned back to her, unable to stop himself. "Oh, Rilsin, I would never hurt you, never put you in harm's way—ah!" He knew he had it wrong, thought he knew why. "Oh, of course! You were afraid for me! What other saedin would think, what they might say—as if I would care, as if that would matter—"

"It matters only what *one* other saedin thinks." They stared at each other. "I must put no one before her, Sola, I must not even seem to do it. You don't know her, not the way I do. She depends on me, wants to be first in my thoughts. Sifuat is no threat to her. You—would have been."

They could not stop staring at each other. Without seeming to realize it, they took steps toward each other, closed the distance between them. Then they were in each other's arms. His lips were firm and cool, his long hair was silky under her hands. He pressed her against him. Her lips opened, her hands ran down the small of his back.

A door opened and closed just around the bend of the corridor, and a servant's voice rose in song as she went about her duties, an old song about the birth of the Baby Sun. Rilsin and Sola pulled apart. They looked at each other, breathing hard.

"We can't," she said.

"I know," he said. "But if you need me, I will come. And we will stay friends."

"Oh yes. Friends."

The servant came into the corridor, whistling now, her hands full of ribbons. "Happy Sunreturn, Dira Sola!" she said.

"Happy Sunreturn," he said to her. "Happy Sunreturn, sae Rilsin."

"Happy Sunreturn, Dira Sola."

Rilsin watched him go. *I wanted to protect him,* she thought. *I wanted to protect myself. All those years. What a waste.*

14

THE MIDWINTER BALL AT THE PALACE WAS A FABLED AFFAIR,
a magical event that resonated down through the ages,
going back, time out of mind, to the first SaeKet who cir-
cled a fire pit in a wooden hut with her tribe. That SaeKet
was priestess as well as ruler of her people and wore the
black robes of death and the red robes of birth, miming the
Mother slaying the Evil One and drinking his blood, and
then giving birth to the Sun. But times had changed. The
palace was no wooden hut, and Sithli was no drab-robed
priestess.

The palace blazed with light, and Sithli herself seemed to
blaze. She was dressed in a tight-fitting, low-cut bodice of
sea-green silk filmed with gold, and her emerald silk
trousers clung tightly to her hips and thighs, to flare away
around her calves with a froth of golden and deeper green
embroidery. Emeralds dripped from her hair, sparkled on
her fingers, glittered at her wrists and throat and on her belt.
Even her slender, green velvet shoes were crusted with
emeralds and gold. She was the center of all activity, the

hub, surrounded by saedin almost as gorgeously dressed as she.

Rilsin surveyed all this from just outside the entrance to the ballroom, steeling herself as if for battle. She was dressed in her customary black, and she felt like the shadow of Death Herself. But her shirt and trousers were black silk, not wool or leather, and she had clipped her silver commander's pin of three crossed swords to her collar, which was closed at the throat. She had no wish to show off her still-healing scar. Her wide, black leather belt had a large silver buckle. This, and the pin, were her only ornaments.

It was a severe impression, she knew, the impression of a person completely dedicated to duty. She had, in fact, taken her duties very seriously tonight, making sure that the palace was well guarded, that there were guards even now watching the SaeKet, and that the city had its own complement of guards patrolling the streets. Even in the midst of celebration, she took no chances with her cousin's life or the safety of the land. But she could no longer hide in work, and she straightened nervously and ran her hand through her short hair.

In the pocket of her trousers was a slim, wrapped package, which she now patted to reassure herself of its presence. She remembered, almost too late, that she and Sifuat must exchange betrothal gifts tonight. It was too late to buy anything, and she had no idea what he liked, in any case. So she selected a book from her library, a small volume of the poems of Ulitin, one of the poets of her grandparents' time. Rilsin was not much of a lover of poetry, although she had been force-fed her share in her years of study. She much preferred works of natural philosophy, but for some reason Ulitin, with his dark view of human nature but his celebration of the beauty of the natural world, appealed to her. She had no idea whether or not this would appeal to Sifuat, but it was all she could find at the last moment.

She stood just outside the entrance to the ballroom, half-hidden behind a fragrant fir bush, which stood in its own pot. The bush glittered with dozens of tiny twists of gold. This was the latest fad in holiday decoration among the rich,

who used gilt paper, but knowing Sithli, the little twists
were probably pure gold. She peered through its branches
into the ballroom, hoping to see Sola.

There were many dira present, mixing with the saedin.
All saedin were invited simply by virtue of their nobility,
but members of the honored class must be issued specific
invitations. Sola dira Mudrin, the foremost inventor of the
land, would of course have been invited, but Rilsin did not
see him. Rilsin had been hoping for the support of his presence, but perhaps he would not come. Petipal was full of
parties and celebrations tonight, and Sola would have invitations to many. Probably he simply went elsewhere.

"Perhaps we should go in together."

Rilsin jumped. Sifuat was peering around the bush at her.

"Most of them," Sifuat jerked his head at the brilliant as-
semblage, "don't know about us yet. We can cause a stir if
we enter together. They think we hate each other." He
smiled, and there was a gleam in his eye.

Rilsin eased herself out of her hiding place. Odd as it
seemed, some of her dread vanished now that she was with
Sifuat, and the notion of flabbergasting the nobility began to
appeal to her. Sifuat saw this and started to grin. Rilsin
found herself grinning back, a coconspirator.

"We owe it to them," said Rilsin. "Let's give them something to talk about." She ran her hand quickly through her
hair and tugged down her shirt. Sifuat, as usual, was gorgeously attired, but tastefully so. He wore lavender trousers
with a darker violet overshirt, all trimmed in silver. Rilsin
remembered that lavender was the Sudit color. She would
have the right to wear this herself, after they were married.
It was an odd thought for someone who did not care about
fashion.

She entered slightly before Sifuat and heard herself announced: "Rilsin sae Becha, first minister of Saeditin, protector of the land."

She slowly descended the long steps, giving time for Sifuat to catch up. Sure enough, he was announced right behind her: "Sifuat sae Sudit, son of Norimin sae Sudit,
defender of the north."

Rilsin paused when she heard him announced. She was partway down the steps, partway to the glitter of mirrors and gems, candles and oil lamps and waiting aristocrats. She turned, smiled at him, and held out her hand. The assembled guests, who had quieted to watch her entrance, were now treated to the sight of Sifuat smiling in return at the woman he nearly killed and taking her hand. Companionably, they linked arms and descended the rest of the way, cheerfully seeming not to notice that they were greeted with open mouths, a flurry of whispers, and even a few gasps. They glanced at each other, and Rilsin fought a sudden, almost overwhelming urge to laugh. The urge faded when she saw the SaeKet, who frowned, perplexed. Rilsin wanted to wink at her, but she couldn't, so instead she gave her cousin a big grin. Sithli's frown deepened.

Norimin greeted them as they reached the floor. The defender of the north took her son's arm as Rilsin released it, and gave Rilsin a slight bow.

"I am pleased to see you take him in hand already, Sae Rilsin," she said.

Rilsin felt herself flush. Norimin's voice was not pitched to carry farther than the three of them, but Rilsin was annoyed. She avoided looking at Sifuat, feeling embarrassed for him.

"I hope you can encourage him in better use of his time," Norimin continued. "I have not had much success. My son unfortunately takes after his late father, who never had much of a mind, except where it did not matter. I am afraid Sifuat is too old to learn better, but perhaps you will fare better than I."

Rilsin had had enough. "Do I understand that you are pleased with this match, Sae Norimin? The truth please; I will not be offended."

Norimin looked surprised. "I am more than pleased, Sae Rilsin. I am delighted."

"Then please do not treat my future husband as a fool. I am sure he is quite capable of many things, including managing his own life. And I believe no one is too old to learn." She looked pointedly at Norimin.

As Norimin stared at her, thunderstruck, Rilsin took Sifuat's arm again and virtually dragged him into the crowd,
away from his mother. After a moment's brief resistance, he
followed her.

"Now you've done it," he said. There was a mixture of
admiration and dread in his voice.

"I don't care. What can she do?" Privately, Rilsin was
afraid that there was a lot Norimin could do. She had just
gotten off to a very bad start with her mother-in-law. "Let's
pay our respects to the SaeKet."

They did not have long to play their game of shock-the-
nobles. Sithli saw them approaching and held up her hand
for silence.

"Saedin and dira," she cried in a voice that carried to all
corners of the room, "I announce to you a joyful event: the
betrothal of Sifuat sae Sudit to my cousin and dearest
friend, Rilsin sae Becha. They will be married in the spring.
Rejoice with them and with me!"

There was a smattering of applause and a few cheers,
which grew in volume as people realized that this was no
joke. Sithli held out her arms to them, to give them the official blessing of her embrace. Then she took their hands
and placed Sifuat's in Rilsin's.

"Rilsin sae Becha, do you promise to wed Sifuat sae
Sudit, to receive his person and his lands and his honor, and
to care for them as your own?"

"I do."

"Do you agree to share yourself and your life with him?"

Sithli did not mention the third part of the promise,
which was to share her children with him, and Rilsin was
grateful. She could see Norimin from the corner of her eye.
"I do," she said.

"Sifuat sae Sudit, is this agreeable to you, and of your
own free will?"

"It is."

What else can he say? thought Rilsin.

"Norimin sae Sudit, do you agree to give your son to this
woman?"

"I do, with great pleasure," said Norimin.

"Give him a kiss, my dear, to seal it." Sithli's eyes were bright, and her voice still carried.

"A kiss!" cried some of the nearby saedin, and the call was taken up.

This was traditional. Rilsin pulled Sifuat closer and then stretched up. It was odd, but she had not realized that he was taller than she. She gave him a cool, dry kiss on the cheek.

"Oh, you can do better than that!" The gleam in Sithli's eyes was not entirely pleasant.

Rilsin stretched up again and pulled Sifuat's head down. She gave him a gentle kiss on the lips. To her astonishment, Sifuat responded. His arm went around her waist, and he drew her closer. He returned the kiss strongly, almost passionately, forcing her lips open.

Rilsin wanted to push him away, but she couldn't; she knew how that would look. She felt his tongue in her mouth like a hot probe. And then, to her greater astonishment, she felt herself responding, kissing him back with even more force. The saedin began to cheer and hoot with raucous approval. Rilsin and Sifuat broke apart and stared at each other. Both were flushed. They placed their hands on their hearts and simultaneously bowed to the SaeKet.

"I thank you for your great gift," said Rilsin formally. She did not look at Sifuat, but she did see Norimin in her peripheral vision. The old woman was smiling. And she did see Sithli. The nasty gleam had faded from her cousin's eyes to be replaced by the look of perplexity again.

It was later that night, after much wine, much dancing, many congratulations, and many overheard incredulous comments, that Rilsin and Sifuat broke away. A chain dance was in progress, rowdy and drunken nobles and honoreds snaking through the room, pulling the unwary into their line. Sithli, who was laughing and urging them on, was pulled unresisting into the line by a handsome noble, and Rilsin, who had been at her side, stepped back before she, too, was grabbed. Sifuat, too, had uncharacteristically avoided the dance. It was a good time to slip out, and they made for the terrace doors. Rilsin accepted the salute of the guard at the door and stepped outside. Sifuat was right behind her.

It was bitterly cold outside. The stars gleamed like hard diamonds, and an aurora danced above them, casting a wavering green and lavender glow on the ice-bound trees, creating strange and shifting shadows. Dawn was not many hours away, when the faithful would go to the temples to celebrate the birth of the sun and the new year. Rilsin took a deep breath of the still, icy air. She began to shiver. She had not thought to find her cloak before coming out, but Sifuat had his, thick and fur-lined. He opened it, offering to share it with her, and after a moment's hesitation, Rilsin accepted. She wrapped herself in the end of it, carefully keeping as much distance as she could from him. They looked out across the frozen gardens in silence.

"I am sorry," Sifuat began, "about the betrothal kiss. I meant only to surprise the others, and Sae Norimin, and Sithli SaeKet. I did not mean—I am sorry—"

"Don't be. Don't apologize." So he meant to surprise his mother and Sithli; it was done in the spirit of rebellion. "It surprised me, too, but I am not sorry for it."

"Nor am I, truly."

They looked at each other, looked away again. Sifuat suddenly remembered something and fumbled under his cloak. He brought out a package wrapped in gilt paper. Rilsin remembered her gift and brought it forth, feeling embarrassed. Sifuat was not as tough nor as calloused as he made out, and she hoped she did not hurt his feelings by a gift with too little thought behind it. It belatedly occurred to her that Sifuat did not have a reputation for deep thought or much learning, and he might take her gift of classic poetry as a slap at him. So it was with trepidation that she gave him her package and received his in return.

She was afraid that he would give her the traditional betrothal necklace, which she would have to wear over the scar on her throat. But she could tell as soon as she accepted his package that it was a book. Surprised, she unwrapped the paper and pulled out the book. In the wavering light of the aurora, she saw that it was a book of poetry, a book of Ulitin's poetry.

"He is one of my favorites," said Sifuat. He unwrapped her gift and held it with incredulous delight. It was, at least, a different volume of verse from his gift to her. "I had hoped you might enjoy his verse, but I never dreamed—" his eyes reflected the changing aurora, and he was smiling. "I write verse, myself. Sae Norimin," he hesitated, as if realizing at last how formal it sounded, "my mother, has no use for poetry. She says it is an occupation for dreamy fools. I must admit I was afraid of what you would think, and I am glad to see you are not of that opinion."

Actually, Rilsin was of that opinion. She happened to agree with Norimin, but for different reasons. She believed that poetry had little use in the modern world, despite her fondness for Ulitin. "I would never say that poetry is an occupation for fools," she said carefully.

" 'The inward fire, the gift of the heart
'And the mind's delight,' " he quoted.

" 'A beacon under darkening skies,' " they finished together.

He was so pleased that Rilsin could not help but smile back at him. Impulsively, he reached for her hand, drawing her closer under the heavy cloak. It was at this moment that the door to the terrace opened again, and Sithli came out.

"So you *are* out here!" she said.

Sifuat pulled back, hiding his book under his cloak as if it were something to be ashamed of. Rilsin, suddenly cloakless in the cold, shivered.

"You will freeze solid out here," said the SaeKet, who was wrapped in a cloak of ermine and valley slipe, whose winter fur was soft and blindingly white, "and besides, it is getting near time to go to the temple for the dawn rites. We need to change clothes, Rils, or I do, anyway, and have a snack before we go. I'm famished! Sae Sifuat, your mother is looking for you; go and find her." She dismissed him with a quick wave, and he put hand to heart and went in.

Rilsin watched him go. She was suddenly exhausted and would have liked nothing better than to go home and go to bed and ignore the dawn rites. She knew she could not do this; it would be unthinkable for a saedin of her standing to shirk this duty. Many commoners would line the route to the temple, and the gallery open to the commoners would have been packed for hours now. They were all waiting, not just for the rites, which would be celebrated in many locations at dawn, but for a sight of the SaeKet and her cousin, the Sword of Saeditin. Rilsin couldn't let them down. On top of that, the priests would have something to say about it, and Rilsin was not willing to roil that nest of ants.

"Rilsin! I am speaking to you! You look a thousand miles away. I said, I see you have found that Sifuat has his good points."

"Indeed he does, SaeKet, indeed he does."

Sithli gave her a sharp look, but Rilsin made no further comment. They went inside where the party was at last breaking up, celebrants parting and drifting away, streaming out of the ballroom slowly, like tendrils of fog. Some would be going to the dawn rites with the SaeKet or in other parts of the city, but most were going home to bed. In other times, the priests would have imposed severe penalties for such disrespect, but not in this changed and degenerate age.

Norimin and Sifuat were conversing in a corner. They would be going to the main temple. Rilsin had no idea whether Sifuat had strong religious feelings, but Norimin was known for her piety. She was also defender of the north, the chief of one of the most important saedholds, and as such must put in an appearance.

Rilsin realized that she would be standing beside Norimin, her future mother-in-law, for the rites, and suppressed a wince of distaste. She decided to ask Sifuat to stand beside her or at least to try to arrange it somehow. But she had no chance to speak to him again before they left. Sithli whisked her away for a private supper, a tradition they had shared for years, and she must stay with Sithli while Sithli changed into clothes more suitable for the rites, and then they were leaving, going to the courtyard where grooms had the SaeKet's carriage, and it was too late.

Norimin and Sifuat were nowhere to be seen, and Rilsin concluded that they had already left for the temple.

Rilsin rode beside Sithli's carriage through the predawn streets. She waved and nodded at the crowds, marveling as always at the numbers of people who braved the cold and the early hour to see the SaeKet's procession. A handful of picked troops surrounded the carriage and Rilsin herself, as even on this occasion Rilsin did not dare leave the SaeKet unguarded. But the crowds were always respectful and quiet. They were watching the passage of the Mother's representative on earth, for Sithli was the titular head of the temples, although it was the priests who truly administered all rites.

For Rilsin, tired as she was, this short journey was dreamlike. The light of the fading aurora mingled with the light of the late dawn, giving streets and faces in the crowd a strange cast. Her horse's breath froze on the bitter air in clouds, as did her own. The cold cut through the silk of her trousers where her cloak failed to cover them, and she felt the shaggy winter coat of the horse against her legs through the silk. Her sword dragged at her side. She had an overwhelming sense of something huge and impending, as if the whole land were poised on the brink of an abyss. Something was changing, something would never be the same again.

But when they reached the temple, the feeling faded or at least was pushed aside. In the icy dimness of the temple, where the fires of Sunreturn had yet to be lit, Rilsin saw that Sifuat and Norimin had indeed preceded them. Norimin stood in the high saedin's section, in the front, where the SaeKet would stand. And sure enough, Sithli, with a smile, insisted that Rilsin stand between them, between her SaeKet and her mother-in-law.

Sifuat was there, too, but he was toward the back of the section, leaning across the bar that separated the lesser saedin from the dira. He was flirting with a young dira woman, whose giggle could be heard even at the front of the temple. Rilsin was annoyed, and more. She remembered telling him that discretion was necessary in his future love affairs, but her annoyance was far more than his brazen flaunting of her request should provoke. She was actually angry, burning with a heat that brought color to her face. And then, beyond the giggling young woman, she saw Sola. He was looking straight at her, and she felt still more color rise.

Their glance broke, the giggles stopped, and the low buzz of conversation ceased as the priests entered the temple. They carried the torches to be kindled with the sun-fire, and they prodded forward the bound captive who represented the Evil One, the captive whose blood would stain the altar just as the sun rose on the shortest day of the year. Rilsin focused on the priests and on the terror in the captive's eyes. Anything was better right now than the confusion of her own thoughts.

15

THE LAND WARMED SLOWLY TOWARD SPRING. MIDWINTER passed, with its vicious storms, and the days began to lengthen. The minor Festival of the Snowflowers, which celebrated the first signs of growth in the cold, passed. Rilsin immersed herself in trying to rally support for the new trade with the Runchot and with training her troops and preparing for the campaign against the northern barbarians. Just after the equinox she would march north. The land would still be frozen, especially to the north of the capital, and the tribes would not be expecting her. With luck, she could put a stop to the annual barbarian raids.

When she was not engaged in these occupations, she had all the other duties of a first minister, mediating, overseeing, and planning all the myriad facets of government. Whenever she let herself rest, which was not often, she spent her time with Sithli, who expected it of her, or with Chilsa, haunting the frozen woods and fields like ghosts before dawn or after dusk. She saw Sola only when she must, which was often enough, as he was a major force behind the trade movement, and politics brought them together. Sifuat

she saw frequently but more formally. She made it a point
never to see him alone, or at least, not for long. He was polite and friendly with her, and although she never mentioned
it again, she knew Norimin had forced him to give up his
lovers, but she could not feel any happier over their coming
wedding.

The wedding was planned for the equinox itself, the balance point between light and dark. As the date approached,
Rilsin grew ever more glum, a contrast to Sithli's increasing
animation. In some perverse way, Rilsin's unhappiness fu-
eled her cousin's gaiety. Rilsin told herself that Sithli had
simply found, in the wedding plans, a distraction and relief
from the grief of her father's death. And it was now, as it
happened, that Rilsin must officiate at the execution of another saedin.

It was a cold day with the bright blue skies and huge
winds that marked the boundary between winter and spring.
The condemned was a woman who had sought to keep her
levies from the SaeKet. Her lands had been taken, and her
children and husband sold to the Runchot. In Rilsin's mind
this was punishment enough for a refusal to pay taxes, but
Sithli had no mercy for those who flouted her.

This was not Rilsin's first execution as first minister, but
it was not easy. Although Sithli had become accustomed to
the shedding of noble blood, Rilsin had not. She put on a
good front, however. Although she still felt ill, there had
been no recurrence of the scene after Zechia's execution, no
need to hide in the bushes. She appeared stern and in complete control. It was what people expected of her.

So on this day she performed her duty. Her soldiers
brought forward the sobbing, pleading saedin, who
screamed when she saw the knife and the goblet. The crowd
hushed to hear her, thrilled with the drama. The sacrifice
proceeded as it must. Rilsin avoided the glance of the death
priest and carried the sacred goblet to Sithli, who wet her
lips with the scarlet blood. The tip of her pink tongue could
be seen as she delicately tasted the thick, salty red. From
fear and horror, Sithli had come to enjoy this part of the ritual, or so it seemed. Rilsin poured out the remaining blood,

knowing it would freeze on the still-frozen ground, knowing the red stain would remain until after the spring thaw. Her soldiers bundled up the body. She felt tired and thick; dull, as she always did after a sacrifice.

The SaeKet left with her guard, and Rilsin turned to leave. Her own guards formed around her; commoners had no opportunity to mob her, not since the first time, at Zechia's execution, years ago. So it was with surprise that Rilsin, who was thinking only of getting home and taking a hot bath, saw that someone was trying hard to enter her cordon. The guards were not using force to stop this person; they were arguing, barring the way. Then the guards began to give way. Furious, she was about to countermand this, when she realized it was Norimin.

"Let her through," she said. She had spoken, as she must, with her future mother-in-law, but she still had no rapport with the old woman, nor did she expect any. She could not believe Norimin was there to offer her any sort of help or support. The only person to whom it might occur that she would need support was Sola, and he no longer attended executions.

"You must go to be purified," said Norimin. "I trust that is where you are going."

"I am going home to bathe." Rilsin had already turned in that direction, but Norimin reached out and pulled her back. Swords came hissing out of guards' scabbards. Norimin let go hastily, as Rilsin shook her head at her defenders, who resheathed their weapons. "What is it, Sae Norimin." Rilsin decided she must be patient.

"You are marrying my son; you cannot go to the bridal altar with blood on you."

"I said that I am going to bathe." Rilsin almost added that the wedding was still not for days yet and she would hardly go to it filthy, when she realized what Norimin meant. She was speaking of ritual purification.

"Have you a priest waiting?" Norimin saw that Rilsin did not. "There is one at my shrine who will do this, Sae Rilsin. Come; it must not wait."

Rilsin opened her mouth to protest. This was the last

thing she wanted to do, to go to the private Sudit shrine and
let Norimin's pet priest drone over her. She had no faith in
the power of priests to wash evil from her or to banish the
malevolent power of the ghosts of the executed. She did not
believe in ghosts and their powers, malevolent or otherwise.
But she couldn't say that to Norimin, who had a reputation
for piety and religious orthodoxy. And Norimin was so urgent about this, it was obviously so important to her, that the
protest died on Rilsin's lips.

"Then let us go," was all she said. After she said it, she
could see that her guards were pleased. Most of them were
not only orthodox, which was the only safe thing to be, but
truly religious, as far as they had it in them.

Norimin had a carriage waiting, and her own guards, so
Rilsin dismissed hers. It would not be polite to bring them
all, and keeping one or two would make no difference. Besides, Norimin was to be her mother-in-law, so some trust
was in order. And she could scarcely ask her soldiers to run
behind Norimin's carriage. The carriage was stuffy and
close and smelled of the lavender scent that Norimin used,
and Rilsin was glad the ride was short.

Sifuat was waiting at his mother's house. He greeted
them formally and ushered them in, careful, Rilsin saw, not
to touch her. He obviously did not want to undergo the purification himself. As soon as the servants and guards dispersed, however, he grinned at her.

"I was not certain Sae Norimin could convince you to
come," he said.

"She has more sense than you," snapped Norimin. "She
is not one of those Motherless modernists who believe in
nothing but themselves. Sae Rilsin knows how necessary
purification is."

Oh, indeed, thought Rilsin, *which is why I have no priest
waiting, why I do not even have a shrine in my house.* She
wondered if Norimin saw this irony. Sifuat did, because
when his mother's back was turned, he raised his eyebrows
slightly and then waggled them at her. This was so incongruous and took her so much by surprise that Rilsin almost
laughed out loud.

The shrine was small, not what Rilsin would have expected from the opulent scale of the rest of the Sudit mansion, but it was richly appointed, having both the sacred pool and the sacred fountain, and the priest was waiting. Norimin stripped without hesitation for the purification, which surprised Rilsin until she remembered: Norimin touched her right after the sacrifice. Norimin was marked with scars from long-ago duels, and the pucker of an old arrow wound. The wound was earned in the Civil War, fighting for Rilsin's mother, fighting for the Sae Bechas. Rilsin had cause to reflect again on the craft and power of Norimin, the survivor. She was not a bad ally to have, if Rilsin could force herself to be properly friendly, and for the first time Rilsin wondered if Sithli really knew what she was doing by insisting on this marriage. Naked herself now, she shivered despite the warmth and the steam rising from the small sacred pool.

Norimin was first, since her purification was so much simpler. The priest, a pleasant young man, whose plump face was creased by laugh lines, was not at all the sort of person Rilsin would have expected to find in Norimin's employ. He washed Norimin with air, by wafting a feather around her, and then with incense. The sound of his chanting began to make Rilsin drowsy. Finally Norimin stepped into the heated pool, not much more than a bath itself, and the steam partially obscured her from view. When she emerged, she gave a perfunctory bow to the little priest, took a towel from the side of the room, and began to vigorously dry herself. Now it was Rilsin's turn.

Her drowsiness was shattered as soon as the priest touched her with the ritual feather. He jerked back with a gasp and dropped the feather. He reached forward and grasped her hands with surprising strength.

"It is true! Too much malevolence!" he exclaimed. "Oh, Rilsin sae Becha, you are muffled by the evil of others; you are swathed in ill wishes! That your spirit shines at all is a blessing of the Mother! You must be cleansed!"

This was a bit overstated, Rilsin thought. But it was true, she had not been purified of any of the deaths over which she had presided as first minister. This priest undoubtedly knew that.

"Purify me, my brother, of the sprits over whose deaths I presided." It was what she was expected to say, and she felt bored again.

"I fear we are dealing with much more than that here," said the priest in a conversational tone. "Sae Rilsin, you have powerful ill wishes on you from the living, which can be as hard, or harder, to banish. I do hope you will let me do my best." He still had hold of her hands.

"Of course." Rilsin was momentarily startled out of her boredom and her expectations. "Do what you must."

"It will not," said the priest, with a smile, "take all that long." His eyes twinkled; he had read her mind. "But it will be rigorous."

"It will take as long as it takes, Mage. I want her completely clear." Norimin, dressed, watched from the side of the shrine. "Do not forget the matter we spoke on."

So the little priest was not just a brother, he was a mage, Rilsin realized. It made sense, of course. Norimin would have as high a rank as she could get. She fought back a sigh, willing herself to patience. If Norimin wanted a full purification, with all the trimmmings and gilt, then this was what she would have, and Rilsin must simply make the best of it.

As the rite progressed, Rilsin slipped into a sort of trance. It was not her previous drowsiness but a more dreamlike state. She felt completely relaxed in the hands of this priest, this mage, completely willing to let him waft her with feathers and incense, chant over her, sprinkle her with herbal water. It was strange, but she thought she could feel layers of griminess and lethargy being scrubbed from her soul, if she had such a thing. The mage's hands had real power in them, and his kindly face was intent on his task. Beyond the safe circles his hands made, Rilsin saw dark mists and threatening faces. It occurred to her to wonder if she had been drugged, but she couldn't imagine how this could have been accomplished. When he led her into the warm water, through the veils of steam, she felt a shock. It was like awakening from a dark sleep.

"Take a breath," he said, and then pushed her completely under the water.

While she was beneath the surface, she rubbed her arms and legs and shook her head, feeling her short hair float up. It was wonderful. She surfaced, smiling, and opened her mouth to thank the priest for whatever it was he did. But he shook his head at her.

"Not yet. Don't speak. There is one more thing."

He led her to the back of the shrine. The sacred fountain was there, gurgling and splashing. The priest motioned her to go beneath it, so she did. She was aware of Norimin watching this intently. She could see the Sae Sudit from the corner of her eye, but more than that, there was the sense of Norimin's eyes burning little holes into her. But she didn't have time to puzzle over this. As soon as she stepped beneath the fountain's spray, she became sick.

It began as a slight queasiness, but in seconds it was full-blown nausea. Rilsin hadn't felt this bad since the long-ago slop nights, thankfully in the past. She lurched to escape, but the priest's hands pushed her back, strong as iron. He was chanting something again, but she was too sick to pay attention to it. If she didn't get out, she was going to vomit. The feeling of those long-ago evenings in Nefit's chambers was overwhelming; she felt as if she had just downed the ghastly mixture, only much stronger than it was ever made, even for her.

Rilsin flailed, then tried to draw a breath. She would fight her way out if she must, priest or no priest. She snapped her wrist back, breaking his grasp. The effort was just what she did not need. Before she could stop herself, Rilsin sae Becha, first minister of Saeditin, leaned over and vomited into the sacred fountain.

She threw up until there was nothing left, not even a weak dribble of bile, and then sat gasping, weak and dizzy, under the spray. She was so wrung out that she couldn't move at first, not even when the priest tried to help her to her feet. Eventually, she realized what he was trying to do and managed to stagger up, slipping slightly on the wet stones. The mage steadied her.

"That is good," he said. "It's almost over now, Sae Rilsin. You are free, and you should feel free."

A towel, huge and thick, somehow materialized in his hands, and he draped this around her. Since she was shaking and still unsteady, he guided her back from the fountain to the shrine's altar, where a fat white candle was burning. Beside it was a green candle, unlit, in the shape of an egg.

"Light the candle, Rilsin SaeKet Becha, drawing flame from the Mother's candle." He gave her a twist of tinder.

Rilsin was still too shaken to be sure of what he said. Perhaps she only imagined what she heard. She took the old-fashioned tinder twist and poked it into the white candle's flame, and then, when it caught, touched it to the wick of the green egg candle. The wick caught and flared into light. Rilsin felt strength begin to come back to her, and her mind began to function again. She looked at the green candle and realized what she had just done.

"Rilsin sae Becha," said the priest, "you are free of ill, free of all the old curses. Live free, that our land may be free, by the blessing of the Mother."

He reached up and placed his hands on her wet head. Rilsin paused, in the act of wrapping the towel more tightly around herself. The little mage was right, she did feel free. She felt wonderful. But more than that, she was aware, for the first time, of something that had been muffled all of her life. She could feel, up through her feet, through her skin, through the top of her head where the priest touched it, all over her body, and deep within her mind, a magical, rich suffusion of impressions. There was no way to describe what she felt except perhaps to compare it to music, with its texture of themes and countermelodies. Rilsin was hearing the song of the land.

It was later, dressed in clean clothes borrowed from Norimin and slightly too small, that Rilsin confronted her hostess.

"That was not just a purification; that was a fertility rite," she said.

They were seated in Norimin's informal parlor, which was decorated in velvet brocade and silk. Nothing in the Sae

Sudit town mansion was truly informal. Rilsin sipped a hot stimulant tea while Sifuat, in a chair as far from his mother as he could get without being obvious, munched his way steadily through a small mound of fried cakes.

"It was a rite to restore fertility, to open the womb, yes." Norimin was perfectly at ease.

Sifuat stopped chewing and stared at his mother. Rilsin felt herself beginning to flush.

"You could have asked me first," she said. She was recovered enough now to begin to feel angry.

"You would have refused it, would you not?"

"I would. I would certainly have refused to be drugged!" She looked at Sifuat, who grunted in surprise. "There was something in the steam," she told him. "It made me violently ill. I haven't been that sick since—I have never been that sick! Sae Norimin, this went too far!"

"There was nothing harmful in the steam. The rite simply purged you of the compulsions and limitations set on you by others. Wrongly set on you, against the will of the Great Mother."

"I see you didn't know," said Sifuat. He gave his mother a sideways glance. "Sae Norimin, *Mother,* has been lighting egg candles for you every day, praying for grandchildren." He was trying not to smirk.

Rilsin's anger was met by an equal dose of compassion. Norimin and Sifuat were all that was left of the Sae Sudits. "I can understand how much you must long for grandchildren. I am more sorry than I can express to you that you will not have them. Not through me." She couldn't resist a glance at Sifuat, who found something fascinating and attention-absorbing about his boots. "I would agree to adoption, some time in the future, with the agreement of the SaeKet." Who would never agree, because the children would be Sae Becha. But Norimin would never be satisfied with adoption.

"Naturally I want grandchildren, legitimate grandchildren." She did not glance at her son. "And I will have them, for the Mother is good. She is also just, and it was cruelly and outrageously unjust that the true SaeKet should be prevented from her natural right, by drugs and by evil. You spoke of drugs, Rilsin SaeKet, Rilsin, my daughter; that is how you were drugged, not by me but by your enemies, as all of Saeditin knows. Today we undid an evil."

Rilsin got to her feet. She was still not completely recovered from the rite, but she wanted their full attention. "Listen to me, Sae Norimin; you, too, Sifuat. Listen well. I know what you lost in the war, Sae Norimin, but consider what you saved. I am not the SaeKet; I will never be the SaeKet. You must not think of me that way or speak of me that way. Never. I am the true servant of Sithli SaeKet Melisin. As you must be. That is the future, Sae Norimin. The other . . . is the past. I want your promise on this. Promise me, Sae Norimin. Promise me."

"Sit down, Sae Rilsin, sit down. Yes, I lost much, but as you say, I have much left. No one lost more in the war than you, my child. But of course we are loyal citizens, Sifuat and I. And I will never mention again what might have been, not if you do not wish it. Even Sifuat knows better than to refer to you in public as — by your true title. Neither he nor I shall ever let it pass our lips." She looked hard at Sifuat, who finally met his mother's eye and winced. "But you know how I think of you, Sae Rilsin." She left a conspicuous pause after "Sae."

"Do not think of me that way."

"As you wish."

"This is not a light matter."

"Indeed it is not." Norimin smiled. "I know that, never fear. And as for grandchildren — well, there will be no more Sae Sudits, but I *will* have grandchildren. Legitimate Sae Becha granddaughters. No, no, you need say nothing! Do not attempt to disabuse me of this, my child! Let me have my fantasy! Forgive an old woman for bringing you to the rite unwarned! I had only the best in mind. I would like us to be friends, Sae Rilsin, since our families will be joined." Norimin was smiling again.

"We will be friends," said Rilsin. "Of course we will be friends. And as for the other — well, no harm was done. In fact, I feel quite well now." This was true. She felt better than she ever remembered feeling. She got up to take Norimin's hands and press her cheek against Norimin's. *Old woman, indeed!* she thought. Norimin sae Sudit could outthink and outmaneuver most people half her age. And it would be best if Rilsin remembered this. She was conscious of Sifuat's eyes on her.

16

THE MORNING AFTER HER VISIT TO NORIMIN, RILSIN awakened early. The days were growing longer, and the winds blew across the city from the forests and plains beyond, carrying a scent of pine and a hint of the newness of spring. Rilsin was anxious to be out of the city and into those woods, anxious to give vent to some of the energy she felt bursting up inside her before she faced her day at the palace. So she almost leaped out of bed in the predawn hour, before her clock could awaken her. Chilsa, who slept on her bed again, jumped down, catching some of this energy. Rilsin threw on her clothes, ran her hands through her hair, and hurried to the kitchen for her quick breakfast. In the kitchen Meffa was arranging an enormous bunch of flowers in a crystal vase. There were snow-roses and rock-jumps and daffodils and cat-lilies and the delicate, spotted bloodsprays, a profusion of blooms, some of which had to come from a hothouse.

"Good morning, Meffa. Those are truly beautiful, but they must have cost far too much." Rilsin enjoyed flowers, but she was death on extravagance. Meffa knew this and paled slightly.

"I did not purchase them, Sae Rilsin. They are a gift."

"A gift?"

"To you. This came with them." She held out a note. "From Sifuat sae Sudit." She saw Rilsin's look. "I, I did not read it, Sae Rilsin. A Sae Sudit servant brought them!"

Rilsin knew Meffa could read now, and she had been encouraging her, offering her library. She also knew that she could be intimidating sometimes when she did not mean to be.

"That is fine, Meffa. I never thought otherwise."

She took the note, read it as she downed a large piece of warm cranberry bread with honey. It was a standard sort of note to one's betrothed, wishing health and joy, but Sifuat added that he wished to speak to her alone. Rilsin frowned and put the note in her pocket. She would think about it later. All she wanted now was not to have to think for an hour or two, to be outside where she could feel. Chilsa butted against her legs, having caught her mood.

It was still cold, even though it was, by the Saeditin calendar, officially early spring. It was a fine, frosty morning, and Rilsin wrapped herself in her fur-trimmed woolen cloak and went to the stables to select her favorite horse. This morning she did not want to walk; she wanted to go fast and far. It was only when she was well away from Petipal and out into the fields that she realized she was being followed.

As usual, she had no guard with her. Her horse was fast, and she might be able to lose her follower, but she was not in the mood to try. Instead, she reined in her horse and gave Chilsa a quiet command.

Her horse was standing in the middle of the field, cropping the the wisps of grass that poked through the melting snow when the following rider came up, but Rilsin was nowhere to be seen. It was strange, because there didn't appear to be anywhere for her to hide, not in an open field. There was no sign of woman or cat. The man on the horse frowned in brief puzzlement before he registered danger from a shadow behind a clump of frozen grass, and by then it was too late. A huge silver streak leaped from nowhere, causing his horse to snort and paw, knocking him from the saddle.

"Chilsa! Stop! Stop!"

Rilsin was on her feet, shouting, grabbing for the reins of the horses, but she saw that no damage had been done. Chilsa stood over his victim, his huge paws pinning the man to the ground by the shoulders, but instead of ripping out his captive's throat, he was sniffing his face in a puzzled manner.

"Are you all right?" Rilsin held out her hand to help him up as Chilsa backed away.

"I'm a little sore from the fall, but I suppose it's better than I deserve. It's lucky Chilsa likes me." Sifuat smiled ruefully. "Didn't you get my note?" He allowed her to help him up and proceeded to brush crusted snow from his maroon woolen trousers, which were tucked into matching maroon leather boots.

"Your note? Oh, your note! With the flowers!" She was aware of it now, in her pocket, like a live thing. "The flowers are beautiful; thank you."

"I said I wanted to see you alone."

"I didn't know you meant right now, that you were going to come up behind me like an assassin. Sifuat, we have got to stop almost killing each other."

"Yes." He looked uncomfortable, finally, as it dawned on him how his approach seemed.

"You wanted to see me alone. Here I am. What is it you wanted?"

Sifuat shuffled, looked away, flushed. He was not at ease with what he wanted to say, and Rilsin's brusqueness was not helping. "I wanted to apologize for Sae Nor—for my mother. For yesterday. Sae Norimin and I are both loyal to Sithli SaeKet, you must be assured of that. It is just that my mother has her dreams. Allying our family with you, even though we are all that is left of it, is very important to her. As for grandchildren . . ." He paused for breath and then did not know how to continue.

Rilsin looked at him. She had gone to steady the horses,

and held the reins of both. He was defending Norimin, something she would not have expected of him. He was afraid for his mother, she saw, but there was something else, something she didn't understand, something that was making his eyes glow, making him fidget. "I understand that, Sae Sifuat, all of it, including the desire for grandchildren. Your mother took me by surprise on many counts; that is all." *As have you,* she thought. She would not have credited him with caring much about Norimin, let alone having insight into her mind.

"I have no wish to diminish her sense of importance concerning this marriage, as long as there is no sign of disloyalty to the SaeKet. Especially since I must disappoint her when it comes to grandchildren."

"It will be good for her to be disappointed in something," muttered Sifuat, reverting to his familiar attitude.

"Well," said Rilsin, "dawn is almost here." She whistled, and Chilsa who had been crouched, ears back, watching a rabbit, reluctantly came to her. "There is not much time for riding today, after all. Will you ride back to Petipal with me, Sae Sifuat? To the palace?" She swung herself up onto her horse. The wind whipped her cloak back until she grabbed it, one-handed, and fastened it down. Her cheeks stung from the cold.

"I would be delighted. But there is more I wished to say. Please, Sae Rilsin, hear me on this." He mounted his own horse, took the reins. He looked ready to flee if all did not go well. "I want . . . I wish for us to have a good marriage. You know that I keep no more women."

"I know," said Rilsin before she could stop herself. "Sae Norimin made you send them packing."

"Is that what you think? She had nothing to do with it! *I* 'sent them packing'! Oh, I know what you saw at Sunreturn, in the temple, and I know my reputation. At Sunreturn I was angry at Sae Norimin and even at you, Sae Rilsin. I had heard things about Sola dira Mudrin from my friends, untrue things, as it happens. They talk." He waved a hand dismissively. "My friends, well, perhaps I am outgrowing them, and none too soon, as my mother would say. But this is not her idea. I want us to have a chance at our marriage, I want us . . . I want us to be happy!" He drew a deep breath and leaned toward her across the neck of his horse. His face was flushed, intent. He was willing her to listen, to understand.

"I have not been able to stop thinking about you, not since Sunreturn, and seeing you only formally, only in the company of others, and you never look at me . . . Rilsin, you spoke to me before as if I were someone whose thoughts you valued. You were kind, and you are the most beautiful woman I have ever seen! Rilsin. I am trying to say that I love you."

Rilsin sat on her horse as if turned to stone. The wind feathered her hair away from her face. Chilsa sat on the ground, looking up at her expectantly, his ears twitching toward the plain where he knew there were rabbits. The sun was rising now, casting a deep red-gold light over everything. And Sifuat the beautiful was there, telling her that *she* was beautiful. The most beautiful woman he had ever seen. Sifuat had seen a lot of beautiful women. She wanted to laugh.

"I know we think alike, Rilsin; I know we do. I have been studying your essays on natural law and on astronomy, and they have made me think. I have been wasting my life! I love you, Rilsin. Believe me, please! Give me a chance." His eyes were intense, earnest, pleading.

She *was* going to laugh. It was awful. He meant every word; she could see it. He radiated sincerity and passion. Passion for her, for Rilsin the disinherited, Rilsin the captive, Rilsin, Sithli's shadow, Rilsin the plain. This man who could have any woman he wanted, who had any woman he wanted. She made a sound, tried to smother the laughter she was sure would emerge. But she couldn't smother it. The sound came out, and to her horror it was somewhere between a laugh and a sob.

"Oh, Rilsin, sweetheart!"

He couldn't reach her from horseback; her horse danced back when his edged closer. And then there was Chilsa, who paced, watching Rilsin, knowing she was upset. Sifuat stretched out a hand to her; Chilsa growled warningly. He liked Sifuat, but enough was enough.

"It's all right, Chilsa. He's a friend." She leaned down, touching the cat on the head to calm him. Dealing with the cat helped Rilsin get herself under control. Sifuat loved her. Sola loved her, but she couldn't have Sola. She had been avoiding Sola. She had been avoiding Sola because she couldn't have him, and she had been avoiding Sifuat because she must have him. But Sifuat was in love with her; Sifuat thought she was wonderful, thought she was beautiful! Or so he said.

"Give me a chance, Rilsin, that's all. It's all I ask."

"A chance, Sifuat. We all deserve a chance." She pulled away, backed her horse away when he tried to come close again. She would give Sifuat a chance to prove himself. She would give herself a chance to believe him. She turned and rode for Petipal as if demons were behind her, with Chilsa a silver streak beside her.

For most of the day she managed not to think about Sifuat or his declaration of love. Sithli had Common Audience today. Most of the day was devoted to hearing the concerns of the commoners, those Saeditin without any other access to the SaeKet. In theory they might bring a case even against saedin, but this rarely happened. Most cases were commoner against commoner, or commoner against dira, or, more frequently these days, commoners complaining of injustice in the laws themselves. Sithli hated these audiences. She frequently asked for the advice of Rilsin, who stood beside her. Sometimes she abdicated her responsibilities and left them to Rilsin, but she could not do this often, for fear of comment.

Rilsin was genuinely interested in the lives of the commoners. In part, Sola was responsible for this. There had been so much change in so little time, due in some degree to the invention of his machine. Refinements in condensing the steam helped him design a far more efficient engine, which was now being used not just in mining and heating but in grinding flour and in the great sawmills of the west. As a result, saedin who kept to the old-fashioned ways were losing some of their farmers to the cities of saedin with mills and factories. Problems that resulted from these changes were likely to end up in Sithli's Common Audience.

Today was a bad day in the Audience. The petitioners had been coming relentlessly all day. It was now well past midday, and Sithli had not eaten. She was tired, hungry, and irritable, and Rilsin, whose feet hurt from standing all morning beside her, saw with relief that Sithli was going to call a halt. She knew she would have to persuade the SaeKet to resume the Audience after a meal, which might be hard to do, but at least there would be time now to sit, to ease aching muscles, to eat.

The SaeKet rose, putting an end to the Audience. Her guard stepped forward. Rilsin, who discovered that her left foot had gone to sleep, tried not to limp as she followed her cousin. And then there was a sudden commotion, a wailing cry, almost a scream. A woman threw herself forward out of the ranks of the petitioners who had not yet been heard. Rilsin knew why: she was afraid the SaeKet was ending the Audience for the day, that her chance for aid in whatever desperate matter brought her here was vanishing.

"SaeKet, hear me!"

The woman sobbed, stretching out her arms. It was to no avail. Guards had her now, were dragging her away. She began to scream, until a guard hit her hard across the mouth, drawing blood. The few saedin and dira present, all court officials, turned away, bored.

"Another one for the Runchot," said Sithli in disgust. The woman began to weep pitifully.

"Wait." Rilsin was barely aware of countermanding her cousin, of the guards obeying her without confirmation from Sithli. She studied the woman, who sagged in the grip of the guards. She was a commoner dressed in plain gray wool trousers and overshirt, worn and mended but clean, obviously the best she had. Her face was lined and thin from a hard life, and her hands were red and chapped, and at first glance she seemed old, but Rilsin realized that despite how she looked, she was probably in her early twenties. *She's not much older, than I am,* Rilsin thought. Her face was twisted in hopeless grief.

"What is it, ria?" The honorific used for the common people seemed misplaced here. "Bring her forward," she instructed the guards.

The guards had to drag the woman forward. It was then that Rilsin thought to glance at her cousin. Sithli was not happy.

"By your leave, SaeKet," said Rilsin, her voice carrying. And then, more softly, "Sithli, please."

"Make it quick," said the SaeKet sourly.

"What is it, ria," she asked again, "to cause such grief? Don't be afraid to speak." She had every reason to be afraid to speak, thought Rilsin, glancing at Sithli again. But the woman seized her chance.

"It's my child," she sobbed. "My little daughter." With a valiant effort she controlled herself. "She is only five years old, and she has done nothing! Please, Mother of the Land, help her! They took her, they are going to sell her; I know what the Runchot do to girls! My baby!"

"Who took her, ria?" Rilsin was conscious of Sithli fidgeting. She had to conclude this before Sithli concluded it for her.

"Sae Kepit, Kepit sae Lisim."

There was a stunned silence. A commoner had accused an aristocrat, and a powerful one. The Sae Lisims were one of the few saedin families who no longer had a saedhold outside of the city. Instead, they had become landlords in Petipal, owning dwellings, guild houses, and businesses.

"Why, ria?" Rilsin tried to urge her on. She was pretty sure she knew why, and it was the same old story.

"We owed Sae Kepit, owed her money for our room. I couldn't make enough with the washing," Rilsin glanced again at her chapped hands, "and Frek . . . my husband . . ." She was trying not to cry, but the tears were streaming down her face anyway. "Frek hurt his back unloading wagons for the market. He couldn't walk, sae! I had to care for him!"

Sithli sighed pointedly and looked away toward the door.

"So you did not have the money, or goods worth the

money, and Kepit sae Lisim sent someone to take your child," Rilsin finished for her.

"But I did get the money! It was late. Late by days, but I got it, and I gave it to Sae Kepit's man, but they came anyway! They killed Frek, said he was no use to them! They ran him through with a sword right there in his bed! And they took everything, my water jar, my cook pot, everything! And they took my Gisi! She was screaming for me! And they took me, too, but I kicked and I bit one of them and they let me go and I ran! I hid overnight with my sister until I could come here. Help me, please, Rilsin sae Becha! Sword of the Land, give me justice! Help me, Sithli SaeKet!"

Sithli was interested now in spite of herself. "It could not have been servants of Kepit sae Lisim," she said, "not if you paid your rent. You were attacked by robbers."

"But it was Sae Kepit's men, Sithli SaeKet," said the woman doggedly. "They were her personal guard, and they wore her colors. And they were laughing about getting more out of me, about how Gisi would bring so much more than the rent, and Sae Kepit would reward them for this!"

"Where is Kepit sae Lisim?" Rilsin looked around. "She or a representative should be here to answer these charges." But it was obvious that neither Kepit nor a designate was present.

"She is not here," said Sithli, "because this is not believable. A saedin would not behave in this manner. If she took your child for sale to the Runchot, it is because you owed her for many months or even years of rent."

"It is not true, SaeKet!" The woman dropped to her knees. "And Gisi did nothing! She is only five!"

"Old enough to be trained for—whatever the Runchot wish. Your child was your property until you went into debt. Now she is no longer yours. Your husband's death sounds like an accident, although, as you say, he was useless. As for you yourself, Sae Kepit overreached herself. You could not have owed her more than the value of the money you gave her and the value of your child."

"And my water jar and cook pot and my good coat," said

the woman. Sithli glared at her, and she swallowed and was silent.

"As I say, that is too much. But you have brought unfounded charges against a saedin of the land, and for that you must pay. That is a crime against the land of Saeditin and against the SaeKet, against me, the Mother of the Land. For that, your person is forfeit. You are my property now, to do with as I please. I will give you to the border warden in the south. He will decide whether you will be used here in Saeditin or sold to the Runchot yourself. Perhaps you will find your daughter if you are sold. Take her," Sithli turned to the guard, "and cut her hair. And brand her, for the trouble she has caused."

The woman began to sob again, but she did not resist as the soldiers pulled her up. She stumbled as they grasped her arms and began to take her away.

"What is your name, ria?" said Rilsin. The woman did not reply, and the guards were dragging her out.

"Your name!"

The woman looked at her, jolted briefly from despair. "Cilla," she said. "Cilla the washerwoman, from Blue Street."

The guards pulled her out. Sithli sighed. "I need my luncheon. This took far too long. You indulge your desire for knowledge of the commoners at the worst times, Rilsin."

Sithli and Rilsin went to Sithli's private parlor, where Sithli immediately sank into a chair, pulled the emerald-studded comb from her long hair, and began to massage the back of her neck. Food appeared promptly: roast meats, new bread, teas, cider, and wine. Sithli barely waited to be served before she started to eat. Rilsin watched her.

"Eat, Rilsin." Sithli passed her some bread. "I forbid you to free that woman. I know you do not approve, but I forbid you to free her. Not after I sentenced her."

"Of course not, SaeKet. I will not free her." Rilsin ripped off a piece of new bread and dipped it in gravy.

"But you do not approve."

"You know I do not. You did not investigate the matter,

SaeKet, you simply ruled on it. The administration of justice is under the hand of the first minister, Sithli. This was
not justice."

"The administration of justice is under your hand only
when it is not under mine. All of my rulings are just."

"I believed Cilla."

"Who? Oh, the washerwoman. Rilsin, it does not matter!
She is a commoner! They cannot be encouraged to bring
charges against saedin!"

"I have heard stories about Kepit sae Lisim twice before,
but each time I try to investigate, something happens. Wit-
nesses disappear, my own people, my guards, well, one of
them turned up dead! In a bad part of town, it is true—"

"Well, there you are." Sithli carved a piece of meat, put
it on Rilsin's plate.

"We need our commoners, Sithli. We need our workers.
It is not right to bleed away our people, our own heart's
blood, to the Runchot! Not for any amount!"

"Don't start on this trade matter with me again, Rilsin.
Not now. I am tired, and I am sick to death of hearing about
this. The Runchot want slaves; we can supply them. They
pay well, and it keeps the peace. I notice you like your cotton well enough in the summer. And the commons are stupid, Rilsin, stupid as those rocks you read about! We have
more than enough."

"We do not have enough. Not for farms, and not for factories. We will have more mills, more factories in the future;
I can see it, Sithli, I can see it coming. And we will need the
army, even more than before. And a better navy, for more
trade with the cotton lands across the sea, without going
through Runchot. The commoners are not stupid, they are
just uneducated. We should teach them to read, Sithli."

"To read! What, all of them? Rilsin, eat. Your brain is ad-
dled from lack of nourishment. And I will hear no more
about the Runchot trade today!"

17

It didn't look as though Sifuat was going to leave. He sat talking to Rilsin in her private parlor, trying to engage her in a discussion of poetry. Rilsin was too distracted to pay proper attention. It was late, since Sithli had kept her at the palace through a formal dinner and afterwards, so she now felt pressed for time. Midnight was approaching, and after that it would be too late. She had not had the chance to complete her instructions to Meffa before Sifuat arrived.

"Indeed." Rilsin had no idea what Sifuat just said, but the pause in his conversational flow alerted her to the necessity of some sort of response.

Sifuat regarded her steadily for a moment and then rose with a smile. "It's late," he said, "and I can see you are tired. I understand that days of Common Audience can be especially wearing. You need your rest." He leaned over, reaching first toward Rilsin but drawing back, only daring to stroke Chilsa before he rose. "Let me leave this with you, for an odd moment's diversion." He placed a book, undoubtedly the book he was attempting to discuss with her, on the table near the fire.

"Thank you. That is very kind." Rilsin did not even glance at it. "You are right; I am tired. I am sorry not to be better company."

"Rilsin, there is no need for formality with me. To me you are always good company. I hope that soon you will trust me enough not to feel the need to hide the true state of your thoughts."

Rilsin frowned at him, but he was already straightening his overshirt and trousers—not the maroon wool he wore in the morning but a deep forest-green velvet—and turning to leave. Perhaps the remark was innocuous, and it was only her sense of passing time that made her anxious.

"No need to see me out," he assured her, but she did. He sent for his escort, who were drinking hot cider in the kitchen, and headed out into the night.

Rilsin waited until she saw the light of their lanterns fade down the path to the street. Then she looked around her.

"Meffa!" The name echoed down the hallway. No answer. Rilsin turned back toward the kitchen. "Meffa!"

The cook's young assistant, Bik, was the only one in the kitchen, a young man whose face was scarred by an all too recent adolescent battle with acne.

"She left," he told her. "She said something about it being too long wait for the poet, uh, Sae Sifuat, to leave."

"Did she take anyone with her?"

He shook his head, confused.

"Guards, did she take guards!"

"I think she went alone, Sae Rilsin. There aren't that many guards here; only four, I think. She wouldn't leave you unprotected. And she said she knows the streets of down-city."

"Great freezing Runchot hells!" It was her own fault for keeping so few staff, especially so few live-in staff.

She left the cook's assistant staring after her. She ran to the hallway, snatched up her sword and cloak, and belted the sword on as she ran through the door. She didn't bother with a lantern. Her night vision was excellent, and she, too, knew the streets, both of fashionable up-city, and of down-city. There was a waning moon overhead, still fat enough to cast some light into the darkness of the narrow alleys through which Rilsin ran in her effort to catch up with Meffa.

In her haste to leave, she forgot to ask how long ago Meffa left. It occurred to her that she might overtake and pass her chief servant without even realizing it if she continued to take shortcuts, so she slowed down and crossed back to the more frequently used side streets, the ones she thought Meffa might take. But the clanging of the big bell on the temple up in the better parts of the city reminded her how close it was to midnight, how close it was to the time when she must be at the Traitors' Prison. It would be hard enough to do this without calling undue attention to herself in any case.

Belatedly, she realized that she had no money. She was not accustomed to carrying much, and Meffa had all the funds she set aside for this. If Meffa was not at the prison, and if she could not find her, she would have to forget her errand, call up guards from the palace barracks, and mount a search for Meffa.

The better part of the city was far behind her now, as were the sections where the poorer dira and the few wealthier commoners lived. She was in a definitely seedy part of town, and it only got worse the closer she got to the prison. There were taverns here that remained open all night, selling the cheapest of beer to the roughest of clientele. Some of the alleys were the home turf of the women and men who sold their bodies, and these Rilsin avoided, as she knew Meffa would. She moved silently from shadow to shadow, avoiding the light, avoiding all passersby with an ability born of much practice and familiarity, a familiarity that would have greatly surprised the SaeKet, if she could have seen her cousin now.

But as so often happens when good luck is needed, only the worst luck was available. Rilsin saw Meffa, or a woman she was certain must be Meffa, only a few yards ahead of her, in the narrow lane into which she had just turned. Rilsin was hastening to catch up with her when a tavern door opened suddenly, spilling light and customers out into the cold night. One of these customers, a tall, heavy man with the muscles of a laborer, saw Meffa ahead of him in the lane. In the light from the open doorway it was apparent that her clothes were of good quality, and also that she was young and good-looking.

"Ho there!" shouted the laborer. "Wait up, little whore! Here's business for you!"

It was Meffa, Rilsin could see it in the way she hunched up her shoulders and turned her head. She lengthened her stride in an attempt to outdistance the men, but it was no use. Five of the tavern's customers ran forward and surrounded her, drunk and laughing.

"Leave me alone! I am no whore, so take your business elsewhere!"

"No whore, indeed! Then what is it you do tonight? Look at her fine trousers, such thick, soft wool! You have done well for yourself, but you are too good for us, heh?"

One of the men pulled aside Meffa's cloak and tried to yank at her trousers. This was when the money belt came to light. There was a moment of silence, and then the men began to shout, pulling at the money belt, pulling at Meffa's clothes, at Meffa herself.

"Leave me alone! I am on an errand for the first minister!"

The men howled with laughter. They were laughing so hard they did not hear the sound Rilsin's sword made as she came up behind them and drew it. But one of the men saw her and shouted, and they turned. Some of them had time to fumble out knives, and one had a sword.

Rilsin wasted no time and no breath in words. She went after the man with the sword first, sliced the weapon from his hand, ran him through the shoulder and then, as he stumbled, hamstrung him. She continued this movement up, to engage a man with a long knife, taking off his hand at the wrist. One of the remaining three men managed to go for Rilsin's stomach with his knife, but she was no longer there, and his knife caught in her cloak. She ran him through the heart. By this time, Meffa had picked up the wounded man's sword and was waving it furiously, as the last two men shouted for help.

"Saedin!" one shouted. "A saedin for the plucking!"

"That's no saedin," the one less drunk protested. "Look at her hair! She's a prisoner escaped!" No one listened to him.

Help arrived. The lane was the home of two taverns, as it happened, and the doors to both now disgorged men and women looking for a brawl and for plunder. As the night's bad luck would have it, Rilsin and Meffa were cut off from both sides of the alley.

"Back to back!" shouted Rilsin. Meffa obeyed, almost leaning against Rilsin, panting. She still had the sword, but Rilsin knew she had only the vaguest of ideas of how to use it.

The crowd began to close in. Rilsin lunged forward as soon as anyone was in striking distance. The first she reached was a woman of about thirty, who was swinging the long metal hook she used for unloading bales of hay. She was too drunk to be cautious, and she posed no problem for Rilsin, who simply cut the hook out of her hand, then turned her sword flat side out and smashed the woman across the side of the head. The woman staggered back and sat down on the packed dirt of the alley, holding her wounded hand and sobbing.

"I don't want to hurt any more of you," Rilsin called. "Just back away and let us through."

The crowd looked at her uncertainly. No one seemed willing to be next. But then the wounded woman screamed, "Kill them!" A middle-aged man shouted something inarticulate and snatched up the baling hook. From the way he moved, it was obvious that he had some skill at fighting. Others began to move forward after him, and from the way Meffa tensed, they were coming from that direction as well.

"Keep the sword close to you," Rilsin told her in a low voice. "Don't overextend your reach, and try to come in low. Go for something vital. You'll do fine."

"I'll try. I'm sorry, Sae Rilsin."

Rilsin wanted to reassure her, to tell her it didn't matter, but there was no time, and it wasn't true. The crowd rushed them, and she was suddenly very busy. She did not try to

beat them away with her sword but took her own advice and
went for whatever vital spots she could find, as many as
possible, on as many people as possible, as fast as possible.
Behind her, Meffa was screaming like a lunatic.

She took a cut on the hand from a man who sneaked
around the side of her. She responded by running him
through the stomach. She barely noticed. The man with the
baling hook had her attention. He kept just out of her reach,
but the hook combined with his own naturally long reach
made him a significant danger. And on top of this, more
people were coming out of the taverns, and some were entering the alley from the outside. For the first time Rilsin
began to consider that she might be in over her head. She re-
doubled her efforts to get the man with the hook. If she
could take him out, perhaps they could fight their way out
and run.

"Rilsin! I'm coming! SaeBecha!" It was Sifuat. He
shouted her name, her family name, fighting his way
through the lane with six of his own guard.

The mob began to part and fall back, and then Sifuat was
there, appearing at Rilsin's side just as she finally skewered
the man with the hook. Sifuat grinned at her cheerfully, obviously enjoying himself. As the crowd fell back, he swung
his sword in a whistling arc, more impressive than dangerous.

"We should go," he told her. "It's almost midnight."

Rilsin stared at him. She was breathing hard, her cloak
was torn, and the knife slash on her hand was still bleeding.
Then she looked around.

"Meffa?"

Meffa was bent over, still holding her sword, shaking.
One of Sifuat's men was beside her, talking to her.

"Meffa, are you all right?" Rilsin took her by the arm,
made her look up.

"I, I killed two of them! Two of them, Sae Rilsin!" She
looked at the sword in her hand and then dropped it in re-
vulsion. Sifuat's guard, lightning quick, snatched it by the
hilt before it hit the ground. Miraculously, Meffa seemed
unhurt.

"Good for you, Meffa. You had no choice. Don't be sick now; wait until we get out of here." She turned to Sifuat. "Thank you."

"My pleasure."

The mob had split up, but the smaller groups were still there, in the doorways to the taverns and ranged along the side of the lane. Rilsin heard muttering. She wanted to get out of here, now. They started to go, one of the guards helping Meffa. One man detached himself from a group at the mouth of the tavern.

"Sae Rilsin," he said. He planted himself right in front of them, looking askance at all the drawn swords. "We are sorry, we apologize," he said hastily, "we did not know it was truly you." He backed away from them, his eye still on the swords.

"It should not matter who it is," Rilsin snapped. She looked at the bodies lying strewn in the alleyway, all the dead and wounded. "A waste!"

"It's almost midnight," said Sifuat. "We need to go and hope there is no more of this."

"We will go with you, SaeKet," said the man. "We will be your guard tonight, wherever it is that you go."

"She is going to the Traitors' Prison to rescue the woman sentenced today." Sifuat's voice carried through the alley before Rilsin could speak. "What was her name?" he asked her, lower.

"Cilla. How did you know? And why, Sifuat, why did you tell them?" She looked at their impromptu "guard," the band of tough carousers from the taverns that was forming around them. They didn't seem to care that they had to step over bodies to reach her.

"You don't think this won't be all over Petipal by tomorrow anyway?" Sifuat grinned.

"Rilsin SaeKet does not own slaves," shouted a gray-haired woman. She was muscled and tough, with a scar down one cheek.

"*Sithli* SaeKet has forbidden her to free Cilla," Sifuat shouted, his emphasis on *Sithli*. "She has no choice but to buy her! Before midnight! Let us go!"

They made their way out of the alley. The toughs cleared the way; there was nothing and no one impeding them now. If they reached the prison by midnight, Rilsin could buy her prisoner legally and without fuss, although certainly not without notice now, as she had hoped.

"How did you know?" Rilsin asked Sifuat again. She couldn't think who could have told him. Only a few of her staff knew, and she didn't think there was time.

"No one told me." He guessed what she thought. "I just tried to think what you would do. I heard about the Audience today. That's all over Petipal, too. And tonight, I realized I was distracting you, that you probably hadn't had time to make all the arrangements. I don't know what made me think you might go yourself. The Mother must have been guiding me."

They reached the prison just before midnight. They attracted more people along the way, more of the same sort, although there were a number of prostitutes in this new bunch as well. All were prone to shouting Rilsin's name at the slightest provocation, sometimes with "SaeKet" attached, until she commanded them not to. They waited outside the prison while she and Meffa and Sifuat and his men went in.

Before she went in, Rilsin looked back at them, a huge crowd, muttering in the light of the torches outside the prison walls, glaring up at the guards patrolling the walls. The empty square around the Traitors' Prison was filled with them, or so it seemed. She felt the hair rise on the back of her neck. Surely the guards on the walls must feel the menace.

The people of Petipal, the commoners of the city, of the whole land, were like a pot about to boil over. She had been out prowling the city at night before, she had known there was discontent, but never had she felt it this clearly. She felt it behind her even through the outer walls of the prison compound, and it was not until the heavy doors of the prison itself closed behind her that the prickle between her shoulder blades vanished.

The Traitors' Prison was a huge fortress of despair. It housed common prisoners convicted of all manner of serious crimes, prisoners who would be hanged from the walls, or sold into labor to saedin or wealthy dira, or sent south for sale to the Runchot, or who would never again see the light of day. And beyond this, it housed also those saedin and dira who had been marked for sale across the border for their crimes. They were kept in thick stone cells with only what was necessary to keep them alive until they faced their punishment or died. The very air seemed thick with sorrow and hopeless anger.

The prison governor had been alerted and was waiting for them. Despite the dismal surroundings, he was a chipper man, a member of the honored class who had made a fortune from his position, from what he skimmed from the sale of those condemned to slavery, either in Runchot or in Saeditin itself, and from whatever he could extract from prisoners or their families in exchange for extra food or blankets. He had them shown into his personal apartment, which was beautifully appointed.

"It is an honor and a true pleasure to have you here," he told them. He had already sent for Cilla, and he didn't seem to mind that it was past midnight and technically illegal for him to make this sale. If it were anyone but the first minister, the SaeKet's cousin, Rilsin thought, he would demand more money.

"I want the daughter, too," she said.

"That, regrettably, I cannot help you with." The governor leaned back in his velvet chair. The golden light of at least half a dozen oil lamps gleamed on his long brown hair, which was braided with amethysts. His hands were impeccably manicured, and they glittered with rings.

Rilsin felt unkempt and a little the worse for wear. Although Sifuat, somehow and despite everything, was still smooth and unrumpled in his green velvet, her cloak was torn, as was her overshirt, and her hand, hastily bandaged, hurt. With her short hair, lack of jewels, and torn clothing of plain black, she was uncomfortably aware of how similar she must look to some of this man's charges.

"I want the daughter," she repeated.

"The daughter is already at the border, or should be by

tomorrow. Her sale is already promised to a Runchot gentleman of . . . very good connections. You might arrange to purchase her back from him for a suitable price, but perhaps not. A child so young and beautiful, surely you are aware of her beauty, Sae Rilsin, is worth a great deal, a very great deal, to such a man."

"And just what sort of man is he, this Runchot gentleman?"

"Ah." The governor smiled at her. "He is very well known, has a great many establishments throughout the northern part of Runchot."

"Establishments?" said Rilsin, her voice like iron. She saw Meffa, who was in the room at Rilsin's insistence and who had been huddled in a great, overstuffed chair, flinch at her tone. Meffa closed her eyes.

"Rilsin." Sifuat, in the chair beside her, leaned forward. "Let it go, Rilsin."

"What sort of establishments?" she insisted.

"Brothels, Sae Rilsin. Brothels, of course." He was tired of playing this game. If the first minister wanted to be crude about it, then crude he would be. But he couldn't resist adding, "Some of them are the finest in all of Runchot. And young children, well, they are at a premium."

Rilsin was rigid in her chair. Sifuat's hand was on her wrist, squeezing hard. She felt him willing her to let it go. She felt a sudden loathing for him. How could he condone this? She glanced at him. He did not condone it. It was something else. Before she could speak, the governor rose from his chair and went to the door of the apartment. Sifuat seized his chance.

"Sithli's percentage," he whispered. It came out as a hiss.

Rilsin frowned. She started to say, "I'll pay her percentage," but he cut her off.

"She gets a percentage from the governor's profit," Sifuat whispered, "as well as from the Runchot. *Don't* speak of it now."

The governor motioned someone into the room. It was a guard, bringing Cilla. Her hands were bound in front of her, and her hair was as short as Rilsin's now, but more ragged.

Through her torn shirt the red welt of a brand could be seen on her shoulder. Her eyes were red from weeping. The guard brought her to a halt just inside the door.

"Here she is," said the governor, "and our price is agreed." He looked again at the coins that lined the inside of the money belt, which he picked up from the table beside Meffa. "There is no need for your seal, since you yourself are present." The seal was what Meffa had lacked when she left Rilsin's house.

Rilsin was on her feet, Sifuat beside her.

"You are the property of Rilsin sae Becha," the governor told Cilla. There was a weary distaste in his voice, although he still stroked the money belt. "Your body and your life are hers to do with as she pleases. Serve her well."

"Thank you, dira," said Sifuat promptly. "We are finished here." He shifted his grasp to Rilsin's elbow, and he tried to pull her forward. Rilsin shook him off, ignoring his desperate warning look.

"For now," she said.

They were escorted out. The governor offered a further escort or a carriage, back up-city, and at first Rilsin declined, but after looking at Cilla, she doubted the woman could walk. Meffa, too, was exhausted, so she accepted the carriage. The crowd was still waiting for her, she found. When they saw her on the steps leading down from the wall, they cheered, and when, in the light of the flaming torches, she cut Cilla's bonds, they cheered again.

"Rilsin SaeKet Becha," shouted a woman, "let us see you home!"

"Rilsin sae Becha!" Rilsin called back. "I am the servant of Sithli SaeKet, as are you all! I have accepted a carriage for Cilla, but I thank you."

"Sae Rilsin!" It was the same woman's voice. "When you are tired of being a servant, remember us!"

The cry was taken up by others in the crowd. "Remember us!" they shouted. But they dispersed when Rilsin asked them to, just as the carriage arrived and the prison guards were coming out.

18

"SO YOU PREVENTED A RIOT LAST NIGHT AT THE TRAITORS' Prison." Sithli waved her servant away and poured herself some more tea.

Rilsin stood before her cousin, feeling exhausted, and with good reason. She had had very little sleep last night. She was very aware that Sithli had not asked her to sit down and had not offered her breakfast as she usually did.

"A potential riot that would not, could not possibly have had a chance of occurring had you not gone to the prison as you did."

"It was bad planning, SaeKet. I apologize. But there was no riot."

"You don't sound as though you are apologizing. You sound the way you do when you are upset with me. If you have something to say to me, Rilsin, then say it." Sithli put down her cup and stared at her cousin.

Sifuat had warned her to say nothing, to do what she must to make this pass. And Sola, whom she had not seen privately in weeks, showed up at her house early this morning, disrupting the only chance she had for a little sleep, to say the same thing. News traveled fast in Petipal, it seemed, for he had heard all about her escapade of the previous night, with some embellishments. He joined forces with Sifuat, who was still there, to try to convince her to avoid a confrontation with Sithli. Rilsin was not convinced, and now she would not back down.

"The governor of the Traitors' Prison, and others, I understand, have been acting illegally. They have been skimming profits from the sale of prisoners and, I believe, have been selling prisoners who should not be sold. And more than this, SaeKet. Someone, in your name, has been taking a percentage, not just of the sales but of the governors' profits." She watched Sithli carefully, and she saw the beautiful face pale behind its powder and then flush slightly. Sithli's eyes began to flash.

"This is outrageous, Rilsin! No one could sell prisoners not sentenced to slavery without a report being made to me! Are you saying that I knew? And are you claiming that I profit twice from these sales?"

"I am not claiming that you knew, SaeKet. But I am claiming that it happens! That someone knows! I told you my people had disappeared!"

"Investigating Kepit sae Lisim, you said, and we all know there are some rough customers in some of her streets. As for profit skimming, Rilsin, that has gone on forever. It is to be expected, and it harms no one, so long as it is kept within bounds. You cannot take it seriously. As for the rest, do you have proof?"

"I will have it. I will have it soon. I am bending all efforts, now that I have some idea where to look—"

"You will cease those efforts immediately! You will cease because there is no proof!"

Rilsin drew a deep breath. Despite herself, her suspicion began to harden. "I am first minister, SaeKet. Justice for the people is under my hand."

"When it is not under mine! And what is this about 'the people,' Rilsin! The people that matter are saedin and dira! Oh, I will grant you that most of the commoners are good and law-abiding people, and yes, they are citizens, as you are so fond of pointing out, but many are descendants of freed criminals and captives!"

Rilsin deliberately ran her hand through her short hair. Sithli stopped. Then her color began to rise. Her golden skin mottled with rage.

"You push me to the limit, Rilsin! I warn you again not to go too far!"

"I'm sorry, Sithli." Rilsin held out her hands, an appeal. Nothing could be gained from her cousin in this mood, and it was stupid to provoke her. She must try something else. "Do you remember when I took you to meet Sola for the first time, that hot summer day in the forest?"

"Of course. Yes." Sithli was startled from her rage. "The day the assassin tried to kill me." Her hand rose in an unconscious gesture toward her scar, dropped again.

"Before that, in the woods, do you remember what it was like when we realized we had no guards, and we were unarmed? That we could have been kidnapped? Kidnapped and sold?"

Sithli frowned. "I haven't thought about that. It could not have happened, would not have. It did *not* happen."

"But it could have! Did you ever think, Sithli, what it would be like to be a child, a Saeditin child taken away from everything she knows, and sold? Sold to foreigners, or to enemies, to never again have her birthright? How many Saeditin children face that today? Face that illegally because of greed on the part of . . . officials?" Rilsin was out of breath, carried away, more passionate than she had planned.

Sithli looked for a long moment at her cousin. Rilsin had the chance to hear the echo of her own words, to hear how, in her passion, she had phrased this. The word *birthright* seemed to hang in the air. The silence stretched. At last Sithli leaned forward.

"It could not have happened to me, Rilsin. I am the SaeKet, protected by the Mother. I ensure that only those who deserve punishment receive it. All those who stand against me, She gives into my hand, whether they are commoner, dira, or even saedin. Even saedin, Rilsin. They are traitors, to be dealt with as I please. All lawful Saeditin are my servants, all else are traitors. Which are you, Rilsin? I saved you from the knife. For all these years I gave you my protection, and you have been my first and foremost servant. Are you tired of being my servant, Rilsin sae Becha?"

Rilsin looked into her cousin's eyes, heard the crowd outside the prison, heard the woman's loud voice soaring up from the mob to ask the same question.

"Is that what you think, Sithli?" Rilsin stepped forward, right up to her cousin's chair. "I know what you heard. Where did you think your reports on last night's incidents came from? My people, my agents. They came through me. I have promised you more than my obedience, more than my service. I promised you peace, I promised to keep the land in peace." She saw Sithli remembering the first time she promised this, in the room full of blood and death, with Sithli's mother, the rebel SaeKet, lying in her own blood. Could anything ever justify breaking that promise? She pushed the thought down.

Rilsin stepped back from the chair. She turned away from her cousin, looking out the window. A late spring snowstorm had begun, and fat white flakes swirled around the glass, obscuring the view. She felt strangely detached. A sound made her turn back. Sithli had been so unpredictable, even for Sithli, since her father's death, and Rilsin wondered what she would do. At this moment, somehow, she didn't care. But when she turned around, Sithli was weeping.

"I don't know what I would do if you ever betrayed me," she sobbed. "Don't ever betray me, Rils. I couldn't bear it!"

"Oh, Sith! I never will! You know that!" Rilsin went to her cousin, knelt by her chair, and put her arm around her, ignoring a flash of uneasiness. "Stop crying, stop. You have an audience with some ships' owners, Sithli, and look, your powder is all streaked." The appeal to save her makeup worked, as Rilsin knew it would. Sithli stopped sobbing and brought out mirror and powder to repair the damage. After a moment she looked up, smiling slightly, tears gone.

"You will not have time for an investigation, Rils. You

are going to be married! And then I will hold you to your vow to keep the peace. You will go north the day after your wedding to push back the barbarian tribes from our border."

"The day after—but Sithli! That is too soon! It is only days away! I planned to go soon, but not that soon!"

"Then you will be busy. Wedding first, and then the campaign. Go, Rils, go." She made shooing motions. "You have work to do."

THE WEDDING FELL on the equinox itself, an auspicious day, another turning of the tides of the year. It was a beautiful day, with blue sky, gold sun, and birds returning to Saeditin from the south. Anyone who could, turned out to see the wedding procession or to cram into the temple, which was filled by dawn.

It would be quite the spectacle, as the SaeKet had spared no expense for her cousin's ceremony. Banners lined the streets, flapping in the stiff springtime wind, banners the green and gold of the Melisin, but in honor of Rilsin. Flower petals covered the steps to the temple. Since two people had already slipped and almost fallen on these, some of them had to be swept away so that no accident would befall the wedding party.

Rilsin and Sifuat, who had been undergoing purification in the caverns beneath the temple since the previous night, emerged to clouds of incense and crowds of waiting priests and saedin spectators in velvets and silks, and Sithli smiling, raising her hands in blessing. Sifuat was dressed in purple with a trim of lavender and gold. His fair hair was braided with amethysts. Rilsin modified her standard black to include grays. Her overshirt was a gray so soft that it hinted at blue. This bordered on the dangerous, but she was convinced that Sithli would not notice. She wore her pendant, but today she also had a silver ring, a wide band set with a flat star ruby, a gift from Sifuat. Sifuat wore a ring of identical design but with a pale gray sapphire, a gift from Rilsin.

To everyone, from the high saedin at the front of the temple to the lowest of commoners at the back, it was obvious that the bridal couple was in love. They looked away from each other only when they must, and when their hands brushed by accident, both blushed. Rilsin promised to guard Sifuat's honor, and Sifuat promised to aid Rilsin in all undertakings. Once again, all reference to children of the union was forgone. Their hands were joined at last, by Dremfir sae Cortin, the little mage from Norimin's household, who had somehow been given this honor even above more senior priests, and both bride and groom could not stop smiling. They left the temple for the waiting open carriage and the procession to the cheers of the crowd and to Sithli's comment that she had never seen Rilsin so infatuated, and she wondered how long it would last.

Rilsin waved at the people from the open carriage. The wind feathered her hair back from her face as she tossed traditional gifts of coins and sweets into the crowd, which shouted her name and Sifuat's. She was very conscious of Sifuat beside her, waving, of the warmth of him, of his incredible beauty. When the carriage stopped for a moment, held up briefly by the mass of people ahead, a woman darted past a distracted guard and thrust something at Rilsin. The guard recovered in time to snatch it up, but Rilsin motioned him to show it to her. It was a charm, a twist of wheat straw and river pebbles, an old-fashioned charm for health and fertility.

"The Mother bless you!" shouted the woman. "Such a beautiful couple!"

Rilsin took the charm, smiling, and tossed her a coin.

"You are more than beautiful," whispered Sifuat. "You are radiant."

Rilsin felt herself blushing again as the carriage began to move forward. Sithli's carriage was ahead of them, and she felt her cousin's eyes as Sithli turned to look at them. Overcome with a feeling of lightheadedness, she waved at Sithli, but there was no response. Then Sithli's carriage moved on, leaving them behind. It was a morning of many delays, as people thronged the streets, but Rilsin and Sifuat tolerated it with good grace.

All the same, it was with a feeling of intense relief that

Rilsin saw her own house at last. She had only today and tonight with Sifuat, since tomorrow, in obedience to Sithli's command, she rode north. But once down the drive from the street, she could safely block out the rest of the world for a few hours, at least. So it was with an unpleasant shock that she was greeted by Meffa with the news of visitors.

"Sae Norimin is here," Meffa told her in a low voice as Rilsin handed her her gray velvet wedding cloak.

"Not for long," said Sifuat. "I'll see that she leaves." He made as if to go past Meffa, but she put out a hand, appealing to Rilsin.

"The SaeKet is here, too," she said. "They are in your formal parlor, having cakes and tea."

"I don't see how we can get rid of *her*," said Rilsin, "but I'll see what I can do. What can she want?" How like Sithli to demand that Rilsin, even on her wedding day, focus on her.

"I wanted to wish you the best," Sithli told her, when she entered the parlor, "and to see you today," she smiled, "in a nonritual setting. I am going to miss you, Rils. Make it a short campaign!"

"As short as I can." Rilsin was puzzled. She knew there was more here than met the eye; she smelled it. Norimin was looking at her without smiling.

"Sit down, Sae Sifuat." Sithli patted the gray velvet sofa beside her. Her green and gold velvet blazed against the gray. "I know you will miss your bride. This will be a lonely house for you until she returns. Perhaps you will visit me as a distraction." She fluttered her eyelashes at Sifuat, who looked astonished but then went to sit beside her with a gallant if uneasy flourish.

"It will be a great honor, SaeKet."

"An honor of which my son must avail himself at a later date," said Norimin. "He is coming north with me to Sudithold. I need his help in some legal matters, as I explained to you." She smiled imperturbably at Sithli. Sifuat looked surprised. It was obvious to all of them that he knew nothing of this.

"So you did, and I agreed with you. But these matters are not urgent, surely."

"Indeed they are, since they involve the transfer of Sudit property to Sae Rilsin, your cousin. I am old, and death may come at any moment, and I am unwilling to chance fate in this matter."

"Well then, he will have to leave soon," said Sithli, looking put out. "But he can stay awhile for me to console him."

"We go north tomorrow, since all the arrangements are made," said Norimin blandly, "but we will not remain more than two or three months at most, and probably much less. Only as long as we must."

Only about as long as the campaign, thought Rilsin, looking at Norimin with awe. There was no doubt in her mind that they would be traveling with her. And no doubt that she would be able to see her husband, at least some of the time. She would not be chasing barbarians every minute. She saw that Sifuat, although still sitting beside Sithli, managed to edge slightly away from her. He caught Rilsin's eye and smiled faintly.

"How pleasant for Rilsin." Sithli looked sour, but then she brightened. "Come and sit down, Rilsin. This is your own house, after all; you needn't stand there. I have decided to give you and Sifuat another wedding gift."

"You have already given us more than enough." This was true. Rilsin, perched on the edge of her chair, had no desire for any more gems or velvets or cottons, nor for any more land, since Sudithold would be—was—hers.

"I am giving you the position of minister of mines and factories. You will be able to direct all these modern inventions for the good of Saeditin. You will be subject only to me."

"Thank you, Sithli! That's wonderful."

"And you can appoint whomever you please. I know you will appoint Sola dira Mudrin to something, perhaps under minister? And I know you will work very closely with him." Sithli smiled more broadly, as she saw Rilsin's face close up. "And now, we must follow custom, and you must give me a present in return, to celebrate your good fortune."

Rilsin was surprised and confused. She had already given her cousin a present of the emeralds she loved. Sithli saw the surprise and continued.

"Oh, I know you have given me the beautiful emeralds, but there is one gift I truly crave, one small thing you can give me to show your happiness with the marriage I arranged, which obviously suits you so well."

Rilsin saw that Sifuat had edged even farther from her cousin, and the look on his face suggested that he was afraid that he might be the gift Sithli desired. But not even Sithli would go that far.

"What is this small item?" She couldn't imagine what it could be. Everything Sithli desired, she already owned.

"Your captive. Your slave. I cannot get her from my mind, and I want her for my own."

Rilsin gaped stupidly at her smiling cousin. *What captive, what slave?* She didn't keep them. Then it dawned on her. "You mean Cilla?"

"Surely you won't deny me that pleasure. You can purchase so many more with the wealth I have given you."

For a moment Rilsin continued to stare at her cousin. She could not deny this request. It would have been stupid to attempt to do so, all the more because it was not a request at all.

"Of course," she said at last. "I will have her sent to you as soon as the opportunity arises." There was a slim chance that Sithli would forget this, and she could send Cilla away.

"I will have her now." Sithli rose, smoothing her green velvet with fingers that blazed with rings. "I must go and leave you two sweethearts alone." She smiled fondly at Rilsin and reached out as if to touch a lock of Sifuat's hair, which had escaped his braid, pulling back just before she completed the gesture. "There is so little time before you must leave for the north, where you will have so little chance to be with each other, poor things."

All of them went out to Rilsin's entrance hall, where she gave the necessary orders. Sithli's golden carriage was brought up for her, swarming with her personal guards, and they went out. Sithli draped herself in her long green velvet

cloak and took Rilsin's hands in hers, and gave her a gentle
kiss on the lips.

"Blessings on you both," said Sithli.

Rilsin, held in her cousin's embrace, saw from the corner
of her eye the flurry of activity at the SaeKet's carriage.
Cilla had been brought out, wearing the plain off-white
woolen trousers and shirt with which Rilsin had provided
her, but cloakless in the cold. Her hands were bound behind
her back, and in her eyes Rilsin saw absolute terror. Sithli
turned from Rilsin and strode out to the carriage. One of the
escort helped her in. Cilla was thrown across a guard's
horse, tied behind the saddle like a piece of baggage. As the
carriage left, Sithli waved.

Rilsin stared after her, feeling helpless, feeling sick.
"Damn it, Sithli, damn it," she whispered.

Norimin looked at her, concerned but not surprised.
"Rilsin, my daughter," she said, "don't take it so hard.
Surely you, of us all, know how the SaeKet is."

"Yes," said Rilsin. "I do. This was my fault. Sithli wants
me to have only that which she gives me. I must owe all to
her. I went about this all wrong, but it is poor Cilla who pays
the price."

"We *all* pay the price," said Norimin, but so softly that
Rilsin was not quite sure she actually heard it.

19

THEY LEFT IN THE EARLY MORNING, RILSIN AT THE HEAD OF fifteen thousand troops, Sifuat and Norimin traveling separately, but at the same pace, with their own guards. Rilsin spoke briefly with Bilma, whom she delegated to attend to some of her duties while she was gone. Sithli saw them off from the main balcony of the palace, after a private audience with Rilsin. Nothing was said about Cilla, much about a quick victory. Sithli even requested a supply of northern captives.

"I will do whatever I can to safeguard our borders and to insure peace," Rilsin told her. It was a measure of how she felt that the thought of taking even barbarians as slaves was unsettling.

Rilsin was exhausted from her wedding night, which she had been in no mood to forgo, even though she knew she would pay for it this morning. She was happier than she wanted to admit that she was not leaving Sifuat behind. If only she could, she would have liked to think of nothing but Sifuat, but she didn't resent that there were matters that prevented this. She had come to the conclusion that she could not have the conversation she would have liked to have with Sithli, not now, which meant that it must wait until she returned. She was concerned about Sithli's moods, which had been growing ever more erratic, but perhaps while Rilsin was away from the capital, Sithli would find peace with herself. Perhaps Bilma, in his old position, could help to calm the SaeKet.

When Rilsin had mentioned this to Norimin early this morning, her mother-in-law simply shook her head. Sifuat put his hand on Rilsin's arm and told her that he was glad to be leaving Petipal for a time, glad to be away with her. As they smiled at each other, seeing no one else, Norimin shook her head again, but she smiled, too.

By early afternoon Rilsin was well away from the capital, although the line of troops snaked backward for some few miles. Norimin and Sifuat, with their own small entourage, were somehwere up ahead, and Chilsa was riding on a nearby wagon, since Rilsin was reluctant to leave him behind. Some of her officers looked at her askance, expecting her to be in a filthy mood at finding herself without a honeymoon, but Rilsin didn't see it that way. The farther away from Petipal she got, the better she felt. She found it hard not to smile.

They were marching through the fields and small towns that surrounded Petipal the way the rings surrounded the moon: a thick cluster of towns, which became a thinner cluster of villages, which thinned out in turn until there was only a sprinkling of farmsteads and then an occasional village, like a star beyond the rainbow rings. Saeditin still had large tracts of forest, too, although these were not nearly so vast as they had been only a generation ago. The army kept away from most of the villages, heading northward as fast as it could. It marched through fields only when it must, even though it was still too early for spring plowing.

In fact, it was not as early as it might have been. The thaw would be soon, a week or two early, and Rilsin knew she must make up for lost time. It was important to reach the border and to make a decisive strike against the barbarians before they began their annual raids. It would not only be nice to have peace along the border, but the coal routes must be secure. She motioned to the young officer who rode slightly behind her.

"Send word ahead to the saedhold seat," she said, "that we are not stopping until near nightfall, and we need the SaeKet's Road clear for us. They will be expecting us to stop sooner."

The officer was Essit sae Tillit, of the borderlands himself, her ally in the trade battle.

"Yes, Commander." He wheeled to ride ahead.

"Wait! Send someone to the Sae Sudit party with the same message; you needn't go yourself." Rilsin had not forgotten the ill will between the two families.

"I'll see to it myself. Sae Sifuat and I are trying to mend fences." Essit smiled broadly at her, whistling as he rode away, and she realized that her good mood was infectious.

The journey went well and quickly. It went too quickly for Rilsin, even though she was the one urging speed. It went too quickly because after that first day, Sifuat rode beside her most of the time. The nights were spent either as the guests of local saedin or in her tent, set up in an open field.

As honeymoons went, Rilsin wouldn't ask for anything else, only more of the same. Flocks of birds were flying northward. They filled the trees and the fields with singing. Snow-roses bloomed beside the road and under the trees in the orchards, filling the air with their heady, sweet scent. Sometimes Chilsa ran beside her horse, and sometimes Sifuat quoted poetry to her, when he thought no one else was close enough to hear. And Norimin made herself scarce, with more tact than Rilsin had been willing to credit her. She stayed exclusively with her entourage, and she and Rilsin saw each other only when they met at dinner in the house of a local saedin.

The nights in camp were the best. The cold moon waxed in the center of its rainbow rings, gleaming like a polished pearl. Rilsin spent time with her troops and then retired to sit by her own fire with Sifuat. But soon enough the fire was out, and they were in the tent, bundled into heaps of down quilts, trying to keep silent so the sentries wouldn't hear them.

Early in the morning, almost every morning, well before dawn, Rilsin rode out into the countryside with Chilsa, always alone, to return before the camp stirred. And all the while the border grew closer. Soon it would be time for Sifuat to join Norimin for the journey to Hoptrin, while Rilsin proceeded to the edge of Saeditin territory, between Sudit and Tillit saedholds. Rilsin tried not to think about this inevitable parting, but she couldn't keep her mind from it, especially on these predawn rides with only her cat for company, before the business of the day began, coordinating the march of the army northward. It was one of these early morning excursions that put an end to all this well-ordered progress, that was to change the history of Saeditin.

It was a chilly morning, with frost still standing on the fields and woods, sparkling on the snow-roses, which grew in profusion where the land was once cleared and then abandoned. The waning moon was a thin crescent in the east, gleaming faintly in its rings, rising shortly before the sun, but the sky had just begun to lighten with false dawn. Rilsin and Chilsa had been out hunting deer and rabbits by the light of the stars, with no luck but for the large snow rabbit Chilsa caught and had for his breakfast. Rilsin was ready to return when Chilsa stopped suddenly, growling low in his throat. He sniffed the air and then looked up at Rilsin, mouth open slightly, lips drawn back in a grimace, tasting something on the wind. Now she smelled it, too, the smell of charred wood and ashes, the smell of something burned.

She gave Chilsa the hand sign for silence, which he had learned as a kitten in training. Luckily, she was on foot this morning, and there was no horse to hide. She glided into the cover of the frost-spangled brush, relying on the old skills, silently making her way toward the smell, which grew stronger with the freshening breeze of dawn. Chilsa was equally invisible, but she knew he was there.

The brush thinned at the edge of an orchard, which was still spotted with patches of unmelted snow. The sun was just below the horizon now, casting a faint golden glow over the land. At the foot of the orchard Rilsin saw the source of the charred smell. A farmhouse once stood there, and sheep pens, and an outbuilding, a typical borderland farm. Cautiously, Rilsin crept forward, coming into the open only when she must.

The charred wood of the farmhouse was still warm in spots. Rilsin felt the hair rise on the back of her neck. She saw Chilsa now, investigating something at the angle of two charred lines, the remains of the fence that enclosed a sheep pen. Suddenly the cat snorted and jumped back. Rilsin ran to him, then pulled back at what startled him. It was the burned body of a girl of about eleven, horribly disfigured by fire but not so much that Rilsin could not see the gaping wound in her thin chest, a wound made by a sword. It was obvious that the barbarians had sneaked across the border to begin their raids early this year. As Rilsin realized how badly she had miscalculated, the sun rose, shedding its light across the ruined farm.

There were other bodies. Behind the remains of the farmhouse, the body of a woman shielded the corpse of an infant. A boy in his early teens must have tried to fight; he still clutched the pitchfork he had wielded, its tines covered with dried blood, before his head was split open from behind. Some of his blood was still wet. And the ground around was trampled with fresh hoofprints. This raid was less than a day old. Some of the raiders might still be nearby.

Now Rilsin regretted not being mounted. She needed to get back to the army as fast as possible. How could she have been so stupid as to come out here alone, this close to the border? Why had the scouts not reported that barbarians had crossed the border early? She could not afford to be captured. She faded back quickly through the orchard into the brush. When Chilsa came up beside her, she took the woolen scarf from her throat. It was gray, embroidered with lavender, Sudit colors. She tied this around Chilsa's neck, knotting it in the pattern that meant *enemies*. She considered tying another piece of cloth with the knot pattern for *near*, or for *north*, but she decided this was obvious, especially if she didn't make it back.

"Go back," she whispered to the cat. "Back to camp." It was after dawn, and her absence had certainly been noticed already. "Go, Chilsa!" And she gave the sign for silence again. Chilsa went.

Chilsa was at camp when Rilsin arrived safely, having encountered no raiders, no survivors, no one. The camp was in uproar, and at first Rilsin assumed this was because of Chilsa's arrival and the deductions that had been drawn from the scarf. But it seemed this was not entirely the case. Chilsa's arrival had thrown fresh fuel on an already burning fire. Sifuat, contrary to his habit, had awakened early this morning and decided to follow his wife, perhaps because he knew there was little time with her remaining. He took two soldiers with him and set out to find her. One of the soldiers had since returned, wounded, with a story of raiders and ambush. When Rilsin talked to him, he was certain that Sifuat was still alive but a prisoner.

THEY HADN'T KILLED his horse, and they let him ride, for which he supposed he should be grateful. Barbarians had been known to make their prisoners run behind the horses until they fainted and were dragged along by the ropes that bound them. That they were not doing this was a cause for gratitude. But Sifuat sae Sudit couldn't shake an overwhelming feeling of resentment, resentment that sometimes even overpowered his fear.

Why was it that bad luck always happened to him, and not just bad luck, but bad luck that made him look like a fool? He was the one who insisted on following the tracks of the raiders, even when he knew what they were, over the objections of his escort. When they had tried to turn back, he forged ahead, forcing them to follow him. He had wanted so much to be able to bring the information to Rilsin, not just that there were raiders, but how many, and anything else he could find out. He had a fantasy of overpowering the barbarians, of bringing back captives to his wife. It couldn't have gone more wrong.

Ahead of him was the wounded soldier, Gest dira Happin, he thought his name was. Gest was badly wounded, wounded in defense of him, but he was still alive. But Gest was in need of medical attention, which he was not likely to get any time soon, and of water, which he also did not seem likely to receive. Gest was tied to his horse, not to keep him from escaping but because he could no longer ride. Every now and then he whimpered. A moan would be one thing, but the whimpers set Sifuat's teeth on edge.

Sifuat, too, was bound to his horse. His hands were tied in front of him and tied to the saddle as well, and a rope around his waist was attached to the saddle, and then trailed back to link him to one of the raiders. He had been gagged, too. In case the raiders decided they wanted silence, they didn't want him to spoil it. It was humiliating.

Worse still, they knew who he was. They knew his name, which they learned during the brief, fierce fight in which he was captured, and they knew that he was Norimin's son, that he was Rilsin's husband. The leader of this little band of twenty raiders was very pleased with himself. Every so often he glanced at Sifuat and smiled.

They rode until well into the afternoon, keeping to the woods. They rode until they must stop for the sake of the horses. When they did stop, Sifuat was stiff, not just from all that time bound in the saddle, but also from the cut he took on his shoulder, which had stopped bleeding; it was not serious, but it still stung in the cold. Gest had stopped whimpering long ago, and Sifuat saw that he was limp across the back of the horse. He feared the worst.

"Get down." The barbarian leader untied the ropes that bound Sifuat to his horse, but he did not untie his hands. Awkwardly, Sifuat slid from the saddle. He almost fell, but the raider steadied him.

"You must be thirsty, yes?" The man spoke a pretty good Saeditin, despite the northern accent. He pulled the gag from Sifuat's mouth and offered his own water skin.

For a moment Sifuat considered refusing, but his thirst was too great. He took the water skin with his bound hands and drank deeply, keeping his eyes on the barbarian. When he finished, he gave it back.

"Your wife follows us," said the barbarian conversationally, taking the skin and drinking. Despite himself, Sifuat glanced back. The raider grinned. "She won't catch. But we must ride again soon. We need extra horse. I explain this to you so you will understand what I do. What I must do. We need extra horse." He nodded to one of his men, who pulled Gest from his mount.

When Gest hit the ground, he moaned, so Sifuat knew he was not dead. But he thought he knew what was coming, and he was desperate to stop it.

"Don't kill him!" he cried. "Keep away from him, you filth!" He lunged toward Gest, but one of the raiders grabbed him while another hit him across the face.

"Enough!" said the leader. "Enough!" He looked at Sifuat. "We will not kill him. Why should we kill him? I hope he lives. We leave him here for Rilsin sae Becha. If he lives, perhaps he will slow her down. We must leave him behind. You understand this, son of Sae Sudit?" When Sifuat said nothing, he shrugged and turned away to oversee what they were doing to Gest. Only later did Sifuat wonder why the man should care if he understood or what he thought.

Sifuat studied the barbarian as best he could with his eyes watering and his ears ringing from the blow. The barbarian leader was a tall man with dark hair and the pale skin of Saeditin commoners and some of the old dira and saedin. If it were not for the fact that Rilsin had this coloring, Sifuat would hate it. The leader had a scar down his left cheek that made him look older than he actually was, which Sifuat reckoned to be somewhere around thirty.

They rode again as soon as the horses were rested and watered. Gest dira Happin was left on the ground, wrapped not only in his own cloak but in one the raiders provided, stolen, no doubt, thought Sifuat sourly. They gave Gest some water and even treated his wounds, at least superficially, but Sifuat knew that if Gest were not found soon, by Rilsin or by someone, he would die.

By nightfall, which came early this far north, they were

into wild country, very wild country, and Sifuat knew with
a sinking heart that they had crossed the border. He was in
the barbarians' land now, and that made it all somehow
much worse. The barbarians felt better about it, however.
They laughed and joked quietly, although Scarface, as Sifuat thought of the leader, wouldn't let them light a fire.
This gave him a little hope, making him think that Rilsin
might be close.

They took him from the horse and tied him to a tree, with
his hands behind the trunk and his feet straight out in front
of him on the ground. He was extremely uncomfortable, but
he gritted his teeth, determined not to complain, not to ask
them for anything. He only hoped they would give him
something to eat, or to drink, at least, since they didn't seem
to plan on killing him now. Sure enough, just before all the
light left the sky, Scarface came over to him with a waterskin and a large chunk of something in his hand; cold roast
meat, Sifuat hoped. Scarface squatted down in front of him.

"If I untie you and give food, you must not run, understand?" When Sifuat said nothing, the man sighed. "You
would not get far. Look." He waved at the sentries posted,
and at his men, who even in relaxation, looked alert. Some
watched their leader and the prisoner with interest. "You
would be hurt badly, killed, maybe. You don't want that. I
don't want that. Besides, then you can't eat." Scarface
chuckled slightly. It was a joke. "So. If I untie you, you
promise. Yes?"

"Yes," said Sifuat.

Scarface looked at him intently, determining whether or
not he really meant it. Then he put down the waterskin,
drew a wicked-looking knife from his belt, and cut Sifuat's
bonds. He gave Sifuat both the waterskin and what did, in
fact, turn out to be a chunk of roasted meat, but he didn't
back away while Sifuat ate. He simply squatted there, knife
still in hand, watching. When Sifuat was finished, he picked
up the ropes again.

"Wait." Sifuat had no plan in mind, but he didn't want to
be tied to the tree again. "I have to, uh, relieve myself."

At first, Scarface looked blank; then understanding

dawned. But he called over three of the raiders, *three,* thought Sifuat, in disgust, to guard him while he did what he must. They took him only to the very edge of the little camp. Since Sifuat did need to do what he claimed, and very badly, he did it. His guards relaxed slightly and even glanced aside to give him just a little privacy. Sifuat seized his opportunity and tried to run into the woods. They caught him almost immediately and brought him back, slamming him back against his tree before they tied him to it, making him wince from the pain in his wounded shoulder.

"Oh, Sudit," said Scarface, "that was predictable. And I had hoped for better." He squatted down again and took Sifuat's face in one hand. With the other hand he slapped him hard across the face, first one way and then the other, but his palm was open. "No more," he said. "No more." He slapped Sifuat's face again and held him tightly by the chin, watching as the involuntary tears ran and Sifuat blinked. "Fool!"

"Why don't you just kill me and get it over with?" Sifuat's fury at being called a fool overcame his good sense. He knew better than to antagonize his captor, and he really didn't want to die. But Scarface just looked at him for a long moment.

"I want you alive," he said. "You are my prize," he said. "Why I crossed border." He stalked away, leaving Sifuat to ponder this remark for the rest of the miserable, uncomfortable, freezing night.

20

BY MORNING SIFUAT WAS SO STIFF HE COULD BARELY
move. Despite the cloaks with which the raiders covered
him during the night, he suffered from the cold. His muscles
had cramped and seized, and his shoulder was painful.
When they untied him, he could barely stand.

"You will not run today," Scarface told him, not without
sympathy. He tore off a chunk of bread from the piece he
held in his hand and offered it to Sifuat, who took it, feeling
miserable, his hand shaking, his teeth actually chattering.

"Let me see shoulder." Scarface leaned forward and
grasped Sifuat by the arm when he tried to pull away. "Ah,"
he said, as he prodded, surprisingly gently, at the wound.
"Not bad, not bad, just stiff from cold. Good it is not your
sword arm, yes? With luck, you live to fight again. You are
a most excellent fighter."

There was sincerity in Scarface's voice when he said
this. Sifuat knew he meant it, but it didn't make him feel any
better. On the contrary, it made him feel worse. All his life,
it seemed, he put too much faith in his physical abilities, but
they were all he had, if you didn't count poetry, and he

didn't. In a strange way they were the reason he was not in the army himself. He could fight brilliantly, but somehow, when it came to strategy on a broader scale, he just couldn't think, just couldn't see it. And in the army, saedin were officers, high officers. Sifuat knew he would not be an officer, could not be an officer, that he just couldn't do the job. And now, because of his foolishness, no, his *stupidity,* as Norimin would be the first to point out, he was in the hands of Scarface, being taken north into the Mother knew what.

"Tonight," said Scarface, "you will be warm. We will all be warm. We can make fires, eat hot food. By afternoon we will be out of the reach of Sae Becha. We will be through the Throat, and then we will wait. If Sae Becha comes, and tries to go through the Throat, we will catch her, we will swallow her!" He grinned at Sifuat, delighted with his own humor, and he made chewing and swallowing motions. Sifuat looked away. "If I catch Sae Becha, oh, that is very good! That will be best! But if not, if she does not come, I have you."

Sifuat closed his eyes. And then, surprisingly, Scarface patted him gently on the arm. "Don't worry," said Scarface.

THE THROAT WAS a narrow, rocky valley in a thin line of rocky hills surrounded by freezing marshland. The marshes were not frozen, at least not completely, and to try to go north through them would be foolhardy. Many an unwary traveler had gone into the marshes, never to be seen again. Only the hills, with the Throat as the highway through them, were passable. An actual road, or something like it, a cleared way, had been made in the Throat valley, and it was toward this that the raider band was headed. Once through the Throat, they would wait for a while to see if any Saeditin troops had followed them. If they had, the raiders would ambush them.

By afternoon, as promised, the raiders and their prisoner reached the Throat. There was no longer any sign of pursuit, Scarface regretfully informed Sifuat. Once they were through, they would wait, but he feared it would be in vain.

"Sae Becha knows it is not safe to follow into marsh-

lands. So I will take you home with me, Sudit." He shook
his head at Sifuat's expression. "Wilfrisin don't have
slaves." Sifuat was unfamiliar with the term, so Scarface explained. "Northerners," he said. "Barbarians." There was an
ironic glint in his eyes. "We have no slaves. You will be a
prisoner, but that is not so bad, with us. We will see what
Sae Becha will give for you."

"Ransom," said Sifuat. "That's why you took me. Ransom."

Scarface smiled at him. "In a way, Sudit. In a way."

The raider scouts came back. The Throat was clear. It appeared that no one had been this way since their own party
came through some days before. There was still no sign of
pursuit. Sifuat was bound and gagged again, this time with
his hands tied behind his back, which increased his discomfort and made him work harder to hold his balance on horseback but gave the raiders even more control over him. After
his failed escape attempt, they didn't trust him. He rode behind Scarface and another raider, tethered to the second
raider. The stony hills rose around them, still brown and
seemingly lifeless; spring had not yet arrived here.

Sifuat kept his eyes on the raiders ahead of him and tried
not to think. Every scrubby, rocky patch of earth they covered reminded him that he was being taken away from
everything he knew and cared about, and depression settled
on him like a gray fog. So he was slow to react when the
first arrows whistled around them, and the raider to whom
he was tethered slumped in the saddle. Scarface screamed
something in the barbarian tongue, but Sifuat didn't have to
speak it to know what it meant. "Ambush!" was what it
meant. The arrow protruding from the chest of the barbarian ahead of him was notched in the distinctive pattern of
the Saeditin army. Scarface dragged him from his horse.

Sifuat dropped to the ground like a sack of lead, unable
to protect his face or his stiff shoulder. Raiders cried out,
rolling and diving for cover among the rocks at the side of
the trail, trying to return the fire. But they were caught in the
natural trap of the Throat, the trap in which they had hoped
to catch the Saeditin troops. All around and above them on

the barren, rocky hills were Saeditin archers, and the barbarians dropped, silent or screaming, but they dropped.

Scarface pulled Sifuat in front of him, like a shield. Sifuat was beginning to get his breath back despite the gag, despite the pain of his bonds. He struggled against the man's hands but ceased abruptly when he felt the bite of a knife blade against his throat.

"Hold still," panted the raider chief, "or I kill you! I will if I must!"

Sifuat believed him.

"Stop shooting," shouted Scarface to the listening hills, "stop shooting or I kill him!"

The shooting stopped. All around was quiet but for the gasping moan of a wounded barbarian. Sifuat felt his skin begin to crawl. He knew his countrymen, and they were not going to let Scarface get away with this. That Sifuat might die in the confrontation was undesirable, but it wouldn't stop them now that they had committed themselves to this fight. Victory was more important. This barbarian couldn't know what he was facing. But it seemed he guessed, because he shouted out quickly, before whatever was going to happen could happen.

"Sae Becha, come out! I know you are here! I want to talk! I have of interest more than just the life of this man, this Sudit husband!"

There was more silence, a long silence, too long. Sifuat tensed against the knife, tensed against whatever was coming.

"I am sure you do," said Rilsin. From the sound of her voice she was just behind and slightly above them, but Sifuat couldn't turn to see. "Don't turn around, Wilfrisin. If he dies, so do you." Then she said something else, something in the barbarian language. There was another pause, and Scarface seemed to be thinking. Rilsin said something else in an unintelligible flow of sound.

"I must trust," said Scarface, in Saeditin. "There is no choice."

The knife was gone, and the barbarian no longer held him. Sifuat lost his balance and sprawled. There was a rush of footfalls. Someone pulled him up, pulled the gag from his mouth, stood him on his feet. It was a Saeditin trooper, and behind him was Rilsin, looking dirty, tired, and grim, but relieved. The barbarian chief had been disarmed, and now *his* hands were being tied.

"Are you all right?" Rilsin looked at him.

"Fine. Someone untie me." He jerked his head backward at his hands, and the soldier beside him cut the ropes. While this was happening, Rilsin spoke to the raider again in the barbarian language. Sifuat looked around. Of the twenty raiders, only three seemed to be alive, the leader and two others, and both of the others were wounded, one badly.

"Sifuat!" Rilsin had been speaking to him, and he didn't hear. His thoughts were elswehere.

"I said, what is this man's name, since he seems reluctant to tell me! And what else do you know about him?"

Sifuat stared at her, feeling a flush start to creep into his cheeks. It never occurred to him to find out the leader's name or anything about him. He had been content to think of him as Scarface.

"I am Bilt of the Wilfrisin," said the barbarian with a slight smile and a glance at Sifuat. For a man who might be dead at any moment, he seemed very at ease.

The name obviously meant something to Rilsin. She looked at him more carefully. "And what," she said, "is the leader of the Wilfrisin doing this far south, in the territory of the Clinsi, on a raiding mission that is more suited to the youngest and most untried of men?"

Sifuat frowned. It had never occurred to him that the differences between barbarians were of any importance. Ever since Scarface—Bilt—told him the name Wilfrisin, he assumed it referred to all barbarians.

"I came to talk to you, Sae Becha. To get your attention."

"You got my attention, all right. But if you wanted to talk to me, why not just ask?"

"You know why. Saeditin do not talk to barbarians. *Saedin* do not talk to barbarians. You fight us and you kill us—if we do not kill you first—and you take us as captives and steal our children to work for you or to sell to the lands in the south. But you do not talk. So I came to steal a saedin, and if I could, a saedin important to you, Sae Becha, to make you come and talk with me."

"And what makes you think I will talk to you now, barbarian, now that I have him back and have you as well?"

Rilsin had flushed slightly at the barbarian's catalogue of supposed wrongs, Sifuat saw. He assumed she was angry, since he was. It was foolish for barbarians to question the use saedin had for them.

"You will talk, or at least you will listen, because Sae Becha hates injustice, or so I have heard. And because Sae Becha wants peace for her people. As I want peace for mine."

"If you want peace for the Wilfrisin, why raid Saeditin farms, why kill Saeditin children, why kidnap a saedin?"

She was angry, Sifuat saw, but there was something else there as well. In a moment, and with some surprise, he identified it as something like embarrassment.

"I do not raid. I merely steal this saedin, this Norimin Sudit son, when he puts himself in my hands like gift." Bilt frowned. "If there was a raid, it was not mine. Maybe Clinsi, young Clinsi men. I would stop that."

"You would stop that! And how would you, a Wilfrisin, stop a Clinsi raid?"

"Ah, Sae Becha, that is subject for my talk with you!" Bilt shifted, and the muscles in his arms bunched. He wanted to use his hands when he talked, but they were tied behind him. "I have many Clinsi friends, and many friends in Trift lands as well. I want Wilfrisin, Clinsi, Trift, all, all to be together. One land with one leader, as is Saeditin. I can do this better if Saeditin troops do not kill us, and better still if Sae Becha sends Saeditin troops to help me."

He had finished and was waiting for a response. Rilsin said nothing. She merely stared at this tall, scarred northerner with her mouth slightly open, as if she couldn't believe what she just heard. In fact, she couldn't. Saeditin soldiers glanced at one another, glanced away again. No one spoke, and the only sound was the moaning of the wounded raider.

"Let me get this clear," she said at last. "You want me to help you make war against the other tribes so that you can unite them."

"Yes."

Rilsin laughed, a puffing sound, more an exhalation than a laugh. She held up her hands in rejection and refusal and started to shake her head. "No," she said, "Oh no. I'm not getting involved in barbarian tribal conflicts!" She didn't get any farther. Bilt broke in.

"Not much conflict, Sae Becha, truly, not much! I have many, many friends who think as I do. Just knowing Saeditin troops will help me should discourage my enemies. And then there will be peace. Peace in the north, and peace with Saeditin. No more raids across border, no more killing of children, burning of farms."

Indeed, thought Rilsin, *just a united nation to the north, under a strong leader.*

"I will sign a treaty," said Bilt. "We have amber and salt and wood." He paused and smiled at her. "All of which go south to our ally Saeditin. You will still be much stronger than we will be. And Saeditin never worries about the north again. All armies can look to southern lands. To Runchot. If Saeditin needs help, the north will come."

Rilsin was not smiling anymore. "And if Bilt needs help?"

"If the north needs help, Saeditin comes. But I tell you, Sae Becha, I think I will win this war even without your help; it will just take longer. With your help, it will be fast. We help each other, and we trade. We all eat well, get rich, and not waste," he paused, thinking, then shrugged, "not waste everything in fighting. And no more children get taken. Not by us, not by you. And maybe you will give us the machine that burns the coal to make heat for our homes. Winter is very long and cold."

"Maybe," said Rilsin. She knew Bilt was a strong leader and was surprised to find him here. "This is a big gamble you took."

"But a gamble I will win. And you will win, too, if you help me."

"Not so fast. I can make peace for Saeditin, yes, but only the SaeKet can approve the conditions."

"Which she will do, if you explain to her why. You came to pacify the north, yes? This is how."

"This is what I will do. First of all, I will give you your life. And I will give you your freedom. I will not pursue you, attack you, or attack any northern village. We will stay on our side of the border unless we are forced to defend ourselves or to stop raids. If you can stop the raids, and if you come close to uniting the tribes, Bilt, then we will help you. It is not what you ask, but it is all I will give and more than you have a right to expect. What do you say?"

"I say, agreed. This is not a thing you will regret, Sae Becha."

"We will see."

She nodded to a soldier, who cut Bilt's bonds. Bilt immediately went to kneel by the seriously wounded raider, putting his hand on the man's brow and whispering something to him. Rilsin came up beside him.

"He will not live," she said, "but he will linger."

"No," said Bilt, "he will not." He whispered something to the wounded man, who tried to grasp his hand and nodded.

Rilsin, standing close enough to hear what was said, drew her knife and gave it to Bilt. Several soldiers started forward when they saw this, but she waved them back. It was over very quickly, and Bilt did not draw back from the blood that coated his quilted shirt. When he rose, he had tears in his eyes, but he said nothing. Rilsin gave him and his one remaining warrior their horses, they put the body on another, and there was silence as they rode away to the north. Rilsin turned and looked at Sifuat.

"Time to go home," she said.

It was only later that he learned how the ambush was accomplished.

"We hid down in the marshes on either side of the Throat," Rilsin told him, "until we were sure Bilt had checked it and found it clear. They didn't think to look in the icy water; they didn't imagine we would hide in that. Then

we had to hurry, to scramble up there before he got you
through the Throat. I took a chance that they wouldn't look
in the water, and I took a chance that they wouldn't hurt you
when we attacked." She looked at him over the fire that
burned, once again, outside their tent. "I don't know what I
would have done if I had been wrong."

RILSIN KEPT HER word. No Saeditin troops crossed the border to the north, and they took no northern captives. Rilsin
did send her spies, and they reported to her that Bilt of the
Wilfrisin was making great progress. His idea was one
whose time had come, it seemed. The Trift joined him willingly, without a fight, due to ties of marriage and kinship
between the two peoples, as well as a shared dialect. Bilt
announced the birth of the Wilfrisin Confederacy and invited the Clinsi to join on equal terms.

"Something like a saedhold," Rilsin's agent old her, "but
with more powers."

The Clinsi refused. Bilt held out the threat of Saeditin in-
volvement, which the Clinsi did not take seriously. Rilsin's
agents told her that he would, indeed, win in time, so she did
two things, as she had promised. She sent a second, in-depth
report to Sithli, and she went north as Bilt's ally.

She had more troops than she could possibly use. As it
happened, Norimin's personal and saedhold guard num-
bered twenty thousand, a fact that her mother-in-law deliberately let slip to her over dinner one night in her Hoptrin
mansion. Rilsin had thought there were two thousand.

"Oh, they are not all under arms at one time," she said
when Rilsin goggled at her, "but as protector of the north, I
never know when they might be needed. If the SaeKet
wants them, they can be called up at a moment's notice." It
was necessary for her to report only those held under arms
to the SaeKet, which accounted for the difference. "If you
need them, Rilsin," said Norimin, "they are yours. They
want to fight for you."

Rilsin stored this information away to think about later.
She would not need them for this campaign, nor would she
need the troops from Tillit saedhold, whose actual and re-

ported numbers tallied at three thousand. She had had time
to pay her respects to Essit's family as well, in the weeks of
waiting. She and Sifuat thoroughly enjoyed themselves, and
so did the army, which had only drills and training and lib-
erty in the towns, but no real war. By the time they marched
north, spring was in full swing, with trees blossoming and
the skies filled with light.

"It's a time for lovers," Sifuat told her, "not for war. It's
a time for us."

"All times are times for us," Rilsin said. She couldn't
help smiling when she looked at him. "This will be over
soon, and I will be back for you. Norimin seems more mel-
low these days; surely you can stand her for a few weeks
until I return." In love though she was, Rilsin did not make
the mistake of asking him to accompany her. "Believe me,
sweetheart, this will be fast. If the reply does not come in
time from Sithli SaeKet, I don't know how long I can stall.
I should have heard by now."

But the reply came just before she left, by sun-flash. "All
necessary authority is yours," the mirrors told her. Confirmation by courier came later and followed her north.

21

It was green and cool in the deep northern forest. It seemed peaceful; a false impression, Rilsin knew. A large Clinsi column, the bulk of their best fighters, along with some badly needed supplies for Clinsi towns whose supply routes had been cut by the Wilfrisin and Saeditin, was making its way toward them right now. If Rilsin and Bilt stopped this column, the war would not last much longer.

She lay on her stomach, her face partly concealed by a monstrous fern, which was obscenely larger than its Saeditin relatives, her black and gray uniform pressed into the spongy moss and cool forest floor. All around her, unseen, her troopers, dressed the same way, were doing the same thing, awaiting her signal. She was awaiting the signal from the Wilfrisin scout.

"We have to trust them," Rilsin had told Essit, when he objected, saying they should send their own scouts and not rely on the barbarians. "The whole point is mutual trust. You must stop thinking of them as barbarians. They are our allies."

"They fight like barbarians," Essit said, "like wild animals lurking behind trees, not like human beings, in armies."

"Well, Sae Essit, we shall fight that way, too, if we want to live to see Saeditin again. Blundering through the woods is a sure way to get killed." Rilsin found it elegant to combine woodcraft with battle in a way that she found difficult to explain to other Saeditin but that she suspected the northerners understood.

So now she, and Essit, and two hundred Saeditin soldiers lay hidden in this forest, waiting for the signal from a Wilfrisin scout. It eventually came: a marsh hawk's cry repeated four times in rapid succession. It was like something out of a children's tale, thought Rilsin, but her palms were damp and her heart sped up. She waited a few seconds and then reached out a hand to find Essit's shoulder, giving it a squeeze: *Be ready.* The signal was passed. And then she heard something, the crackle of leaves and twigs breaking. Peering around her fern, she saw the first flash of movement down the forest road they flanked.

"Now!" she cried.

From their hiding places in brush and ferns and boulders, the Saeditin archers let loose a volley at the Clinsi. Then the rest of the Saeditin were up and running, crashing into the Clinsi column. The Clinsi were surprised but not as disorganized as Rilsin hoped they would be, or at least they rallied quickly; they were accustomed to the idea of ambush in the forest. It soon became clear that the Clinsi idea of organization was not the Saeditin idea of organization. The Clinsi were infuriated by the ambush, and in their fury each Clinsi warrior tried to prove that he or she was the fiercest of them all. If this led to breaking ranks, the Clinsi didn't think it mattered. But the Saeditin blocked their progress and flanked them, and behind them were the Wilfrisin, or so Rilsin hoped.

Rilsin raced forward. In front of her was one of the tallest women she had ever seen, a woman who had dyed her long hair an odd blue green color and tied it up in spikes, in keeping with some odd northern tradition, and who had stained her teeth red and streaked her face red in honor of the north-

ern battle goddess. She screamed something at the top of
her considerable lungs and brandished a sword and a long
dagger. She had no shield because she was a fore-fighter,
one of the northern best. Rilsin danced just out of her very
long reach. She was nervous and jittery, not at all in the
calm battle clarity she needed.

"Hey," she said in Wilfrisin, the only northern dialect in
which she could think without effort, and one that she was
sure the giantess understood, "are you truly as stupid as you
look? If you are as stupid as you are ugly, how do you know
your goddess will accept you when you die?" She hoped
this would rub the raw religious nerve of her opponent.
Some of the fore-fighters, she knew, were first in battle out
of guilt over crimes they committed or because they were
otherwise outcasts at the margins of their tribes and hoped
to win the favor of the gods this way. She wanted her opponent to lose caution and rush her, letting down her guard.

"She will accept me because of the sacrifices I give her,"
said the Clinsi, "sacrifices like you." She spoke not in Clinsi
or Wilfrisin dialect but in good, unaccented Saeditin, and
she followed her answer up with a feint at Rilsin and then a
low cut aimed under Rilsin's guard.

Surprise slowed Rilsin down, almost too long. She recovered just in time to avoid a serious wound but not in time
to avoid the long dagger that followed the sword, but from
the other side, slicing up through the cloth of her sleeve and
drawing a long cut in the underside of her upper arm when
she threw her left arm up, at the last moment, to defend herself. Her breath came in a hiss of pain. The Clinsi laughed.

Well, thought Rilsin, *so much for getting her to let down
her guard.* And then: *Perhaps Essit was right, and I should
not be risking myself in this battle. I could have stayed back,
as he suggested. How will Sithli manage if I don't come
home, and what will Sifuat do?* Following these thoughts
was a throb of concern for Saeditin itself. Saeditin needed
her. Anger followed this thought. With the anger came the
clarity she needed, that calm place where time slowed
down, where she saw every move her opponent made almost before her opponent could think of it. She said noth-

ing but moved in closer, fast, almost as if she were dancing. She smiled slightly, no longer feeling the pain in her arm.

It was only a moment before the Clinsi giant realized that everything had changed, but it was a moment too long. It seemed to her that the Saeditin woman was everywhere, anticipating her every move, drawing blood not once but three times. Nonplussed, she tried to retreat, to give herself time to think, but the Saeditin saw this, too, and somehow when she stepped back, the Saeditin woman was there, and then she was on the ground, with the Saeditin woman kneeling on her, pinning her sword arm.

"I'm sorry," said the Saeditin just before she cut her throat.

Rilsin took her opponent's long dagger, noticing as she did so, with some strange detached part of her mind, that the woman's blue green hair was blonde at the roots. But her victory had been noted by other Clinsi, and she was rushed by two of them. Rilsin was on her feet, killing first one and then the other. The Saeditin saw this, as well, and they began to shout her name. Rilsin fought her way down the Clinsi column, which was a column no longer but a ragged mass of warriors, fighting bitterly.

Her soldiers followed her, and the world narrowed to a succession of encounters with sword and dagger, all of which Rilsin won. After a while, she realized that there were fewer Clinsi to fight, and then there were none, except right ahead of her, where a group of Clinsi had surrounded two Wilfrisin, who fought desperately. All around there were overturned wagons, dead and wounded horses, the wounded ones still screaming, and there were human wounded as well, some of them still screaming, too. Rilsin and her Saeditin had fought their way back to the Wilfrisin, in the process killing or capturing virtually all of the Clinsi. There were still a few knots of Clinsi here, however, fighting small knots of Wilfrisin, like the one right in front of her. Rilsin realized why she was so interested in this group. One of the Wilfrisin under attack was Bilt.

As she realized this, she also realized that she was now alone, that there were no other Saeditin with her after all.

Somehow she had left her soldiers behind her. Now one of
the Clinsi noticed her, noticed her and recognized her. He
gave a shout that was more like a scream, and Clinsi broke
off from other groups to rally around him. He pointed at
Rilsin, and she heard "Sae Becha." When she heard her
name, the clarity, the light around her that had guided her
through the battle, left her, and exhaustion took its place.
She felt her arm begin to throb from the wound.

In less time than it took to think about it, Rilsin was surrounded. She had just time to back up against a pile of overturned wagons, one smouldering slightly from someone's
attempt to set fire to it. She held her sword at the ready, but
her left hand, the one with the dagger, dragged from the pain
of the wound in her arm. Her opponents began to taunt her,
"Sae Becha! Sae Becha!" in high voices. A few of them
were painted, and all wore patchworks of leather and linen
and fur. They looked like barbarians.

"Saeditin!" she shouted. "Here! Saeditin!" But her voice
was hoarse from exhaustion, no longer strong. There was no
response to her cry for help, except from her enemies, who
began to taunt, whining, "Saeditin! Sae Becha!" There were
five of them, four men and a woman. They meant to finish
her, but they also meant to take their time and enjoy themselves doing it.

"You take her left," said the woman to one of the men, in
Clinsi, "and I'll come from the right. Jas can come in the
front under her guard. When I give the word!"

She never gave the word. Rilsin pushed herself away
from the wagon, ran her through the throat, pulled her
sword free, and cut the first man open from stomach to rib
cage. Jas she got at the last moment, with the dagger, which
she thrust through his eye into his brain. It stuck there, and
she had to abandon it. Her remaining two opponents
stepped back, giving her a wider berth, but they kept her
hemmed in.

"She must speak Clinsi!" said one to the other, as they
glanced in disbelief at their dead friends.

"Not perfectly," said Rilsin in that dialect, "but well
enough to get by."

Without so much as a glance at each other, the two men rushed her. Rilsin ducked and struck, wounding one, but not seriously. Her shelter of wagons now seemed more like a hindrance. What she would have really liked to do was run, but she was stuck between the wagons and the enemy, so she gritted her teeth, tried to ignore her throbbing arm, and deal with the two Clinsi. They were not as easy as their friends, however, and Rilsin barely managed to keep them off, taking several minor nicks and cuts. She heard someone breathing heavily, almost gasping, and when she realized it was herself, she knew she had to finish this fast.

With what felt like the last of her strength, she jumped back out of reach and then fell back against one of the wagons, propping herself with her wounded arm, looking as if she were going to collapse any minute. Her sword drooped toward the ground. She thought of it as a ruse, but it was very close to the truth.

With a shout, one of the men lunged toward her, not waiting for his friend in his haste to be the one to finish off the enemy commander. At the last possible moment, she ran him through the heart. She turned to face her final opponent and realized that she was too late. He was already inside her guard, too close. In another moment she would be dead. He was, truly, her final opponent. With a cry and a look of absolute astonishment on his face, the Clinsi pitched forward. Rilsin pulled back just in time to avoid having him fall on her. A sword protruded from his back.

"Sorry to be late," said Bilt. "I heard you call before, but I have business." He looked at her. "Business was successful, as was yours, I see." He waved at the bodies that littered the ground around them. Rilsin just stared at him, breathing in great rasping shudders. "Hey, Sae Becha, you look terrible."

Rilsin found her voice. "So do you," she said. "You're covered with blood."

"And what is that all over you, then?"

She looked at herself. He was right, she was a gory mess. "Most of this isn't mine."

"Most of this is not mine, either. I hope my sword did not

break in that stupid Clinsi. I like that sword." He put his foot
on the dead Clinsi's back, grasped his sword hilt with both
hands, and pulled. It came free, and it was not broken.

Rilsin looked around. All the fighting had ceased. There
were a few Clinsi left alive, but they were prisoners. The
Saeditin were coming up now, having caught up with her at
last, and she saw Essit coming toward her, looking relieved.

"Bilt," she said, "thank you. You saved my life."

Bilt looked up from examining his sword. "We are allies," he said.

"I know. Thank you."

"We are also friends." He smiled at her and held out one
large hand. Rilsin clasped it.

"Yes," she said.

After this it went even faster and better than Rilsin imagined it could. The Clinsi had no desire to face a well-trained
Saeditin army, and they fled from her until they were caught
again between her force and Bilt's. There was another battle, in which the Clinsi were easily defeated, with few casualties to Rilsin or Bilt. Then there were skirmishes with a
few holdout bands, but before long they had all been hunted
down, and Rilsin prepared to sign the peace treaty and return home. High summer had just begun.

On the morning of the treaty signing, Rilsin woke early
after a restless night. Her head ached and she felt dull and
tired, as she had for the past two weeks. Her arm was healing well, but she suspected it had given her some sort of lin-
gering illness, an exhaustion she just couldn't shake. More
likely, it was camp fever. There had been a minor outbreak,
which she thought she had escaped. Obviously she had not.
But today was the treaty signing, and she needed to look
alert and well, a suitable representative of Saeditin and the
SaeKet.

Rilsin heaved herself out of bed and rushed for the corner of the tent where the night pot was kept. She barely
reached it in time and knelt down, clutching it, fighting the
urge to vomit, and losing. When she was done, she felt
shaky and weak, but she knew from experience that this
would pass. It was one of the marks of this illness.

She wiped her mouth and dressed, forcing herself to think about eating something for breakfast. Right now, even more than Sifuat, she missed Chilsa. When she was sick, the cat always seemed to know, and he followed her around and rubbed against her to comfort her. But Chilsa was back in Hoptrin, under Sifuat's care. By the time she left the tent she was convinced she looked well, or well enough.

"Sae Becha, my friend!" Bilt was waiting for her, well before the time the little ceremony was due to start. He had come to her own camp with just a few of his warriors. He was resplendent in leather trousers stitched with gold thread, and a fur-trimmed shirt, which must have been unbearably hot even in this northern summer. He held out his hands to her.

"First Man Bilt," Rilsin smiled and took his hands. She had become very fond of the big, scarred northerner during the past weeks of their joint campaign, and she was certain he felt the same way about her.

"Today we make it all official," said Bilt. "Saeditin and Wilfrisin Confederacy become allies, and enemies no longer! Have you eaten?" When Rilsin shook her head no, he had a suggestion. "Yesterday my men make a kill, a big buck, for the feast. They roast it last night, and look, I have some here, my own breakfast." He pulled some from the depths of the fur-trimmed shirt. "You share with me!"

"Thank you, no." Rilsin thought she actually felt the blood leaving her face when she looked at the greasy lump he held. "I'm not hungry."

Bilt watched her. "It is not as though I offer you the special treat of the eyeball," he joked, "since I ate them both myself." When he saw the sweat break out on her face, he became serious. "It is true, then, the reports. You are ill. You must see my physician as soon this treaty is done."

"I'm fine." Rilsin was embarrassed. "Well, no, it is true, I have been feeling a little off. That is quite the intelligence system you have, my friend." Bilt grinned at this. "But it is nothing serious, only camp fever, and I will be going home soon."

"My physician is good; he is never wrong. We are not barbarians, as you truly know, Sae Becha, my friend."

"I know, I know—"

"But perhaps it is only that you miss the handsome Sudit son. I remember young love!"

"You are not that old, First Man!"

"I am the grandfather of my people now, so I must be wise."

The banter carried them past the awkward moment, but Rilsin resolved to see a physician, a Saeditin physician, if the malady did not pass soon.

The treaty signing was in what passed for the main square of the Trift town. In fact, it was the only square. There were no trees to shade the tables, one with papers and ritual implements, the others groaning with food for the feast, from which Rilsin hastily turned away. Members of the new Confederacy were everywhere, dressed in their finest furs and leathers and linens, and some of them, the very richest, in imported cotton. The town was crammed to its limit with visitors, most staying with relatives or friends, since the small inn was the first to fill, and others camped in the fields at the edge of town or in the surrounding woods.

Rilsin entered, dressed in her black and gray uniform. Essit, her second in command, was beside her, and they were followed by a small squad of Saeditin soldiers. The people cheered Rilsin and the Saeditin almost as much as they cheered Bilt; Rilsin's popularity had been growing ever since the first fight in the forest. She and Essit and Bilt and his officer sat in the chairs set for them, unfortunately in the full sun. At least her soldiers and Bilt's warriors were able to stand back toward the crowd, where there was a little more shade.

The proceedings went faster than Rilsin had feared they would. There were the requisite blessings by priests of both nations, but the sacrifices had thankfully been dealt with previously and elsewhere. She and Bilt must each make a brief speech, and she made hers in Wilfrisin, for the benefit of the crowd, which cheered her with enthusiasm. Then there was the treaty itself to sign, several copies on paper,

laboriously written out by hand, since they were far from
the printing presses of Saeditin, and one copy on actual
cured sheepskin, as all documents once were in Saeditin as
well as the north. Then it was time for the celebration. Not
only was Rilsin anxious to get out of the sun, but she was
actually feeling hungry now, and she looked toward the
laden food tables with anticipation.

"Sae Becha."

The gravity in Bilt's voice caused her to turn and face
him, remembering that there was one more serious matter to
be dealt with. Beside Bilt was a woman a little younger than
he, blonde, and as fair-skinned as he and as Rilsin herself.
Although she had powdered her face, Rilsin could tell she
had been crying. She held a little boy of about three years
tightly by the hand.

"My wife," said Bilt, "the lady Ticha. And my son
Lendis."

"Hello, Lendis," said Rilsin, bending down. She held out
her hands. The child shrank back against his mother, who
pulled him close.

"Let him go to Sae Becha," said Bilt. There was such
grimness in his voice that Rilsin flinched.

"This is not my choice," Rilsin said, straightening. She
spoke first to Bilt, then to Ticha, whose gaze she held.

"It is custom," said Bilt, "and expected. It was agreed."

"I would not hold you to it, did the SaeKet not insist. I
can assure you, I *promise* you, that he will be treated well.
He will be in the SaeKet's household, and she will treat him
as she would her own son." Rilsin suppressed a sudden
doubt about how Sithli would treat a son of her own, if she
had one.

"I do not doubt that, my friend," said Bilt. "I would ask
you—"

"Rilsin sae Becha," Ticha broke in. "I put my Lendis into
your care, not the care of Sithli sae Melisin, called Sithli
SaeKet." Her Saeditin was pure and unaccented, so much
better than Bilt's that Rilsin blinked. "I charge you with his
care and well-being, even though he will not live with you,
but in the household of Sae Melisin. And I charge you with

more than that. Love him, if you can, Sae Rilsin." She stroked Lendis's hair with such tenderness that Rilsin's heart ached. "He is only a little boy, and he has never been away from me before. He needs love, a mother's love." She fought back tears. "You would understand if you had a child of your own. Please. Take care of him. You, not Sithli SaeKet. Please." She thrust Lendis's little hand into Rilsin's, turned, and strode away. By the time she reached the edge of the crowd, she was running.

"I apologize for my Ticha." Bilt followed his wife with his eyes.

"Don't," said Rilsin softly.

"Mama." It was almost a whimper, a little despairing cry. Lendis looked after his mother, one small fist clenched. The hand that Rilsin held spasmed, twitching like a little animal. Rilsin felt a stab at her heart. Another child losing another mother. She dropped to her knees.

"Lendis, sweetheart, don't cry! I'll take care of you!" She spoke in Wilfrisin and gathered the child into her arms, where he stood stiffly, still sobbing. She looked up at Bilt, and saw, to her horror, that he, too, was fighting back tears.

"I would have given you anything else," he said, "anything but my favorite child, my son. I would have given you my daughter, but she is less than a year old, and not heir. Not my heir." Unlike the Saeditin, the northerners preferred that boys inherit. "And your SaeKet, she holds me tight." He held up his hand, squeezed his fist to show how tight. "It is high price for peace." Tears leaked from the corner of his eyes. Lendis saw this and cried harder. "Sae Becha, do not let him forget who he is. He will come home someday. Someday he must be Wilfrisin again, true northerner. Do not let your SaeKet make him Saeditin!"

Rilsin stared at him, taken aback. It never occurred to her that anyone would not want to be Saeditin, if they could. "I will do what I can, my friend, what I can. He will understand both worlds. We are not so different."

Bilt shook his head, looking bitterly into the distance. "Different enough," he said, "but peace was my plan. Mine. And it was only way."

"You are right." Rilsin decided to be candid. "Soon, not this year, not next, but soon, we would have marched north and conquered you. You have saved your people, First Man." She looked at the child in her arms. "I will make sure Lendis has everything. Including love, Bilt. Including love. And I will make sure he doesn't forget you."

Essit had been watching the little drama from a distance. Now he came forward.

"I will take the child, Commander." He held out a hand.

Rilsin got to her feet, feeling exhausted again. She still had Lendis's hand in her own. "Not yet, Sae Essit. He can stay with me for now, and he can go to his parents tonight, if they wish. We won't take him until just before we march south, tomorrow." She looked wearily at the child, who still sniffled. "Don't cry, Lendis, please don't cry, baby." Without thinking, she spoke in Saeditin. To her surprise, Lendis pulled himself away from her, drawing himself up to his small height.

"Not baby!" he said in Saeditin. "Not baby! Big boy!"

"Good!" said Rilsin. "Good for you, Lendis! Would you like some honey bread?"

22

PETIPAL WAS DECORATED TO THE TEETH AND STREWN WITH flowers to welcome her home. It was a brilliant, sunny summer day, and the roads to the city were lined with cheering crowds. Rilsin expected a celebration, since she knew her people loved a pageant, but nothing like this, especially since the Saeditin were more interested in victories than in treaties signed and conflict averted.

"You deserve it," Sifuat told her. "And it is a victory, sweetheart, against the Clinsi. You fought hard. The people have missed you." He had spent the months of her northern campaign working with his mother's troops in Hoptrin, which kept him from the boredom he tended to experience away from the capital.

"I wonder if Sithli has."

Sithli's mood and Sithli's welcome were on her mind for most of the march south. The official messages were all congratulatory and pleasant, but there had been no private communications from Sithli, and Rilsin felt she had reason to be concerned. She would meet her cousin officially at the palace, the emmissary told her, after she paraded her troops through the streets. Rilsin was not in a celebratory mood, herself.

"Let's get this over with," was her only comment.

She rode through the streets on horseback, in her black and gray uniform, with Sifuat beside her in the gray and lavender of the northern guards, and Essit sae Tillit riding slightly behind her. On the saddle right in front of her, dressed in plain, unbleached cotton trousers and overshirt, sat Lendis. She pointed things out to the child every now and then: the great market square, the shrines, the old guild quarter, the more recent lending house. She spoke only in Saeditin. The little boy's eyes were wide, and sometimes, when Rilsin waved at the crowd, he waved, too. One woman was so enchanted by the child that she rushed up, almost beneath the horse's hooves, to hold up two garlands of roses.

"For you, Sae Rilsin, and your foster son!"

Rilsin accepted the garlands, smiling, and put one around her own and one around Lendis's neck. But Lendis was not her foster son. Lendis belonged to the SaeKet, as tradition demanded; he was the SaeKet's foster son.

It seemed as though the entire population of the city turned out for the parade, and more. They were dressed in their best, cheering and waving and throwing flowers at her, at Sifuat, at her troops, and at the few astonished and unhappy Clinsi prisoners they brought back, the very last northern captives. Underneath the perfume of all the flowers lay the pervasive smell of the city in the summer, the mingled scents of horses and horse dung, slightly rotting garbage, cooking, and human beings crammed together in close quarters. On top of this was the drift of incense from the shrines and temples. It smelled like home, and Rilsin smiled.

The main temple was the first stop, so that Rilsin and the troops could be blessed and undergo a very rapid purification. The procession halted in the temple square, with most of the troops spilling out into the street. Priests walked quickly down the lines, wafting incense over the soldiers,

cleansing them from whatever blood they had shed. A
trickle of coughing marked their progress.

Rilsin, Sifuat, Essit, and a few other officers dismounted
and climbed the steps to the temple itself. Rilsin carried one
of the copies of the new treaty to deposit in the temple.
Lendis trotted along, his hand in the hand of one of the officers. When she was momentarily distracted, he ran forward and pulled at Rilsin's uniform. She looked down,
smiled, and took his hand.

The temple was dim and cool, and it, too, was wreathed
with flowers. But the first thing that Rilsin noticed was that
she would not be meeting Sithli at the palace. Sithli was
here. She stood behind the priests, dressed in her formal
green and gold, all silks and jewels. She smiled at Rilsin
with clear and obvious delight.

Rilsin presented the treaty to the priests. She allowed
herself to be censed and smudged and sprinkled. She was
conscious of Sifuat beside her and her officers behind her,
and of Lendis, bowing his head, kneeling, holding out his
hands, just as she coached him. But the center of her attention, throughout all of this, was the beautiful, blazing figure
of her cousin. The small ceremony did not last very long,
but when it was finally finished, Rilsin felt as though she
had been standing in the temple for an eternity. The priests
moved aside, and she was face-to-face with Sithli.

"SaeKet," she said, putting her hand to heart, bowing her
head. In the next moment she was surrounded and engulfed
in silks and jewels and scented, elegantly braided blonde
hair.

"Oh, Rils, I'm so glad you're back! I've been miserable
without you! Petipal is such a garbage heap! Wait till you
see the new bracelet I had made! And I had one made for
you, even though I know you won't wear it much!"

Rilsin laughed, feeling some of the tension melt away.
She embraced her cousin. "I've missed you, too! I sent you
all those letters—"

"I know. And I sent you only official answers! You know
I'm not much for writing! Now that you're here, we can go
out to my new palace in the hills, where it's cooler!"

"Sithli, I just got here! We just got here!"

Sithli took the hint and turned to formally greet Rilsin's officers. As she did this, Lendis moved forward, for the moment ignored and overlooked by everyone. He had been watching everything, but he was particularly fascinated by the beautiful blonde woman in the glorious green. He had never seen anyone like her. Her clothing shone, her hair looked so soft, and she smelled wonderful. While Rilsin was distracted, carefully watching Sithli give Sifuat a sisterly kiss of welcome, Lendis stepped up to Sithli and grasped her silk overshirt just below her waist. It felt as soft and smooth as he had imagined it would. He reached up to touch her long hair.

Everything froze. Sifuat, smiling at Sithli, Sithli turning to look down at the child, Essit, his mouth partway open in surprise and dismay, the other officers, starting to react. Rilsin reached down and detached the child's hand from her cousin's hair. She started to pull him back, but he wriggled like a kitten and pulled free again.

"You are most beautiful lady!" he said to Sithli. "Are you my new mama?" He stopped, wrinkled his smooth child's brow in thought, as he worked out what he wanted in the unfamiliar Saeditin language. "Will you be my mama till I can go home?"

Sithli's frown of displeasure, just beginning to form, evaporated as she looked down at the little boy. She reached down to smooth his tousled hair.

"Yes," she said. "I'm your mama now. And you are home, Lendis. You belong to me and to Saeditin."

CHILSA WOKE HER up, wanting to go out for his morning romp. Rilsin eased from the bed so as not to disturb Sifuat. Her head hurt again, and she knew she was going to be sick. She slipped into the privy room quietly, sure she had not woken Sifuat, but when she emerged, light-headed and weak, he was sitting up in bed.

"You promised to see Nefit. We have been back in Petipal for more than a week, and you are not better, Rilsin. You must see her."

Rilsin sat on the edge of the bed, stroking the top of Chilsa's head as he lay on the floor by her feet. Every morning she wondered if she could continue with the day, but it always passed.

"I was so sure it would pass, that it was only an illness from my wound." She touched the scar under her left arm, but the wound was healed, and there was no infection. "You are right, love, I must see her. Yes, today." She smiled at him. "It is strange, because in every other way, I have never felt better. I have even put on a little weight, which should please you." Sifuat worried that she was too thin.

It was not until almost evening, the late evening of a Saeditin summer, that she kept her promise. Even though she had been back for a week, there was still too much to do. Bilma had done well in her absence, but he was getting old and was glad to return the responsibilities of first minister to her. All week she struggled to catch up with the myriad details that had escaped notice for the past months. She met with saedin and dira almost too numerous to count, and all week, during all the meetings and the little ostensibly social chats, and all of the parties, she looked for the one face she hadn't seen. She asked, since she was minister of mines and factories, and was told that Sola was in his workshop on the palace grounds, where he was extremely busy and did not wished to be disturbed.

Nefit was waiting for her when Rilsin finally went to the physician's rooms. They were the same rooms she had always had, and going there reminded Rilsin, unavoidably, of times she would rather forget. Maltia was not there. He was an apprentice no longer. Nefit was alone, expecting her, and for some reason Rilsin felt her heart speed up with unaccustomed fear. *Ridiculous,* she told herself. *I have nothing to fear.*

It was not much later that Rilsin left Nefit's chambers. She brushed off two saedin who had discovered where she was and wished to discuss something with her and hurried toward escape, toward the palace gardens, out, anywhere away from people. She was glad, and more than glad that she had not mentioned her plan to visit Nefit to Sithli, since

Sithli would have demanded an immediate accounting. But she would have to know, thought Rilsin with something like despair. She would have to know.

She considered using the old tunnel to freedom near her old room, but it was easier to take the less used corridors. She was out in the gardens at last, in the last light of the summer day, with the late sun riding the edge of the horizon. Fall would be coming soon. The evening breeze had a distinct edge to it.

Because there were people in the gardens and she wished to be alone, Rilsin wandered back through the formal and the less formal gardens until she found herself back by the horse pastures. Without actually deciding to, she headed toward the woods, reverting to the patterns of childhood. True dusk was finally falling when she was on the path to the old hunting lodge.

The woods were still much as they were, green and windy, but the path to the lodge had been widened and cleared. The lodge itself was officially Sola's retreat now, his private workshop and study. He had another workshop as well, one much bigger and with more equipment, but the old lodge was still his favorite place for quiet thought. It had, in fact, been restored and enlarged, so that it only somewhat resembled the dilapidated structure in which three children played so many summers before, or the lodge to which Rilsin and her mother had come in even older times, times almost and perhaps best forgotten.

The lodge sat empty in its little clearing, and the door was locked. Sola, she knew, was at his main workshop, so of course this one would be closed and secured, and it was unreasonable of her to think she could just walk in. She sat on the log bench that stood in the clearing where no furniture used to be and tried to sort out her thoughts.

She tried, but she couldn't seem to make sense of anything. She knew she must go home, that she must tell Sifuat. She loved Sifuat, but it seemed to her that she was always comforting Sifuat, listening to Sifuat, keeping Sifuat happy, advising Sifuat, managing Sifuat. Right now she wanted someone to comfort her, to give her advice, someone she could lean on. And besides, after Sifuat came Norimin, and she shied away from the thought of talking to the old lady. Norimin would be coming south to Petipal any day now. Then there was Sithli. It was this last thought that caused Rilsin to put her head in her hands and moan aloud.

"Rilsin, what is it, what's wrong?"

Rilsin was on her feet, sword drawn and ready before she realized that it was Sola. Sola standing there in the dimness of the twilit woods. He didn't move, just waited for her to sheath her sword with trembling hands. Then he came to her and put his hands on her shoulders, and then, before she could think about it, she was in his arms, and he in hers. She tried desperately not to cry, and after an endless while, she succeeded. She pulled away from him, sniffing. Sola pulled a handkerchief of snow-white linen from his pocket, like a pale flame in the dusk, and handed it to her.

"I looked for you everywhere," she said.

"You didn't look for me at home. You didn't send me a message. But Rils, I didn't want to be found. I thought I should leave you and Sifuat—your husband—alone. I can see I was wrong."

"Oh, Great Mother! What am I going to do?" She sat down on the bench again suddenly, as if arrow-shot. Sola sat beside her.

"You'd better tell me."

She looked at him. "I can't. No one else knows yet. No one but Nefit."

"I heard you were sick, something you picked up in the north. But you're not, are you." It was not a question.

"No."

There was silence for a moment.

"Rilsin, most people, most women, especially, would be pleased."

She looked at him from the corner of her eye without turning. "I'm not most women, Sola. All those years of slop night, for nothing!"

"You didn't guess?"

"No, I didn't guess. I—my moons have not been regular, not ever. Beltrip can do that. *This,*" she emphasized the word, "was the farthest thing from my mind." A part of her couldn't believe she was talking about this with him, but another part of her found it perfectly natural. "Oh, Mother, what will Sithli say? What will Sithli do?"

"If it weren't for what Sithli thinks, you would be happy?"

She thought about this for a minute. "Yes. Yes, I think so. Yes, I would. I never thought about this before. I tried not to. Since I could never have children, I never wanted to think about them." Her voice strengthened. "I want this, Sola. I want this child." Without realizing it, her hand went protectively to cover her stomach. "Sithli can't make me—" She couldn't even finish the thought.

"No, she can't. You are a citizen, and a saedin. She can't make you abort. I'm not convinced she'd want to. She loves you, and she will be your baby's second mother."

"You're right. Of course you're right! That's what I have to tell her, how I have to say it! Thank you, Sola!" Then caution came back. "A Sae Becha child. Oh, Mother, my line is not dead!" It was not clear to Sola if she called on the goddess, or on her own mother. "I will have to be very careful."

"Yes, you will. Very careful. I will help you any way I can. And Sifuat will help you, and Sae Norimin; she's crafty enough. You have many more friends than you think you do. But Rilsin, I have to say—you know I'm not religious. Far from it. But this, well, I don't think this is chance."

Rilsin stared at him, striving to see his expression in the gathering darkness. Scenes flashed across her mind, the purification in Norimin's shrine, the little priest, the egg candle. Did the Great Mother listen to Norimin's prayers, Norimin's schemes? *That way lies folly,* she thought. She said it aloud.

"Perhaps. But I know how it seems."

Looking at him in the growing darkness, Rilsin had a horrifying thought. If that was how it seemed to him, unreligious as he was, how would it seem to the great masses of commoners, most of whom were devout? She began to shudder and then found she couldn't stop.

"Oh, Rilsin!" He put his arm around her again. "It will

work out!" He had the same thought she had, it seemed, for he said, "you should get the word out soon. You and the child will be safe once the commoners know. Even Sithli SaeKet will not risk their anger."

He was right, but Rilsin couldn't speak; she could only shiver. She had a sudden vision of herself fleeing north, with Chilsa and Sola—why Sola, and not Sifuat?—to take shelter with the Wilfrisin Confederacy. But that was impossible. Sithli would hunt her down for sure and destroy the Confederacy in the process. *She has no commanders to match me,* whispered a part of her mind, but she put the thought aside. She could never leave Saeditin, let alone bring it to war for her sake. Her teeth began to chatter.

"Rilsin, come inside, you're freezing. I'll build a fire." When she didn't respond, Sola pulled a key on a thong from around his neck. He unlocked the door, then came back and took her hands, helping her to her feet.

Once the fire was lit, Rilsin found that her mind began to work again. She looked around at the once-familiar room, now flickering with golden firelight and shadows. There were chairs, bookshelves, a big worktable, curtains on the windows, and, in the corner, a bed. The light also flickered over Sola, over his fine brown hair, done in a plain and undecorated braid down his back, with little hairs escaping at the temples. He wore dark linen trousers and a cream-colored short-sleeved cotton overshirt that accentuated his wiry build but also showed that his years of manually struggling with his machines had built up his muscles.

With part of her mind Rilsin planned what to say to Sithli, how to get the news out publicly, how to handle herself. And the other part of her mind told her that Sola was beautiful. As she thought this, he turned and looked at her.

"Come sit near the fire." He pulled a chair in front of the flames and came and took her hand, intending to lead her there. Without conscious will they were in each other's arms again.

What is wrong with me? Rilsin wondered, just before she kissed him.

After a few endless moments, they broke apart.

"We can't do this, Sola." Her voice sounded breathless and high, even in her own ears.

"No," he agreed, "we can't."

Why was she so unhappy that he agreed with her?

23

"NEFIT SAID YOU LEFT HER CHAMBERS WELL BEFORE SUNSET. She would not say what is making you ill, only that you would tell me! No one knew where you were."

Rilsin looked at her husband. Sifuat's big hands were knotted together. He loomed over her in his concern, standing above her where she sat in her parlor. He really had been worried about her, and in his concern he alerted the Mother only knew how many people to the possibility that there might be something very wrong.

"I am fine. But there is something I must tell you. Sit down." She patted the seat beside her on her big sofa. Chilsa, who had been sitting at his feet, immediately took this as an invitation to him and jumped up, so the next few moments were spent sorting out places for people and cat. By the time this was accomplished, Sifuat seemed slightly less nervous. But when she told him, he said nothing at first, merely sat, staring into the fire.

"It can't be true," he said at last. There was something strange in his voice. It wasn't fear for her, nor was it simple disbelief.

"That's what I thought, but Nefit assures me it is."

"So my mother gets her way again."

"Your mother!" Rilsin felt heat begin to flood through her. "Sifuat, this is my child and yours, not Norimin's, whatever she may think!"

"It would be better if you were ill! Now you will have no time at all for me!" He was up and out of the room before Rilsin could do anything more than look after him, openmouthed. It crossed her mind that Sifuat himself was scarcely more than a large child.

SITHLI WAS WAITING for her, and it was obvious that she knew. She was in her formal garden, wearing green and gold. She had dressed for this meeting specifically to make a point. Her guards were out of earshot but within calling distance. Rilsin was their commander, but they were the SaeKet's guards. They would not hesitate to arrest her if Sithli ordered it. How could Sithli know? Who could have told her? Sola would not have, and Sifuat had not yet had the chance.

"Nefit told you," Rilsin blurted. Her nervousness increased as she watched Sithli's eyes. Her cousin's expression was tight and hard.

"There was no need. The Mother Herself told me. She began to whisper to me as soon as I heard that you were ill." Sithli's expression did not change. "I am the SaeKet, and She protects me."

Rilsin swallowed nervously. Of course Sithli would have guessed. Sola had guessed. Sithli was far from stupid, and she was certainly sensitive on this matter. Rilsin would not be surprised if everyone in Saeditin had figured this out before she had. She swallowed again, wishing her throat were not so very dry.

"You knew because you will be the child's second mother." Sola's words came back to her, and she seized on them. "The Great Mother has made this gift not to me alone, but to you." She felt sweat begin to trickle down her neck. Now that she had said it, it sounded feeble. If only she had a better plan! But she had not planned for this, because it had been the farthest thing from her thoughts, literally unthinkable.

"A second mother." Sithli was mulling this over. "No. I will be her first mother. It is for you to do the work of bearing the child; it is for you to give her to me," Sithli smiled suddenly, a pleased smile edged with strangeness.

Rilsin suppressed a shudder. There was something about her cousin that was alien and frightening. A stranger looked out of her cousin's eyes. Just as suddenly, the strangeness passed.

"You will do the work; I will spoil the child! I think that's fair!" Sithli laughed, and now she sounded like herself again. "I can spoil her, but give her back when she cries! What do you think, Rils?"

"I think you have the best of the bargain." Rilsin smiled back at her, her uneasiness fading only a little. "I might have a boy, you know."

"A boy. Yes. Much better than having to go through birth myself and then having to actually live with the little brat."

"I don't understand. I thought you wanted dozens of children."

"Not when you see what they are really like!" Sithli made a face. "There was a rash of births after you left, and I use that word advisedly; I am godmother to three little girls now, Rils, and they all cry and whine! And it doesn't get much better when they age a little, from what I can see. Lendis spends far too much time moping."

"He misses his parents."

"I am his mother now. Anyone else would appreciate being my foster son, but I have had to have Lendis whipped twice already. I don't envy you, Rils. When I have my own, I will have plenty of nurses and tutors for those first few years, to make sure she is civilized properly." Sithli leaned over and idly picked two full-blown summer-roses and began to pull their petals off, one by one. "You should do the same."

Rilsin felt a flash of concern for Lendis, but that must come later.

"I thought you might not be happy about this, Sith."

"You mean, you thought I might be jealous, because I don't have my children yet. I will have them, Rils. A beautiful girl, anyway, that much at least. I have a new lover, you know. I think he's the one. I'm not worried about losing Saeditin to you. I know you too well. You will die before you wrest the land from me." Sithli's expression had gone flat again.

Rilsin stared at her cousin. "You are right, of course. I would die before I harmed you or let any harm come to you."

BY THE TIME Norimin reached Petipal, the news had spread across the land. Rilsin knew that there had been several offers to assassinate her, which Sithli had turned down angrily. The last person to so offer had disappeared, into Runchot, Rilsin's private sources informed her. Rilsin was subjected to advice, concern, and careful scrutiny every day from friends, jealous saedin, awed commoners, gossiping priests, and, of course, the physicians, so she did not expect that Norimin would be able to add anything to this stew. Of course, Norimin did.

"The news reached me on the road," her mother-in-law said. She sat in Rilsin's formal parlor, very much at ease, dressed in fine cotton trousers and overshirt of gray with a purple trim. She looked comfortable and smug, like the cat that swallowed the partridge. "But I have been expecting it, so I was not unprepared. I have made you a little gift, Rilsin, in honor of the coming birth of your daughter."

"It could be a son." Rilsin hoped it was a boy. A son would allay the dynastic fears Rilsin knew Sithli to have, despite her reassurances. A son would cause some of the feverish attention that had focused on her to vanish. A son would be safe.

"It will be a girl." Norimin spoke with calm certainty. "And this is for her. I made it myself." She held out a bundle wrapped in fine gilt paper. Sifuat, looking bored, took it from his mother and passed it to Rilsin. There had been an overabundance of infant gifts in the past weeks.

Rilsin's first thought as she unwrapped it was that this

gift took much time to make. Norimin must have begun work on it shortly after the purification ceremony, even before Rilsin and Sifuat were wed. *That's faith,* thought Rilsin, amused.

The gift was a blanket of fine wool, beautifully woven. Rilsin had no idea that Norimin could weave or that she could do it so beautifully. That was her first thought. It was the realization that followed this that made Rilsin turn first cold with fear and then hot with anger. Norimin had woven a pattern into the blanket. Against a field of dark Sae Becha blue, golden hunting cats frolicked amid silver and lavender grasses beneath a golden sun. For a moment, Rilsin could not speak. When she could at last, her voice was choked.

"This is not wise," she said. "It is very beautiful, Sae Norimin, but not wise. I cannot and will not accept it."

Sifuat sat up when he heard the tone in her voice. He reached over and took the blanket from her, and when he looked at it, his golden skin paled. That even Sifuat saw the danger there said much.

"Do you hate Rilsin? Do you hate my wife, Norimin— Mother? Because this will get her killed! This could get us all killed!" He grabbed up the blanket, and it looked as if he would throw it at Norimin. Rilsin reached up hastily and rescued the blanket. Although her sentiments were the same as Sifuat's, she didn't want to see the fine work harmed.

"Don't be a fool!" Norimin looked at her son with contempt. "It is not for public display. It is for use in the child's crib, at home. As for the blue—well, Sae Becha lives; the Mother wishes the line to endure as it should, everyone knows that now."

Norimin's feelings were hurt, Rilsin saw. This surprised her, as if she hadn't thought Norimin could be hurt.

"It really is not wise," she said more gently. She stroked the blanket as she spoke. "It is not just the blue, Sae Norimin, it is the golden cats. Sithli SaeKet—well, I must be very careful. For my sake, your son's sake, your own sake, and the sake of your grandchild. Surely you can see that."

"They say Sithli is pleased."

"She seems so. But Norimin, you must know, Sithli SaeKet can never be taken for granted." *Less so now than ever,* Rilsin thought, but then she put it from her mind.

"You are right, of course." Norimin took back the blanket, folding it gently and carefully. "I do not know what I was thinking. I would not risk my granddaughter's life."

"I am sorry, Norimin, truly I am." Her mother-in-law's sadness touched Rilsin. "That is beautiful work, fine work, but even if it never left the nursery, word would get out." She was more than touched by Norimin's sadness; she was concerned. This tough old woman was to have been a major ally. Now she seemed more like a liability. She was getting old, thought Rilsin, and then, no, she was showing her age. But in fact, Norimin did not seem old, she seemed young and somehow fragile. Rilsin would see age manifest itself this way again, but now it surprised her.

"Yes." Norimin folded the blanket and wrapped it carefully back into its gilt paper. "We will say nothing more of this."

By the time Meffa came to offer them chilled tea, the blanket, in its paper, was out of sight.

AUTUMN HAD DEFINITELY arrived. The leaves had turned and were beginning to drift down, keeping the palace gardeners busy raking them up again. The days snipped shorter, and the nights were chilly with winds that blew down from the north.

Rilsin's pregnancy began to show, and she had to have some of her trousers let out, to her great annoyance, and she even had some new overshirts made. She still walked every morning, and occasionally rode, and she hunted with Chilsa. She still did weapons practice most days, too, but unarmed combat practice ceased, not only by Nefit's orders, but by Rilsin's choice. All of her physical activities slowed, and most nights she fell asleep as soon as she climbed into bed, which she did earlier every night. But at least the nausea was past, and Sifuat was very solicitous of her health and comfort. There was no recurrence of his surprising outburst, and he now seemed just as pleased about this unexpected child as Rilsin.

Sithli, too, was more like the Sithli of old. She was as unpredictable and vain as ever, but the evil moods and sulks that followed her father's death all but disappeared. Rilsin began to hope that they were a fleeting phenomenon, and that they had vanished with the hot weather, but unlike the hot weather, never to return.

The people of Saeditin, most of the commoners and even some of the dira and saedin, concerned Rilsin the most. They treated her with an almost religious reverence. They still called her "Sword of Saeditin" and "Sithli's Sword," but more often now she heard "Mother-blessed," and even whispers of "true SaeKet." It was this last that made her blood run cold, and it was these whispers that were largely responsible for her backing away from any confrontation with Sithli. This stance included a retreat from her leadership of the trade faction.

"I cannot, not now," Rilsin told Essit when he urged that she persuade Sithli to send a delegation south to Runchot. "The SaeKet has said she is not ready to hear us on this."

"She is never ready," said Essit with frustration, "but you have a way of talking to her where others fail. And I tell you, Commander, you have seen the reports as well as I. If we do not make an attempt to reopen negotiations with Runchot, there may be consequences we do not wish."

"I know there is a faction, in northern Runchot particularly, that wants war, that thinks it can win a war, the fools! But I do not think they are strong yet, Essit, and they may never be strong. Yes, all right, I agree with you, we must talk with them, even if not about a trade treaty. I will see if I can convince the SaeKet to send an ordinary mission, at least."

But she didn't. She put it off from day to day, telling herself that one day more or less made no difference. Sithli was in a mood for celebrations and festivities, which she insisted that Rilsin attend, and which Rilsin found increasingly wearying. The priests were not pleased with Sithli's gaiety, for they were entering the solemn time of the season of

Death, the great ritual when all in Saeditin honored their ancestors. All but Rilsin. Her ancestors could not be honored, except for those she shared with Sithli, and it was considered unwise to have her at the ritual and at the temple, where she might invoke the attention of unwanted ghosts. So she was left free from all demands for the three days of the ritual, which suited her. She was exhausted.

The three days gave her time with Lendis, who also had no Saeditin ancestors to invoke. Sithli was pleased to turn him over to Rilsin, although in truth she had little enough to complain about on his account, since she delegated virtually all care of him to others.

"Well, Lendis, what shall we do for three days?" Rilsin sat in the small garden behind her house, watching Chilsa play with fallen leaves. Sifuat and Norimin were gone for the ritual, as was most of her staff, although Meffa and Bik, the junior cook, would return later. There were still guards around the perimeter of the grounds, however, as was normal for saedin of any standing.

Lendis stared at her. "You spoke in Wilfrisin. Sithli SaeKet has told me never to speak in Wilfrisin. She had me whipped the last time."

"Well, then, do not speak it to Sithli SaeKet. To me, you may speak it, if we are alone. We just won't tell the SaeKet."

Lendis considered this for a moment, and then decided to trust her, at least for the time being. "You took me from my mama, and you gave me to Sithli SaeKet," he said, in his own language, "but I don't like it. Will you take me home again?"

"I wish I could, Lendis, I wish I could. You have to stay here, at least for now, because you help to guarantee the peace. I don't know if you understand that."

"But why?" Lendis looked as if he were considering tears.

"Because that is the way things are done, and because the SaeKet knows that your father will keep his promises if she has you here."

Lendis thought about this for a minute. Then he said, "I do understand. I am a hostage."

Rilsin looked at him, taken aback. It was a harsh but accurate assessment from a child, a baby, of not yet five years. "Yes," she said, "you are, but an honored one. Your father is my friend, Lendis. He saved my life once. I promised him I would help in any way I could, but unfortunately, that does not mean I can take you back."

"My papa said if I needed anything, I should ask you. And Mama said you would learn to love me, as much as a childless woman could."

Rilsin drew in her breath again. "I hope you are not quite so candid with the SaeKet," she said, "or with anyone else." Then when she saw he did not entirely understand, "I hope you don't say what you think all the time."

"No. I know better. But Papa said to trust you, Aunt Rilsin."

While Rilsin blinked at her new title, Lendis came over to her and looked down at her stomach, swelling under the thick woolen overshirt.

"Besides," he continued, "you won't be childless. That is a baby growing in there, isn't it, like the way my sister grew in Mama."

"Yes, it is. And he's kicking right now. Want to feel him kick?"

It was the beginning of a friendship. Rilsin took the precocious little boy under her wing. By the end of the three days, they had gone hunting — briefly and unsuccessfully — with Chilsa, gone to the cat pens to meet Kerida, who still presided there over a small army of apprentices, to see if there were any kittens (there weren't), visited the huntsman's lodge (the huntsman was at the ritual, but his wife, who had come home early with her infant, demonstrated the use of a crossbow), and watched Bik make fruit pastries for the coming winter feasts, although many of those same pastries turned out to be destined for immediate consumption instead of storage.

At night Rilsin told Lendis stories, sometimes in Saeditin, sometimes in Wilfrisin, before she tucked him into

THE SWORD OF THE LAND

bed. Rilsin decided she liked having him there, especially as he was so obviously reluctant to go back to the SaeKet's palace. Sifuat, who came home from the rituals in the evenings, also took to the little boy, despite his initial reluctance to care for the son of the man who had kidnapped him. He remembered his own unhappy childhood and determined to try to make Lendis's less sad, and he felt sympathy for the child who had no one to care for him except former enemies.

Even after Lendis returned to the palace, Rilsin made a point of seeing him often, and soon it no longer caused comment to see the Wilfrisin child tagging along after the first minister. So well-behaved was he when he was with Rilsin that he sometimes slipped unnoticed into meetings with saedin or dira, where he listened quietly until he was sent away. He was still Sithli's charge, and he lived in the palace, but he avoided the beautiful SaeKet as much as he could.

24

THE FIRST SNOWS OF WINTER CAME EARLY. THERE WAS much discussion that this would be a bad winter, made worse by a partial crop failure in the east. A lack of rain plus the exodus of so many commoners from the countryside to the cities, to work in the new factories, had a crisis brewing, with eastern saedin appealing to Petipal and the SaeKet for help. Rilsin organized convoys of food to the afflicted region, and she sent teams of oxen-pulled plows to keep the roads open against the first heavy snowfalls.

Also taking up her time, without Sithli's knowledge, or so she hoped, was the investigation of Kepit sae Lisim. Sae Kepit, it appeared, had her hand in many of Petipal's less savory enterprises. She was the real owner behind several of the city's brothels, hiding behind the owners of record. This was perfectly legal, although surprising. Continuing a family tradition, she was also a slumlord. Her six siblings; five brothers and one younger sister, took her orders and had their own tenement holdings, all subject to Sae Kepit. All of this was legal, too, if unpleasant. One niece, Jullka, was

Kepit's favorite and heir apparent. Great care was necessary in dealing with the Sae Lisim.

What was not legal was the hint of darker things. There were rumors, amounting in some quarters to hysterical certainty, that the Sae Lisims were kidnapping commoners. The understanding was that the unfortunate victims were sold across the border and were never seen again. Innocent commoners, or at least commoners who never went through the courts, whether saedin or the SaeKet's. No matter how hard she tried, and she put her best agents on it, Rilsin could not come up with any hard evidence. This disturbed her. It was obvious to her that Kepit was protected, and the only person with the power to protect her from Rilsin was the SaeKet.

She had to talk to Sithli about it, but she couldn't, not without hard evidence. She knew what Sithli would say. And she was afraid of what she would find when she did get her evidence. She decided to devote as much energy as possible to getting the evidence first. Once she had it, she would decide how to approach Sithli.

It was in this way that the winter progressed. Sunreturn approached, and with it, the birth of Rilsin's child. Nefit told her the child would be born sometime after the great festival, as the season turned to its coldest, and she advised Rilsin to stay warm and cut back on her activity. Rilsin surprised herself by being glad to follow this advice. Her back hurt her, especially in the late afternoons, and she tired easily. She was glad to go home to spend the bitter evenings in front of the fire with Chilsa's warm bulk stretched out beside her, listening to Sifuat read to her or tell her about the gossip among the nobles. It was on one of these icy nights a week before midwinter, long after she had gone to bed under two down comforters, that Rilsin was awakened by a pounding on the door.

"Sae Rilsin! Wake up! Sae Rilsin! Sae Sifuat!"

"Meffa! Stop the pounding!" Sifuat sat up and reached for the candle, which he finally lit. But Meffa continued to knock and then finally opened the door a crack.

"Get out!" Sifuat was furious. "Unless the house is burning down, it will wait till morning!"

Rilsin pulled herself deeper under the covers while the commotion raged. Her back hurt, and now she had a headache, too. But when Chilsa sat up beside her and growled softly, she felt anxiety begin to dig its needles into her. Chilsa would not growl at Meffa.

"Sae Rilsin! Commander! I am sorry to wake you, but you must come!"

Essit stood in the doorway, half pushing Meffa aside. He tried not to look at her, but whatever it was, it was obviously urgent.

Rilsin sat up. Whatever it was was not only urgent, but outstandingly so. Chilsa continued to growl, and Sifuat was puffing up with anger.

"Chilsa, enough! What—"

"Have you no decency, Sae Essit! Can this not wait for morning!"

"Obviously, it can't." Rilsin was in no mood to coddle her husband, and she was trying to get her mind to work. "What is it, Sae Essit?"

"Signal fires from the south. The Runchot have invaded."

Iᴛ ᴡᴀꜱ ᴛRᴜᴇ, as Rilsin soon saw for herself. Bundled in wool and fur, the hood of her cloak pulled down over her head against the biting wind, she heaved herself into the saddle and rode through the snowy streets to the main temple. The priests ushered her into the warmth, and then she and Essit climbed, Essit easily, she panting slightly, up to the high tower. Sure enough, there was the blaze on the summit of Watchers' Peak, to the south. Following soon after came the courier with the details, a courier who had ridden so hard that he killed two horses but made it up from the south in two days' time. Rilsin was with Sithli by this time, along with a few other saedin, as the news spread fast. They received the exhausted messenger, who had not even removed his cloak.

"We are outnumbered," he told them. He was a member

of the border saedin family. "They took us by surprise. No one could imagine they would attack in this weather! Most of our troops were home with their families."

"They will have been mobilized by now, no doubt." Sithli was swathed in a green and gold silk robe, and her hair was combed and braided, but for once she had no jewels but her emerald-thick bracelet, which she obviously wore while she slept, and in her haste, she had forgotten her powder. The scar on her face showed plainly, a white slash on the gold of her skin.

"The farms are burning, SaeKet, and the people are out in the cold. The Southern Guard will mobilize where it can, but the Runchot are moving fast. They are coming north. Toward Petipal."

"How could this happen? What of the border watch? All the troops? Why were so many simply . . . not there!" Rilsin had a hard time containing herself.

"No one expected this, First Minister! We thought it safe to let our soldiers go home. They have never attacked in the winter before."

"Well, they have now! This is what comes of too much autonomy for local guards, Sithli!" Rilsin remembered where she was and added, "SaeKet." She turned back to the messenger, who was actually swaying on his feet. "They are coming north? You are sure?"

"The local guards will slow them down, but they are a huge force, First Minister! They want Petipal."

"They won't have it. Get this man some food and a place to rest. With your permission, SaeKet."

"Yes." They watched the messenger as he left, stumbling, catching himself on his guide. "Poor man. Rilsin, what can we do? I should leave Petipal! We have to do something!"

"It's already being done. I sent out orders, and all the southern saedin between Petipal and the border have some warning now, if they didn't before. Don't leave Petipal unless I warn you it's time to go! You could start a panic! But they won't get here, Sith. I'm going south myself, tonight. I'll leave some troops to guard Petipal, but most I'll take with me. All of the southern forces will rally. Sae Bilma, I need your help here, to keep calm in the city and advise the SaeKet while I'm gone."

"I will, Sae Rilsin. But," the old man looked pointedly at her swollen stomach, "is it wise for you to go?"

"What choice is there, my friend?"

"She has to go!" Sithli was agitated. "She has to stop the Runchot! She has to!"

"I will do everything I can, SaeKet. Stay calm, Sithli. The people need you. Help her, Bilma." Rilsin's thoughts were already moving ahead. If she could not stop the Runchot long before they got here, Sithli's state of mind wouldn't matter.

Before she left, with her hastily called-up troops, Sithli took her aside.

"I know you will come back, Rilsin. I know it." She looked significantly at her cousin. "The Mother Herself told me. She told me you will save Petipal, and you will return. But changed, much changed." She smiled slightly. "Without this." She leaned forward and touched Rilsin on the stomach.

It was a light touch, barely perceptible through all the layers of her clothing, but Rilsin flinched back. It felt as though the light brush of Sithli's finger was burning its way through the cloth to her skin. Without thinking, she covered the spot with her hand. And then Sithli reached out again, and pulled the collar and scarf away from her neck.

"You still wear your mother's pendant over the scar Sifuat gave you. And you wear his ring. But nothing of mine, Rils." Rilsin tried to think what to say. Before she could, Sithli removed the emerald bracelet from her wrist. "Wear this. Do not remove it until you come home safely." She took Rilsin's hand and pushed the thick, gold, gem-encrusted cuff onto her wrist. Sithli gathered her into her arms.

It was dawn when she left. Sifuat saw her off. Instead of going with her, he was to help organize the defense of the capital. Chilsa was to stay with him, although the big cat whined and yowled when he realized that he was not going with Rilsin. Sifuat, seeing this, felt the hair rise on the back of his neck. Chilsa sensed something, he thought. Cats knew things before humans did. Then he tried to forget this, to unthink it.

"Don't worry so." Rilsin saw his expression. "I am not going into battle myself. I will come back, sweetheart. I'm not going to put our son in any danger." But as she left, she could hear Chilsa's yowls.

Soon after leaving Petipal, Rilsin switched from horse-back to carriage. It was really more like a modified chariot, built for speed, but at least Rilsin was able to sit behind the driver. There was not much between them and the icy ruts of the road, however, and she must continually brace herself against the jars and shocks, which she found more exhausting than riding, so after a while she was back, cumbersome, in the saddle.

The troops mustered quickly from the southern saed-holds, and they gathered to her. She left some to protect each saedhold, but most she added to her own force. She wanted to overwhelm the Runchot, to defeat them as quickly as possible, and decisively. There must be no recurrence. Guilt made her wonder if this attack could have been prevented by the diplomatic mission Saeditin never sent, the mission she neglected to urge Sithli to send.

Reports came in to her steadily. The Runchot kept mainly to the roads, trying to move north as fast as possible. They burned farms and a few unprotected villages, but they left the larger towns and the saedhold seats alone. It was obvious that they were making for Petipal. They wanted the capital, and they wanted the SaeKet. It was also obvious that they expected to face the Saeditin army or whatever of it could be mobilized in time. But they knew that Rilsin was expecting her child soon, and they did not expect her to be capable of much. On top of it all, the weather turned bad. As Rilsin and the army approached the Runchot, on the second day after the news of the invasion, the skies were growing dark, and a blizzard was brewing.

"At least," Rilsin told Essit, "it will snow on them as much as it snows on us."

"None of us will move until the weather clears," said Essit sourly.

They were camped on a high plain near the steep southern hills, the hills that formed a partial border between Saeditin and Runchot. Tents were being put up and brush shelters hastily erected for the shaggy Saeditin horses. Evening was approaching, but so was the storm. The first winds began to howl down from the northeast, and snow was beginning to fall in stinging gusts and sheets.

Rilsin pulled her fur-lined cloak tighter. The smoke from the fire rose through the tent's smoke hole, and the tent was actually relatively warm, but these days Rilsin was always cold. At least, her feet were cold, and she moved closer to the fire.

The camp was settled in and secure by the time the full force of the blizzard hit. Darkness descended well before nightfall. The soldiers ate in their tents and ventured out for very little, keeping to the guidelines strung between the tents and shelters when they must go. Everyone but the sentries went to bed early.

It was some time during the night that Rilsin woke. The storm was still howling outside. She listened, but that was all she could hear, and she couldn't determine just what dragged her from sleep. The child in her womb was quiet, resting. She threw her cloak around her and went to the overlapping tent flaps, pulled at them, and peered out. She was rewarded with a faceful of stinging snow but also with the sight of the sentry, his back to her, huddled in his cloak, clutching his firepot and staring at the wall of white.

Rilsin went back to bed. But just as she drifted off to sleep again, she heard it: something pulling and scratching at the tent. She sat up now, lit the lantern, and reached for her sword. She approached the side of the tent cautiously, ready to strike but unable to imagine what could be causing the thick skin tent to shudder and move the way it did in just that section. Her imagination began to call up the demon legends, the winter demons that accompanied the Evil One just around the time of Sunreturn. She pulled back the skin of the tent: no demons. But what she did see made her gasp.

It was a hunting cat outside, a cat almost overcome with cold, a cat crusted with ice and snow. It looked only remotely like a cat, covered as it was with snow and sleet and ice. But when the animal looked up at her and gave a rasping meow, a strangely incongruous sound from such a large cat, she cried out. Dropping the sword, she pulled Chilsa into the tent. It took most of her strength to do this, because the cat was at the end of his own considerable strength, frozen by the blizzard.

"He tracked you all the way from Petipal," said Essit, stating the obvious with amazement. He had come after the sentries had heard their commander cry out, and roused him. "I don't know how he found you in this storm."

Rilsin shook her head. She didn't know, either. She busied herself getting the cat warm and dry and giving him meat. It became obvious that Chilsa was recovering from his ordeal. He ate and then settled down in front of the fire to sleep. He gave Rilsin a look that said he was pleased with himself and closed his eyes, purring. She had hoped to leave him in the safety of Petipal, but now that he was here, she was glad of it. When she at last tried to resume her interrupted sleep, the camp bed sagged under a sudden weight. Rilsin moved over, wedging herself against the side of the bed to give the huge cat room. She was resigned to staying awake, but to her surprise, the warm, familiar bulk of Chilsa relaxed her, and she drifted easily into sleep.

Morning was not much different from night. The skies lightened slightly to a charcoal gray instead of black, but the snow continued to fall. Blizzards like this one had been known to last for days, and Rilsin and her officers gathered together to discuss the problems of supply for the troops and of strategy. It was then that fate intervened, with the news that a scout had returned.

"He insists on seeing you right away," the sentry told her. "He says it can't wait."

When the scout came in, he looked much as Chilsa had the night before. Icicles were frozen into his beard, and his clothing immediately began to drip in the warmth of the tent. Some of the officers edged away from the growing puddle. Many of them thought it insanity to be out in the blizzard.

"You risked your life," said one, "for what could wait until the storm ends."

"Why don't you let me judge that for myself," said Rilsin sharply. She was aware of how awkwardly she sat in the camp chair that had been set up for her, and she was aware of how she must look: ungainly and huge. And she was aware of how she felt: bloated, and her back hurt. All of this made her temper short.

"The Runchot, Commander," said the scout, "are camped just in the valley between East Arm and West Arm Ridges. They are waiting out the storm, and they have no idea that we are here."

Automatically, almost everyone in the tent turned in the appropriate direction, or at least glanced that way. There was nothing to be seen but tent, of course, and even if they ventured out, there would be nothing to be seen but snow. But if the storm should let up, when the storm let up, the Runchot were almost within hailing distance.

"We need to move quickly when the storm ends," said Essit. "We need to be ready to move right away, before they know we are here."

There was a consensus on this point, the officers murmuring in agreement. But Rilsin sat silent. For a moment, no one noticed. Then Essit looked at her and fell silent, and gradually the others did, too.

"No," said Rilsin, "not after the storm is over. Now. Now while the storm still rages. Now when they least expect it." They looked at her as if she had lost her mind, even Essit, and Rilsin felt herself getting angry again. With an effort, she controlled it. "We can march through the snow. It isn't far; this man made it, after all!" She waved at the still-defrosting scout. "They will not be expecting us. They will be holed up against the storm just as we are now. What better time!"

"Tomorrow night is Sunreturn," said Niffa sae Delf. She was a young captain, promoted to her position for talent, and she was very religious. "We cannot fight on the solstice, on the very night the Mother births Her child!"

Rilsin looked at the young woman and had the satisfaction of seeing her flinch.

"The Mother Herself fought on the solstice, if you recall," said Rilsin acidly, "and we shall do the same."

"She fought against the Evil One," protested Niffa, intimidated but unwilling to give up.

"And so shall we." She relented a little, seeing Niffa's expression. "We shall have victory before nightfall," she said, "and celebrate the solstice in peace." Her words fell into the silence like a prophecy rather than a promise, and Rilsin was perhaps the only one who didn't hear it.

They attacked the Runchot camp before nightfall, descending on them out of the strengthening storm. Just as the scout reported, the entire enemy force was camped in the valley between the Arm Ridges, the valley known unofficially to the locals as the Armpit, not just because of its position but because of the tough and rank-smelling grass that grew there in the summer. It was uninhabited and used for grazing.

True to her promise to Sifuat, Rilsin did not join the battle herself. She stayed back with some of her officers, directing, doing the best she could to coordinate the attack. It was difficult to see anything from her position slightly up on the East Arm because the storm was so severe, and she relied on the steady stream of messengers. Even the flashing of light signals would not reliably pierce the storm.

The Runchot were better prepared than they had a right to be. They rallied quickly, despite the storm, despite surprise, and the rapid victory Rilsin promised did not seem likely to materialize. They fought like the demons she had compared them to, and the battle went on into the darkness of the early midwinter night, the screams of the wounded and dying echoing across the frozen battlefield, which was lit by the flames of some of the Runchot tents, set afire by Saeditin troops. Rilsin thought the Runchot were right. There was a hell, and this was it.

But by morning it was clear that the Runchot could not

win. The storm began to abate at last, and in the growing
light a grotesque sight could be seen: bodies frozen into the
snow. Arms reached upward, solid as trees, but more brittle,
some of them still clutching weapons; icy eyeballs stared
sightless at what passed for dawn. It was like a field of
frozen, twisted statues. In the midst of this icy horror, some
of the Runchot managed to regroup and were desperately
fighting their way south toward home, trying to break trail
through the enormous drifts in the uninhabited valley.

"Let them go," said Rilsin. "Let them go until they are in
the narrowest part of the valley, under both Arms. Don't
pursue them. Send a few soldiers up the ridges; no wait,
only the East Arm; that will do. When the Runchot reach the
narrow valley, shout. Shout, and blow the trumpets."

"Shout?" Essit looked at her. Despite the fact that he was
at her side during this fight and had not actually engaged the
enemy himself, he looked as bad as she did: haggard, cold,
and exhausted. He stared at her for a moment, and then the
import of her words came through. He looked around him
at the soft, deep drifts of new snow and up the ridges, where
the snow piled even deeper on the steep slopes.

"If any escape the valley, let them go. I don't expect that
many will."

Essit continued to stare at her. He was cold, so cold and
tired, and he felt the beginnings of sympathy for the Runchot.

"Give the order," said Rilsin.

Because she knew what the end would be, what it would
look like, and because suddenly she very much did not want
to see it but also because she had cramps in her stomach
now, she decided to go back to camp. Surely others could
handle this little ending.

"You see to it, Sae Essit."

Essit watched her climb onto her horse and ordered a
few soldiers to go with her, to escort her back to the Saeditin
camp. He worried about her. She looked awful, and she
could barely stand without staggering from exhaustion.
Once in the saddle, she hunched over, looking ill. She
needed to get back to camp, to get warm, dry clothes and

food. And rest. The very thought of rest made Essit's bones ache.

"I will deal with this," he promised her.

"Thank you." Her voice was barely audible over the wind.

25

Essit assigned ten soldiers to ride back with her. There was no conversation among them, no rejoicing at their victory. All were tired, glad to leave the battle's aftermath and the cleanup to others, glad for the chance to return early to camp. All were cold and hungry.

They rode in silence. Rilsin did not trust herself to speak. The stomach pains were getting worse, and she gritted her teeth to avoid showing her pain. They were hunger cramps, she assumed; pregnancy gave her a voracious appetite, and her body rebelled when it was not fed. She hadn't eaten during the long battle.

To make things worse, the wind picked up. The snow had ended, but for the occasional flurry, but the storm winds continued, picking up the fallen snow and flinging it in blinding sheets into their faces and across their path. Tonight would be solstice night, when the rest of Saeditin should be celebrating. All Rilsin and her escort could think of was warmth and a chance to get out of the snow. These thoughts, and the blowing snow and the shrieking wind, contrived to hide their danger from them.

A band of Runchot had not been content to retreat through the valley but made its way out in the confusion of the defeat and the storm, to cut back toward the camp of their enemy. They knew they were going to die, and they wanted to take some Saeditin with them. It was this small group that launched itself out of the blowing snow at Rilsin and her escort.

One moment Rilsin rode, head down, enduring the pain, thinking vaguely of the fire in her tent and of seeing one of the physicians, perhaps. The next moment, there was chaos. None of her escort, not one, was alert enough to spot the attack before it happened. Four of the ten Saeditin escort died immediately. The remaining six surrounded Rilsin to try to fight off nine attackers.

It said much for Rilsin's condition that she couldn't, for a moment, make sense of what was happening. When the man beside her went down, with his horse under him, she awoke to the danger. She had just time enough to draw her sword.

She fought desperately, ignoring the pain in her abdomen, which came now in waves. She fought through the waves, drew breath and strength between them. She killed two Runchot, and saw, or thought she saw that three more were down, either dead or wounded too badly to fight. But three more of her own exhausted troops suffered the same fate. They had been forced from the trail, forced off into the wilder terrain of the ridges. Rilsin's horse, although bred for the bitter Saeditin winters, slipped, and a Runchot cut the animal's throat. Rilsin managed to roll clear with the screams of the dying horse ringing in her ears.

She felt the strength of rage and terror flow into her. She attacked in a fury, her lips drawn back in a rictus of pain and exhaustion; killing two more Runchot. Then there was a moment, a quiet moment to draw breath. Only one Runchot soldier was left, and he was moving in for the kill on the one remaining Saeditin other than Rilsin herself. With a last spurt of strength, Rilsin ran the man through the back. When she tried to tug her sword free, a cramp seized her.

When it released her, she left the sword in the body and knelt down beside her last soldier.

"I am sorry, Commander, I'm sorry." The soldier died with her eyes open, and the apology still on her lips.

Rilsin reached out after a moment to close her eyes. "No," she said. "I am the one to be sorry."

No sooner had she spoken than a cramp worse than all the earlier cramps seized her. She doubled over, gasping, and when it finally released her, she felt a flood of warm liquid running down the inside of her thighs, soaking through her trousers. No, she had not been suffering from hunger pains. Or perhaps she had, but there was also this. *How fitting,* she thought. *I did not know I was pregnant, and now I can't recognize labor.*

She looked around her. There was nothing but rocky, icy, terrain, stinging, wind-blown snow, and the corpses of people and horses. She would have to somehow make her way back to the trail, and from there to camp. She hoped to find some of her own troops in the process. But what if there were more Runchot? It occurred to her that she hadn't heard the shouts or the trumpet blasts that should have heralded the doom of the remaining enemy troops, but this meant little. The noise of the fight around her and of the wind could have masked it.

She actually managed to walk a few steps back in the direction of the trail, or in what she thought was the right direction. But another cramp stopped her, and as it was passing, she heard something. She held still, drawing her breath in tight little sips between her teeth. There it was again, and now the source of the sound was plain. Someone was coming through the snow.

"Is anyone there, anyone alive?" The words were Saeditin, then in Runchot, then Saeditin again. The Saeditin was unaccented, seemingly the speaker's native language, and Rilsin felt a pang of relief so sharp it was almost painful.

"Here," she called. She was shocked at the sound of her voice, so much weaker than it usually was.

Someone loomed up out of the white: someone in the

russet of the Runchot winter army. Not a Saeditin after all. She was looking at an enemy soldier, a tall man with a thick reddish beard and a drawn sword. He did not waste time looking long at her but lunged for her immediately.

Rilsin stepped back. She was unarmed and in no condition to fight. She dodged clumsily and tried to retreat again, but she slipped on the snow and went down. Her enemy shouted in triumph and stepped toward her.

A sound came from behind him, something between a snarl and a roar, a threat so plain and so overwhelming that Rilsin felt the hair rise on the back of her neck. The Runchot gaped, eyes widening in fear, and he began to turn, but there was no time. Something that seemed part of the blowing silver snow hit him hard from behind, and he went down under a huge, sleek, silver-furred body.

There was a brief struggle. The Runchot was resourceful and quick. His knife was already in his hand, and he struck at the cat, who twisted and took a cut along the left shoulder. Rilsin cried out, but there was nothing she could do. It was all over soon, in any case. Chilsa sank his teeth into the man's throat, the knife fell from his slack hand, and after a moment, he ceased to struggle. Chilsa continued to hold him by the throat, growling dangerously, until there was no question but that he was dead. Then Chilsa got to his feet and went to Rilsin without a backward look.

Rilsin was in the grip of another contraction. It felt as though something was trying to tear her apart from inside, and she bit down hard on the sleeve of her woolen overshirt to keep from screaming. No one told her it would be like this; this was worse than battle.

Chilsa stood over her helplessly, the blood from his wound dripping onto her. When the contraction finally passed, she was weak and dripping with sweat, but she took her cloak and gently wiped the blood from the cat's wound. It did not look too severe, but it would be best if she could get treatment for him. She tried to rise to her feet, but there was another contraction, equally strong. Rilsin realized she was not going to make it back to camp, barring a miracle, before she gave birth to her child. She needed shelter and she needed help, but neither was anywhere to be seen. Another contraction came, and she moaned, reaching out for Chilsa, the only comfort in the barren snow.

But Chilsa backed away from her. He looked at her for a moment and then turned and disappeared into the snow. Rilsin did not have time to be astonished at this abandonment. The contractions were too close together now, and it took all of her remaining strength just to breathe and not to scream. She barely felt her hands and feet, and it occurred to her to wonder about frostbite, but there was nothing she could do now. And despite the cold of her extremities, sweat ran down her back and pooled under her breasts. She found herself alternately damning Sifuat and wishing she had been forced to take even more beltrip. Perhaps an even higher dosage might have worked, might have prevented this hell. *I am going to die here in the snow,* she thought in one lucid moment. When she closed her eyes, she saw flashes of yellow and red. She felt more sticky liquid flowing down her thighs, and she knew that this time it was all blood.

Something was breathing into her face. Something was making a chuffing sound, like a steam pipe. She opened her eyes and saw Chilsa standing over her. He chuffed at her, breathing on her, wanting her to get up. Perhaps he brought help. She forced herself to sit up. But no one was there, no one came out of the wind to help her. But Chilsa would not leave her alone. He wanted her up and following him, so perhaps he found something after all. Whatever it was, it must be better than lying in the snow, where both she and the soon-to-be-born child would die.

What Chilsa had found was a small cave, set back into the rocky line of the ridge. Luckily it was neither far nor difficult to climb into, or Rilsin could not have managed it. When she half fell, half crawled into it, Chilsa gave a grunt of satisfaction and lay down just inside the small entrance, blocking most of the wind.

It was warmer inside the small cave, a change of temperature that felt almost pleasant after the bitter cold of the open air. A small pile of dried leaves had been deposited inside by the winds of autumn, and a clump of long grass had taken root in the entrance and then died. Rilsin managed to pull this up and spread it with the leaves to form a sort of bed. As she did this, she saw the light begin to fade. Somehow she spent all day in labor, and now the longest night of the year was beginning.

She got her trousers off, despite the fact that they were stiff with frozen blood. She worked between the continuing contractions, and just as the trousers came off, there was another flow of blood, which left her feeling dizzy. *How much blood can I have?* she wondered. The answer came as a vision of an execution in the Mother's Square, with blood overflowing the crystal goblet: a lot of blood. She moaned, and in answer, she heard Chilsa's hoarse meow. She was not in the square, she was in the cave Chilsa found for her. If not for this cave, if not for Chilsa guarding her, warming the air with his body heat, she would be dead already or soon to die.

The light faded, and there was only darkness. Rilsin wished desperately for a match, or for an old-fashioned firestriker, but there was nothing to burn but the leaves and grass on which she sometimes sat, sometimes reclined. She thought again of the winter demons, but the dark-against-dark shadow of Chilsa in the cave's mouth was reassuring. Nothing would come in, not even a demon, while Chilsa guarded the entrance.

Contractions came and went. She felt her belly ripple and heave, but there was still no child. Delirium came and went, too. Why was it that no one had found her? Did the Runchot somehow rally, had her army been defeated after all? She dreamed a nightmare of the Runchot marching north, of Petipal burning, of Sithli captured, killed. But no. Of course not. She simply strayed too far from the trail in the fight with the renegade Runchot. Search parties had been looking for her, were no doubt looking for her right now. Unless they thought she was dead, killed in the skirmish, or dead in these hills. *Which I may be yet,* she thought.

In one gasping moment of rest she became conscious of something hard, cold, and uncomfortable on her right wrist. She fingered it, pulled it off. She couldn't see it in the darkness, but her hands told her what it was: Sithli's emerald and gold cuff. As pain seized her again, she dropped the bracelet into the darkness.

In another, later moment, she wondered why this was so hard. Surely not all women went through such long agony for their children. The answer was the beltrip, of course. The herb damaged her. It hadn't prevented fertility, as was intended, but it damaged her, made it so hard to give birth. Now, instead of wishing she had been given more beltrip, she cursed Dinip for decreeing that she take it at all.

"It was the only way," Dinip said to her, "that I could let you live. I did not know then what I know now."

"You should have killed me," Rilsin answered her uncle. "Better even the square and the knife and that horrible goblet than this."

"You must live, little Rils." It was her mother. "You must live, you and Reniat. Saeditin needs you both."

"Mama!"

Chilsa meowed in distress at her cry. He came to her, and she felt his warm breath, his wet nose. She sat up now, and clutched the big cat around the neck. Holding onto him in the darkness, Rilsin got to her knees. Chilsa permitted this, did not back away. The contractions came again, and Rilsin, kneeling, bore down hard. The contractions came in rapid waves. She was being torn apart. She couldn't help it now, couldn't resist anymore. She screamed, bearing down as hard as she could.

The enormous pressure eased a little. Rilsin reached down between her legs, felt something there. Something round, soft: the baby's head. She pushed again, and managed to catch the child as it slid from her in another gush of blood.

She saw Chilsa in the faint light, saw the child in her hands, slippery, with the cord still attached. There was one more contraction, not so strong: the afterbirth. Rilsin looked around. She could see. There was light. Dawn.

There were some pebbles in the cave. She smashed one to make a sharp edge, cut the umbilical with this. She wiped the child off with snow from just outside the cave, saw her open her eyes, heard her begin to cry. There was a tuft of golden fuzz on the top of the baby's head. She would be golden-haired like Sifuat, like Sithli. But her skin was as pale as Rilsin's own. Rilsin felt a flood of love.

"Reniat," she whispered. "Little Reniat." She put the baby to her breast and wrapped herself in her cloak.

Chilsa came over, sniffed at her, at the nursing child. Rilsin smiled at him, reached out to him. Chilsa bumped her hand with his huge head, then leaned down and picked up something in his mouth. It was Sithli's bracelet. Holding this in his mouth, Chilsa left the cave. Rilsin saw him go, was too exhausted to stop him. Wrapped in her cloak with her new daughter, she drifted into sleep.

IT WAS WARM, and she was lying on something soft. Through half-closed eyes she saw the flickering of an oil lamp. For a moment she was disoriented, then she remembered: the cave, the cold. Her baby. With a gasp, Rilsin sat up.

She was in a tent. Her tent. There was a fire burning beneath the smoke hole, and Chilsa slept in front of it. In a chair near the fire was Sola. This was so surprising that she couldn't help herself, and she called out to him.

"Sola!"

Sola jerked awake.

"How did you get here? Where's my baby? What happened to the army?"

"Reniat is fine. She's sleeping." He came to her side and nodded toward where Chilsa slept, and she saw something incongruous in an army tent: a crib. "She's fine. Really."

"How do you know her name? How did I get here?"

"You told me her name. Or rather, you told Sae Essit and me her name. He went crazy when he found you were missing, sent search parties everywhere. Still, no one found you until Chilsa showed up yesterday morning with Sithli's bracelet. Then Sae Essit went out and brought you back. I came as soon as I heard you were missing." He took her hand, and she clutched his like a lifeline.

"Yesterday! The army—the Runchot—"

"There isn't much left of the Runchot." Essit came in, a physician with him. The physician looked at Rilsin while Essit talked. "The avalanche killed most of them. The few who were left, we let go, as you said, and I sent word of our victory north. We should receive a peace emissary from the Runchot soon."

"Our casualties?"

"Seven hundred killed, more wounded. The Runchot lost three thousand. It could have been much worse."

There was something different about Essit, about the way he looked at her. Perhaps he was embarrassed about the way she was when he found her, hidden in the cave. But that didn't seem like Essit. And why couldn't she remember?

"Why can't I remember?"

"You were exhausted." The physician eased her back against the pillows. She was a small woman, but her hands were strong. "I'm surprised you survived at all. You owe your life to the hunting cat and to the protection of the Mother."

Rilsin saw Essit's face when the physician said this, and now she knew what was different. Essit was in awe of her.

"I want to see Reniat."

The doctor placed the sleeping baby in Rilsin's arms. She was even more beautiful than Rilsin remembered, and the flood of happiness took her breath away. The thought of the four thousand lives lost in the battle, the memory of the cave, the coming peace talks, all faded for the moment. While she gazed at her child, Chilsa padded over and climbed up on the bed with her. No one made a move to stop him or even protest. As he settled down, Rilsin saw that the wound on his shoulder had been cleaned.

"I will have food sent in, Commander," the physician told her. "You must eat." She left, and Essit turned to go with her.

"Wait, Sae Essit. Thank you for bringing me back. Now that I try, it seems I do remember you in the cave. I am very grateful."

"It was an honor," he said formally.

"It was a big relief for me," she said, and he smiled finally.

"For me, too. I had search parties everywhere. We found where you were ambushed, but we couldn't find you. More snow fell and covered your tracks. When Chilsa came back with the bracelet, Dira Sola and I went out to find you. I was afraid we wouldn't find you alive. But to find you alive and the sun-child . . . it was a miracle."

"Sun-child?"

Essit blushed. "That's what they're calling her. Reniat the Golden, born on the solstice. It's a miracle." He saw her expression. "And it makes a good story." He grinned at her and left.

"Is that true, they're saying that? Who is 'they'?"

Sola pulled his chair up beside her bed. "The army. And all of Saeditin soon, if they're not already."

"It does make a good story, but it will pass. I will see to it that it passes." She looked down and saw that she had taken his hand again. Something occurred to her, something she should have thought of long before. "Does Sifuat know?" She found she needed another breath. "And Sithli?"

"Sae Sifuat should be here soon. He couldn't leave as soon as I could, but by now he knows you have been found. And that he has a daughter." Sola found he had to look away from her.

"And Sithli knows by now, too."

"She knows." He looked back at her, at the child in her arms. "You are safe, Rilsin. Both of you. The SaeKet must say she is pleased; she may truly be. You are safe. They are not just calling Reniat a sun-child, Rils. They are saying that Sae Rilsin, the Mother-blessed, drove evil from the land and gave birth to a golden child on solstice night. You are a legend, Rils, and not even Sithli SaeKet would dare to harm a legend."

26

Rilsin waited outside the formal audience chamber with Reniat in her arms. Sithli had not seen Rilsin or Reniat since their return from the south three days before, and Rilsin was nervous. She told herself that Sithli would not harm her, at the very least because of her victory and her popularity with the people, but she was less than completely successful at convincing herself.

Reniat slept, bundled in fine-spun woolen blankets. Occasionally Rilsin stroked the golden fuzz of hair on her daughter's head. When she wasn't doing this, her hand would drift absently to her sword hilt. She was still permitted to bear arms in the presence of her cousin, which was encouraging. Her hand lingered there every time she considered the possibility that Sithli might threaten her child. She did not realize that she did this, and she wondered why the eyes of the guards kept shifting to her.

Rilsin nervously pulled at her hair. It was growing out, and she had plaited it into a short, tight, plain braid. Keeping it short had begun to seem an affectation, so she was letting it grow, but she was not used to it yet. When she tugged at her braid, she had to shift Reniat in her arms, and the baby gurgled and gave one brief cry before settling back into sleep. Rilsin wished she could sit, but the chairs had been removed from the room. Sithli was making another point.

"The SaeKet will see you." The guard had entered the room without her noticing. Rilsin straightened her shoulders. It was not good to allow herself to be distracted.

As she passed the guard, who turned to escort her in, she heard him whisper, "Good luck, Commander."

Sithli sat on the formal SaeKet's chair, surrounded by guards. She was dressed in green and gold velvets and silk, her blonde hair cascading down her back, sparkling with artfully entwined emeralds. Rilsin was immediately conscious of a spot of drool that Reniat had left on the shoulder of her uniform. She smiled at Sithli, but her cousin did not smile in return.

Rilsin walked to the foot of the chair, shifted Reniat to her left arm, put her right hand over her heart, and bowed. For a moment, Sithli regarded her and said nothing. Then her gaze shifted to the baby in Rilsin's arms.

"Give her to me." She held out her hands.

Rilsin could not afford to hesitate. She straightened, took a step forward, and held out Reniat.

Sithli took the baby. She gently pulled aside the blankets and looked down into the tiny face. At this moment, Reniat awoke. But instead of crying, she yawned, opening her little toothless rosebud mouth. Sithli poked her gently, and Reniat's tiny hand grabbed the SaeKet's finger tightly. Finally, Sithli smiled.

"My daughter," she said. She held Reniat to her, cuddling the infant, and then suddenly beamed at Rilsin. "Well done, Rils! She is beautiful!" Reniat made little gurgling noises and then began to cry. Sithli looked nonplussed. She bounced Reniat twice, but when the baby's wails grew stronger, she abruptly held her out to Rilsin. "Take her, Rils. How can something that small make that much noise!"

Rilsin relaxed slightly. "That's about all she has to say for herself so far." She smiled at her cousin. "That will change soon enough." She rubbed Reniat's back gently, and the crying subsided into little hiccups.

"Let's get out of this drafty old room." Sithli stood abruptly. "We can have something to eat in private. I think we deserve a small celebration on two counts. You have saved the land from the Runchot, and you have given us a daughter to share."

She swept down from the chair and out of the room. Holding Reniat, Rilsin followed her. Sithli did not see Rilsin's smile fade as soon as her back was turned.

"YOU WILL HAVE to go north to see her. I can't; I don't dare leave Petipal, especially with Sithli in the mood she's in. You can wait until the roads are cleared again, a couple of days at the most, but you will have to go." Rilsin settled herself back among the pillows in front of the fire. Chilsa shifted beside her, allowing her a little more room. Reniat slept nearby in a basket, while Sifuat paced the room.

"I don't want to see her! You know how she is! She goes on about what a disappointment I am to her, the old weasel."

"She's still your mother," said Rilsin mildly. "And she's ill." The thought of Norimin ill was disconcerting. She had seemed like such a solid fixture, whatever one thought of her, part of the foundation of the world.

"She won't miss me." Sifuat glared resentfully at the small stack of innocent logs beside the fire, and then gave one a petulant kick.

"Sifuat, sit down," she said abruptly.

Something in her tone caused him to stop his pacing and look at her. After a moment, he sat beside her on the couch, causing Chilsa to shift again.

"I need you to go north, but not just for Norimin. For us." She almost said, "for Saeditin." For once, Sifuat said nothing, merely looked at her.

"Norimin is old, and now she is ill. She will not live forever. No, wait; listen, please." She put her hand on her husband's arm, forestalling him as he opened his mouth. "It is hard to imagine Norimin not in Hoptrin, as she has always been, but in the arms of the Mother. When that happens, Sifuat, the north must be secure. I would go, but I can't. Sithli —" she paused, shook her head. Sithli had been growing even more unpredictable.

"Sithli will not let me go; she will barely let me out of her sight. The north must be secure. There are Norimin's troops to consider." Rilsin paused, uncertain how to proceed.

"There are very many troops. More troops than Sithli Saeket realizes," she said at last.

"And you wish them disbanded." Sifuat interrupted, looking slightly bored. "Norimin has said that you would want as much someday, over her strong objections, but I do not understand why you need me to see to it. And why now. Surely it can wait."

"You misunderstand me, Sifuat. I want the troops kept under arms. I do not want them disbanded when Norimin dies. We may need them someday. And there is no need for Sithli to know about them. She must not know about them yet. She has enough on her mind these days."

Sifuat sat up. He smiled slightly. "I can see to that."

Rilsin studied him. She hoped she was right in trusting him, but there was no one else for this task, not now. She did not intend to move against Sithli, but she could not allow the unrest to worsen in the land. How could she resolve this? She had sworn to protect Saeditin. Her mother-in-law's army could be of help, one way or another.

SiFUAT GAZED OUT the window at the blowing snow. Another blizzard had roared down from the northeast, and Petipal was again under a blanket of white. The roads would be closed for another day or two, until the horse-drawn and oxen-drawn plows could dig them out. But he was no longer reluctant to leave the capital. He knew his mother had been hoping that someday Rilsin would organize and move against Sithli, although she had admitted to doubts that Rilsin ever would. He had thought it would never happen. Now that it seemed it might, he tried to sort out his feelings.

Excitement was paramount. Boredom had been the bane

of Sifuat's existence. The alleviation of boredom had been a driving force in his life. If his wife began an armed rebellion, life would be far from boring. It would be dangerous, but Sifuat had never been afraid of physical danger. Rilsin might need him to help command her troops—no, she *would* need him to help command the troops. It would be glorious.

And then, afterwards, after the victory he would engineer, he would be the consort of the SaeKet. Sifuat smiled to himself. He wondered if Norimin had thought of this aspect, that the son she despised would stand beside the SaeKet's chair. Of course she had thought of it, he realized; she had just never mentioned it to him. All that had mattered to her was a granddaughter, not the fact that he would be the father of the SaeKetti, the consort of the SaeKet. For the first time, he thought of little Reniat with a certain amount of pride.

There was, of course, the possibility that the revolt would fail. That could be a disaster. It could be, but it would not be, not for him. Sifuat had a contingency plan. Rilsin's relationship with Sithli had its ambiguities, but he was close to someone who was in turn close to Sithli, someone closer and more important to Sithli with every passing day, someone on whose favor he could depend, if all else failed. Sifuat smoothed his lavender velvet appreciatively. He was charming, he was handsome, and despite what Norimin and Rilsin thought of him, he did know how to intrigue. His future, one way or the other, was secure.

"THE ROADS ARE clear. I have to go tomorrow." Sifuat shoved his hands deeper into his vest, wishing it weren't so damnably cold, wishing he had had the nerve to do this somewhere warm. "Norimin is ill and needs me. Will you miss me?"

Jullka sae Lisim smiled. She looked warm and comfortable, her fur hood pulled up close around her face, fur-lined trousers tucked into fur-lined boots. In point of fact, she was almost as cold as Sifuat, and she was also annoyed, although she couldn't show it. If Kepit hadn't assigned her the responsibility for seeing that Sifuat fit into their plans, she wouldn't be standing in his summer pavilion, at the back of Rilsin's tiny town estate, in the freezing dead of winter, trying to pretend she was attracted to the first minister's husband. Sifuat had sent word that he didn't dare meet her anywhere but here, on his own property. Or rather, on Rilsin's. Of course they couldn't meet in the house, where it was warm, and they might be discovered. Aunt Kepit was getting too old, and she didn't know what she asked. It was almost time for Jullka to take control of the Lisims into her own hands.

"Of course I will miss you, Siffy. But Norimin doesn't need you to go to Hoptrin. Rilsin is the one who should be going."

Sifuat blushed and coughed. "Uh, Rilsin can't go. Her duties keep her here, so I must go in her place."

"You don't have to pretend with me, Siffy." Jullka looked concerned, but inwardly she was amused to see Sifuat squirm. "You don't need to pretend; I grew up with you." Jullka smiled, reached out, and tucked a stray strand of Sifuat's hair behind his ear. She watched him flush even more. *At least someone is warm,* she thought. "I know that Norimin never thought highly of you. It's hard when your own mother underrates you. We have that in common." In fact, Jullka was not underrated by any of her clan, but Sifuat was too self-centered to know that. "I don't think even Sae Rilsin appreciates you as you should be appreciated, Siffy. She is a lucky woman. If it weren't for Rilsin—" Jullka sighed and tried to look lovelorn.

"Rilsin won't know. Rilsin never has to know." Sifuat put his arm around Jullka. It was not easy, as both were bundled into their heavy winter clothing. Jullka was dark-haired, golden-skinned, sharp-featured, and slender to the point of being thin. Sifuat had long been attracted to her, but he had had no reason to think the feeling was reciprocated until recently, when she began to pay him flattering attention.

"We can't, Siffy." Jullka pulled gently away, but not too far. "I wouldn't hurt Rilsin for all of Saeditin." *I hope the*

Mother doesn't strike me dead, she thought. She knew she had confused her target, so she waited a moment to let Sifuat's perplexity deepen.

"I wouldn't hurt Rilsin, because that would mean hurting you, Siffy dearest. We need to wait for a better time, a time when you have the power you deserve. You deserve to be in command. You were born for it. To command the SaeKet's armies. Go to Hoptrin and take command of Norimin's troops, Sifuat." She lowered her voice, even though there was no one anywhere near to hear them. No one else would have the foolishness to meet in such freezing circumstances. "You think I don't know that Petipal is uneasy, that all of Saeditin is uneasy? You think I don't know how the people feel about Sithli SaeKet, and how they feel about Rilsin? If you move, Sifuat, I will support you. The Lisims will support you."

"You know how dangerous this is." Sifuat found it hard to catch his breath. He was almost unbearably excited. Jullka would not have said what she did unless it were true. Kepit and the whole Sae Lisim clan were behind him, would support him. "What if I fail?" He could have kicked himself as soon as he said it.

"You won't fail, Sifuat. I won't let you. We won't let you. And afterwards, then we can think about Rilsin. She will be Rilsin SaeKet only because of you. She will owe you."

"Yes." Sifuat allowed himself to think of this. Surely then Rilsin would allow him whatever he wanted. She could not refuse him.

Jullka could almost read his mind. She had long ago ceased to be astounded by the ability of people to delude themselves and to see what they wanted to see. Allowing them to delude themselves was her stock in trade. It was a good thing Sifuat was going north tomorrow; if he stayed, he might let something slip to his wife. Rilsin, too, could be deluded, but not by Sifuat, or not for long.

"Go north and take command, Sifuat, while Norimin still lives. When the time is right, you will move. Saeditin will be waiting."

"How will I know when it's time?" Sifuat wanted to seem suave and cool, but his anxiety showed.

"You will know, Siffy. I will let you know. Remember, Sae Lisim supports you. And I support you." Now she leaned forward and kissed him. "You can't lose."

"No," said Sifuat, "I can't." He returned the kiss passionately.

27

It was a glorious day in late spring. The air was still cool, but the sun was strong. The garden was thick with blossoms, and Rilsin was glad she had decided to come home for her brief midday meal. She fed Reniat the last spoonful of porridge and fruit and then wiped the baby's face.

"There!" she said. "What a good girl!" She tickled her daughter gently, and Reniat laughed, a pure baby's laugh. Rilsin hugged her and then reluctantly handed her to Meffa.

"I'm sorry little sweet pear, but Mama can't take you now. Uncle Sola's workshop is no place for someone so little. Be good for Meffa until I get back:"

"She's always good." Meffa smiled, as much at Reniat as at Rilsin. Meffa knew it was a great honor to care for Rilsin's child, the sun-child, but she also loved the little girl.

Rilsin glanced back at them as she left. Reniat had added a whole new dimension to her life. She begrudged the moments she must be parted from her child, and, in fact, she often took the little girl with her to meetings. Reniat was usually well-behaved, and people tended to spoil her. Some

simply liked children, but some wanted to curry favor with
the first minister. Others, Rilsin knew, had religious reasons,
due to the circumstances of Reniat's birth. These reasons
were never mentioned, but Rilsin knew how widespread
they were, especially among the commoners.

As she glanced back one last time, she saw that Chilsa
had come up to Meffa. Reniat was pushing one tiny fist into
the big cat's fur, and she was laughing. Chilsa was unfail-
ingly gentle with her.

She walked through the streets toward Sola's workshop,
not the old hunting lodge, but his official workshop near the
palace. She went alone, even though most saedin these days
preferred not to walk the streets of the capital without an escort. Rilsin was as safe as a saedin could be, given the times.
She was recognizable in her black uniform, and although
her hair was growing out, she did not adorn it with gems, as
most saedin did.

Petipal had been quiet recently. Although the unrest was
there, not far below the surface, Rilsin chose not to see it.
Her investigation of the Lisims, of Kepit and her ever more
powerful lieutenant Jullka, had languished. Sifuat's reports
from the north had been reassuring; Norimin still lived and
was even regaining strength. Rilsin had time, and time was
what she needed: time to secure her position, time to secure
the safety of her child, time to reassure Sithli.

Sola was alone when she arrived. This was surprising.
Saeditin's foremost inventor had several apprentices, and he
was besieged by young people who wanted nothing more
than to work with him. Some of the younger generation, especially sons and younger daughters of rich dira, had their
own workshops, where they enthusiastically pursued various projects, everything from improving the steam machines to attempting to turn lead to gold.

"Where is everybody?" Rilsin found Sola working
around an object that was covered with a thick cloth. The
guards posted at the perimeter of the workshop's grounds
had admitted her with no questions.

"I sent them away. I have only one apprentice who
knows anything about this project, and he is sworn to tell no

one. I had everything made separately, and I assembled it here. No one really understands why. This is most dangerous, Rilsin."

"Greetings to you, too." Rilsin's grin faded when she saw how serious Sola was. "All right, Sola, I'm here. You had best explain."

"I'll do better. I'll show you. But Rilsin, I don't think this invention should be used. I was going to destroy my notes and show no one, but I had to show you, Rils. You will understand. You have supported my work."

"The SaeKet has supported your work. I administer the funds."

"Sithli, least of all, should know of this." He waved off her questions. "You will see why."

He removed the cloth from whatever it had been covering. On one table rested a little contraption that seemed to be basically a small tube. Opposite it was a mound of earth.

Sola was fiddling with the tube thing, putting something into it, so Rilsin went to see the mound. It was, in fact, a pile of earth, heaped rather solidly. In front of it were several old pottery jars and also shards and scraps of broken jars. Rilsin picked a few of these scraps up and dropped them clinking back to the floor, confused. She glanced back at Sola and his tube. It looked unprepossessing, but so had the original steam machine. It was like Sola to take something ordinary in appearance and make of it a magic as great as any in the old tales.

Rilsin walked back to the table. A piece of twine came out of Sola's tube, which he had just finished packing with powders, and with little round, leaden balls. As she watched, he lit a match and touched it to the twine, which began to spark and fizz. Intrigued, Rilsin leaned over and peered down into the tube.

"Get away from there!" Sola grabbed her and unceremoniously dragged her back behind the table.

The twine burned into the tube. There was a flash of light and the boom of a small explosion. Almost simultaneously came the crack of a breaking jar. Rilsin's ears rang, and she shook her head, trying to clear it. Two of the jars were broken, and some of the earth was plowed, as if it had been dug with a stick. She reached out gingerly to touch the smoking tube: it was hot. She pulled back abruptly. She stared at the tube, then at the smashed pottery, but she did not go to examine it. Doing so would have required that she pass in front of the tube.

"It's safe now," Sola assured her.

"What?" Her ears were ringing.

"I said, it's safe now!"

But Rilsin did not move. She stared at the broken pottery, her mind in a whirl. Sola watched her, saying nothing. Eventually, she shook herself.

"Can these be made in different sizes? Larger, and smaller—even more portable?" Her hearing was returning, but the room still buzzed slightly. "Must lead balls be used? Have you tried how far this tube will shoot the balls? What are the powders that fuel this machine? I think we could have the smiths turn these out rapidly; is a special kind of iron required? Can you refine the aim?"

"Rilsin!"

She blinked and looked at him. "This is amazing, Sola; truly amazing!"

"I cannot let this invention leave this room. I told you I have thought of destroying my notes; I will do so."

"You can't, Sola. Why would you?"

"Think of what this could do!"

"I am." She was hearing herself give the order to sound the trumpets against the Runchot on the eve of Sunreturn, the trumpet blasts that had precipitated the fatal avalanche. Would that have been necessary if she had had these tubes? Would this have been worse? Why?

"One question." She looked at him with frank curiosity. "Why did you make this," she waved her hand, "fire-tube? Why, if you don't want it used?" She almost asked, *And why show it to me?* But she knew the answer to that one. He had shown it to her because there was no one else, and he couldn't bear the knowledge alone.

"I made it because I had to know if I could. Once I imagined it, I had to know if it would work. But in the wrong hands, Rilsin—" he almost said, "in any hands."

"What wrong hands? It will be in my hands. I command the armies."

"They are the armies of Sithli SaeKet."

They looked at each other for a moment.

Sola hurried on, before Rilsin could speak. "It's not just Sithli." Sola sighed and ran sooty hands through his hair, leaving streaks on his face. "Imagine kidnap rings with these. Imagine highwaymen and thieves with these. Imagine saedin fighting duels with these."

"Imagine facing the Runchot with these. Sola, I will not keep this secret. How common are these . . . powders, here?" Rilsin gingerly touched the little heap by the tube.

"Very common. We use them in matches."

"Then it is just a matter of time. If you do not announce this, one of your apprentices will discover it, or one of your many imitators. You have begun a craze for invention. The army must have these. Imagine if the Runchot got these first."

"Perhaps. No, no, you are right." He sat down heavily. "But not yet. Please, Rilsin. I have never asked anything of you, but I'm asking this. Just give me a little more time."

"I can't refuse you. I don't like it, but I can't refuse." Rilsin frowned. "A little time, Sola, just a little."

She turned and left before she could be tempted to say anything else, or before he could. She made her way by habit through the streets of Petipal, deep in thought, almost unaware of those around her. She understood Sola's fears, or she thought she did. The vision of such a device in the hands of many was enough to give anyone pause. But the device would be in her hands. She stopped abruptly, causing pedestrians to turn and look at her. What if Kepit sae Lisim had this? Would Sithli give it to her? Once Sithli knew, once Sithli had this device, what might Sithli not command?

Had she, in fact, been too cautious these past weeks? She had told herself it was for the sake of Saeditin, but was it really for Reniat's sake and for her own? Perhaps there was less time than she thought.

28

THE LAND MOVED EARLY INTO SUMMER. IT SEEMED AS though spring ended suddenly, after only a few days. Sifuat did not return from the north, where Norimin, although ill, still clung to life. It was possible she was not recovering, as Sifuat claimed, but this was hard to prove. Rilsin's agents informed her that Sifuat had a mistress in Hoptrin, a young saedin woman, the third daughter of a minor family. Rilsin did not mention this when she wrote to Sifuat. She was not surprised, but she found herself sometimes feeling sad. She thought of the early days of their marriage, their honeymoon time, as if it were long ago. Sometimes she told herself that Sifuat would change, but she could not believe this with any conviction.

Sifuat trained with Norimin's troops. He did not just keep the troops at full strength, as he had assured Rilsin he would, he augmented them. Rilsin sent word that she intended to go north as soon as she was able to, presumably to see Norimin before she died.

The mood in the city was becoming ever more dangerous. Tension seemed to rise with the heat, and Rilsin realized that whatever action she took, she was going to have to take it soon. She had kept her promise to Sola and had said nothing of his new invention, but her own silence on the matter disturbed her. As a result, a coolness had descended on her friendship with Sola, a chill at odds with the mood in Petipal.

Sithli seemed oblivious to the mood of the people. She kept Rilsin close to her, and in some respects the relationship was as it always had been, but Rilsin knew she was not her cousin's only close advisor. Kepit sae Lisim was frequently in the SaeKet's quarters, almost always when Rilsin was not there. It disturbed Rilsin that her agents were unable to unearth any conclusive proof of the Lisims' illegal activities. Also, no one seemed to know the whereabouts of Jullka. Kepit could not feign ignorance, but Rilsin was never able to question her directly. Some of Rilsin's sources claimed she had been spotted near Hoptrin, which was unsettling, if true. She wanted to write to warn Sifuat, but what what would she say? Worse, what if Sifuat already knew? What if Jullka were there, not for political reasons, but for personal ones? The reports remained unconfirmed, and she did not write.

"I need you to leave today, Sae Essit. Can you manage that?"

"Immediately, Commander."

They stood in her formal parlor. Essit held the glass of cool berry juice, which Rilsin had offered him as refreshment, but he was dressed for the road, with high boots, thick trousers, and a belted shirt, uncomfortable in the heat.

"No, my friend, not in daylight. It must wait until dark, just a few more hours, for your own safety. Keep your route secret, as we discussed. Do not take the main roads. I do not want you found with a knife in your back. Being my friend is not safe these days."

"The Lisims would not be so bold without Sithli's backing."

Rilsin nodded. "True. And I will remedy that. I have a meeting with the SaeKet in the morning."

"Sithli SaeKet does not listen to reason or sense. The time for talk is rapidly passing." Essit tapped his foot impa-

tiently and shifted his weight. Everything about him said
that he longed to be gone. Rilsin put her hand on his arm.

"I know it is. That is why I need you to go. Take command of your own troops in the north, and of Norimin's. If
Sifuat balks at my directive, tell him it is a joint command,
but see that you give the orders, Essit, until I get there. I will
prepare the Guard in the city. Sithli has her new Elite, under
Lisim command." She sighed. "I hope it does not come to
this, but if it does, we must be prepared."

Essit looked at her. It would come to it. He knew it. He
was glad Rilsin was finally willing to take action, but he
wished she would act now. Immediately. He had the sense
that too much time had passed while Rilsin struggled with
her vow to keep the peace and support the Sae Melisin
regime. Everything had seemed to accelerate since the Winter Solstice Battle: Sithli's distrust of her old friend, the increasing Lisim influence over the SaeKet, the assaults
against commoners and even dira, and the unrest of the people. But at least Rilsin was acting at last.

"Come north with me, Commander:" He spoke impulsively, but he wished she would. He was uneasy with her remaining in Petipal.

"I can't, Essit." Rilsin sank into a stiff-backed chair. She
ran her hands through her hair, pulling strands from her
short braid. At times she forgot that it had grown, and she
needed to take more care of it. "We are not ready to move,
and to tell the truth, I hope there is no need. I have always
been able to talk Sithli SaeKet to sense before. I will come
north when I can, Essit, and I will bring as much of the
Guard with me as I can."

Later that evening, as the sun set at last into the summer
haze over Petipal, Essit sae Tillit rode out of the city and
into the countryside, taking the back roads to the north. He
rode alone, and he made sure that he was not followed. For
these reasons, he missed the messenger racing south from
Hoptrin.

THE ĐAY ĐAWNEĐ even hotter than the ones preceding it.
Rilsin took Chilsa for a walk well before dawn and fed Re-

niat when she returned. Today would be a bad day for her meeting with Sithli. The heat invariably put her cousin in a bad mood. It was likely to bring on one of Sithli's headaches, and Rilsin pondered delaying the meeting, but she knew she had delayed too long already. She saw Reniat settled into Meffa's care and Chilsa sprawled out on the cool tiles of the kitchen floor, and she envied them both. Her black shirt was cotton and short-sleeved, but it would not do much to help her remain comfortable in what promised to be a scorching summerlike day.

Rilsin arrived at the palace early. Her own guards saluted her at the entrance, but within the palace itself, the guards of the new Elite showed no such formality. They did not dare, however, to bar the way to the first minister.

Sithli was awake and up. This was unusual. Also unusual was the fact that Rilsin was asked to wait. The SaeKet, she was told, was in a meeting. Just after sunrise? Sithli liked her comforts, which included rising late, and Rilsin had fully expected to meet Sithli fresh from her bed. When at last she was ushered into Sithli's presence, she understood. Kepit sae Lisim smiled slightly at her as she left. Rilsin nodded in return. Neither spoke, and despite the heat, Rilsin felt a chill run over her. She was not surprised that Sithli would see the Lisim without Rilsin present, but why so early?

"Come in, Sae Rilsin."

Sithli was dressed in formal green and gold, and her hair was done up in the customary emeralds, but she looked haggard, as if she hadn't slept, and the scar stood out on her cheek. She was slumped in a cushioned chair, but she straightened as Rilsin entered. Three guards of the new Elite stood against the walls, looking alert, their hands on their swords. Rilsin felt a wave of uneasiness wash over her.

"Are you well, Sithli?" Rilsin touched hand to heart, but looked at her cousin with concern.

"Do you know some reason I should not be well, Sae Rilsin?"

"I know of none," Rilsin was confused, as much by the formality as by Sithli's words, "but you do not look well, SaeKet. Perhaps it is only the heat."

"Perhaps the heat of treachery!"

Rilsin stared at her. For a brief moment she wondered if her cousin had read her thoughts over the past weeks. But she had done nothing disloyal. Her preparations had not taken her that far, for she still hoped that Sithli would see reason.

"What treachery, Sith?" Rilsin would have to calm her and reassure her.

"How can you ask me that?"

Sithli sounded sorrowful as well as angry. Her gaze shifted to a point behind Rilsin, and Rilsin turned to look. Kepit sae Lisim had reentered the room. Rilsin glanced behind her in time to see the Lisim nod once at Sithli.

"You are the traitor, Rilsin! There is word from the north, through Jullka sae Lisim. There is insurrection in Hoptrin. Sudit troops are moving south!"

Rilsin gasped. She could feel the blood draining from her face, but otherwise she felt numb. She did not doubt the news; even had she been inclined to, the look on Kepit's face would have erased any uncertainty. Essit had not had time to reach Hoptrin. Sifuat had moved on his own, and Norimin had permitted him to. How could he have been so stupid! Why had Norimin permitted this?

"How can this be? There is a mistake, SaeKet!"

"No mistake, Sae Rilsin. The troops are moving south to Petipal. But they will not reach the city. I will see to it." Kepit took it upon herself to respond. She was smiling slightly. Rilsin ignored her.

"I will put a stop to it, Sithli! Sifuat has done something stupid without my knowledge." Inwardly she was seething. "I will go north immediately—"

"You will do nothing, and certainly not go north!"

Of course I can't, thought Rilsin. *But wait until I get hold of Sifuat. I have to stop him!* "I must stop Sifuat!"

Kepit stepped forward. "What is more important, Rilsin sae Becha, is that you be stopped. Guards, arrest her."

Rilsin looked at the Elite guards standing against the wall. They were not her guards, but they hesitated, nonetheless. They hesitated until Sithli herself gave the order.

"Arrest her," said Sithli, "and take her to High Prison."
She looked directly at Rilsin. "You betrayed me, Rils." Her
voice was cold and passionless. "You owe me your life, and
now you will pay it back."

Rilsin watched the guards advance. It occurred to her to
draw her sword and fight her way out, but she put the
thought aside. She might win free of the room, but she could
not win free of the palace or its grounds, and she might die
trying. If she were fast, and she could be very fast, she could
kill her cousin first, before they took her. But her throat
closed with sorrow at the thought, her love for Sithli rising
in spite of all. They took her sword from her and bound her
hands behind her back, while Rilsin thought of Essit, riding
north, and how she had declined to go with him.

HIGH PRISOΠ HAÐ not changed since Rilsin had been incar-
cerated there as a child. It was the same solid, bulky stone,
graceless and ugly, and Rilsin wondered how her ancestors
could ever have called it home. It was much better suited as
a prison than as a palace.

To reach the prison they had to march her through the
streets, surrounded by Elite guards, with a growing crowd
of sullen commoners trailing behind them. The ominous
muttering of the people surrounded the guards who surrounded Rilsin.

The guards were nervous, and the two beside her kept
their hands on her arms at all times. Rilsin found it impossible to think. Fragments of thought fluttered through her
mind like tattered rags, only to drift away on the winds of
shock. The one fragment that stuck in her mind, remaining
foremost, was that she must contact Meffa. Meffa must take
Reniat and Chilsa and leave Petipal. She had to get word to
Meffa.

In the prison they marched her up a winding staircase to
a tower at the peak of the old building. It was not the same
room in which she had been imprisoned as a child. If anything, this one was smaller, being at the tower's tip. There
was a high, small window set into the stone. It was barred
but had no glass. There was a straw pallet in one corner for

a bed and a curtained alcove with a chamber pot. The jailer
and his two assistants were waiting for her. Rilsin almost
expected to see the old man of her childhood, but he was
long dead. This jailer was a chubby, red-faced man of the
honored class, Pilsopnit dira Froz. His appearance, was
jovial, but his reputation was harsh. His assistants were a
young man and woman of the common class.

Without much ado, one assistant cut her bonds. The
other brought a rough stool and pushed her down onto it.
Drawing a sharp knife, he grasped Rilsin's braided hair.
Rilsin jerked, thoughts of the Mother's Square rushing into
her brain.

With a quick twist, she lunged to her feet and feinted for
the knife. The stool crashed onto the floor. The jailer's assistant tripped over it, and suddenly the knife was in
Rilsin's hands. The other assistant, the young woman,
looked startled and slightly awed.

"Stop her!" shouted Pilsopnit, and he waded into the fray
to aid his subordinates. It was to his credit, thought Rilsin,
that he did not leave all of the dirty work to others.

As Pilsopnit came at her, she ducked under his arm and
jabbed him hard in the solar plexus with the hand that did
not hold the knife. Simultaneously, she stomped his foot
with the hard edge of her boot. Pilsopnit swore. The assistant she had tripped had pulled himself up from the floor.
Rilsin held them at bay with the knife held low in front of
her. She would not use it, but they did not know that.

"I don't want to kill you," she said, "but neither will I
have my throat cut here."

From behind her, she could feel the young woman jailer
gathering herself for a belated attack. The outcome was a
foregone conclusion, but Rilsin was not inclined to give up.
She started to turn, but she was too late. Sure enough, the
woman jumped on her from behind, and the two men took
advantage of this to rush her from the front. The knife was
pulled from her hands.

"We are not going to cut your throat, traitor, more's the
pity," snarled Pilsopnit. He held one hand over his bruised
stomach. Rilsin was slightly gratified to see that he was

puffing and out of breath. "We are only going to cut your hair, as befits a prisoner of the SaeKet."

They held her tightly, the young man twisting her arms behind her painfully and forcing her back down on the stool, which had been righted. The young woman had the knife now. Despite the pain and discomfort, Rilsin began to laugh. After all these years, she thought, when she had finally decided to grow out her hair, when she had at last stopped thinking of herself as Sithli's prisoner. The jailers looked at her uncertainly.

She regained control as she felt the woman begin to hack at her disheveled braid, and she sat still, barely breathing now. Pilsopnit watched her from as far away as the small room would allow.

"Forgive me," whispered the woman softly, as she cut Rilsin's hair. "Forgive me." The whisper was so soft that even her young male partner could not hear it, let alone Pilsopnit, who stood farther away. "Forgive me, SaeKet."

After they cut her hair, they left. Rilsin heard the heavy wooden door swing shut, and the slap of the bolts as they shot home, and the clank as the key turned in the lock. She looked down at the small pile of hair on the floor; the jailers had not swept it up. She ran her hands through her newly shorn hair. *The worst cut I have had in years,* she thought, *the worst cut ever, since the very first.* She walked to the window. It was too high for her to see out of it, but they had left the stool. She carried this to below the window and stood on it to look out.

Below her was a short expanse of Petipal Street, patrolled now by Elite guards. In the back of her mind Rilsin noted that Kepit did not dare let the army or the Petipal Guards have this duty. But most of her thoughts were focused on the shock of the view from her window. The street led straight to the Mother's Square. Her view was of the place of execution.

The sound of the bolts being drawn brought Rilsin from her dark trance. She had no idea how long she had stood, gazing down from her small window. She stepped from the stool and stood with her back to the wall as the door opened.

Pilsopnit and the young jailer's assistant stepped inside. The apprentice carried a pitcher, a cup, and a slab of bread. She looked around nervously, not at Rilsin, but behind her, at the door, which she kicked shut.

"Put the food by the bed," ordered Pilsopnit.

She put the food down near the pallet, barely taking her eyes from Rilsin as she did so. Then she turned, following Pilsopnit to the door.

"Dira Pilsopnit." Rilsin's voice sounded strange in her own ears. The jailer turned. "I need you to take a message from me to the SaeKet. If you would bring me paper and ink and see that it is sent, I would be grateful."

"There will be no messages, by the SaeKet's orders. Besides," Pilsopnit smirked, "such things cost."

Rilsin stared at him, startled. He wanted to be paid for this? "I will pay you whatever you wish, Dira."

"With what?" Pilsopnit barked out a laugh. When he saw Rilsin's confusion, he laughed again. "You own nothing, Becha, but what is on your person. Your property and estates have been seized by Sithli SaeKet."

Rilsin swallowed. Of course. She took a rapid inventory of her sole possessions: a black cotton uniform shirt and trousers, her boots. Her commander's pin and her sword were gone. She had her mother's pendant. Sifuat's ruby marriage ring. She looked up to find her jailers leaving, the door almost closed, with the young woman pulling it shut.

"Wait!"

The door cracked open. "What is it!" Pilsopnit seemed to have lost patience.

"Is there bedding?" Rilsin looked at the straw of the pallet, which was none too clean.

"It costs," said Pilsopnit, and shut the door. The bolts rang home.

Rilsin sank down on the stool and put her head in her hands as the reality of her situation began to come clear to her. She heard the sounds of the street below her, heard when the guards were changed, but she did not move. At last the summer day faded into its late, light dusk. There was the sound of someone at the door, the bolts being drawn again. Rilsin looked up.

It was the young woman jailer. She carried a broom and dustpan, to sweep up Rilsin's hair. There was a coarse woolen blanket over her arm.

"For you," she said. "I will tell Dira Pilsopnit that you gave me a brass button for it, should he ask." She laid the blanket on the pallet and began to sweep.

"What is your name, ria?"

"Lellefon." Her eyes were wide and clear blue, looking into Rilsin's eyes. She was almost as tall as Rilsin, pale-skinned, with dark, braided hair. The old Saeditin stock, as Rilsin was.

"Ria Lellefon, I need your help. Please." Rilsin stood abruptly, feeling her unused muscles cramp, as the woman began to edge away.

"I know it is dangerous, but with a little care you will be safe. And I will give you this." She drew off Sifuat's ring. The ruby caught the last of the daylight and glowed, as she held it out. Lellefon gasped.

"No, Sae Rilsin, I cannot." She continued to back away. "I cannot take a message to Sithli SaeKet! Not to her!"

"Not to Sithli. Not to the SaeKet. Do you have children, Ria Lellefon?"

The woman blinked with surprise at the unexpected question. "A son," she said. Her features softened as she thought of him. "Drenit. He was four years this last Snowflower Festival."

"Then you will understand. I want you to take a message to my good friend, the woman who cares for my daughter."

Lellefon's gaze sharpened, and she ceased edging away.

"I cannot get you paper and ink, Sae Rilsin, and I cannot write."

"It does not matter, if you can speak the message yourself. If you will do so. I trust you." She remembered Lellefon calling her "SaeKet," but the truth was that she had no choice. "Will you do this?"

"I will," whispered Lellefon.

Rilsin felt a piece of darkness lift slightly. "Find Meffa

ria Shonfa. She may not be at my house; it may be difficult.
Find her and tell her to take Reniat and Chilsa—my child
and my cat," she said, wanting to be clear, momentarily forgetting that everyone in Petipal would know who they were.
"Tell her to take them and leave Petipal. Tell her to go—"
Rilsin paused. Where would be safe? Would Meffa's family
in the countryside be safe? "Tell her not to go to her family;
it may not be safe; they may be watched. Tell her to go
north." Rilsin drew a breath. "To the Wilfrisin Confederacy.
If she can, tell her to get Lendis, and take him and take
Reniat, take both children, to First Man Bilt of the Confederacy."

She met Lellefon's clear blue eyes, and the woman nodded slightly.

"Take this for your trouble." Rilsin again held out the
ring.

"I cannot." Lellefon backed away. "I will find Meffa ria
Shonfa, and everything will be done to get the sun-child to
safety. And the hunting cat and the barbarian's child." She
looked at Rilsin intently. "My family is Notliss, Sae Rilsin."

Rilsin frowned; the name was familiar. Just as it came to
her, Lellefon spoke again.

"My mother is Notliss, but my father is Shonfa. He is
Crenfa ria Shonfa, Meffa's brother. Meffa is my aunt. She
does not know I am in Petipal, for I ran away from home
two years past, hoping for fortune in the city. This," she
glanced around her, "is all I found for work. Now I see the
Mother's purpose."

29

Sifuat looked down into the valley from the crest of the little hill and smiled to himself. It would be the perfect place. Behind him massed Norimin's troops, *his* troops, and for the first time, Sifuat felt himself to be truly in charge, truly doing something of value, contributing to the history of Saeditin.

Norimin had not wanted him to do this, but his mother was dead, and now she could not stop him. He had kept up the fiction that she was ill but recovering, but the word would soon be out. The news had come that Rilsin was imprisoned by Sithli. Rilsin would not have wanted him to do this, either, to begin a revolt, whatever her plans may have been for the future, but now it was up to him to rescue her and to earn her everlasting gratitude. The coming battle would be just the beginning.

"We will set up camp in the valley!" Sifuat ordered. He watched, gratified, as his orders were repeated, the messengers racing away, the troops beginning to comply.

"You cannot be serious!" Essit had ridden up in time to hear the order. Now he dismounted and strode over to Si-

fuat. He looked down into the valley and shook his head.
"Countermand that!"

"This is my army." Sifuat glared at the young noble. "No
one countermands my orders!"

"Then you countermand them, Sae Sifuat! We cannot
make camp there!"

"It is the perfect place. It is flat, good land for tenting.
There is a stream at the edge for water. No one could ask for
better."

"Sithli's forces are nearby. The Lisim could catch us
down there, Sifuat, which would be very bad for us. You
see," Essit spoke slowly and simply, "that place is a trap."
He knew he should not let his feelings for Sifuat color what
he said or how he said it, but he was too young to keep all
the scorn from his voice.

Sifuat heard it. He heard it and correctly deduced that
Essit thought him an idiot. Any opportunity for listening
with reason and patience fled. He flushed, his golden skin
mottling with a darker purple. His hands clenched.

"I am in command here! And I say that is where we
camp! If it is a trap, it will be so for Kepit sae Lisim!" He
stomped away from the younger man, gathering his lieu-
tenants around him.

Essit watched him leave. Rilsin must have had the patience of the Mother Herself to put up with such a fool. "I
am withdrawing my troops!" he shouted after Sifuat. "I will
not place them in the way of certain death!"

Sifuat heard him, and for a moment he let concern slow
him. The forces of Tillit saedhold, which Essit commanded,
were significant. But Sifuat's forces were greater still, and
he knew his own personal fighting abilities. This time he
would gain the glory he sought.

Essit gathered his troops and retreated into the woods up
the hillside. It was safer to camp there for the night, with a
good view of the surrounding land. He could not see Sithli's
army yet, under its Lisim command, but his scouts had said
they were near. If Sifuat got himself into trouble, Essit
would come to his rescue, despite what he thought of the
man. Essit's main regret was that Rilsin had not come north

with him when he had asked. It was all so much more complicated now. He needed to gain a decisive victory and to get south to Petipal before Sithli had her executed. When it came to getting Rilsin out of Sithli's hands, his thinking grew a little fuzzy, but he had faith that a plan would come to him.

The late summer darkness found Sifuat encamped in the valley. Essit's troops had faded back into the woods of the surrounding hills, far back from the main body of troops. Sifuat's scouts had informed him of the Lisim advance, but he was not worried. By morning, he and his troops would be rested and fed, prepared for battle. He had sentries posted so that he would not be taken by surprise, and then he went to bed. Sifuat functioned best after a good night's sleep.

Morning came shrouded in mist. Sifuat yawned, stretched, and looked across his camp to the surrounding hills. Dark shapes moved in the fog, darkening the hillsides, moving like dreams or nightmares. Sifuat felt a chill, and for the first time wondered if he had been wise not to listen to Essit. Even as he wondered, the alarms were being blown, the horns sounded, and his troops were scrambling for their weapons. It wasn't until much later that Sifuat learned what had happened to his sentries. All of them had died at their posts, their throats cut.

The enemy did not wait until Sifuat could rally his forces. They poured down the hillsides from all directions. The fog made it harder to coordinate a defense, and Sifuat's troops were in confusion. Screams and cries pierced the fog. He understood now why Essit had refused to camp in the valley. There was no way to regroup and to gain the advantage of the higher ground. Just as Essit had predicted, they were trapped.

Sifuat was able to rally a small force around himself. He was a formidable fighter, and his reputation for courage and ferocity were well-founded. He believed in himself, and he did not intend to lose this battle.

"To me! For Becha!" boomed out through the fog. Soon Sifuat had an ever-growing core around him, trying to force their way through the confusion, to gather more troops, and to make their way to higher ground.

The way was littered with debris and with the bodies of the dead and dying. Some of the tents had been set afire, and their glow and the flames lit the fog. Sifuat pressed forward, his sword moving so fast that it sometimes seemed to have a life of its own.

More of the enemy poured down from the hills above. Sifuat found himself at the front of a tight little knot of northern troops, trying to get to higher ground. For a while, he had no idea where he was, and then he found himself fighting with wet feet: he was at the stream, in a little marshy spot just before the banks widened out. The stream was a little narrower here, and shallow. Beyond it was a short expanse of open meadow, and then the hills. With a glance over his shoulder, he could see that the way was almost clear. If he and the few with him could fight their way across the stream, they could run through the meadow and retreat up the hillside with relatively little opposition, if they were lucky. Then Sifuat could regroup. He could join up with Essit's forces. He had no doubt he could do this. He grinned at the woman fighting beside him, overwhelmed with a love for these soldiers of his.

Then his foot caught on a rock, his ankle turned, and he went down. The woman beside him was run through by her opponent, and she fell half across him, her blood pouring over him. She choked, gurgling, her mouth gaping. The man fighting behind him threw down his sword, surrendering. Sifuat looked up and saw himself surrounded. His sword had flown from his grasp in his fall. He swallowed, closed his eyes, and prepared to die.

ESSIT HEARD THE sounds of combat and knew it had happened as he feared. Sifuat had been caught in the trap. He called his troops into formation, and they marched for the valley. By the time he reached the battleground, the fog was lifting, and he had a good view of the result of the morning's activity.

The valley was a shambles. It was littered with bodies

and equipment, with dead or dying horses, smashed wagons, burned or broken tents. Some bands of survivors were attempting to rally and escape, but Essit could not tell if Sifuat were among them. The largest group of survivors was fighting desperately halfway up on the hills. The sheer numbers of the Lisim troops were overwhelming.

He hoped that Sifuat was among the survivors, or better still, failing that, that he had been killed in battle. He intended to rescue those whom he could, do as much damage to Sithli's forces as he could, and get away again. If he could not escape, it was all in vain, and Rilsin's cause was lost, but he could not leave the surviving Sudit troops to die or be captured.

"Archers first!" Essit cried.

The archers of Tillit saedhold loosed a volley into the enemy below. The beleaguered Sudit troops responded with a ragged cheer when they realized what was happening. Volley after volley winged its way downward into the valley, but the range was not good, and Essit knew he had to close the distance. The archers marched ahead, pausing to fire and then fall back. Essit reined in his horse and drew his sword.

"For Rilsin SaeKet!" he shouted. He spurred his horse and thundered down the hillside.

Essit had the advantage of surprise, but Sithli's forces were larger, and they were well-organized. Essit tried to push the enemy to the center of the valley, but they would not be pushed, and Essit would not commit himself to descending all the way into the confusion. Wherever Essit saw a large enough band of surviving Sudit troops, he fought his way there to rescue them. All across the hillside, Tillit forces were doing the same. The cry of "For Rilsin SaeKet! For Becha!" echoed and clashed with cries of "For Melisin!"

As dusk began to fall, Essit called a retreat. He was exhausted but unhurt, covered with blood, but very little of it his own. He had been careful, and his personal guard had protected him. He was willing to let Sithli's army leave the valley and begin the march back to Petipal in return for his own chance to leave.

"We have saved about four thousand Sudit troops, Commander. We won't have an accurate count until morning." The aide was dirty, tired, and grim. She tried to wipe the sweat from her eyes but succeeded only in smearing more dirt across her face.

"Is that all?" Essit was appalled. "Out of twenty-five thousand?"

"I think so, Commander. There will probably be more, a few stragglers coming in during the night, but not many. We have saved whom we could."

"Great Mother!" Essit slumped on the stool that had been placed near the fire for him. This was his temporary headquarters: a stool, a table, a fire, a pot of stew, and officers and messengers coming and going in a steady stream. There was no tent, no bed, and Essit wondered if he would ever again get the chance to sleep.

"What of our own casualties?"

"Two hundred dead. About five hundred wounded."

Essit sighed and nodded. It was not bad at all. It could have been much worse.

"Any sign of Sifuat sae Sudit?"

"Not yet." The aide did not attempt to hide her distaste. She knew who was responsible for the carnage in the valley. "We have not found him among the survivors. The dead are being searched, but if he is there, we may never find him." Unsaid was the grim fact that not only were there too many dead, but there were too many to bury before wild animals or looters made recovery impossible. This was one of Essit's foremost regrets: that he would not have time to search among the dead and to give them the rites for their final peace.

"If anyone even resembling Sae Sifuat is found, alive or dead, inform me immediately." It had crossed Essit's mind that Sifuat might try to hide his identity. He could not be very popular with his own troops just now.

"Yes, Commander."

"Get some rest if you can." Essit sighed again and then

straightened on his stool. He had made a decision. "We march north at first light." There were too many of Sithli's forces still intact, still nearby. He could not hold this territory. "We march for Hoptrin."

The aide saluted and left. She wished she could rest, but she knew she could not. First light was not that far away. As she was leaving, she remembered a detail, overlooked among so many.

"Commander Essit," she said, "there is a messenger from Petipal. From Sola dira Mudrin. He would not say what it is, but he claims it is of utmost importance, and that he must speak with you. You alone."

"Soon," said Essit. "Soon, but not yet. See to his needs, and if he still wishes to speak to me, have him come north with us." He was puzzled. What could Sola want? He was not a fighting man. Unless perhaps it was news of Rilsin that the messenger brought. "No, wait. I will see him now."

SIFUAT AWOKE IΠ the dark, thirsty and cramped. He could not at first remember where he was or why. The room he was in seemed to be moving. His head was pounding, and there was a sour taste in his mouth. His throat was dry and hot. It must have been some night, for the hangover to be this bad. Who had been with him? Was it Jullka? The sae Lisim heir was insatiable. He would have to stop seeing her. Having two mistresses and a wife was too much. He stretched, and discovered he was chained at wrists and ankles. Memory came flooding back, and he tried to sit up. It was a mistake. The chains yanked him back, biting into his flesh. Nausea rose and almost overcame him. Sifuat was barely able to stifle a moan of pain.

He was in a wagon, a closed wagon of the sort used to carry supplies and weapons, and the wagon was moving. He remembered looking up into the eyes of an enemy soldier, a soldier who would have killed him, had not an officer recognized him at the last instant, before the spear point descended. Instead of death, Sifuat had been kicked in the ribs and kicked in the groin, but it was the kick to his head that had rendered him unconscious. Now, consciousness had returned, unfortunately. The wagon jounced over a deep rut, and Sifuat's head banged against the boards. Despite himself, he moaned.

The wagon jounced on through the night, and Sifuat no longer tried to restrain his moans. For a little while, he lost consciousness again, and then consciousness came and went like the tides of the faraway ocean. During those times when he was awake, Sifuat heard someone pleading for help. It sounded like his own voice. Eventually, the sound would drift away.

Consciousness returned again. He was not moving, or rather the wagon was not moving: a blessed relief. Gray light seeped in through the boards, as best he could tell through half-closed eyes, so it was no longer night, although Sifuat did not know how many nights or days had passed. He tried to open his eyes and turn his head. This took some doing. His eyes were partially gummed shut. The attempt to turn his head made the pounding headache worse and brought the nausea back. He lay still for a moment, with sweat popping out all over his body, and then tried again. This time he was able to turn his head to see most of the wagon.

The wagon was empty. He lay on his back, arms and legs pulled tight. His wrists were chained above him to the front boards of the wagon bed. His legs were stretched out, and his ankles were chained to the side boards. The chains were looped over and through the boards, prompting Sifuat to wonder if he might be able to pull the boards loose and pull the chains free. Then all he would have left to accomplish would be to escape the wagon and escape the enemy camp while still wearing his chains. The thought made him groan.

"I see you are awake. Good morning to you, Siffy."

The rear gate of the wagon had been lowered, admitting early morning sunlight and a visitor. Jullka sae Lisim walked lightly through the wagon to crouch near Sifuat's head.

"Oof, Siffy," Jullka waved her hand in front of her face. "You smell terrible! Worse than on most mornings. But then, your night was a little worse than most nights, wasn't it? I am afraid I cannot offer you the amenities of a bath or clean clothes."

Jullka herself was dressed in the green and gold of an Elite Guard, and her dark hair was freshly braided with gold thread. She seemed to sparkle in the light. She took a large bite of the hard biscuit she held and chewed thoughtfully. If she had meant to torment Sifuat with hunger, it did not work. The sight of the food made him slightly nauseous again. But when she took a long pull from her water flask, Sifuat swallowed dryly. His thirst was overwhelming.

"Thirsty? Poor Siffy."

Jullka leaned over and raised his head with one hand. With the other she held her water flask to his lips and tipped it. Sifuat gulped the slightly acrid-tasting water. After a moment, she pulled it away.

"Don't drink too much now, or you will be sick."

"What are you doing here?" Sifuat's voice came out in a hoarse whisper. "You have to help me, Jullka; get me out of here!" He began to cough, and for a while, he couldn't stop. Jullka leaned over and gave him another sip of water. Then she sat back, capping her flask.

"I can't get you out of here, Siffy." She laughed sunnily.

Sifuat stared at her, blinking, trying to get her in focus. "I know it won't be easy, but you can do it. You obviously have them fooled."

"Obviously have them fooled?"

"Yes, the uniform, your Elite uniform, they must think . . ." Sifuat's words trailed away as Jullka continued to smile.

"I think you are the one who was fooled, Siffy."

"But—" he had to pause. Breathing had become difficult. "But you . . . you encouraged me! Jullka, you told me the time was right to rise against Sithli! You told me you were working against her." She had said she was working against the SaeKet for his sake, but Sifuat did not say this now. "You told me the Lisims would support me, that the time was right!"

"The time *was* right." Jullka leaned over and smoothed his hair back from his eyes. "The time was very right. But not for you. The time was perfect for us. For the Lisims. Rilsin was too dangerous for us; we needed her out of the way. You performed a valuable service, Siffy, a very valuable service. Now she will be out of the way. Permanently. Unfortunately, so will you."

"But Jullka! I trusted you!"

"Trust is such a problem, isn't it? Sithli trusted Rilsin. Rilsin trusted you, even though she knew better. You trusted me. Now, of course, Sithli trusts Kepit. The only ones you should count on are those in your family, but you never knew that, did you, Siffy? Rilsin had no family, but you should have known. It's too bad that you never trusted Norimin, or she you." Jullka brushed off her green trousers, dusted her hands together, and rose. "I suppose I can't blame Norimin. It's hard to trust a fool. She had more sense than Rilsin, at least." Jullka turned to go.

"Wait! Jullka, wait! I thought you loved me!"

Jullka turned. "You thought so?"

"You said you did!"

"Oh, Siffy. Poor Sifuat. You said you loved me, too." She smiled. "The difference is that I never believed it."

30

THERE WAS THE SOUND OF THE KEY IN THE LOCK. THAT first, and then the bolts being drawn. It was a sound she both longed for and dreaded. Rilsin sat up on her pallet and drew her legs under her. The apprentice jailer would be bringing her her meal and taking out the slop bucket.

In the weeks since her arrest she had not seen Lellefon ria Notliss again. She was afraid that the young apprentice jailer had been caught and had lost her position, or worse, but there was nothing she could do. The other apprentice spoke with her only when he must and would not even give her his name. Most of his business with her he conducted in silence, despite Rilsin's attempts to draw him out. He was the only person she saw, except for the guards in the street below her tower, and she could not speak to them.

The apprentice brought her food once each day, mostly bread and cheese and water, but also vegetables and fruit twice a week, and meat once a week. It was more, she was sure, than other prisoners received. It was good treatment. She was fed and she was not tortured, but she was not particularly grateful for the privilege. What she wanted more

than food was information, but there was no way to obtain
it. The lack of news was an agony, as bad a torture, in her
mind, as anything physical they could have inflicted, as was
the lack of anything with which to occupy her time. All she
could do was to worry. When, after four weeks, the apprentice jailer cut her hair again, Rilsin saw that the brown was
mixed with white.

The door swung open on its thick hinges. Rilsin put her
arms around her knees and looked away.

"Sae Rilsin."

She looked up. Hope and amazement arose simultaneously. It was Lellefon.

"What happened to you! I thought—" Rilsin stopped.
She did not want to say what she had thought, to give it any
reality. Lellefon's possible fate had been one of the things
tormenting her.

"I am well." Lellefon smiled slightly, dismissing all of
Rilsin's fears on her behalf. "Only now has it been safe
enough for me to return to Petipal. I took a leave, claiming
illness, first my own, and then a family member's, my little
brother's. It was the only way I could move about more or
less unwatched. I said I had to tend my brother and recon-
cile with my mother. And I have had one piece of unexpected luck. I have in truth reconciled with my mother."

"I am happy for you." Rilsin meant it. "Children should
not be divided from their mothers." Hearing her own words,
she stopped, swallowing the lump in her throat.

"I have your news. I am sorry you had to wait, but I
could not come, and there was no one to trust. Visitors to
this prison are carefully screened."

Why did Lellefon not just say it? Rilsin felt as if she
could not breathe.

"Meffa is in hiding, with Chilsa. She is not far outside
the city, but she does not dare to return."

She drew a breath, and Rilsin watched her, trying to say
nothing. She clenched her fists, digging her nails into her
palms with the effort.

"Sithli SaeKet has taken the sun-child."

Rilsin closed her eyes. The tiny room seemed to spin

around her, and she sank back on her pallet, leaning her head against the hard stone of the wall. Sithli had taken her baby.

"She has not harmed her, Sae Rilsin! Sae Rilsin, please! She has adopted her."

"What!"

"Sithli SaeKet has adopted Sae Reniat. She has declared that the sun-child is no longer Sae Becha, but Sae Melisin. Reniat SaeKetti Melisin. She declared that the Mother always meant for the child to be hers, that you bore the child for her."

Rilsin laughed. It came up from somewhere deep inside her, and she laughed until the tears ran down her cheeks. At last she stopped, wiping her eyes, while Lellefon smiled uncertainly.

"So Sithli would have my child inherit after her. My Becha daughter. Sithli's grandmother swore there would be no more Bechas in the SaeKet's chair. And no matter what Sithli says, Reniat is still my child and a Becha."

"The people know this, Sae Rilsin. They are not happy with Sithli SaeKet. More commoners are missing, and more dira. We know that most are sold over the border, but some are taken to work in the mines in the east. It is getting worse, Sae Rilsin."

Rilsin got up from the pallet. "I can never thank you enough for what you have done for me, Ria Lellefon."

Lellefon's fair skin turned pink, and she opened her mouth, but Rilsin forestalled her.

"I am going to ask you for more, ria. This is dangerous, and I will not think ill of you if you refuse."

"I will not refuse, SaeKet. Not if there is any way I can help. The Mother has placed me here for this. It was Her hand guiding me."

Never underestimate the faith of the commons, thought Rilsin. She hadn't much faith herself, but she was grateful now for those who did. "I need you to go to someone for me. Is Sola dira Mudrin still free?"

Lellefon looked startled. "Of course!" Then she looked surprised. "Sae Sithli knows he was your friend, but he has

been locked away in his workshop. She knows, and everyone believes, that his work means more to him than anything, that he cares nothing for politics. And he is too
important. She would not harm him."

"Good. Can you give him a message?"

"I will die trying, SaeKet!"

"I hope not." She did not smile. "Tell him that his secret
is needed now."

"That's it? 'His secret is needed now'?"

"That's it. And be careful, Lellefon."

SUMMER WAS FADING, and the first chill winds of autumn
blasted through the tower window. Rilsin took the blanket
from her bed and hung it in the window in an attempt to
keep out the cold. She shivered in her cotton clothing, wishing desperately for the warm clothes she had at home, the
home that was no longer hers.

Lellefon had successfully delivered her message, but
Rilsin was unable to speak with her again. For some reason,
the two apprentices had been ordered to come together on
the daily visit to Rilsin's cell; it was never Lellefon alone.
In the company of her fellow apprentice jailer, Lellefon was
as brusque and taciturn as he. The most the young commoner could do was to bring her another blanket, which
Rilsin gratefully accepted.

Rilsin lost track of time. She had certainly lost track of
the moon phases. One brisk morning she heard the sounds
of activity in the streets below. Positioning the stool below
the window, she climbed up and peered out, wrapped
against the chill in her second blanket. The activity was not
in the street below, where the Elite Guards patrolled, but in
the Mother's Square, where the execution platform was
being cleaned and the spectators' platforms prepared. Rilsin
felt a chill that had nothing to do with autumn. It occurred
to her that the stool had been left for just this purpose, to en-
able her to see just this particular view. Now she knew the
moon phase. Tomorrow would be the dark of the moon.

She told herself she would not watch. She told herself
that it did not matter whose throat would be cut, whose

blood Sithli would taste, but she knew she told herself lies.
When the drums began to roll, and the guards lined the
street to the square, Rilsin was at her window. She knew the
guards in the street below her glanced up, smirking, aware
of her presence, but she could not leave.

Sithli was escorted to her chair on the main platform.
The crowd muttered as she passed by and then grew omi-
nously silent. It was obvious that the people bore her no
love. In her window, Rilsin felt the sudden sting of unexpected tears. How had this happened? She remembered
Sithli as the young girl who had saved her from the knife so
long ago, but times had changed. Sithli had changed. She
had known it was happening, but she had refused to see, had
refused to act, and now it was too late.

"This is my fault," Rilsin whispered. "I betrayed my vow
to the land. I could not have kept my vow of peace, but I
could have kept my vow to the land." No one heard her
whisper, no one except the stones. It seemed to her that the
stones of the prison heard her, the prison that had once been
a Sae Becha palace.

They were bringing the prisoner now, the condemned
saedin. The people began to mutter again, and someone
shouted, before one of the Elite Guards lining the streets
and the square silenced him.

"Sudit! Becha!" was the cry.

Rilsin felt time stop around her. Sithli in her green and
gold was clearly in her view, and the death priest was on the
platform. When the prisoner was brought forward, she
could see him clearly, too. It was Sifuat.

He was thin and ragged, and his golden hair had been
chopped as short as hers. But he was still beautiful. Even
knowing how his rashness had cost him everything, and had
cost her, too, Rilsin felt a lump forming in the back of her
throat. Behind her eyes, something prickled.

She should never have trusted him; she knew it now, and
she had always known it. It was too simple to say that love
had blinded her to his faults. It had been more than that, or
less. It had been a desire and a longing to trust, to be able to
rely on someone else, someone with whom she should be

sharing her life. She had always known that Sifuat was not that someone, and she had ignored what she knew. But he was still her husband, the father of her child, and he had loved her in his way. The prickling behind her eyes intensified and then leaked down her cheek.

Someone stepped forward, dressed in Melisin green but wearing a scarlet vest. The new first minister, Rilsin realized, who turned and looked directly up at Rilsin's window. It was Jullka sae Lisim.

"Sifuat sae Sudit," Jullka's voice carried over the square, "you are convicted of treason. You are a traitor to the land of Saeditin, and to Sithli SaeKet Melisin, its true ruler. Do you admit and proclaim your guilt?"

Sifuat drew himself up. "I am no traitor!" His voice boomed out, and he looked around him at the crowds in the square. He ignored Sithli, but he looked up at Rilsin's window. "I fought for the true SaeKet, and I fought for Saeditin, for all the Mother's people, commoner as well as noble!"

Rilsin drew a breath, realizing only as she did so that she had not been breathing. Where had Sifuat come up with that speech? It was so unlike him, but it was, of course, just what he should have fought for.

Two guards seized Sifuat, and one put his hand across Sifuat's mouth.

"In the name of the Mother," Jullka was intoning, "and the land of Saeditin, you must return your life and your blood to the land. SaeKet, will you receive it?"

Rilsin knew the formula; she had recited it often enough. Her eyes were on her husband, who had ceased to struggle and stood straight between his guards.

She heard Sithli say, "I will receive it."

The guards forced Sifuat to his knees, and one pulled his head back to bare his throat. Rilsin wanted to scream. She wanted to close her eyes. She could do neither. She jammed her hand into her mouth to keep from crying out.

When it was over, when Sifuat's body lay slumped on the platform and Sithli's pink tongue delicately tasted his blood, Rilsin, too, tasted blood. It was then that she found that she had bitten her hand.

She remained at the window, unmoving, as the rite ended. Sithli made her way from the platform, heavily guarded, through the silent square. The commoners parted for her, but sullenly. The saedin and the dira on their platforms were silent, too. Some of the saedin looked around them uneasily.

When darkness fell, the square was empty save for the guards, but Rilsin still stood at the window. It seemed to her that even in the darkness she could see the dark stain on the ground made by Sifuat's blood. She thought she could feel it, even from a distance, like heat from a fire. Eventually, she left the window to sit on her pallet. Finally, she lay down, but she did not sleep.

When morning came, she lay there still. She did not move at the sound of her door being opened. She did not move until she heard Jullka's voice.

"Was it a bad night, Rilsin?"

Rilsin sat up. Jullka was there with five guards and the three jailers. It was quite a crowd for a small cell, but that was not all. In the midst of them was Sithli, dressed in green and gold, with emeralds in her hair. She was beautiful as always.

"Sithli." Rilsin's voice sounded old and tired, even in her own ears.

"Sithli SaeKet," her cousin responded, moving aside.

The jailers were bringing things into the cell: a small table, onto which they placed a candle and a paper. Pilsopnit laid a knife beside the candle. He caught Rislin's gaze on him and smiled slightly.

"There are three days of the dark moon, Rilsin," said Jullka cheerfully. "Yesterday was the first. Today, tonight, is the dark mother's height, the time for maximum purification."

Rilsin ignored her. Her attention was all for her cousin. Sithli's face was slightly puffy, and there were dark circles under her eyes.

"You don't look well, Sithli SaeKet." There was a tinge of pity to the words. Rilsin had expected to hate her cousin, but now that she saw her, she felt unaccountably sorry for her. Unfortunately, Sithli heard the pity. Her golden skin flushed.

"Your betrayal has made me ill! Your treason! The only cure for me is your death! So I have been told."

Rilsin's eyes flicked to Jullka. She was pretty sure she knew who was responsible for the suggested cure, but she was tired, so very tired, too tired even to hate the young Lisim.

"It won't work, Sithli; the cure won't work. Killing me, killing Sifuat . . ." She swallowed. "This is just the beginning."

Rilsin glanced away from her visitors, up at the window, the square of blue autumn sky. "Where will this end?" she said, but she was not addressing her cousin.

"It ends now, Rilsin." Jullka held out her hand, and Pilsopnit placed a paper in it.

Rilsin looked at the paper; it was her death warrant, she knew.

"No," she said; "no, Jullka, it does not. How many have died so far? How many battles? Has the war reached Petipal yet? I don't think so, or even I would know. I can feel the mood of the people even in here. I felt it yesterday from the square. If I die, the land will be ablaze; Petipal will burn."

"Not if you die! Not if, Rilsin!" Sithli was livid with anger. She grabbed the paper from Jullka's hands and began to read. "Rilsin sae Becha, you are convicted of treason against Sithli SaeKet Melisin and the land of Saeditin. For this you are sentenced to death. Your blood will be returned to the land, that the Mother may cleanse it," Sithli's voice began to shake, and she stopped, choking. Jullka took the paper from her unresisting hands.

"On the evening of the height of the dark moon," Jullka continued, "you will be taken to the Square of the Mother, to give your life to the land." She slapped the paper down on the table, struck a match, and lit the candle. She picked up the knife and ran it through the candle flame and then held it out to Rilsin. "Tonight, Rilsin," she said.

Rilsin was still watching her cousin. Sithli had stopped

trembling, and she looked back at Rilsin. Rilsin took a step toward her but stopped as the guards began to draw their swords.

"Sithli, let me see Reniat." She stopped, swallowed, and tried again. "Sithli, please, before I die, let me see my child one last time."

"She is not your child! She was never yours! She is mine! The Mother gave her to me!" Sithli whirled toward Rilsin, baring her teeth in a snarl. "You will see her! Tonight, in my arms! Before your throat is cut!"

Rilsin felt tears begin to rise. When Sithli had been unable to finish reading the death warrant, she had thought some of the old bond remained, but what she saw now in her cousin's eyes was only hatred.

"Admit your guilt and seal your death, traitor." Jullka was still holding the knife toward her.

Rilsin glanced at her, then turned back to her cousin. The tears had retreated somewhere deep inside her. She felt numb. "Yes," she said, "I am a traitor; I admit it. Not traitor to you, Sithli. To you I was true, and that is my mistake and my shame. I betrayed the land; I betrayed Saeditin. By trying to keep the peace, I betrayed the peace; by keeping my vow to you, I betrayed it!" The numbness was fading, replaced by fury, not against Sithli but against herself. "My guilt is that I did not act! I put it off, I waited, Sithli! I waited, hoping you would see the right course! Hoping you would act as you should! You are not the true SaeKet, Sithli, and you have never been! If I were true to the land, I would have taken back the SaeKet's chair long ago!"

Rilsin turned on her heel and snatched the knife from Jullka's hands. Belatedly, the guards realized that she was now armed, and they drew their swords, surrounding Sithli. The tiny cell was bristling with weapons. Rilsin ignored them. Two steps took her to the small table. She drew the blade of the knife, hard, across her left palm, ignoring the pain, and when the blood welled up, she slammed her palm down on her death warrant, smearing the paper with red. Then she tossed the knife to the floor.

"Good luck to you, Sithli," she said. "You are in dire need of it."

"We are done here," said Jullka, picking up the paper. "Let us go."

The small contingent left the cell hurriedly, but Rilsin did not watch them leave. Her palm felt as if it were on fire. When she heard the bolts shoot home and the key turn again in the lock, she walked to the wall of her cell, the outside wall nearest the street and the Mother's Square. She pressed her wounded palm against the cool stones. Keeping her palm against the wall, she slowly slid down until she sat on the floor. Then she rested her head, too, against the cold stone.

Despair surrounded her and weighed her down, making it hard to breathe. It seemed that all she could do was regret. She regretted all the times she had not acted, and the times that she had acted to keep Sithli secure. Sithli was right, but her betrayal was even greater than Sithli knew.

She felt it flowing up through the stones, through the walls and the foundation of the old palace. It flowed up from the stones, through her wound, and mingled with her blood. She felt it even in the air around her, that rich harmony of impressions. She could feel the distant woods moving into autumn sleep, and she could feel the life of the city throbbing with her own heartbeat. The song of the land.

Rilsin was not accustomed to prayer, so she whispered instead one stray and forlorn hope.

"Another chance," she whispered. "I would give anything, had I anything to give, for another chance."

31

She could feel the passage of time. Day was drifting toward autumn evening, and soon they would come for her. Rilsin stayed where she was, head leaning against the wall. When she heard the bolts drawn and the door open, she did not look up. Someone came and knelt by her, and she tried to brace herself for the hard grip of guards come to take her to her execution. A gentle hand touched her shoulder.

"SaeKet. Rilsin SaeKet, let me help you." It was Lellefon, and she was alone. Rilsin blinked up at her. "Please, SaeKet, we haven't much time. Oh, your poor hand!"

The jailer's apprentice set down a small basin, opened a flask of water, and poured some in. Then she took a cloth, wet it, and began to gently wash Rilsin's hand. Rilsin was too astonished to stop her. She watched blood and dirt rinse into the basin. Lellefon, it would seem, had no fear of the curse of the SaeKet's blood. Lellefon appeared to catch this thought.

"I know you would never harm me, SaeKet."

Rilsin pushed herself up, away from the wall. "I would never harm you; you are right, my friend." She sighed. "But why are you bothering?" She watched as Lellefon wrapped a bandage around the now clean cut. "In only a little time I will have a wound far worse than that, one which you cannot mend."

"No, you will not." Lellefon finished tying the bandage and sat back on her heels. "But we must hurry. There is no time to spare. Dira Pilsopnit is busy with the preparations for—with the preparations—and I have arranged for Nep to help him. They think I am doing my appointed tasks. I am, but my tasks are those set by the Mother, not by Dira Pilsopnit." She rose to her feet. "Can you stand, SaeKet? You must!"

Rilsin looked up at her. She looked at Lellefon's extended hand and at the door to the cell, open behind her. The haze of despair around her vanished, and hope took its place in a fiery rush that was almost painful. She rose to her feet so quickly that she swayed with dizziness. She had not slept or eaten since the previous day, but the new hope made up for the lack of food and sleep.

"I have a way out of the prison, and I have someone to help us outside. Hurry!"

The corridor and the stairs were empty. It was strange to be out of the cell which had been her world for months, strange to be moving again. Her legs felt light, her head felt like feathers. Lellefon held up a hand at the bottom of the stairs: *wait,* then motioned her to come. Rilsin hesitated, then moved forward. As they rounded a corner, there were voices.

"An extra contingent of guards, even though it is such a short distance to the square. The traitor was right, the mood of the people is ugly." It was Pilsopnit. "We must take no chances tonight. What has happened to all the guards? There should be guards here!"

Lellefon backed up, almost bumping into Rilsin. Rilsin looked around for somewhere to hide. There was a door near them, a heavy wooden door. Without hesitation, she pushed against it. It opened, and she and Lellefon stepped in, closing the door behind them.

It was an office, Pilsopnit's, from the look of it. There

was a large desk, an overstuffed couch, some hangings. They could hear Pilsopnit, still talking, right outside the door. It was obvious that he meant to enter his office, along with whomever he had in tow, and in another moment he would be in. Rilsin looked around desperately. Lellefon saw a knife on the desk, one used for trimming paper and quills, and snatched it up. Rilsin saw nothing she could use for a weapon, and in any event, it was too late.

She flattened herself to one side of the doorway and motioned to Lellefon to do the same on the other side. Unfortunately, the young commoner was either too slow or did not understand. The door opened, and Pilsopnit entered, followed by the other jailer's apprentice. Nep, Rilsin remembered. Lellefon had called him Nep. She at last knew his name.

"Lellefon! What are you doing here? Why are you not bringing the chains, as I —" he stopped, suddenly seeing Rilsin against the wall beside the door.

Nep saw her at the same time. The young apprentice froze, but Pilsopnit opened his mouth, simultaneously reaching for his sword. Lellefon aimed the paper knife and threw. The knife flipped, hilt over blade, and caught Pilsopnit in the throat. He went down with a gurgling cry.

Nep recovered from his astonishment and turned to run. Rilsin jumped him from behind, bringing him down. She rode him to the floor, staying on his back. She felt blood soak the bandage on her left hand as her wound opened again. The landing knocked most of the breath out of her, but she did not hesitate. She grabbed Nep by the chin and snapped his head back, hard. There was a crack as his neck broke.

She felt no regret, only a sense of urgency. She rose to her feet to see Lellefon standing over Pilsopnit. The prison governor was still alive, thrashing and clawing ineffectually at the knife in his throat.

"SaeKet, he won't die!" She was shaking, and Rilsin realized the young woman had probably never killed anyone before.

"Yes, he will," she said. "Excuse me, ria." Rilsin gently

moved Lellefon aside. She knelt to the side of Pilsopnit, trying to push his head to the side, but his hands were still
clutching the knife, trying to pull it out. Rilsin would have
to get Lellefon to help, after all, if she couldn't manage.

"Dira," she said. "Dira Pilsopnit, you know how this
must end. You are dying anyway; there is nothing anyone
can do to save you. All I can do is to make it quicker. I am
sorry."

His eyes met hers. Suddenly, his hands went loose on the
knife. Rilsin grabbed it and pulled it sideways, as hard as
she could. It was only a paper knife, but it was sharp
enough. Rilsin moved back just in time, avoiding getting
blood on anything but her hands, which she wiped on Pilsopnit's cloak. She stood and looked down at him. He had
been preparing to take her to have her throat cut. Fate was a
strange thing. She shook her head slightly, clearing it, and
looked at Lellefon. The jailer's apprentice was staring at her
former master and at her fellow apprentice.

"We had no choice," said Rilsin. "Lellefon, we had no
choice."

Lellefon made a visible effort to control herself. "It
won't be long before he is missed," she said. "Follow me,
SaeKet. We must hurry."

They ran through the corridor and down another flight of
stairs. The air was damp and dank here, chill. They were in
the cellars of the old castle. There were small rooms and
corners piled high with old objects: a storage area. Rotted
barrels and a pile of old, rusted weapons, spears, and shields
lay across their path, and they stepped around them. A little
light filtered in through windows set up at ground level.
Lellefon took her down a dark corridor. Now there was very
little light at all, and Rilsin brushed against earthen walls in
the dimness, but her guide seemed to know where she was
going. The corridor broadened out suddenly, and Rilsin had
a sense of space. She could see nothing at all now, and she
stretched out her hands, searching for Lellefon or for anything.

There was the scrape and hiss of a match. Lellefon lit a
lantern and held it up. In its light, shadows danced and flick-

ered. It was a huge room, vanishing into shadows and dimness. Rilsin stared. She had only her summer uniform, but it wasn't only the chill that made her shiver.

"Where are we? What is this?" She kept her voice to a whisper, as if afraid that someone or something might overhear her.

"We are below the old wing of the castle, SaeKet, a wing that was torn down for a courtyard and guard barracks. They tore it down, but they left the cellars below and forgot them, or they never knew they were here." She held the lantern higher. "I found it one afternoon when Dira Pilsopnit was away." Lellefon was whispering, too. Something she had said struck Rilsin.

"They tore down the wing for a courtyard and guard barracks. Does that mean the barracks are right above us?"

"Yes. This cellar runs beneath the barracks and exits up through a destroyed shop in an alley that runs beside the Mother's Square. We can escape the guards by passing beneath them."

They moved quietly through the vast chamber. Despite the stone and the earth that separated them from the world above, they could hear thumps and sometimes footfalls from overhead. If they could hear what was above, then the guards above them would, in return, hear any noise they made.

They began to move uphill, imperceptibly at first, but then it was obvious that they were leaving the old cellars. The space narrowed, and Lellefon blew out the lantern. A faint light filtered down from somewhere ahead and above. Lellefon dropped to her knees and began to crawl, pushing the lantern ahead of her. Rilsin followed. By the time she caught up to Lellefon and they came into a slightly larger space, she was shivering so hard that her teeth were chattering.

They had exited into a ruin. They climbed over large tumbled stones and out into another cellar, this one shallower and lighter. Through an opening, Rilsin could see a small room with shelves, obviously the abandoned shop of which Lellefon had spoken. A cold wind filtered through the open chinks and gaps in the stone. She wrapped her arms around herself for warmth and moved toward the room. Someone stepped out of the shadows of the smaller cellar and into their path.

The shock was so great that she almost cried out, and from old habit she reached for the sword that was no longer there.

"Ria Lellefon," said a voice she knew, and then, "Rilsin? Rilsin!"

It was Sola. She was enfolded suddenly and awkwardly in his arms. Then he dropped the bundle he was holding and looked at her. "Rilsin, what have they done to you?"

For a moment she couldn't speak, fighting again against the unaccustomed tears. What had they done to her? How could she answer that? She looked closely, as closely as she could in the dim light, at her friend. He was thinner, with tight, haunted lines around his eyes.

"Oh Sola," she whispered. She felt lost and wanted nothing more than to have him hold her again.

"We need to hurry," said Lellefon. "The SaeKet had to kill the governor and . . . and the other apprentice. It won't be long before they find them, and then find her gone, and the alarm goes out."

Sola drew back and picked up the bundle he had dropped. "Then let's not waste time."

The bundle was a cloak, wrapped around some other items. Sola handed her the first of these items: a wig. A long braid of brown hair, twined with sparkling yellow citrines was stitched, with more hair, to a short cloth cap. Rilsin took it but looked at it with distaste. It hung limply from her hand like some strange dead animal.

"Hurry, Rilsin." Sola was unwrapping other items.

Rilsin set the wig on her head. It covered her own short hair completely, but it felt strange. The next item was a vest of gray fur, which Rilsin tried to put on, but she was shivering so hard she had trouble getting her arms through it.

The next item was a sword, which Rilsin strapped on gratefully. She felt a little better now that she was armed. Then Sola handed her the cloak itself. Rilsin stared at it. It was thick wool, deep and warm, with leather fastenings, but it was a bright burgundy slashed with a brilliant, wide silver stripe, and a silver velvet lining. It was ostentatious, something for a showy saedin or a newly rich dira.

"I can't," she said. "I would never wear something like this."

"That is exactly the point." Sola helped her to throw it around her shoulders. It hung down just below her knees, the proper length for a dira, partially hiding the sword. "You are Cedit dira Firit, my wife." He was moving toward the door, and in the stronger light, Rilsin saw him flush. "I am Sipa dira Krat, a cloth merchant."

"We will be recognized." Now that freedom was here, now that she had her chance, Rilsin was reluctant to step out of the ruined shop and into the street.

"Dira Sola may be recognized," Lellefon answered, "but he insisted on coming."

Rilsin had no alternative plan. There was nothing she could do but trust these friends who had saved her life and who risked everything for her. She put her hand, beneath the cloak, on the hilt of her sword and stepped to the front of the shop.

"How are we getting out of the city, Dira Sipa?" she asked.

As she spoke she glanced down at a broken pane of glass, lying aslant a counter. The shop had once been fairly well-to-do, to judge from the amount of broken glass on the floor and the counters. The reflection in the broken glass stopped her. Looking back at her was a woman with braided brown hair, a woman with a pallid, very thin, and slightly dirty face and pain-filled eyes, a woman who looked older than Rilsin's twenty-two years. No wonder Lellefon had said only that Sola might be recognized but nothing about Rilsin herself. A few strands of short-cropped gray hair— gray?—peeked from under the smooth brown of the wig. Rilsin paused to tuck them back and to rub the dirt from her face.

"Tell me the plan," she said, as she stepped out of the shop.

"As we walk," said Sola.

The shop fronted on an alley that now, apparently, was used only for trash. It was a short alley, at the end of which was a broader street, with people coming and going, pushing forward toward some nearby destination.

"Ria Lellefon will leave the city immediately to alert our friends. She should have little trouble leaving. You and I will follow shortly, after we retrieve the horses I have waiting."

"Excuse me, Dira Sola, but I must go, before you and the SaeKet leave this alley." Lellefon looked around anxiously. "I will see you outside the city, SaeKet." Lellfefon put her hand to her heart.

"Wait! Ria—Lellefon—my friend—" for a moment, Rilsin couldn't find the words. "Thank you. You saved my life, and you are a true friend. Whatever happens now, you are a true friend to Saeditin, and to me."

"I try to do the Mother's work." Lellefon had flushed pink. "I will see you outside the city, SaeKet." She put her hand to her heart again, stepped out of the alley, and was gone. Rilsin and Sola waited for a moment and then stepped out themselves.

The street beyond the alley was filled with people, and now Rilsin could see why. She had forgotten what Lellefon had said: that the cellar passageway brought them out near the Square of the Mother. The square was right there, right beside the street where they now stood.

Rilsin stopped in her tracks and stared. They were only a short distance from the saedin platform, which was surrounded by guards. The SaeKet's chair was there, empty now, but waiting for Sithli. The platform itself was still dark with blood in one place: Sifuat's blood, from yesterday's execution. There was a buzzing in Rilsin's ears, and she felt suddenly dizzy. She swayed. It was hard to breathe, and she saw spots in front of her eyes. She raised a shaking hand to brush them away, and Sola caught her elbow.

"You are early, dira; have you a place reserved on the honored platform?"

Rilsin looked up. There was a guard in front of them, a

member of Sithli's new Elite, in Melisin green. He was not
a man she knew, but he looked at her closely. "Are you ill,
dira?"

Rilsin swallowed. The nausea and dizziness brought on
by the sight of her husband's blood receded, but she
couldn't think, couldn't even imagine what she could say.
She waited tensely for him to recognize them. She was
stealthily reaching for her sword, wondering if they could
fight their way out, when Sola spoke.

"My wife is unwell. It should pass. She is with child,
and . . ." he stopped. Rilsin could see that his imagination
had suddenly failed him.

"I forgot to eat today, in the excitement." She smiled
faintly at the guard.

"Is the sausage vendor still in his old spot?" Sola drew
the guard's gaze again. "We should have time to purchase a
little food and return."

"Plenty of time," the guard assured them. "The SaeKet's
procession is not for another . . ." He pulled a watch from
within his cloak. "Almost two hours' time, and they won't
bring out the traitor for a time after that. I don't know where
the sausage vendor is, but you should have time."

"Thank you, sae."

Sola grasped her elbow again and pulled her away. She
let him continue to hold her arm as they pushed their way
against the flow of people, the crowds coming to the square
for the execution. Many of them were not in a festive mood,
as the guard had been, but grim. Rilsin saw one woman who
had been weeping.

"Not everyone will be unhappy when Sithli fails to provide the scheduled entertainment," Sola said.

He was more than right. Rilsin felt her palm throb
slightly. If she wanted to, with only the slightest shift of
concentration, she could hear and feel the song of the land.
Part of the song was the mood of the people. Sithli had far
more trouble than she realized.

It was hard work for a time, going against the flow of
people, but eventually they made their way into lighter traffic. Sola released her arm. Rilsin drew in deep breaths of the

chilly autumn air. She glanced at Sola, striding along beside her.

"Sola, my friend," she said, pulling him to a stop. "I thanked Lellefon, but I haven't thanked you. You are risking everything for my sake, and—"

"Don't thank me yet, Rilsin. When all is over, and you are SaeKet in more than right, when Saeditin is safe again, when no more of our people die in this fight—" he cut himself off. There was a bitter twist to his mouth. "Thank me then. You don't know yet what you have to thank me for."

Rilsin stared at him. In turn, Sola looked into the distance, the lines of anxiety and unhappiness so tight on his face that she wanted to reach out and smooth them away, but she did not dare. She wanted to ask him what had happened, what he had done to secure her freedom, but for a moment she couldn't speak. He had changed, somehow, but then so had she.

"Where are the horses?" was all she asked when she found her voice again.

"Near the cat pens. I have seen to it that two horses will be tied out to graze, with no guards." He began to move forward again.

Rilsin looked around. They were still a few streets away from the palace complex, which she could see they would take care to skirt, until they came near to the horse fields, and then the cat pens.

"We have an errand to do first," she said.

Sola slackened his pace but did not stop again. "What do you mean? We can't stop; we can't go anywhere but to the horses and out of Petipal! The alarm will be raised soon!" He glanced behind him.

Rilsin glanced back, too. She had been expecting to hear the cry and tumult as the deaths of the jailers and her disappearance were discovered, but perhaps they had been discovered, and no cry had been raised. Perhaps the search was proceeding under cover of silence. It did not matter.

"I am going into the palace," she said adamantly. "That is my errand. I am getting Reniat. And I am getting Lendis.

Sithli will not have left for the square yet, and Reniat will be in the palace."

Sola gaped at her. "Rilsin, you cannot! That is insanity! We will be caught! You have no idea how many people have put themselves into danger to get you out of Petipal! And you cannot enter the palace! The palace and its grounds are swarming with guards, even more than in the past; they have been for months, ever since Sithli had you arrested! We can't get in!"

"Yes," she said, "we can. I have a way in, where there will be no guards." She held up her hand, forestalling his continued protest. "And I am going in, whether you come with me or not. I will not leave my child in Sithli's hands!"

She turned away from him and began to walk so fast that she was almost running.

"Cedit! Cedit, wait!"

It took a moment for Rilsin to realize that Sola was speaking to her. There were still people around, although far fewer, so he could not call her real name.

"Cedit, don't run!" He caught up to her and lowered his voice. "Running will attract attention."

She slowed, but only slightly. Now that she was free, now that she had a chance to rescue her daughter, it seemed that every second that it took was a second too long. The sense of urgency she felt was almost explosive.

They could see the lane to the cat pens now, but Rilsin turned away from it toward the horse pastures, and Sola stayed with her. They rounded a corner, and she could see there were guards at the pasture. Immediately, she dropped down into the grass, pulling Sola with her. He was stiff with disapproval and anxiety, but he stayed beside her, and he squirmed through the long, autumn-killed grass after her, trying to remain quiet.

The brush had grown up again for real around the entrance to the old tunnel, tangling with the rotted remains of the old cut brush she had left there years before. She tugged at it, increasingly desperately, still trying to keep a low profile should any of the guards look their way. She felt the bandage on her palm tear and shred, but she did not slow her efforts. Sola came up beside her and gave a mighty yank to the brush. It parted slightly, and cool, dank air flowed out. Without hesitation, Rilsin pushed through into the tunnel, catching and ripping her cloak in the process. Sola was right behind her. They were in, and the guards had not seen them.

It was completely dark, but Rilsin needed only the light provided by her memory. She grabbed Sola by the hand and pulled him along. When they were far enough from the entrance that she thought they could not be overheard, she began to smile in the darkness. She was sure now that they would succeed.

"This is how I sneaked out of the palace when we were children," she whispered to Sola.

"It seems not to have been used in years," Sola murmured back.

"It should be safe. No one else knew about it."

"No one else?"

"Only Sithli."

The name seemed to breathe at them in the darkness. Then, just as it had in the cellars beneath the prison, the slope of the tunnel began to rise.

They stopped just inside the ancient doorway. Rilsin cracked it open, praying that it wouldn't creak. The door swung smoothly, as if its hinges had been oiled, and she had to catch it before it swung open all the way. There was still a dusty wall hanging covering it. Rilsin peered around this. She could see the entrance to her old room not so far away, and the corridor was clear. She motioned Sola forward, then stopped. She realized they had a problem.

"Where is she, do you know? Where does Sithli keep Reniat?"

Sola shook his head. "I don't know," he whispered. "I have no idea!"

Rilsin stepped out into the corridor. It didn't matter; she would find her daughter. She drew her sword, holding it ready, and moved quietly along the hallway. After a moment, Sola followed her.

Because it was right there, because it had been hers, and because she felt the tug of an inexplicable urge, Rilsin glided to the door of her old room, the one she had lived in as a child. The last she knew, it had reverted to an attendant's waiting room, and then to storage. She should have simply passed it by, but she couldn't. She flattened herself against the wall beside the door and risked a look around the corner.

The room had been converted back to a bedchamber, and there was a child in the room. Rilsin's breath caught in her throat. For a brief moment she thought it was Reniat, unguarded, but it was not; the child was too old. It was Lendis. The little boy looked up and saw her. For the briefest moment he gaped, and then he jumped up.

"Aunt Rilsin!" He had recognized her, of course, despite her attempt at disguise.

"Shhh!" she said, stepping into the room, but she was speaking to the top of his head. The little boy had launched himself forward and wrapped his arms around her waist. He clung to her so tightly that it took a moment and some effort to pry him free. "Hush, Lendis," she whispered.

"Have you come to rescue me?" He whispered back.

"Yes. You and Reniat. Dira Sola is helping me," she added, as Sola slipped into the room.

"Good! I knew you would! Sithli SaeKet is so mean to me; I hate her! I knew you would come to take me home!"

"Get your cloak, Lendis. Where is it? And tell me where Reniat is."

Sola saw the child's cloak and grabbed it up, also taking an extra shirt and pair of trousers, which he was tying into the cloak. Lendis suddenly ran to the bed, which was positioned just where Rilsin had had hers, and took something from the bed and held it out for Sola to tie into the cloak. It was a knitted stuffed toy, a hunting cat, rather like the one Norimin had made once for Reniat. Sola took it without comment and tied it into the cloak, which he tied across his back. Rilsin picked up Lendis and slung him on her hip.

"Tell us where Reniat is," she whispered again.

"In Sithli SaeKet's rooms," the child said. "They made her a bedchamber in what was the waiting woman's room, beside her private parlor."

Rilsin stopped. She took Lendis and swung him away from her, holding him toward Sola.

"Go with Dira Sola," she said. "He will take care of you, and he will get you back to your mother, and to your father."

"Rilsin, what are you doing!" Sola whispered urgently. "You can't get into Sithli's rooms; there will be guards everywhere!"

"I know it, but I must. I am going, Sola."

"Rilsin, you can't! You are throwing everything away!"

As they whispered they continued down the corridor in the direction of the SaeKet's quarters. Their luck had unaccountably held, but now, inevitably, it gave out. A guard in the green of the Elite entered the hallway and stopped at the sight of the strange trio. Rilsin could see he did not recognize her or Sola, but it didn't matter. They shouldn't be there; he knew that much. He reached for his sword and opened his mouth to shout a warning.

Rilsin had no memory of crossing the distance between them, it happened so quickly. She had the guard by the throat before he could draw his sword. She slammed him back against the wall and held the tip of her sword slanting upward to his throat beneath his chin.

"Where is Sithli," she hissed at him, "and where is Reniat?"

He choked but didn't answer.

"Tell me!" She felt her wig slip. Still holding the sword to the man's throat, she took her left hand, matted with blood from the wound on her palm, and ripped the wig from her head. She saw his eyes widen, saw the knowledge in them as he realized who she was.

"Where—is—Reniat!"

"Gone! Gone with the SaeKet! They left not a quarter hour ago, to the square! For the execution—" The man began to sob. "Please don't kill me!" His face crumpled. "Please, Sae Rilsin, please don't kill me!"

"Damn it! Damn Sithli to a freezing Runchot hell!" Rilsin took the sword tip from the man's throat and looked back at Sola. "You are right; we are too late!"

The guard shifted away from the wall. Rilsin turned back in time to see him drawing his sword.

"Help!" the guard screamed, struggling to free his sword. His voice was loud, a fine bellow. "Help, aid! Treason! Sae Rilsin is free!"

Rilsin ran him through the heart. She pulled her sword free of the body and kept it unsheathed. She could hear running footsteps behind them. She grabbed Lendis, whose eyes were wide with shock, by the hand, then tried to hoist him, left-handed, to her hip again, but the pain in her hand made her cry out. Sola turned, grabbed the boy, and swung him up to his shoulders. They ran back to the wall hanging, slipped behind it and into the tunnel, and pulled the door closed. They could hear the thunder of guards running past their hiding place, crying out at the sight of their dead comrade.

"He said Sae Rilsin is free!"

"How can that be? She could not have gone far! Search every room!"

Rilsin sheathed her sword. She took Sola by the hand again and led him back down through the tunnel in the dark. Lendis, riding on Sola's shoulders, said nothing, although he whimpered a little, only once.

32

THEY PUSHED THEIR WAY OUT OF THE BRUSH AND INTO THE
horse pasture. Rilsin went out first, dropping down immediately and looking for the horse guards. Luck seemed to be
with them again, for the guards were gone. Scanning carefully, Rilsin could see them, all four of them, at the far edge
of the field, passing a wineskin from hand to hand.

"Can you crawl with us and do it quietly?" she whispered to Lendis. Trying to carry him while they crawled
would slow them down even more; the boy would do better
on his own. He nodded, his eyes huge. "Good. Let's go."

They reached the edge of the pasture. Rilsin's back hurt,
and she was scratched and sweaty from the crawl. Her hand
was bleeding again, and she was weak and dizzy from lack
of food and sleep and from the sudden and intense activity
after her imprisonment. She stood a little too quickly, and
the motion attracted the attention of the distant guards. One
of them shouted something. At almost the same moment,
there was a trumpet blast and more shouting from the direction of the palace. Rilsin and Sola looked at each other.
Rilsin grabbed Lendis with her good hand and began to run.

She staggered, and Sola grabbed the child up again, and they ran down the lane to the cat pens.

There were two horses, saddled and waiting outside the cat pens. There was no one around, no sign of activity at the pens, no sound from within the cattery. Rilsin grabbed the reins of one animal and threw herself into the saddle. She leaned down and dragged Lendis up, sitting him in front of her.

"Hang on to the saddle, Lendis!" she told him. "Sola, where is Kerida?" It had occurred to her that Sola's mother might take some of the blame for her escape.

"Out of Petipal," said Sola shortly. "She had to flee. There is a price on her head. The cattery has been left to apprentices."

Rilsin stared. Kerida, gone but presumably still alive. There was no time to ask anything more. Sola spurred his horse, and she followed. They were making for one of the many roads out of Petipal, this one not as well-used or as heavily trafficked as most. With any luck, the word would not have been passed quickly enough, and they could get through without being stopped. They thundered through the streets, scattering a few pedestrians. They passed a few poor houses, and then there was the road out, leading north.

"Damn!" Sola reined his horse back.

Blocking the road was a hastily erected barrier of carts, three deep, and a small patrol of Elite guards, a few archers among them. Rilsin wondered briefly if the horses could jump the carts and if they could make it through without being shot. It was a fleeting thought; they obviously could not. Her insistence on going to the palace could have cost them their escape. She reined back, realizing as she did so that she could not easily free her sword, not with Lendis on the saddle in front of her. She spared a quick glance at Sola, long enough to see that he had not drawn his weapon and did not look about to.

"Halt, by the SaeKet's order!"

The guards were around them. Several had drawn their bows and were holding her little party steadily in their sights. One grabbed the bridle of Sola's horse; the guards'

leader grabbed Rilsin's. Looking down, she realized she
knew the man. He now wore Elite green, but he had been
one of the Petipal Guard, formerly under her command. He
stared back at her, then his eyes shifted to Sola, whom he
obviously also recognized, and then to Lendis. Other guards
also recognized them; it was plain.

Rilsin had wound the reins around the wrist of her
wounded left hand, and she saw the man's eyes go next to
her bloody hand, with the remains of its tattered bandage.
Her right hand reached stealthily behind Lendis, going for
her sword hilt, even though she could not imagine how she
would succeed in drawing nor how they could fight their
way out now.

"I am sorry for the inconvenience, dira," said the guard,
"but we have been ordered to stop and question all those
who are leaving Petipal. There has been an escape of, er, an
important prisoner," the guard was staring at Rilsin, at her
head. She realized that she had dropped her wig back in the
palace, not that it mattered now. She closed her hand over
the hilt of her sword. The guard saw this.

"Obviously you are not those we seek." The guard
looked at her directly, then glanced back and made a motioned command. Rilsin knew it: *stand down.* The archers
relaxed, the bows dropped down. "May I, ah, I need your
names, dira, and your business. For my report."

Rilsin's hand seemed frozen to her sword hilt. She stared
into the man's eyes.

"I am Dira, ah, I am . . ." Sola seemed to have forgotten
his name.

"He is Sipa dira Krat, a cloth merchant. I am . . ." Rilsin
frowned. She could not remember her own alias. "I am
Cedit dira . . . ah . . ."

"We are traveling on," Sola cut in, apparently unable to remember her full alias, either. "We are traveling on . . . ah . . ."

"Firit! I am Cedit dira Firit. And we travel on family
business," concluded Rilsin.

"Indeed. Go on your way with the Mother's blessing on
you and your business," said the guard. "Dira." He put his
hand to his heart.

Others in the little troop were doing the same. Rilsin felt her own heart lift slightly, and she smiled. "Thank you, my friends!" The little comedy of the past few minutes came to her and now she could not stop smiling. Sola was looking at her with concern.

"Perhaps we can help you with your 'business,' when you return to Petipal!" called one of the guards, grinning at her as they rode away.

"I will look for it!" Rilsin called back.

THEY RODE HARD and fast through the early gathering dusk of autumn. Rilsin thought they would try to put as much distance as possible between themselves and the city before stopping. They did not. Sola motioned for them to halt long before the horses even began to tire.

"There is a safe place nearby," he told her. "We can hide there for a time and wait for pursuit to pass us by. After a day or two, we will set off for the north again but not by the main roads."

Rilsin swayed slightly in the saddle. The horses might not be tired, but she was. Lendis was obviously tired, too. He clung so tightly to the saddle that he trembled slightly.

Sola led them off the road. They picked their way carefully across a field, and when they came to a small patch of woods, Sola and Rilsin both dismounted to lead the horses.

"Just a little while longer, Lendis, and we can rest," Rilsin told the child, although in truth she had no idea how long it would be or where they were going.

The wind picked up now that darkness had fallen. Leaves blew around them, and branches sighed and creaked. It was getting more and more difficult to see.

"We may have to stop here, Sola. The horses—"

Light suddenly gleamed, almost beside them. Someone was there, holding up a lantern. Rilsin raised a hand to shield her eyes against the glare, and then something hit her, hard, just below waist level. She stumbled and fell to the forest floor, crying out as she stopped her fall with her injured hand. She was pinned down by something huge and furred, something that was chuffing like a steam pipe and purring simultaneously.

"Chilsa!"

The big cat gave her a mighty butt with his large head, and Rilsin scratched behind his ears. The horses were whickering nervously, but someone, she couldn't see who, had helped Lendis from the saddle and was leading the horses and the child away. They seemed to vanish, almost before her eyes. Rilsin blinked, then rubbed at her eyes.

"Sae Rilsin! Thank the Mother! You are safe!" Meffa was helping her up, helping her to fend off the attentions of the big cat.

"Meffa." Rilsin put an arm around her chief servant, leaning against her for support. "Lellefon told me you were safe, you and Chilsa. I have missed you!" Now that it seemed they were safe, now that they had arrived at wherever it was that Sola had arranged, something seemed to let go inside her. Meffa was more than her servant, she was a friend. She had missed her friend, she had missed Chilsa, she had missed—

"I am so sorry, Sae Rilsin, about Sae Reniat! Sae Sithli sent guards to take her! I would have fought, Sae Rilsin, but they came while little Reni was napping, and I was in the kitchen. I couldn't get to her; there were too many. All I could do was get out the back and get Chilsa; he would have attacked them, Sae Rilsin, but I held him back, Rilsin, I am so sorry!" She was sobbing. Rilsin could see, in the lantern light, the tears streaming down her face.

"It wasn't your fault. If you had fought them, they would have killed you, and that—oh Meffa." Rilsin put both arms around her. The two women clung together, one sobbing, the other fighting the tears. "We will get Reni back. We will."

"Rilsin SaeKet, come inside. I knew you would get here safely, but come inside now." Lellefon was standing there. "Aunt Meffa, help the SaeKet in."

Rilsin turned. Now that her eyes had adjusted, she could see that they stood in front of a small hillock in the woods. Vines and shrubs grew over the little hill, but it was hol-

lowed out. They stood near an entrance: vines had been
moved aside to reveal a passageway from which spilled
warm lantern light.

It was a large space, Rilsin discovered, with passages
running off in two directions. The earth had been shored up
with timbers and stone, with ventilation shafts cut to the
surface. From one direction came the sounds of snufflings
and stampings; it was apparently a stable for the horses.
They continued down the other corridor. Small chambers
branched off of this, the openings hung with heavy tapestries or cloth in place of doors. The end of the passage
opened out into a large room. The room was filled with the
light of several lanterns, and there were two large tables
with benches and several chairs. The enticing smell of hot
food filled the room. Lendis was seated at one of the tables,
eating something from a bowl. Everyone else in the room
rose when she entered and put hands to heart. Chilsa left
Rilsin's side and went to a bowl in a corner of the room and
began to lap up water noisily.

"Please, sit." Rilsin stopped in the doorway, with Meffa
and Lellefon beside her, and looked around the room.

Sola had been in conversation with a bearded, pleasant-
looking young man who seemed familiar. He smiled at her,
and after a moment it came to her: Dremfir sae Cortin, the
mage from Norimin's household, the priest who had
cleansed her and later married her to Sifuat, but with a beard
now and seeming rather out of his element. Niffa sae Delf,
the devout young captain from her winter campaign, still
stood in front of one the benches, hand still pressed to her
heart. Beside her, also still standing, was another of Rilsin's
captains, Pleffin sae Grisna, a burly man approaching middle age. He nodded soberly to her. There were others, some
familiar, a few not, but there were two absences that stood
out: Kerida dira Mudrin, Sola's mother, and Essit sae Tillit.
The long weeks without any information, as much as physical privation, had left her at a disadvantage. She was also
conscious, suddenly, of how she looked: filthy, wounded,
with ripped and tattered clothing and shorn hair, as far a cry

from Sithli's elegance as it was possible to get. The thought made her smile, and she saw answering smiles.

"Thank you, all of you. I am more grateful to you than I can say for standing by me when I didn't know I had friends any longer, for keeping faith with me, with the land." Her throat was tight. It must have been exhaustion and lack of food that made her voice waver. She cleared her throat. "I vow to you that I will act as I should have acted long ago, that I will be a good SaeKet, that we will win this fight."

She wondered if she could keep that promise. The absence of Essit, and all it implied, disturbed her. But in the cheers that greeted her remarks she heard something else, heard it and felt it: a deep throbbing from beneath her feet, from the earth that surrounded them. The land was answering. She lifted her eyes and felt her gaze lock with Dremfir sae Cortin's, Norimin's mage.

"The SaeKet needs food and rest." Sola's voice carried across the the murmurs and talk.

Rilsin slid onto the bench beside Lendis, who had continued to eat during her arrival and who now held out his bowl for more. She accepted a bowl from from Meffa. The smell of the food was almost too much; it made her dizzy, and it tasted better than she had thought food could taste. She felt some of the fog around her begin to lift, but she realized how tired she was. While she ate, Lellefon came and took Lendis away, to bed presumably. The little boy had almost fallen asleep over his last bowl of stew. Rilsin knew how he felt. When she had finished, she forced herself to sit up straighter. She could not afford to rest, not yet. Sola and the two captains pulled forward the bench opposite hers.

"Norimin is with the Mother, SaeKet." Pleffin confirmed what she had already deduced. "It was her death that gave Sae Sifuat the impetus to act."

For the first time now, Rilsin heard the tale of the Valley Battle, the battle in which Sifuat had lost his army and his freedom. She heard of the staggering casualties and of Sifuat's capture by Jullka sae Lisim. Essit and his troops were besieged in Hoptrin. No one seemed to want to tell her of Sifuat's relationship with Jullka, but it was not difficult to read between the lines. Rilsin put her hand over her eyes and rubbed her forehead. With one poor judgment, with one mistake, Sifuat had thrown away all his mother had worked and schemed for. He had thrown away his life, and almost hers as well. *I have no right to blame him,* she thought. *I have acted no more wisely than he.*

"No one expected the Lisims to move so quickly, SaeKet." Pleffin was to the point. "They brought troops up; much of the army is there, and they have closed Sae Essit in the city."

Rilsin sighed. "How long can he hold out?"

"Not much longer." Niffa could be as blunt as her older colleague. "They did not have the time to bring in the harvest. If they aren't relieved soon, they will starve."

"What forces do we have?"

Her two captains looked at each other, suddenly reluctant to speak. They looked away, and Pleffin shifted uneasily on the bench. Rilsin felt cold.

"I can see it is bad. How bad?" When neither answered her, she looked to Sola. He looked back at her but did not respond. "How bad?" she asked again. "How many troops do we have?"

"We have none." Pleffin finally answered. "Oh, we have a few here and there, but Sae Kepit has the army, and with you in prison, and Sae Sifuat captured, and Sae Essit bottled in . . ." He shook his head and raised his hands helplessly. "There is much discontent with Sae Sithli, but no one knows what to do or is willing to take the risk."

"We will take the risk now," Rilsin said. "We will lift the siege at Hoptrin and get Essit and his troops out, and we will take a larger army than anyone expects, right to Petipal itself, if we have to."

"Where will we get the troops, SaeKet?" Niffa's eyes were shining. She obviously believed completely in Rilsin's power to change the fortunes of war. She looked as if she expected Rilsin to wave her hands and conjure soldiers from the air.

"From the north," said Rilsin. "We have allies across the border, Sae Niffa."

"The Confederacy is Saeditin's ally, and Sae Sithli's," said Pleffin dubiously.

"It is Saeditin's ally, but not Sithli's. First Man Bilt is my friend. I am bringing his son home to him. If you will excuse me," said Rilsin, "I need to speak to Dira Sola about something along these lines." She had remembered that there might be some magic to call upon, after all. "It is possible that we may have some unusual resources."

When the captains had left, Sola looked at her grimly. "The fire tubes are hidden but not in our hands," he said. "I did what you asked that day in my workshop. When Sithli first took you, I had my apprentices get to work. We have made some numbers of the fire-tubes. I devised them smaller than the one you saw, and it is possible to carry them on horseback, or even on your person. I also made two very large, so large they require horses to drag them on a wagon. I was barely able to get them safely away before Sithli had her Guard raid my workshop. I don't know what she had heard or from whom. They found nothing, but she suspected me. It was hard for me to continue as if I did not care about you but only about my work."

"Thank the Mother you remained safe!" Rilsin reached out and put her hand over his. "Where are the tubes now?"

"Near Hoptrin. I was trying to get them to Hoptrin itself, or rather, have my apprentices get them there, but Sae Kepit cut them off. They had barely time to hide the tubes. Two escaped to bring me the news. One Sae Kepit captured. He killed himself rather than reveal the secret. His name was Nennet sae Jillipa. He was very talented, and he loved the work, and he hated Sithli, and I sent him to his death because I was not more careful." Sola's voice cracked.

Rilsin drew in a breath to speak. He saw her open her mouth to speak and hurried on.

"Hear me out on this, Rilsin. When Sithli took you, I was furious! I would have done anything, risked anyone to help you, to get you free. I told more people than I should; I had to, to get the tubes made. I wanted to get the tubes to Essit, so I sent them north too quickly. If I had taken the time to think, to act more carefully, Sae Essit would have had the tubes; Nennet would not have been killed. Essit could have marched south and released you. Sae Sifuat might not have been executed—" Sola looked away. This last was something he did not much regret, and he despised himself for that.

"Stop blaming yourself, Sola. You acted as best you could at the time. Had you done otherwise, no one knows what might have resulted. Sithli could have raided your workshop and found the tubes. Sithli could have arrested *you*. The worst did not happen. We will have to go north and find the tubes."

"I know where they are, but they will be hard to find without Sae Kepit knowing, and it will be harder still to get them away." He looked at her, but Rilsin knew he wasn't seeing her. He was seeing something that she could not, something that terrified him. "The worst has not yet happened, but these tubes will bring it, Rilsin. I have brought it."

"I think you have saved us," she said, but the look he gave her was so dark that she recoiled. She turned instead to the other question she needed to ask. "Where is your mother? What happened to Dira Kerida?"

"I don't know. She was not careful, either. Sithli sent guards to arrest her on the day my workshop was raided. My mother escaped, but I don't know where she is. I have not heard from her."

"We will find her, Sola, or more likely, she will find us." She meant it, but it was weak, and she knew it sounded weak. "You took a huge risk in coming to get me out today. Surely someone else could have been sent."

He said nothing but merely looked at her for a moment. Then he stood. "With your permission, SaeKet," he said. Without waiting for an answer, he left the room.

Rilsin stood, swaying slightly from exhaustion. The room was empty now, but as soon as she was on her feet, Lellefon was there, offering her a room with a bed, water for washing, and clean clothes. She asked to see Lendis first.

The little boy was sound asleep in a bed in one of the

chambers off the main passageway. He was curled up into a little ball, only his head and one arm outside of the covers. He was sucking his thumb, and tucked under his cheek was the little knitted stuffed hunting cat, the toy Sola had tied into the cloak for him. Rilsin knelt by the bed and gently smoothed back the child's hair, ignoring the tears that streaked at last, unseen and unnoticed, down her face. Here was one child who would go back where he belonged.

33

It FELt GOOÐ tO BE HEAÐiɳG ɳORtH, ÐESPitE tHE ÐAɳGER and despite their slow progress. The three days of hiding in the underground retreat had been necessary, both for eluding capture and for recuperation and planning, but Rilsin was glad to be moving again. The sky was leaden gray and heavy, and the winds were cold. The weather had turned steadily colder during the past days as they moved north, hiding from Sithli's troops. Today the temperature had been dropping precipitously.

Winter would come early, it would seem, which was bad news. They needed to end the siege at Hoptrin and move south in force before the roads were closed by snow. The big projectile tubes would have to go by wagon, too, once they reclaimed them, and they could not afford to have them snowed under.

They traveled in groups of very few to try to avert suspicion. Rilsin had wanted her captains with her, but she had been dissuaded from this. They would meet at an agreed-upon village near Hoptrin, Mills Crossing, but travel separately.

She went north with Sola and Dremfir the mage, and with Lendis, leaving a day before the captains. They walked, so they could stay off the roads, away from patrols. Had anyone stopped them, their identity was that of a commoner family—wife, husband, child, and wife's brother—returning to their farmstead in the north. Rilsin wore a wig again, although there was no one to see, as they avoided contact with anyone. Their supposed commoner status would not explain the swords the adults wore.

They kept to the woods when possible, and to the fields when not. They slept in the open, huddled near one another, under haystacks or shrubs. They ate cold food, as they did not dare to risk a fire. They were usually cold and sometimes wet, and the adults were tired. Sometimes they took turns carrying Lendis. Rilsin worried that the pace and the hardship would be too much for Lendis, but the little boy not only proved tough, he seemed to enjoy the adventure.

Meffa and Lellefon stayed behind, Lellefon with her little son. Chilsa also remained behind, in hiding with Meffa. Rilsin had not wanted to be parted again from her cat, who had cried and whined when he realized she was leaving, but the company of the big silver hunting cat would have proclaimed her identity to anyone who saw them.

"We will have to risk returning to the roads again soon, whether or not it is safe. We are almost out of food." Sola hitched his pack into a temporarily more comfortable position. His shoulders ached, his feet hurt, and after over a week on the road, he wondered if he would ever know what it was to be warm again.

"It will snow." Dremfir echoed his thoughts. "It is too cold, in any case, to sleep outside tonight."

Rilsin glanced at the men and then looked at Lendis, who trudged along beside them. "We should be in SaedTillit, near the SaedSudit border," she said. "The last of Sithli's patrols was three days ago, and if we don't get some food and get warm soon, it won't matter who does or does not recognize us. Let's head for the road and stop at the next farm." One of them always crept close to the road every day to spy on the traffic, but except for the patrol three days previously, there had been very little traffic.

The road was empty when they came to it, a brown gray ribbon winding through empty fields. Although there was no farm immediately in sight, Rilsin frowned. Something was not right. There should have been at least some traffic, a few people headed to town, a farmer's boy with sheep, something. She almost said something about it but decided against it. They needed food and shelter, and they were already alert. Nothing she could say could add to that or change it.

"Do you remember who you are?" she said to Lendis.

"Yes, Mama." Lendis grinned. "You are Ritta and I am Lenfir, and this my papa Sil and my Uncle Dem. And we are going home! We live north of Mills Crossing, and you have a little farm." Lendis had been drilled in this story repeatedly until he was bored with it. Now that he might have to use it, he perked up. "We went all the way to Petipal to get Uncle Dem after Auntie Fillit died. I wanted to see the city, but you said no, because there were troubles, and we left! Before I could see the big market, or eat sweet rolls, or get new shoes or—"

"Don't get carried away," said Dremfir wryly. "If you are asked, keep it short. Try to be a shy little boy."

"I *am* shy. Very, very, very shy!" Getting away from the palace, away from Petipal, but most of all, away from Sithli, had been good for Lendis. Although the escape from the palace had been frightening, he had the resiliency of the very young, but beyond that, he trusted Rilsin completely, and he felt safe as long as he was with her. He knew he was going home, and he had no doubt she would get him there safely.

It seemed to get even colder as they walked up the road. Rilsin pulled her cloak more tightly around her. Sure enough, right on the heels of her thought, the first flakes of snow began to fall. She glanced at Sola over Lendis's head. Being so close to him for the past days had been difficult. The circumstances of travel and of hiding had enforced a certain intimacy among all of them, but the constraint between Rilsin and Sola remained.

There had been opportunities to speak to him alone, but Sola had been uncommunicative. She had not done well herself. She was haunted by the memory of Sifuat's death in the square and by her failure to rescue her daughter. It detracted from her determination to restore their friendship. She remembered how Sifuat had looked up toward her prison window before he died, and she remembered his last speech to the crowd, which was also meant for her. Her husband had obviously loved her, despite his dalliance with other women. She twisted the star ruby ring on her finger. Her second thoughts and self-recriminations were endless but silent.

A farmhouse came into view as they rounded a bend of the empty road. It sat amidst fields and the stone walls common in the north, with a winter-barren garden around its door. Smoke curled from the chimney, and there was the smell of something cooking, something that made Rilsin's mouth water. Light from an oil lamp gleamed out through one window. Obviously, someone was home, but for a time no one answered their knock. Rilsin looked around. Dusk was falling, the early dusk of the north, toward the end of the year, and it was snowing more steadily now. She rapped again at the door, harder this time.

The door opened so suddenly that Rilsin knew that someone had been standing just inside it, probably peering out through a crack, inspecting them. It took an effort not to jump back.

"What do you want?" Their rude welcomer was a man, tall, heavyset, with a thick, rust-colored beard. He carried no obvious weapon, but the threat was there, nonetheless. He stared at them for a moment, and behind him, in the house, Rilsin could see a woman whose red hair was streaked with white. She wore an apron over her woolen shirt and trousers, and she twisted her hands in this.

"We are travelers looking for a little shelter," Rilsin began. The man looked as though he might slam the door in their faces, so she added hastily, "We can pay a little—"

"Come in." The man seemed to have made a sudden decision, and determined to act on it just as suddenly. He took Rilsin by the arm and almost yanked her inside. Lendis, who was holding her hand, was yanked along with her. "You and you," said their abrupt host to Sola and Dremfir, "get in!"

He slammed the door behind them, and they stood in the warmth of the little farmhouse, staring around them. Now Rilsin could see three children huddled in a corner of the main room by the fire. The red-haired woman with the apron moved to stand between them and the children.

"Who are you?" demanded the man. His hands were on his hips. Rilsin could see no weapon on him, but she would have bet that he was armed.

"Travelers," said Rilsin again, "going home to our farm. It is late, and I don't think my son can walk much farther; I don't think we can get to the village, since it is dark and snowing—"

"How did you get past the patrols? And who are you?" When the woman made a sound behind him, he turned. "Easy, Brittal, they are obviously not *hers,*" he turned back to them, "but I want to know who you are and how you got past the patrols."

"We kept to the fields and woods," said Dremfir truthfully. "We left Petipal days ago, after my sister," he glanced at Rilsin, "came for me when my wife died. We left when the trouble began, and stayed off the roads—"

"You must have done more than that," growled the man. He looked pointedly at their swords. "You must have hidden from the patrols, and I doubt you are all you seem."

"We have no reason to love Sithli SaeKet," Sola said suddenly. "We also have good reason to avoid her patrols."

"I knew as much." The man nodded. "And since that is so, you have come to the wrong place. No, no, not for the reasons you think," he saw Rilsin reaching for her sword, "we have no love for the Melisin woman, either, but her patrols stop here, eat here, sleep here. Not at our invitation." He obviously seethed with fury at this. "They are not here now, but they will be back. They will not like this weather any more than you."

"I am sorry," said Rilsin. "We will leave." She turned toward the door. "We have no wish to put you in any danger."

"Let us at least give you what little food we can," said the woman, Brittal, "before you leave."

There was the clatter of hoofbeats outside the door, and shouts.

"Too late; they're here!" said the man.

"Great freezing Runchot—" Rilsin began.

"Out the back!" said Brittal. "Out through the kitchen!"

Rilsin heard her, and something slid in the depths of her memory, and she was a child again. She heard her mother telling her they must leave, she saw the maid come to lead them out through the kitchens. That was the night her mother had died. That night was the true beginning of the Melisin reign. Without realizing it, she straightened. Her jaw hardened, and she put her hand on her sword.

"How many are there?" she asked Brittal. Her voice sounded strange in her own ears. The woman stared at her. "How many in the patrol?" she asked again. "Usually there are between five and ten, depending."

"Five," said Brittal's husband. He looked at her as if seeing her for the first time.

"Will it bother you if we kill them here?" she tied back her cloak and unsheathed her sword. The polite irony of the request hung in the air.

The scrape of the steel leaving the scabbard made Brittal draw in her breath, but she smiled. "I wish you would," she said. "Children, come with me!"

"Lenfir, go with her!" said Rilsin. She looked at Lendis. "I won't leave you, don't worry!"

"Ri—Ritta, you can't!" said Sola.

"Not alone," said Rilsin. "I need your help."

Dremfir nodded at her and drew his sword. His round, pleasant face had gone hard, and Rilsin could see in his eyes the tradition and code of the warrior-priests in which he had been trained. After a brief hesitation, Sola drew his sword.

"You have my help," said the farmer. He drew a wicked-

looking knife from somewhere within his woolen shirt.
Rilsin nodded to herself. She had thought he was armed.
"I'm Bren," he said. "It is good to meet other partisans of
the true SaeKet, Ria Ritta." He had made note of her name.

"Put that away," said Rilsin, nodding at the knife, "or at
least don't let them see it when they come in."

She glanced around the room. The walls were covered
with heavy woolen hangings to help insulate the room from
the bitter northern winters. The thick hanging in the doorway between the main room and the kitchen had been
pulled aside. Rilsin motioned Dremfir behind it. She motioned Sola behind the hangings to one side of the front
door. She took the other.

"Open up, farmer! We are hungry, and our horses need
tending!"

Bren moved out of Rilsin's line of sight as he went to
open the door. She tensed. The door swung open. A blast of
cold air swirled in, along with snowflakes. The patrol's captain came in first.

"Where is your wife, man! Send her out to deal with
horses!"

Rilsin waited. Acting too soon would be as bad as not
acting at all. Patience had its reward: the rest of the patrol
followed hard on the heels of their officer.

"Colder than a Runchot hell out there!" said one of the
men, echoing Rilsin's favorite curse.

Rilsin stepped from behind the hanging and ran him
through the heart. She had just enough time to pull her
sword free before a second guard had his own sword free
and engaged her. From the corner of her eye she saw that
Dremfir had taken out one man, and Bren, their host, had
pulled out his knife and had jumped the only woman in the
patrol. Sola had taken on the captain. Dremfir came to help
him just as Rilsin finished with her second man. It was over
quickly. She looked around at the carnage.

"Anyone hurt?" she asked. There was a flurry of denials.
"We may have created a greater problem for you," she told
Bren. "Since Sithli SaeKet controls the roads, you will have
another patrol to answer to, or worse."

"Pull them out into the yard," said Bren, pointing at the bodies, then grabbing one himself. "No, you have not created trouble. We will claim you threatened us and bound us, and threatened our children, when they ask. We will tell them it was a whole troop of brigands." He grinned at her. "It is worth dealing with the mess and the trouble, well worth it."

Dragging the bodies out into the snow was hard work. Sola took the horses and led them around behind the house, and when they went back into the warmth, they found that Brittal had already mopped up the blood from the floor. She was in the kitchen ladling out her stew into bowls, handing them to the children, who were seated around the big wooden table. Rilsin went into the kitchen to help her.

"How far are we from Mills Crossing?" she asked.

"Three days' walk."

"A little over a day, then, if we ride," said Rilsin thoughtfully. "We are close. We can take the patrol's horses."

"You can't leave; you will be stopped for sure." Bren came into the kitchen, the other men close behind him. "The Melisin woman's troops control the roads and much of the towns. With our Sae Essit stuck in Hoptrin, there is no one to rally to, and no one is organized. Were you riding north with a message for Sae Essit?"

"You can hide here until it's safer," said Brittal. "We have a barn."

"We can't stay," said Rilsin, "but we won't be stopped, either." She took another bite of stew from the bowl Brittal had handed her. It was chicken stew, made with an old and scrawny chicken, but it tasted good, amazingly good. The kitchen was warm and comfortable. "This snow will help us."

"You can't count on the snow hiding us," said Dremfir. "Besides which, it will not last for long. It will snow tonight, then warm again. I can feel it. I know it."

She stared at him. She did not need to ask how he knew. Some priests had a feel for the weather, an attunement. It was an extremely valuable talent, although not a very reliable one, unfortunately. Often when it was needed, it failed.

Rilsin had not known that Dremfir had it. By the looks their
hosts exchanged, she could see that they knew the signifi-
cance of Dremfir's remark and realized that they had a
priest in their midst.

"More stew, sae?" asked Brittal deferentially.

"Thank you." Dremfir held out his bowl, not bothering
to deny either his rank nor his occupation. "Ritta, we can't
rely on the snow to mask us."

"Not just the snow," said Rilsin, "although I admit I
hoped we had more time and did not have to ride tonight.
We can't stay off the roads any longer. We do have to ride
tonight, since we need the snow to help disguise us, but we
will ride as Sithli's Elite, or as close to it as we can manage."

For a moment they all stared at her. Then the realization
came to all of them at once.

"The uniforms!" said Sola.

"Whatever of them we can salvage that is neither too
torn nor blood soaked. And whatever will fit."

It was the matter of some very cold minutes to go back
into the yard and strip the bodies of the salvageable items of
clothing and shake the snow from them. Back inside again,
they looked at what they had. There were enough usable
cloaks, in Melisin green. Rilsin took the captain's, slashed
with his rank. She saw the farmer couple looking sideways
at her; they had obviously expected Dremfir to take this.
Sola and Dremfir found regulation trousers that would fit
them, but Rilsin did not. The female guard's would have fit
her, but they were soiled beyond immediate use when the
woman's bowels had let go during her death struggle. Rilsin
took the captain's vest and shrugged into it, even though it
was too large for her. They scarcely looked like a bona fide
Elite unit, not on close inspection, but it was the best they
could do.

"Lenfir will have to stay as he is, although we can wrap
him in a cloak. I hope we will not have to explain the presence of a child with us." Rilsin glanced at Lendis, who had
fallen asleep near the fire. She was sorry to have to take him
away from this comfortable haven, but there was no choice.

She woke him gently and wrapped him in the guard's cloak. Sola hefted him onto his shoulder.

"Thank you both," she said to Brittal and Bren, who stood together watching this procedure. "If you will allow us, we can give you a little coin for your help."

"Ria Ritta," said Bren, "it was an honor to help you in any way. We will not be paid for aiding the envoys of the true SaeKet." He paused and cleared his throat, turning to Dremfir. "Can you give us any news before you go? I have heard rumors — you come from the capital, perhaps you can tell us if this is so — Rilsin SaeKet herself is heading north, that she has a secret army hidden."

The rumors were close enough to the truth that Rilsin was taken aback. Dremfir was not.

"The SaeKet will come north," said Dremfir, "when it is the proper time. I know nothing of any hidden army, unfortunately."

"They say," Bren continued, "that she will not only bring back justice but will teach us commoners to read." He looked hopeful.

"And what good would reading be to us?" his wife snorted. It appeared they had had this discussion before. "We have gotten along fine without it. Justice, though, is another matter."

"You have heard right on both counts," said Dremfir. To his credit, he did not glance at Rilsin.

The storm had picked up in intensity. They were not glad to be heading out into it, but Rilsin was pleased that at least they were riding, not going forward on foot. She had a feeling, growing in intensity along with the storm, that she needed to get north as quickly as possible. She climbed into the saddle and saw Dremfir and Sola mounted also. Sola took Lendis up in front of him on the saddle.

"Go with the Mother," said Bren. "Tell Rilsin SaeKet she has our prayers."

"The SaeKet won't care about our poor prayers," said Brittal.

"She does care," said Rilsin, "and she will know."

By the time they were only a little way down the road,

they could no longer see the farmhouse behind them. The sky, the air, the land, were darkness and white snow. Dremfir held up a lantern to help illumine their way, but it did little good. Rilsin felt as if they were wrapped in soft white silk, blinded by it. She had to trust that the road was there beneath them, that it would not vanish and suddenly plunge them into some vast abyss. The snow blew into her eyes, despite the hood of the cloak, which she had pulled forward over her head. The snow blew into her mouth and nose, although she had wrapped a woolen scarf across her face. She wondered if Dremfir really knew that the storm would not last. After a time she stopped wondering and simply endured. She knew the others were still with her only because she could see the lantern Dremfir held, and in its light she could see him, and she could see Sola, with Lendis before him on the horse. She could not hear anything but the wind and the hiss of the snow. They were the only inhabitants in a strange, cold, white land.

Thus it was that they were on top of the checkpoint before they knew they were approaching it. The guard unit, not as lucky in its accommodations as the unit they had just slaughtered, had been huddled in a shack beside the road, a shack that had once been the toll booth for those leaving SaedTillit roads for SaedSudit. Rilsin had a flashing memory of the seemingly long-ago Council meeting when the maintenance of roads had been discussed, the meeting at which her alliance with Essit sae Tillit had begun to solidify.

Lantern light flared; figures dark against the light and against the driving snow poured at the last moment from the toll shack into the road. Most were too late, but two of the figures grounded spears against the roadbed, and the points threatened the horses.

"Out of the road!" shouted Rilsin. She could see the green cloaks of the guards coated with snow in the short time they had been out; she wondered what her party looked like. Snow demons, most likely. She brushed at her cloak to reveal its color and marking, and shouted, "Stand clear! SaeKet's envoys!" She slowed her horse but did not stop.

The spears were pulled back and away. They thundered through the checkpoint, with Sola hunching low over Lendis's bundled form. There was no pursuit. There was nothing but a shout, "The Mother's blessing, poor souls!"

Well past the checkpoint, they slowed. The storm was even worse, if that were possible. The horses inched along nervously, and the three riders clustered together:

"We were lucky back there," shouted Sola against the wind.

"I don't know how we can keep on." Rilsin motioned them in closer. They stopped, with the small pool of light from Dremfir's lantern in the center. "We should be in Sudit lands now, but I don't see how we can make Mills Crossing. We have been lucky so far, but our luck may have run out here."

"It has indeed." Someone spoke from the darkness just beyond their pool of light.

Figures converged on them out of the snow. Drawn swords gleamed in sudden torchlight. There was nothing they could do. They were stopped in the road, and they were outnumbered. They had no time to draw their own weapons, and they were too cold and stunned to make the effort. The leader reached up to grab Rilsin's bridle.

"Down, Saeditin! Off horse and give up sword!"

Rilsin stared down at the man who had grabbed her reins. He wore no uniform, but leather and fur. He spoke Saeditin, but his accent — she began to grin. Then she laughed.

"Humor? Funny? I do not see it! You will not laugh, Saeditin spy, when I bring you to our general. Our general is First Man Bilt. You have heard of him, yes?"

Rilsin slid from the saddle. Two Wilfrisin made to grab her arms, but she stepped back. "Be easy," she said in Wilfrisin. "You can have our swords." She looked at Sola, who was still on horseback, fighting to keep his seat against the hands that tried to pull him off. "Get down, Sola," she called. "Lendis! Wake up, Lendis! We found your papa!"

34

By dawn the storm was over. Not only was it over, but as the sun rose, the temperature began to rise also. Snow began to melt, dripping from the tents of the Wilfrisin camp, forming slushy puddles and then fields of mud. Rilsin stood in the dawn, wrapped in the fur cloak the Wilfrisin had given her, and watched the camp come to life, absently twisting her marriage ring.

Bilt had been awaiting word from her, but when it never came, he had mobilized the army and marched south over the border. He knew Essit was besieged, and when he heard of her death sentence, he took a contingent and headed south, afraid he would be too late to save her.

"I should know they could not kill you," he had told her with a grin the previous night, but he was obviously relieved.

Rilsin was touched. She knew it was politics—Sithli was not the sort of SaeKet who was good for the new Confederacy—but it was also friendship. He was also ecstatic to have his son returned to him. He had shed tears at the reunion, and when Lendis flung himself into his father's arms, Rilsin had had to turn away.

"I owe you more than I can repay, friend Rilsin," Bilt told her. "If I can, I will help you get daughter back."

Rilsin thought about this as she shivered in the growing light. She had an army now, but it was not hers, it was Bilt's. She wanted nothing more than to take all the troops he would let her take and rush south to Petipal to get Reniat back. She could not. Saeditin itself came first. That meant saving Essit and Hoptrin.

Breakfast was a strategy session in Bilt's big tent. They perched on stools eating some sort of fried bread, which was a Wilfrisin staple, and drinking mugs of herbal tea. There were two other surprise guests: Niffa sae Delf and Pleffin sae Grisna had been intercepted by the Wilfrisin and brought to the camp. It was a relief to Rilsin to know that they were safe.

"We have to get Sae Essit out, with his troops. That should be our first order of business." Rilsin took another bite of the fried bread. It was good.

"It will be hard," said Bilt, "but you are right; we must."

Rilsin glanced at Sola. "There may be something that will make it a little easier," she said. "Explain your device, Sola."

"You want me to explain it to all of them?" Sola looked both upset and amazed. He had kept his secret for so long that he had become accustomed to hiding it.

"Yes," said Rilsin. "To all of us, Dira Sola. Please."

He did, since she commanded it, but with obvious reluctance. No one laughed. Rilsin had half-expected they would, so preposterous-sounding were the tubes. Since it was Sola, however, with his reputation as the man who had changed Saeditin, he was given the complete attention of everyone in the tent, and complete, if astonished, belief.

"Magic," said Niffa. She looked with a mixture of awe and fear at Sola.

"Not magic," said Sola, "science." He could see that there were many who were of Niffa's opinion, or worse, who could not distinguish the one from the other. "If they work as they should," he added, to no one in particular.

"They won't work at all unless we have them in our possession," said Rilsin. "Tell us where they are hidden, Dira Sola."

He did, showing them on a map. Bilt exchanged glances with some of his officers. Rilsin knew what this meant before he spoke. If the tubes were not already behind Kepit's lines, they were close.

"They are hidden near the main camp of that Lisim Kepit," Bilt confirmed. "We will have to send a party to sneak them out."

"Sae Pleffin, Sae Niffa," said Rilsin, "you are with me for this enterprise, with any troops that First Man Bilt will lend us. Sola will stay here until we return, when the tubes will go into his care."

"No," said Bilt. "You cannot go, friend Rilsin." Rilsin stared at him, taken aback. "You are now leader of Saeditin," Bilt explained. "You cannot risk life in this. You are more important than tubes. You are first man of Saeditin. You are SaeKet."

Rilsin closed her mouth with an almost audible snap. He was right. She frowned.

"I will go," said Sola before Rilsin could respond. "I know how the tubes should be handled, as well as where they are."

"I agree this is good idea," said Bilt. "You will take orders from my captain, that I will send, but my captain will listen to advice."

"With your permission, SaeKet," said Sola.

Rilsin looked at him. His eyes were hard and his mouth tight. She did not know what he was thinking. "You have my permission," she said. Her voice sounded odd, even to her own ears.

The mission was organized. She approved the arrangements, watched the party set out, and clenched her hands beneath her cloak. Bilt stood beside her, watching her as much as he watched his mission leave the camp.

"Do not fear, my friend," he said, "there will be plenty of fighting still for you. For both of us."

"I know it," said Rilsin grimly.

The melting snow was an impediment to travel. The roads were muddy, the fields were soggy, and Sola wished it had remained cold. Not snowing, just cold. They were riding. Since they needed horses and wagons for the two big tubes in any event, the decision had been made for all of them to ride the small, tough, strong, shaggy horses of the north.

It was a fairly large contingent: twenty-five soldiers, fifteen of them Wilfrisin, ten of them Saeditin loyalists or rebels, depending upon your point of view, Sola thought. Two of the soldiers were Pleffin and Niffa, but all were under the command of a Wilfrisin, Chif. Chif had been a Wilfrisin fore-fighter, on the outskirts of his society, fighting alone and shieldless in the vanguard, seeking redemption for the murder of two men in a drunken brawl. He had been accepted back into the army and had worked his way up to captain, but he still kept the dyed blue blond hair of a fore-fighter. His hair contrasted oddly with his beard, which was red. He was a huge man, not fat but massive, with arms like tree trunks and enormous hands. His voice was one of the gentlest and most musical Sola had ever heard. Chif motioned Sola forward.

"We split off here, Sola Dira," he said. "You go with team and most horses over fields there," he pointed with his chin, "to reach tubes. I take my team and make distraction. Smaller team follows with wagons. Enemy troops are very near; there is post around bend of road. Very surprised am I we have not met them yet. Victory goddess smiles on us. All the same, much luck to us all."

"Much luck to us," Sola agreed.

He set off over the fields with his team. There was a tremendous amount that could go wrong, but Sola tried not to think of it now. His thoughts were, in fact, not as purely on this mission as they should have been. He was on the mission because he was needed, but he was also there to

prove a thing to Rilsin. It would help him if he could clar-
ify to himself just what it was he wanted to prove to her, but
whenever he started down that road, his thoughts inevitably
became more tangled rather than less. What he finally realized was that he was angry at her.

She had almost lost everything—Saeditin, her child,
even her life—and why? Because of her husband. Unaware
that he did so, Sola snarled to himself and dug his heels into
the side of the horse. Now that she knew what her misplaced faith in Sifuat had cost, it made no difference, not as
far as Sola could tell. She was more loyal to his memory
than she had been to the man himself. Sifuat dead was
worse than Sifuat alive. Sifuat alive would have made more
mistakes. Sifuat dead could do no more wrong.

Only when he heard the snorting of the horses of his
team laboring to come up behind him did Sola realize that
he was outstripping his escort. He reined back. Rilsin
seemed to have forgotten how he felt about her, and she
seemed not to realize what her freedom and her life was
costing him. He knew he could not envision everything that
would come of his newest invention, but some things he
could envision. To a limited extent, Sola thought he saw the
future, and he did not like what he saw.

"Right up there." Pleffin had pulled up beside him, and
Sola pointed out the snowy, brush-covered hillside they
were approaching. "There is a little cave behind that brush,
and the tubes are in there."

"Let's go."

Pleffin set the crew to work, and Sola pitched in. They
hauled brush back and stomped down snow to make it easier to get the wagons closer from the road. The tubes were
just as Sola and his apprentices had left them, in crates covered with heavy canvas, well back in the shallow cave.
Pulling them out was heavy work. Sola had removed his
cloak, and now he removed his heavy outer shirt, perspiring
despite the chill.

When they had the crates out of the cave, including the
crates for the two big tubes, there was still no sign of the
wagons nor of any of Chif's contingent. The sun was past

midday now. While the others drank water and wrapped themselves again in their cloaks, Sola pried open the crate that held three of the medium tubes. Although the crates showed no sign of tampering, he was anxious to know that they were unharmed. The others gathered around him, curious to see this new, important magic. Even the lookout walked in from his spot on a small hillock nearer the road. Since there was no longer any secrecy about it, Sola explained his invention again. He had brought with him some of the powdered fuel in a pouch, and he explained how the tubes were to be loaded with lead balls, "from that crate, there," he pointed, and how it all worked. So fascinated were all of them that it was several moments before the sound of approaching hoofbeats registered.

When they turned, it was too late. They were afoot, weapons sheathed, tired from their work, and the enemy was mounted and close in. The delinquent lookout was the first to die. He ran forward with a shout and was run through by a woman in Elite green, the enemy captain.

Swords were out, and Sola's remaining nine soldiers were engaged with a much larger enemy party. Sola ran in under the hooves of the captain's horse, trying to reach up and yank her from the saddle. It was a dangerous and incredibly risky thing to do, and he fully expected to die. The captain danced her horse aside, and with a command prevented him from being trampled or kicked by the well-trained warhorse.

"Stop right there, Sola dira Mudrin!"

Sola realized he knew her. She was a saedin of a minor family, a client family to the Lisim, and he had seen her in Petipal. He looked up and found three archers sighted on him and him alone. She had recognized him, and she wanted him alive. He knew there was a price on his head.

"Cease fighting and surrender," she shouted to his team, "or Sola dira Mudrin dies!"

Pleffin sae Grisna lowered his sword. Niffa followed, and slowly, the others did also. Sola stood frozen in place. The enemy captain dismounted, came to him, and took the sword from his hand. As she did, he remembered her name.

Jeffa sae Chint. She had been in Rilsin's army once. He remembered her as being one to always grab an advantage for herself, which was undoubtedly why she had thrown her support to Kepit and Jullka sae Lisim.

"See how valuable you are," she told him. "No one wants to see you hurt, Dira Sola. Sae Kepit will be glad to have you, and Sithli SaeKet will be happier still to have you back." Two of her soldiers came and took his arms. "What do you have in these crates, dira?" she asked. She drew her knife and stroked it under his chin, forcing his head up.

"You can see for yourself," shouted Niffa, "but just what they are and how they work, you will never know!" She was trying to get Jeffa's attention away from Sola, and for a moment, it worked.

"Fool! Keep your mouth shut!" Pleffin glared at her.

"It doesn't matter what she says." Jeffa turned from Sola to Pleffin. "anyone can see that Dira Sola, in company with strange objects, means something of great importance. Saeditin's greatest magician has some new magic here. What is it, dira?"

Sola set his jaw and looked to the side.

"We will all die before we tell you!" Niffa spat at Jeffa.

"You will die," said Jeffa, "one by one, if you must, but I am betting that Dira Sola will not stand for that. He has a reputation for softness. I am betting that he will tell me rather than see you all die before his eyes. Am I right?"

Sola still said nothing. He could see that she not only wanted the benefit of delivering him to the Lisim commander, she hoped to personally gain even more from whatever he had. Jeffa took two strides and was before Niffa. Two of her men held the young saedin while Jeffa reached up and cut her throat. Niffa sagged, and the men dropped her to the ground.

"Who is next?" said Jeffa. "You choose, Dira Sola, who is next to die."

"No one." Sola's voice was hoarse. It was an effort to speak. "I will tell you what you want." It seemed he couldn't look anywhere long, not at Niffa's body, not at Jeffa.

"No!" shouted Pleffin. "You cannot! Damn you, Sola, we will all die first!"

"You will not, if I can help it." Sola looked away from Niffa's body. "We will all live, and perhaps Sithli SaeKet will take pity on us." He looked straight at Jeffa. "You are right, Sae Jeffa. This is a big magic. There are tubes in those crates—"

"No!" shouted Pleffin again.

"Silence him," said Jeffa.

"Don't kill him!" cried Sola.

"Don't kill him," agreed Jeffa, "as long Dira Sola cooperates." Her men gagged Pleffin. "Go on, Dira."

"Tubes," said Sola. He cleared his throat. "The tubes bestow protection. I have a powder." He stopped, swallowed. "I have a powder, which I put in the tubes. I cannot explain it to you, but when it is done correctly, it protects those in its aura from harm for some days. It is not perfected yet. I will demonstrate it to Sithli SaeKet, to give her this protection."

"You will demonstrate it to us first. Here. You can do that, can you not, dira?" Fascination and greed were plain in her face. She was not a subtle woman.

"Well, I suppose, but it will not be easy." Sola could not help it; he glanced at Pleffin and then at the rest of his troops. The men stood silent, looking down, but Sola saw the quick gleam in Pleffin's eye.

"It will take a few moments to set this up. It is not easy, Sae Jeffa."

"So you just said. Do it nonetheless."

"I will need help to move my, ah, apparatus."

"Use whomever you wish."

With some help from his own troops, under Jeffa's watchful eye, Sola positioned one of the medium tubes. His own men said nothing but did exactly as he told them. Every so often, to what he hoped was good effect, Sola muttered things under his breath, hoping they sounded sufficiently magical. Pleffin was still gagged and held by two of Jeffa's men, but he no longer struggled.

"I don't know if this will work," he said, when the preparation was complete. Sola's worry was genuine. "These, ah magic tubes have been here for a long time."

"You were trying to get them to Hoptrin, to give the rebels some immunity from our attack. Too bad. See if they work now, dira." Jeffa looked fascinated, eager.

Sola set the elevation of the tube, loaded it, and prepared to light the wick. "It is necessary to stand within a certain distance for it to work," he said. He lit the wick. He motioned Jeffa and her troops closer, nearer the muzzle.

"Show me," said Jeffa. She stood back, out of the way, although her squad edged cautiously closer.

Without hesitation, Sola stepped in front of his tube. The wick fizzed, burning down to the barrel. He took care not to look at anyone. He did not want to see how his own troops were responding; he did not want to see if Pleffin began to struggle again.

"Enough!"

Jeffa rushed forward, pushed Sola violently away, and took his place. Her troops now crowded in around her. There was a flash and a deafening explosion.

Sola staggered, his hands to his ears. Jeffa, or what was left of her, lay on the ground, along with several of her troops. It seemed that the shot had fragmented as it left the tube. Blood and body parts were scattered over the snow. Those of Jeffa's troop who were unharmed were stunned.

His ears ringing, Sola wobbled forward and grabbed up a sword. He didn't know whose it was; it didn't matter. Some of the remaining enemy troops were screaming, some had silently dropped to their knees, their hands to their ears. Sola lunged forward and ran one through. He looked up to find Pleffin free. He and his men were taking care of the rest of Jeffa's company. It did not take long. The survivors were in shock and in no condition to resist.

Eventually, sound began to return to the world. Sola sank down atop one of the crates, letting his sword slide from his hand. He put his head between his knees, trying not to breathe too deeply. Hoofbeats thudded across the packed snow. Chif and the wagons had arrived. They looked around

them in amazement. Chif said something heartfelt in Wilfrisin.

"Dira Sola's work, most of it," said Pleffin. There was a
mixture of pride, awe, and fear in his voice. Sola did not
look up.

"We had trouble," said Chif. "Lost some good men. We
knew you have trouble, hoped we not too late to help. As we
can see most plainly, you do not need help. Except perhaps
to get crates on wagons. Sola Dira, were you injured?"

Now Sola did look up. Chif loomed over him, all incongruous blue hair and red beard and concerned expression.

"No, I am unhurt." He waved off Chif's proferred help
and rose. He felt chilled now and looked for his cloak. It appeared in someone's hand, and he took it. He sheathed the
sword; whose ever it had been, it was his now, and he accepted without comment the waterskin someone handed
him. Then he looked around and began to direct the loading
of the crates onto the wagons.

Rilsin had been right, the fire-tube was inevitable. It was
fitting that he be the one to first put his new invention to
use.

35

In the warming autumn days they marched to Hoptrin, to break the siege. On a morning filled with the mists of melting snow, the Wilfrisin army camped not far from the old walled saedhold capital, beyond the ring of the Lisim blockade.

"They know we're here, of course," said Bilt. "Scouts, even Sae Lisim scouts, cannot be that bad." He poked at a map of the area around the city, sketched in with the position of Sithli's army, under its Lisim command, as well as the outlying farms and fields of Hoptrin, some of them now burned. It was just before dawn, and it was chilly in the big tent. All of those attending this conference were wrapped in their cloaks, huddled near the brazier.

"They do not seem to realize how many of us there are. Or perhaps they do not care. There are more of them than of us, but care they should, all the same."

"They don't realize our numbers yet for good reason," Dremfir spoke up.

Rilsin frowned, then sighed. Her bias against anything

flavored with the supernatural would not stand her well with either her own troops or the Wilfrisin.

"Sae Dremfir—Mage Dremfir—please explain." She nodded at Dremfir, present at this meeting, as he had been at all of them Rilsin had attended. He was the SaeKet's mage, and thus entitled, but he said little. Now he stepped forward from the rear of the tent, where he had been quietly sipping a mug of hot cider.

"I have masked our numbers," he said simply. When he saw that the Wilfrisin did not entirely understand him, he elaborated slightly. "The army, Sae Sithli's army, Sae Kepit's army, looks past many of us. They do not see us. It is as if something distracts them when they look. We are here, but they do not see us."

"Magic," said a Wilfrisin officer.

He looked slightly nervous, as did many of those present, Wilfrisin and Saeditin alike, although some of the Saeditin looked smug. It was patriotic pride, Rilsin realized. Pride in Saeditin magic, which they considered better than Wilfrisin magic.

"Call it magic if you like, although I do not," said Dremfir, unwittingly supporting Rilsin's skepticism. "It is a matter of combining concentration, meditation, prayer, and chant. Belief, training, and technique."

"Magic," said the Wilfrisin again.

"Whatever it is," said Rilsin, "it seems to be working for us. I suggest we make use of it before the enemy manages to get us in their sights, one way or the other."

"When the battle begins, they will see us. Unfortunately, it would take far more than my simple ability to mask us then. Or to mask us for long, in any event. The good weather should hold for two more days, so we should act quickly," said Dremfir.

"We attack today," said Bilt.

"We attack now," said Rilsin simultaneously.

"HAND ME THE glass." Kepit sae Lisim held out her hand for the long-glass, then peered through it toward the enemy encampment, which had sprung up seemingly overnight. It was not close enough to see, but she peered in that direction anyway. Something told her—not her scouts but a feeling—that the Wilfrisin might move today.

She was not particularly happy to be in the Mother-forsaken north with the army, and she was even less happy to have been here so long. Who would have guessed that Tillit boy could have held out like this? It would be a true pleasure to take him back to what waited for him in Petipal, if she didn't kill him first, herself.

Kepit sae Lisim was a more than adequate captain, and in her forty five years had seen more duty with the troops than most people who were not career soldiers, but she did not like it, and it was not her strength. Politics was her strength. She should have been in Petipal. She should have been first minister. This was what she had planned and schemed after for years, the first ministry for herself, and the Sae Lisims the most important family in the land, after SaeKet Melisin. Since Sithli SaeKet Melisin could have no children, it seemed, Sae Lisim was even more important than SaeKet Melisin, although it could never be admitted. This she had achieved, and a Lisim was first minister, but it was her niece Jullka who had wormed her way into the SaeKet's favor. If the scheming little cat thought she could manage without her aunt's advice, she had another think coming.

"Damn fog," Kepit muttered. "What do they think they are doing? Bunch of barbarians! Do they think they can take on the Saeditin army?" She handed the glass back to her aide. "There are not that many of them, and all Wilfrisin. They must think it is a spring raid! We will make short work of this. Take two contingents and engage them. I will stay here, just in case Sae Essit takes it into his head to use this diversion to try to break out of the city."

"He wouldn't get far," said the aide, "even if he had the strength."

"He may try." Kepit rubbed her forehead, then tugged on her braid. It had been a deep brown, but it was now mostly gray, and she did not bother to twine it with gems the way most nobles did.

There was something odd about this situation, but she couldn't quite put her finger on it. It wasn't just that the Wilfrisin had come over the border in support of the rebel Rilsin. That was as understandable as anything the barbarians did, and more understandable than most. The barbarian chief was the rebel's friend. But why would even a stupid barbarian engage the whole Saeditin army? Rilsin had escaped execution in Petipal, but no one knew where she was.

"Sae Essit will be getting desperate now, knowing he must surrender soon, and he may think this is his last chance."

There were figures moving in the mist. It was not her imagination; they were there now, in truth. The mist lifted, as if by command. The rolling fields around Hoptrin were filled with troops. Most were obviously Wilfrisin, but there was a contingent in the front that flew a blue and gold banner, a Sae Becha banner. Rilsin had not simply escaped Petipal, she had come north and joined with the barbarians. She was here.

"Sound the alarm!" shouted Kepit. She didn't need to. The aide was already running for the trumpeter.

RILSIN SAT HER horse in the midst of her small Saeditin contingent, atop a small hillock, one of several that dotted the rolling fields. Runners were ready to take messages to Bilt, who was not far away, in the midst of his own troops. She heard the trumpets of the Saeditin army camped outside the walls of Hoptrin. Kepit could not be permitted to organize her troops.

"Send the archers first," said Rilsin.

She watched as the archers, both hers and the Wilfrisin, went forward, shooting, pausing, shooting again. Horse troops followed them as the archers fell back, all as arranged. The foot soldiers followed. If all went as planned, Kepit's troops would be pushed back against the city walls with no avenue of escape. Unfortunately, Kepit was too good a captain for that.

Kepit had managed to rally her troops, and the defense solidified. Rilsin even knew where she was; she could see

the bright, emerald-green Melisin banner under which
Kepit fought, just as well as Kepit could no doubt see her
banner. Rilsin knew that despite her element of surprise,
Kepit had an advantage: she had the Saeditin army. For all
their courage and for all their individual skill, the Wilfrisin
warriors lacked the training and the teamwork of the
Saeditin. Northern warfare had never demanded it. Bilt had
begun to teach his troops the methods of his southern neigh-
bor, but they had no experience. The relatively few Saeditin
in the attack could not hold them together. As Rilsin
watched, their attack began to fragment. Frustrated, she
looked toward the walls of Hoptrin.

"Get Dira Sola up here! Now!" The idea had been to re-
serve the tubes, and the tube company under Sola's direction, for its shock value. It seemed to Rilsin that now was
the time.

The two large tubes were pulled forward. Sola called orders, the tubes were adjusted. The lead balls were loaded.

"Can you take out Sae Kepit?" Rilsin asked him. "That
would go a long way toward solving our problem." She had
dismounted and was watching the loading process with a
certain grim anticipation.

"I don't know; I think she's too far." Sola wiped his
brow. "I'll try it."

There were further adjustments. Bilt came forward to
watch this procedure.

"Cannot miss this," he said. "First time use of this new
Saeditin magic!"

Sola could not tell whether or not the Wilfrisin chief was
being ironic, but he was not in a mood to care. His primary
problem, as he saw it, was not merely to hit the Lisim commander but not to hit any of their own troops. The Wilfrisin
did not understand, and it seemed that Rilsin did not understand, either, that the tubes were not a magic solution to this
or any other problem.

"Ready," he said to his own crew rather than to Rilsin.
One of his soldiers adjusted the long wick. "Fire!"

The soldier lit the fuse, and the fuse burned down to the
tube barrel. The lead shot fell short of Kepit's position, but

it landed among her troops, and they could see the results spread outward from the impact like ripples in a pond. Sola's crew cheered.

"Again!" Rilsin commanded.

The firing of the tube lent a strange rhythm to the battle as Rilsin observed it. Their troops pulsed forward in small knots. Essit's defenders had at last appeared on the walls of Hoptrin, and their archers targeted the troops below them. Despite her hopes, however, the effect of the tubes was not what she had expected. The army rallied around Kepit and did not retreat. Rilsin felt a perverse sense of pride. Although they were fighting now for Sithli and under Kepit's command, those were *her* troops. Rilsin had trained them and fought with them; they were her army. She would have been oddly disappointed had they splintered and run.

"We can't keep this up," she muttered.

They couldn't, but Kepit could, unless something changed, and changed quickly. Rilsin looked around her at the battle. She looked toward Hoptrin, and she looked across the burned and snowy fields. If she could not turn the tide of this battle, Saeditin would be lost to her. She felt an infuriated helplessness, and she closed her eyes.

The noise of the battle receded. Had she not stood with her feet firmly on the ground and her hand resting against the side of her horse, she would not have believed she was in the midst of a furious fight or even that she was within the world as she knew it. Silence pooled around her, flowed through her, and then, in the silence, something else. It was not the song of the land, not as she had heard it before. Rather, it was as if the land spoke to her. Rilsin opened her eyes and drew a deep breath. She found the eyes of those around her focused on her. With all of her misplaced reliance on Sola's new weapon, she had ignored a powerful weapon that had been hers all along.

"Cease firing," she said.

She mounted her horse and drew her sword.

"For Saeditin!" she said.

Her company swung into the saddle around her, and

there was the scrape and hiss of swords being unsheathed. Her standard-bearer lifted the Sae Becha banner.

"For Saeditin!" they echoed. "Becha!"

Rilsin glanced to the side and saw Dremfir riding beside her. The priest insisted on remaining close to her, it would seem, no matter what she did. Their eyes met.

"For victory, SaeKet," he said.

KEPiT KΠEW SHE could hold out all day, but that was not the point. She had no desire to hold out, she had only the desire to end this now and to capture Rilsin. Capture Hoptrin, capture Rilsin, end the rebellion, and go home to Petipal in triumph. She also wanted to get her hands on whatever strange new device had been blasting holes and terror into her troops. It was not doing all it should, but Kepit could see its possibilities. She would very much like to get Sola dira Mudrin, the obvious source of this device, as well. Once she had done all that, she would see about getting her niece Jullka reassigned to some other position. Sithli would have a difficult time denying anything to the conqueror of Hoptrin.

Kepit looked back up at the walls of the city. Essit's puny attempts at aiding in his own rescue were fairly ineffective. She had simply pulled most of her troops away from the wall, and those that were closest shielded themselves from the arrows of the city archers by a technique almost as old as siege warfare: linking shields above their heads.

She turned her attention back to the problem at hand: capturing Rilsin. Turning away from the walls of the city, she saw that her problem might be well on the way to resolving itself. The Becha banner was moving. Rilsin was going to come to her. Kepit smiled.

The smile did not last long. Something was happening, something odd and disturbing. She could see a shift in the pattern as Rilsin's company rode down. At first, the skirmishing around the rebel increased, but then a wave began to ripple outwards from the center where Rilsin was. Saeditin troops were turning to her, to the Becha rebel. A sound began to roll across the field.

"Becha! Saeditin and Becha!"

Behind her, on the walls of the city, cheering began. The troops of her personal guard shifted uneasily and drew closer around her. Kepit felt the blood leave her face.

It happened faster than she would have believed possible, had she ever considered the possibility in the first place. There was some fighting, as elements of the army held loyal to Sithli, but most of the troops were turning to Rilsin, everywhere shouting her name. At first, they surrendered to her troops, but soon enough that ceased. Soldiers were embracing one another on the battlefield, and Wilfrisin warriors, confused but happy, were cheering and thumping their new allies on the back. Kepit saw that she had one alternative open to her.

"To me, and ride for Petipal!" she ordered.

36

Rilsin saw the Melisin standard begin to move and then vanish, and she knew what it meant. Kepit was conceding the battle and the city, but she would run. Kepit was far more dangerous off the battlefield than on it, but there didn't seem to be anything she could do. She was mobbed with soldiers, cheering her, congratulating her, and she could not break away to chase Kepit herself.

"I want Kepit sae Lisim," she said, "alive, if possible." Since the whole army, all the armies, were now hers, she knew they would try. She doubted they would succeed. She would see Kepit again, she was certain, when she least wanted to.

Hoptrin threw open its gates, and the starving populace cheered them wildly. People ran through the streets, embracing the soldiers of the relieving armies. The Wilfrisin, Bilt included, looked amazed and stunned, being treated as heroes by their former enemies.

"Makes me sorry I send Lendis home to his mother. He should see this," Bilt remarked to Rilsin. Two women leaped from the crowd and threw their arms and legs around him, clinging like tree shrews. "On second thought, maybe not." Bilt disentangled himself, laughing.

Essit sae Tillit met them on the steps of what had been Norimin's manor. It was really more a palace than a manor, and it had been the administrative center of Sudit saedhold. This was where Norimin had died, and where Sifuat had organized—or failed to organize—the rebellion.

"SaeKet!" said Essit. He put his hand to heart and bowed his head.

"Essit!" Rilsin strode up the steps, grabbed him, and embraced him. "Thank the Mother!" She hugged him hard.

"Commander!" Essit grinned back at her, returning the embrace. "Thank the Mother, indeed! If you hadn't come—but you did!"

It was a different Essit: an older, more hardened Essit than the one she had known, and certainly a much thinner Essit. He had subjected himself to the same deprivation the rest of the city had endured.

"We have supplies," said Rilsin, "enough for now, but Hoptrin will need more brought in for the winter; the surrounding villages, too." It was something to be organized as soon as she returned to Petipal.

Companies of Saeditin troops were set to police the streets, and food was distributed to the people. Fires were lit in the market squares, and the sounds of celebrating and dancing echoed through the gathering autumn dusk. There was a dinner set out for Rilsin and her officers, and she ate and smiled through this, accepting the toasts as SaeKet, but only half hearing what was said. She left early, claiming the need for rest, telling them to continue without her, but reminding them that they would be riding south to Petipal within a day's time.

The room she chose was not the one that had been Norimin's; she could not face the thought of sleeping in what had been her mother-in-law's bed. Essit had claimed one of the primary guest rooms as his own, and his staff had the others. Since she had no wish to displace them, she took the only bedchamber remaining that was meant for nobility. It had been Sifuat's.

She tossed her sword on the corner couch and noted that her cloak had already been brushed and hung in the large, carved wardrobe. Oil lamps had been lit, as well as candles, and the room gleamed softly in their light. It was a room of lavender and silver, the Sudit colors, but on one wall hung a hastily draped Becha banner in deep blue and gold. An enormous mirror covered almost one entire wall, a huge and costly item. Rilsin smiled wryly to herself; Sifuat would have considered the mirror a necessity rather than a luxury. She went to stand before it.

She had not seen herself in a full mirror since before her imprisonment, and she drew in a short breath at what she saw. The image that looked back at her from the glass was not the way she was accustomed to thinking of herself. She had aged. She had days before discarded the wig, and she brushed at her ragged, cropped hair, which was threaded with white. She was thin, almost gaunt, and there was a hardness around her eyes that had not been there before, as well as a shadow of pain. As she thought of Niffa and of others who had already died in this cause, the pain deepened. She thought of Reniat and looked away, then forced herself to look back. She passed her left hand over her face, feeling exhausted, and then examined the hand more closely. The cut was healing well, and she no longer even bothered with a bandage on it. The scar would remain, but the function was not impaired.

"May the land heal as well as this," she murmured.

There was a knock on the door.

"Sola dira Mudrin, SaeKet," Pleffin said, in response to her query. "He says you asked to see him."

"I did indeed," said Rilsin. "I had meant earlier today or later tomorrow. No, no, let him in, Sae Pleffin; now will do after all."

"SaeKet," said Sola, putting his hand to his heart.

"Sola, sit down, please." Rilsin moved the sword and sat on the corner couch, motioning Sola to sit beside her. He looked as if he were trying to think of a way to refuse. The tension between them, where something more than friendship had once been, exhausted her further.

"I have had a message from Kerida," she said abruptly. "She is well and safe. She has found her way to the underground headquarters. I thought you would wish to know."

"Thank you, SaeKet. It is in fact a great relief. Is that all?"

"No." Suddenly she wanted nothing more than to break his composure. "Sola, I want you to give me one of those tubes, one of the smaller ones, the ones that can be carried. I want you to show me exactly how it works, and I want to practice with it."

"Why?" In his shock Sola forgot formality. "They aren't safe yet, Rils! I need to work on them more, improve the design. You were right. Using them is inevitable. But you should let others take the risk."

"You took the risk. You faced that patrol yourself. You could have been captured; you could have been killed!" He did not respond, and Rilsin wanted him to. "We could have lost the tubes!" The words rang in her ears.

Sola rose from the couch. "I will see you have what you ask for, SaeKet."

"Sit down, Sola, please. I'm sorry. I must have sounded like Sithli there, the last thing I wanted." Since he wouldn't sit, and she was tired of looking up at him, she got to her feet.

"I don't blame you for being angry with me. No," she waved to cut him off, "truly. If I hadn't been so blind to Sithli, if I had been willing to act sooner, lives might have been saved. I would be surprised if all of Saeditin were not angry with me."

"The people are not angry with you. You tried to honor your vow to Sithli. If you had acted otherwise, only the Mother can say if more would have died, or fewer."

"But you are angry with me. Sola, you have always been my friend."

"Your friend." He sighed and looked away from her briefly. "Yes, I am your friend. What right have I to be angry with my SaeKet, for her blindness to Sithli sae Melisin? Or to anyone? The people love you, SaeKet. May I leave? SaeKet?"

"Of course. Good night, Sola."

She watched his stiff back as he left, and she sighed. Rilsin walked over to the big bed and sat down, pushing aside the curtains of silver cloth; Sifuat had always had the best when he could. No, Sola was not angry with her for her blindness to Sithli. She twisted her marriage ring. She knew perfectly well why he was angry with her, and she could not help it. She heard him say, "The people love you," and she heard what he left unspoken. Sifuat had been her husband, and impetuous though he was, foolish though he was, he had died for her.

She lay back on the bed without bothering to take off her clothes, without even removing her boots. A big bed, a real bed; it was an incredible luxury. There was something hard, though, beneath the pillow. Reaching under, she extracted it. It was a book of Ulitin's poetry. It was, in fact, the very copy she had given Sifuat as a betrothal gift that midwinter night beneath the aurora. The copy was well-read and -thumbed, and it was obvious that it had been loved. Sifuat had taken it with him when he came north to Hoptrin, but he had left it behind when he marched south on his ill-fated campaign. Why had he left it? Rilsin curled herself around the little book as she felt the tears finally come. Still clutching it to her, she cried herself to sleep.

THEY MARCHED FOR the south, for Petipal, after only another day. The weather, which had held fine as Dremfir promised, now deteriorated again. Intermittent icy rain pelted them, but that was the only impediment. The roads were clear of Melisin troops, recalled south for the defense of Petipal. Essit did not ride with her. Over his initial objections, she appointed him governor of Hoptrin and Sudit saedhold in her absence.

She had one of the fire-tubes now, which she carried stuffed down into the waistband of her trousers. It was awkward, and she agreed with Sola; the design needed improvement. Around her rode her new Guard, under Pleffin's command, all of them armed with the tubes. She practiced with them using the new weapon, both morning and

evening, but she was plagued by one disturbing thought.
She did not want to use the tubes against Petipal. She did
not want to use force at all against her capital. She knew
Sithli would defend it vigorously, but the thought of attacking the city made her slightly ill.

As they passed through the villages and little farms, people came out and cheered them, and some of the younger
men and women ran to join the army. Brittal and her children stood near their gate to watch the armies pass. Rilsin
pulled aside, letting the columns go past her. Sola was
somewhere behind her, riding with Bilt and the Wilfrisin,
but Dremfir was with her, and her Guard.

"Ria Ritta?" said Brittal softly. Her eyes went to the blue
and gold banner that snapped in the brisk wind over Rilsin's
head. She took a step backward and put her hand to her
heart. Behind her, her children did the same.

"Where is Bren?" said Rilsin. "I wanted to thank you
both."

"Killed, SaeKet." Brittal's eyes filled with tears. "The
Melisin troops did it. I would join your army for vengeance,
if it were not for my babies and my farm."

Rilsin felt a stab in her soul. "Do not leave your babies,
ria; I will take your vengeance for you. Sae Sithli has killed
too many husbands." She had a sudden flash of the difficul-
ties involved in running a farm, even a small one, single-
handedly. "Nothing I can do will bring back your Bren, but
I will see you have help for your farm, whatever help you
may need, and I will see that you are rewarded for your loyalty. Loyalty should not have such a high price."

She rode southward in a grim mood, plagued with a
widening vision of the loss her countrymen endured. Sithli
had much to answer for, but then, so did she. She would put
a stop to the loss, and she would would keep faithful, afterwards, to the one part of her vow to Sithli that she still held
dear: there would be peace in the land.

It took far less time to ride south on the roads, even with
the armies, than it had to travel north off-road. There was no
resistance at first, and within two days' ride of the city, she
was joined by Lellefon and Meffa, who had Chilsa with

them. The big silver cat rubbed his head ecstatically across
Rilsin's knees. Kerida also joined them at this time. She
came first to pay her respects to Rilsin, and only then went
to see her son.

One day out from Petipal, they met resistence. Sithli's
troops had blockaded the main road, and according to the
scouts, all the minor roads as well. There was nothing to do
but fight their way through. Rilsin stretched the armies out,
across the fields and between several of the roads, pushing
through. She had no desire to be engulfed by Sithli's forces
closing in from the sides. She delayed using the tubes
against her cousin's troops, hoping she would not find it
necessary.

The rain began in earnest as they sent archers and horse
guards against the blockade. The archers had trouble keeping their bowstrings dry, and the horses had trouble with the
mud. They fought through the day and throughout the night,
and Rilsin's forces had to scrabble for every inch. But when
dawn broke, Sithli's troops had fallen back.

The rain stopped and the sun rose, casting its pale autumn glow over Petipal. Rilsin sat her horse on the small
hill outside the city and looked down at it. The defending
troops were ranged across the road. Everyone was exhausted and wet, but there was no indication that the defenders were considering giving up. Rilsin swallowed. Not
only would she have to invade her own capital, but she
might have to use the fire-tubes.

She turned away from the city. Pleffin and her guard surrounded her; Chilsa, with Meffa and Kerida were with her,
and Sola had brought a large fire-tube forward at her command. Rilsin rubbed at her throat, fingering the scar Sifuat
had given her in their duel. She opened her mouth to give
the order.

"SaeKet! Look!" Pleffin was pointing down at the city.

Rilsin stared. Something was indeed happening, not in
the Melisin lines, but behind them. Something was causing
a commotion, an upset, rolling out from the city itself.

"The long-glass!" Rilsin held out her hand.

It was a commotion, but it was more than that. People

were pouring through the city streets, attacking the Melisin troops from behind their own lines. The rising sun sparked and gleamed off kitchen knives and shovels. Through the glass Rilsin could see even a chair swung up, used as a weapon. A sound like a distant growling of surf or an avalanche in the mountains rolled through the morning air. The Melisin troops were turning to face the new challenge, and then they were breaking, fragmenting. Rilsin felt something warm flood through her, wiping away the exhaustion.

"To the city!" she cried, "but no archers! If the enemy resists, kill them; otherwise, let them go. Petipal itself has risen against Sithli!"

Some of Sithli's troops resisted. Even though she was surrounded by her Guard, Rilsin found herself in combat several times, but not for long. One of her opponents died at her hand, the others surrendered. Then they were into the city. Melisin troops were surrendering right and left, to Rilsin's troops, to the Wilfrisin, to the citizens of Petipal. The last was the most dangerous choice, as some citizens took no prisoners. But slowly, slowly, Rilsin made her way through the city, as the fighting turned to cheering. She heard it, but she knew they had not won, not yet. Not until they had the palace, not until they had Sithli's commanders, Kepit and Jullka, not until they had Sithli herself. Not until she had Reniat back.

"Surround the palace," she ordered. "I want the Sae Lisims, and I want Sithli. Don't let them escape; I want them alive."

The gardens around the palace had been trampled. The blooms were past, as the season was late, but the earth itself had been dug and pitted by traffic and troops. Small saplings had been broken and some of the statues smashed. If Sithli had sense, she would have left the city before the fighting began, but it would never have occurred to Sithli that she might lose. She would be in the palace with Reniat. What was left of Sithli's troops, her Elite Guard, had taken up positions on the lower palace terraces, just below the public balcony, from which announcements were often

made. Rilsin dismounted and walked as close as she could
to the palace without coming within their range.

"The palace is surrounded, SaeKet," Pleffin told her.
"They can't get out, but we will have to fight our way in.
First Man Bilt has the roads blocked in case they have al-
ready left the palace."

"The question," put in Sola, "is where do you want to
start, SaeKet. Are we going to fire-tube the palace?

Rilsin frowned at him. She knew how he felt, but the
question irritated her. She refrained from snapping at him,
with the nagging feeling that there was something that she
had forgotten. She looked around her, at her archers, and the
tube company, faced off against Sithli's Elite. Chilsa
crouched at her feet, growling occasionally. She did not
want to fire-tube Sithli's palace—her palace—but if fire-
tubing would end this more quickly, she would do it. She
drew the hand-tube from her belt, and loaded it and straightened its wick, and cut it very short. She wanted as little time
delay as possible.

"Prepare to fire," she told her company, and watched as
they prepared their fire-tubes, short-wicked.

"Rilsin! You haven't won yet!"

Rilsin looked up. On the public balcony, close, yet not
quite close enough, stood Sithli. With her were Kepit and
Jullka, Jullka close beside her, Kepit slightly behind. They
stood close together, a tight target, but a target Rilsin would
would never take. In Sithli's arms, held forward like the
shield she was, was Reniat.

"Don't fire!" Rilsin's throat was dry, and she found it
hard to breathe. Reniat waved her little arms and laughed.
The archers and the fire-tube company held their poses, but
no one fired.

Sithli was as beautiful as ever. She had dressed and made
up as carefully for this occasion as for any public audience.
Emeralds gleamed in her long blonde hair, sparkled at her
throat and on her fingers, and from the gold and green silk
of her clothes. On her right wrist was the big emerald cuff.
There was a brightness to her beyond the careful wardrobe,
however, an edge of hysteria.

"What would you give, Rils, to have this child back?" Sithli leaned forward slightly.

Behind Rilsin, marksmen, both archers and fire-tube, shifted slightly, sighting on the Lisims. Rilsin knew it, caught Pleffin's eye, and nodded slightly. If they could take Kepit or Jullka without harming Reniat, she would let them. But the Lisims knew it, too, and moved up closer to Sithli again. The Elite on the terraces knew it, and their archers were sighted on Rilsin's troops and on Rilsin herself. Pleffin moved into their line of fire, attempting to shield her.

"Would you go, Rils, and leave Petipal and Saeditin to me, in return for Reniat's life?"

Rilsin swallowed. "You can't hurt her, Sithli." Her voice came out as a croak. She tried again. "You love her, Sithli, you won't hurt her."

Sithli laughed. "Oh Rils, how little you understand. No, I didn't think you would give me the land, even for your own child's life." She drew a knife from somewhere within her sleeve.

"Sithli! No! You can have whatever you ask!"

"Oh no. You don't mean it, Rilsin. I know it, and you know it. You will say anything now, and then go back on your word. On your vow." She held up Reniat by the back of her little shirt and shifted the knife with the other hand. Reniat began to cry. "I will cut her throat while you watch, Rilsin."

Rilsin strode forward, out of her screen of guards, pushing Pleffin aside. She knew her cousin, and she heard the truth in Sithli's voice. Whether or not Sithli regretted it later, she would do as she said.

"No! Rilsin!" Sola shouted and ran forward, meaning to drag her back.

Rilsin held up her hand to stop him. She knew the archers were sighted on her, but it didn't matter. She saw everything in a brilliant light: Sithli holding up Reniat, the two Lisim women slightly behind her now. Sithli was holding Reniat up and out from her body, taunting Rilsin. Rilsin reached beneath her cloak and drew out a fire-striker. She clicked it, and the flint scraped against metal. She held the spark to the wick of her fire-tube and watched the wick catch fire. She seemed to have all the time in the world, and yet it all went by in the flicker of an eye, between one breath and the next. She aimed the tube upward at the balcony.

"Stop it, Sithli SaeKet, stop it!" Jullka was leaning forward, stretching, trying to reach the screaming baby. "This is not how we agreed it was to go. We need the child to get out of the palace, out of the Saeditin! Stop it!" She came directly into Rilsin's line of fire.

"You may need the child, Jullka, I do not! You want her, Rilsin? Take her!"

Several things happened simultaneously. Sithli flung the baby over the side of the balcony. Reniat dropped outward in a long arc. Rilsin screamed and leaped forward, knowing she was too late. There were explosions, more than one, as fire-tubes went off, and there was the twang of arrows leaving bows. A silver streak leaped upward from the ground like a star rising: Chilsa, his upward arc intersecting the falling arc of the child. Sola shouted and threw himself toward Rilsin, his fire-tube, aimed upward at the balcony, firing. There were cries and screams.

Something burned in Rilsin's shoulder and below her ribs. She had been shot twice, she could feel the arrows; one even pinned her to the earth. She struggled to rip it free. In front of her she could see Chilsa's body, arrow shafts poking up from him like obscene flowers, his jaws still closed around Reniat's thick winter shirt. A child was wailing, and someone was crying, "My baby, my baby!" over and over.

"Rilsin, oh Rils, hush Rils, Reniat's alive, she's alive! Get a physician for the SaeKet!" Sola was cradling her, tears streaming down his face.

Something was hot in her hand: the tube, its lead shot fired. She let it go. Rilsin tried to rise from the ground again, found the arrow still there, and broke it off, leaving part of the shaft in her side. She cried out with the pain but managed to sit up.

"Don't move Rilsin, the doctor's coming!"

Rilsin looked around her. Sithli's Elite Guard, shocked by the power of the fire-tubes, was surrendering. She could not see Sithli and the Lisims. Pleffin picked up Reniat and brought her to Rilsin. Rilsin hugged the baby to her with her good arm. It was true; she seemed unharmed.

"The hunting cat saved her," said Pleffin.

Rilsin looked toward Chilsa. Through the tears that blurred her vision, she saw Kerida and Meffa leaning over him. Rilsin looked away, struggling for control. There were things that needed to be done, and done immediately.

Rilsin looked up at Pleffin. "Sithli," she said. "The Lisims."

"Jullka sae Lisim is dead, SaeKet. You shot her with your tube, either you or Dira Sola. Sae Kepit and Sae Sithli ran back into the palace. The palace is surrounded. They cannot escape. There is no exit where we are not waiting for them."

"Oh, but they can," said Rilsin, "and there is." She remembered what it was she had forgotten.

37

THE DOOR TO THE CATTERY'S SMALL VETERINARY HOSPITAL was closed. The guards at the door nodded to him, and Sola squared his shoulders and drew a deep breath. She was inside, alone, but he had her permission to enter, or the guards would not allow it, never mind the almost superstitious awe with which many of them regarded him.

It was dim inside the hospital, but Sola saw her immediately. She was sitting on the ground in front of a large steel cage. When he came up behind her, he could see that the cage door was open, and Rilsin was gently stroking the big silver cat that lay on blankets within. She did not turn, although she obviously heard him.

"My mother says he has a good chance to live."

"He will. He has to." Rilsin turned slightly, looking up, but her hand never stopped its slow stroking. The big cat sighed and shifted. "Today for the first time he lapped a little meat mush on his own." Rilsin had been tending Chilsa herself, force-feeding him both food and water. She shifted her weight and winced a little. "He is as lucky as I am. At least, Maltia says I am lucky."

Her wounds had not killed her, and they would heal, with time. They would heal far too slowly unless she rested, but Sola knew better than to say this. It was warm in the little hospital, and a steam-pipe clanked and then hissed, keeping the cold of late autumn at bay. Rilsin had turned her attention back to the cat.

"Rilsin." He found that despite all his planning, he still didn't know what he was going to say. "SaeKet—" Now she looked up sharply, and he knew it was the wrong thing, but he couldn't take it back.

"Has there been any sign of Sithli and Kepit, any report?"

"None." Rilsin scratched behind Chilsa's ear. "They wouldn't go north. That would be incredibly stupid, and neither of them is stupid. They would not have made it through Bilt's blockade. I have it on good authority that they are not still within Saeditin, so even though we don't know where or how they crossed into Runchot, that is where they must be."

"The Runchot won't harbor them. They have no reason to love Sithli."

"There are many Runchot who, if they don't love her, are at least grateful for the profit she and Kepit brought them in slaves sold. And whatever the Runchot think of Sithli, they love Saeditin less. They will try to find a way to use her, just as she will try to find a way to use them."

There was silence for a moment, and Sola cleared his throat.

"This is not what I wanted to talk to you about."

"I know." Rilsin met his eyes but said nothing further. The silence grew and continued to grow.

"I owe you an apology." Sola found it even more difficult than he had imagined, but he couldn't stop now. "You had every right to feel as you felt for Sifuat." There, he had said it. "Your loyalty is one of the things that I, that the people love. I had, have, no right to resent—" He stopped. It still was not going as he wished.

"You have no reason to apologize for how you feel. What I hoped is that you would tell me just what it is you do feel, Sola. Once—" Now Rilsin was the one having difficulty. "Once." She stopped. She had best be direct. "Once you loved me, Sola." She shook her head, annoyed with herself. It was not coming out right.

"I still love you, Rilsin; I have always loved you. I wanted you to love me; I thought you did, but Sifuat got in the way. I was angry that even when you could at last love me, with Sifuat dead, he still got in the way. I can't compete against a dead man." Sola closed his mouth with a snap, horrified at what he had said.

Rilsin sighed. "You don't have to, Sola. Yes, I did love Sifuat, and I do still love him." She saw his mouth turn down in defeat, and he started to turn away. She reached up to stop him, and gave a little distressed cry at the sudden flare of pain in her side and shoulder. "Great freezing Runchot hells! Wait, Sola." Beside her, Chilsa began to snore softly. She gently closed the door to the cage. "Help me up."

Sola looked down at her. She was seated on an old blanket on the stone floor, dressed in black trousers and shirt, even though she could now wear Becha colors, or any colors at all. He had heard her mention to Meffa that black did not show when blood leaked from her bandages. It had been less than two weeks since the battle at the palace. The ragged crop of her hair had been evened, but it was still short, and she looked pale and drawn. He thought she had never looked more beautiful, and it was breaking his heart to think he could never have her. He extended a hand to help her up, and she grasped it. He pulled her to her feet and then looked at the hand in his. Her marriage ring was gone. She saw where his gaze was and looked down at her hand.

"I will always love Sifuat in a way, but it was a match that should never have been, would never have been, but for Sithli. It is time to move on." She met his eyes again. "Eventually, there will be time for the things that should have been." She smiled faintly. "I may be moving slowly, but I am moving. I just need your help."

"Move at the pace you need. I will always be here to help you," he said.

Since her wounds were hurting her, and it really was too soon for her to be moving much at all, she leaned on him until they reached the door.